Etched in Stone

Veronique Wallrapp

Cup of Tea Publishing
New York

To all my furred and feathered friends:

Cinnamon

Foxy

Lucky

Bella

Meow

Acknowledgements

This book has been a labor of love and time, which can be in short supply when you're a mother of four! Writing stories has been a dream of mine for as long as I can remember, it's hard to believe that it took me until I was forty to move forward with my lifelong love of writing. If you've always had stories in your head and haven't put pen to paper yet, let this be your sign.

I finally got a gentle nudge from my husband and that was all it took. There will never be adequate words to properly thank him for reminding me of my love of literature.

A number of people have helped me enormously during this undertaking by answering my endless questions and offering riveting bits of information. I can never remember them all, but think of them with immense appreciation.

Thank you to. . .

. . . Sienna, Logan, Ethan, and Emmeline, for their patience and support during this process. Without their enthusiasm and questions (yes, you can write a book too!), *Etched in Stone* wouldn't have come to fruition.

. . . Clarisa Benlolo, my mother, for being my first reader, and her unwavering support.

. . . Albert Benlolo, my father, for French translations and help in the subtleties of the French language, as well as instilling in me the confidence that I can do, or be anything in the world.

. . . Noelle and Jean-Paul Benlolo, my siblings, for their unquestioning support.

. . . Natalia Salcedo, my sister-in-law and editor, who is literally worth her weight in gold.

. . . Brittney Brewer, friend and fellow author of *The Legend of the Wildlings Saga*, who inspired me and answered countless questions about the writing and publishing process.

CONTENTS

France

Iroise Sea
Brest
Bay of Brest
Trégoudan
Landévennec
Camaret-sur-mer
Crozon Peninsula
Argol
Atlantic Ocean
Quimper
Bay of Biscay

The English Channel
Landévennec
Paris
Atlantic Ocean
Nantes
France
The French Alps
The Pyrennees
Rousillion
Mediterranean Sea

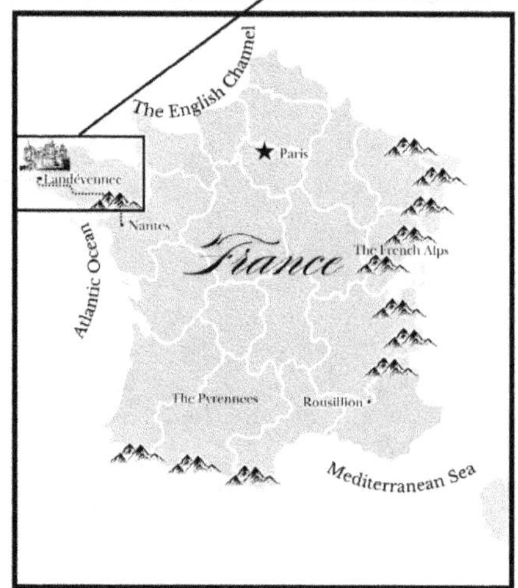

PROLOGUE
WHAT GOES UP, MUST COME DOWN

Dreams can be vicious.

Sometimes they are magnificent, golden, full of warmth and love, so overpowering that you reach out with both hands in a desperate attempt to clutch it, and you hold on for dear life before it inevitably slips through your fingertips. But so often, a dream is bittersweet. It spirals into an all-encompassing, destructive obsession when you aren't paying attention.

When first conceived, a dream is an exquisite thing. Your heart and mind spin a gossamer wish into a solid goal. You set milestones, focus on the obstacles strewn in your path, and plot your course, dodging the dangers hidden beneath the placid surface of the benign, azure water. Your daydreams are spent fantasizing about how marvelous it will be when you finally attain your ebullient aspiration.

Do you pause and ask yourself how it could all go outrageously, unspeakably wrong? Do you imagine your dream might become a nightmare you cannot escape or awaken? Do you ponder what reverberating repercussions you might reap from setting your objective into motion?

No.

You do not.

You focus with a single-minded determination on the effervescent, exquisite beauty of the dream. You rejoice as you cross the to-dos off your list and get inexorably closer to grasping your vision in your hands. Even when you know, all too achingly well, that there is no such thing as the perfect life. Even when you know that the wheel of fortune goes around and around. What goes up, must come down. Even when you've already experienced the cruelty of reality, providing with one hand whilst robbing with the other.

What do you do. . . when your dream, becomes your nightmare?

ONE
WHEN IT ALL GOES WRONG

Somewhere in the North Atlantic

October 20th, 1987

I threw my head back and laughed as the salty spray kissed my cheeks and glistened in my hair. My eyes squinted in the sun as I caught the shock on Carri's face as an enormous, breaking wave swamped her. The brisk air caught curly tendrils of my hair, tugging them from my careless French braid, whipping them about my face, and sending them dancing in the wind.

"You saw that one coming!" Carri accused, her summer blue eyes laughing.

I shook my head and languidly dove under the next wave. The sunlight played through the gin-clear water of the Bahamas, and I watched, mesmerized by the shimmer of tiny sea life floating above me. I held my breath, swimming lazily, and pretended I was a mermaid, like Carri and I had done as children. Only when I felt my lungs begin to burn and I could hear my heart pounding in my ears did I reluctantly come to the surface.

I opened my eyes. Somehow, I had survived the night. I rubbed the sleep from them blearily. *How did I manage to fall asleep during the gale the last night?*

Scarlet, tangerine, and peach streaked out from behind menacing purple clouds. The colors played off the rolling swell of the ocean like liquid stained glass. Thank God, the clouds were now in the distance, no longer threatening my survival. I lifted my face to the sky, drinking in the feeble sunlight on my skin before the full horror of the previous night came crashing down on me.

Lashing rain, wind, and waves had pummeled the boat mercilessly. We fought to stay upright for hours as the ocean tossed us about viciously. Visibility had been nonexistent, the endless black surrounding us punctuated solely by threatening flashes of violet light. The wind had howled so loudly it'd been impossible to hear anything over its roaring.

Overcome with sudden nausea, I closed my eyes and fended against the memory and the bile it brought to my throat.

The starboard jib sheet was loose, banging violently against the side deck and lifelines in the unrelenting wind. Carri reached out and miraculously caught it in her hand.

"Take it!" she screamed hoarsely, but her shout was lost in the storm's clamor.

Intuitively, through years of sailing together, I grabbed the line and bent over, securing it to the winch. I picked up the winch handle and began grinding. The sky lit up ominously as the yacht pitched perilously to the right, and my stomach heaved with the boat. Unnerved, I looked up.

"Carri!" I reached my hand out and felt my fingertips brush against hers for a fraction of a second before she slipped.

In slow-motion horror, I watched as my best friend got swept into the never-ending black of the sea.

Images of the previous night haunted me as I recalled throwing every flotation device we had into the water and turning the boat back in a desperate, futile search for my friend. The panicked calls I'd made on our radio for help had gone unanswered. For the rest of the storm-tossed night, I clung to the boat's lifelines, the cold metal biting into my skin, as I screamed Carri's name into the unyielding wind, soundlessly, frantically searching for any sign of her. Had I stood there for minutes? Hours? Certainly, it'd been long enough to scream myself hoarse. . . my throat was still raw and achy. Long enough to nearly get swept off the boat myself.

It hadn't mattered though. I had never caught so much as a glimpse of Carri again. I must have fallen into an exhausted sleep sometime before the sun rose, though I couldn't recall laying, or even sitting down in the cockpit. Everything between the moment Carri had fallen overboard and the moment I had woken up this morning, had passed in a nightmarish blur. I closed my eyes, my stomach cramping painfully. The critical second when she'd slipped re-played in my head in an unrelenting refrain.

Abruptly, I rolled over and ran out of the cockpit and up onto the deck, seconds before becoming violently ill over the side of the boat. Shakily, I lay down on the side deck and clung to the lifelines as my stomach roiled. My gaze was unfocused on the horizon, seeing Carri slip again and again in my mind's eye. When I stood up, I had no idea how long I'd lain there. I wiped my mouth with the back of my shaking hand and made my way to the boat's helm.

The storm hadn't been in the forecast. I mentally reviewed the night. *Did the boat get struck by lightning?*

I shook my head uncertainly as I double-checked the lines. A quick look up at the sails assured me that the boat was still in the heaved-to position I'd left it in during the wee hours of the morning when the impossibility of finding Carri had fully set in.

The ocean swell was a solid three to four meters high, but nothing compared to the ten-meter waves we'd experienced overnight. I briefly scanned the horizon and ascertained that the boat was in no danger of hitting anything. I unclipped my fluorescent life jacket, stowed it by the helm seat, and shakily walked below deck.

I shivered and realizing that I was still wearing my sodden rain gear, I stripped down hastily, leaving it in a soggy pile on the wood floor. The chilly autumn air raised goosebumps all over my body and I hurriedly grabbed my favorite jade green, wool sweater and pulled on dry jeans. Now what? The boat was still upright, but I was a wreck. My eyes burned with unshed tears, and my stomach was in shambles. I had no idea how far off course the storm had blown me, but I knew I should figure that out as my first order of business. I was utterly alone on the vast, indigo ocean. I'd always loved the feeling of freedom on the water, but right now, I wished myself anywhere else.

Trying to stay busy, I began to put the boat to rights. I knew if I thought about Carri, I would sink into the overwhelming feeling of despair threatening to engulf me. *I have to get to land to get help.*

I had to get to land because our radio didn't work. I had to get to land as a last-ditch, desperate effort to organize a rescue search for Carri.

I repeated this over and over to myself as I gingerly stepped around food items, cleaned up shattered bits of crockery, placed our books and charts back on their shelves, and folded or hung our spare clothes. Every few minutes I paused to poke my head above deck and scan the horizon, but there was no sign of any other vessels as far as I could see. I kept picking up the radio, hoping to get through to someone, but it was persistently staticky. The storm must have fried it somehow. I tried to concentrate on the task at hand, but flashbacks of the night before kept my mind in turmoil.

Carri, I thought in anguish. My knees gave way as I sat down suddenly. My best friend in the entire world, Carrigan, was gone. There was no way she could have survived the night. A tiny part of me screamed that there must be hope. . . She'd been wearing her life jacket; surely, she might have washed up on some French beach. Even as I refused to accept what I knew must be true, hot tears welled up in my eyes and effortlessly rolled down my cheeks.

Deep down, I knew that the odds of Carri surviving were slimmer than slim. A person overboard in the middle of the night in calm conditions was a death sentence. In a force ten gale like last night, with the wind whipping at fifty knots or more and waves ten or more meters high, I knew in my heart that Carri didn't stand a chance. Miserable, I wondered if they'd even find her body.

We'd known each other since we were little girls growing up next door, and we had shared a mutual love of the sea. Our parents had often teased us that we were as inseparable as twins. During the summers as children, we could be found playing along the shore every single gloriously warm day. For years, the two of us had pretended to be mermaids washed ashore. My heart felt like a frozen stone in my chest as I smiled sadly at the memory.

We had learned to sail together; we'd gone to college together and saved every penny in our piggy banks, pooling our riches. Since childhood, we had tenderly nourished the dream of one day exploring the world on a sailboat. Then, on a random Thursday night, I got a phone call that changed everything.

'I'm sorry miss but you should head to the Anne Arundel Medical Center immediately. Your parents were involved in a car accident on Route 50.'

They hadn't made it. I'd been lost in a sea of grief after that. I probably wouldn't have survived the agony of it if it hadn't been for Carri's steady, unfaltering friendship.

The corners of my mouth tipped up as I remembered how she came home from work to our shared apartment with my favorite tacos when I was having a difficult day. How many times had she sat at home with me, watching some horrible movie we got from the video store, digging into a shared pint of our favorite chocolate, raspberry truffle ice cream? How many days had I spent in her quiet presence while I sobbed and railed at the world and God for taking my parents away from me? Who would sit with me while I cried for Carri?

Eventually, I had healed enough to realize that tomorrow was promised to no one. After that, I'd been galvanized to leave on that life-changing trip we'd talked about for years. Combining my inheritance with the money Carri and I had saved over years of babysitting and college jobs, we finally had enough to buy a seaworthy, liveaboard sailboat and could afford to spend a few years exploring the world. In hindsight, I knew that planning our circumnavigation and Carri's faithful, unswerving friendship had been why I had survived that first year without my parents. I had pushed Carri hard, to leave as soon as we could. The guilt crashed down on me, making my chest tight. Maybe Carri would still be here if I'd been willing to wait just a little longer.

Exactly one year after becoming an orphan, Carri and I bought our boat together, named her 'Freedom', and set off on the adventure of our lives. Together. At the time, we had said that my mother and father must have been smiling at us from above. We'd been searching for the perfect boat for months before finally finding the one for us. We were sure it was a sign that my parents were bestowing their blessing on our voyage from heaven.

Never in a million years could I have imagined that just a few short months later, we would encounter a gale so strong that one of us would lose our life. *Now, I am truly alone.*

I could feel myself beginning to spiral, staring down the precipice into the depths of depression. I knew the signs well and forced my mind back to the immediate situation. I would think about Carri later.

I wiped my eyes angrily, gritted my teeth, stood up, and finished setting the boat to rights. On my way back above deck, I swiped a handful of crackers and forced them down with a tepid glass of water. Before I did anything else I needed to figure out where the heck I was and get myself back on course. *Thank God the boat doesn't appear to have suffered any major damage. I better check all the lines and rigging for chafe and signs of wear.*

I paused in the cockpit, shrugged on my life jacket, clipped the tether to the harness, and shakily moved forward on the yacht, stopping to check every line I could and breathed a sigh of relief when I stepped back into the helm station.

Misery threatened to swallow me whole. I held on, closed my eyes, and lowered my forehead to the smooth leather that encased the wheel. I took several deep breaths and fought down bile. It wasn't seasickness that made me nauseous, but the constant thoughts and reminders of Carri.

After a few minutes, I felt steady enough to open my eyes again. I sat in the helm seat and forced myself to breathe and think. I couldn't let the boat drift hoven-to forever. Resolutely, I reached for the sextant, aligned the tool with the brightly shining sun and horizon, and carefully noted my findings in my water-stained notebook. I grabbed our worn nautical almanac and consulted it, making corrections based on the month— late October, and on the part of the world I was in. With my notebook in my hand, I headed downstairs to check the coordinates on the charts. I squinted and shook my head; those numbers couldn't be correct.

I ran back up to the cockpit so quickly that I nearly tripped on the stairs. I glanced at my watch before pointing the sextant back at the sun. In a slight panic, my heart beating rapidly, I marked down the numbers and marched back down to compare my new findings to the ones I'd made mere moments before. After a few minutes, I impatiently scratched my head. Was it truly possible that Carri and I had been blown so far off course?

We'd been making our way south from the UK to winter in the Mediterranean. Living on the water meant we had to follow seasonally nice weather whenever possible to avoid getting caught in storms like the one we'd encountered. All sailors knew that a storm at sea was infinitely more dangerous than a storm on land.

Ideally, we should have left England by mid-September, but we'd been caught in port waiting out one unseasonable, late summer storm after another. Not that we had minded too much. Carri and I had spent our extra time in England exploring the small, charming coastal towns. The winding, cobblestone streets, and the neat little houses and restaurants had captured our hearts.

We'd spent days walking the windswept cliffs along the ocean, picnicking on hikes with picturesque views, and waiting patiently for the weather to turn, taking the extra time to plan for all the places we would explore in the coming months. We intended to stay in Morocco over the winter, and we were excited to see the souks, explore the desert, hike the Atlas Mountains, and eat our fill of mouthwatering Moroccan cuisine.

By the time we had a weather forecast favorable enough for our crossing, we'd lost three weeks and were halfway into October. This posed issues, as the weather in this area of the North Atlantic was notoriously dangerous and known to get worse during the autumn months.

Initially, our plan had been to leisurely hop down the coast of France on our way south, but since we had lost so much time waiting in southern England, Carri and I decided to shoot for a more extended passage and hopefully make it to Finisterre at the northwestern tip of Spain before stopping. This meant crossing the Bay of Biscay in one fell swoop, a passage most sailors regarded as difficult and uncomfortable regardless of the season.

We had been at sea for nearly two days, and we were about one hundred and twenty miles off the coast of Brittany last night when the weather had turned. The timing was shitty. We were in the Iroise Sea, a part of the Celtic Sea known for its powerful currents and rough sea conditions. We spent a few hours consulting our charts and considered running for the closest port. We were nearly a day from Brest, which was our best bet for a safe harbor. Based on our projections, we knew we didn't have enough time to make it to the coast. Additionally, this coastline was known for rocks, reefs, and shipwrecks.

The simple truth we had to acknowledge was that we were safer at sea, where there was no chance of running aground. Accepting that there was no outrunning the storm, we set about discussing safety protocols. We reefed the sails, checked the rigging, and did everything possible to prepare the boat and ourselves. As seasoned sailors, Carri and I knew we were in for a long night by looking at the menacing, greenish sky. As it turned out, it had been far worse than either of us could have imagined.

Impatiently, I pushed my windblown curls out of my face and tied my long, dark hair back in a messy ponytail. Decision made, I glanced at the charts one last time. I would have to adjust the course and put in for Brest. The gale had essentially blown us back toward the direction we had sailed from. I had dozens of miles to make up, plus the hours lost drifting hoven-to so far today. At best, I calculated I *might* make it into Brest before sunset the next day. Luckily, the wind had clocked around and was with me. I adjusted the sails, turned the boat southeast, and went below to give the radio another shot.

My stomach rumbled loudly, a reminder that I'd only put a few measly crackers in it today. I glanced down at my watch. *Damn it!*

Somehow, it was already nearly one in the afternoon. I cursed creatively as I picked up the radio for another attempt.

"Mayday, mayday, mayday, this is sailing vessel Freedom. We are a forty-five-foot sailboat located 48.5 degrees north and 6.9 degrees west. We have a man overboard. Over."

I waited for a reply, impatiently tapping my foot. There was nothing but static in return.

"Radio check, radio check, this is sailing vessel Freedom. Do you read me?"

Again, nothing but static.

In a fit of temper, I threw it aside, ignoring how it bounced off the settee and clattered onto the floor, strode back into the galley, and rummaged around for soup. I found a can of my favorite chicken noodles and opened it, my hands shaking. I dumped it unceremoniously into a pot and started warming it over the propane stove.

While I waited impatiently for it to heat up, I refilled my water bottle and pulled out a pretty blue earthenware bowl for the soup. I tried to banish the endless refrain in my head as I tested the temperature of the soup cautiously. I deemed it hot enough, turned off the burner, and poured the piping soup into my bowl. I carefully balanced my meal in one hand and gripped the companionway ladder with the other as I climbed back into the cockpit to keep watch while I ate.

The meal warmed me through, and I felt an unexpected moment of peace as I sat and watched the wind fill the sails. Similar to being in the deceptively quiet eye of a hurricane, I temporarily forgot my sense of imminent danger. I sat back and lost myself in the play of golden light on the azure water, watching how it capped each wave's crest in reflective silver. I was emotionally and physically exhausted, and the hypnotic movement of the swell slowly lulled me to sleep.

Two
Red Sky at Night, Sailors' Delight Red Sky at Morning, Sailors' Take Warning

My dark, silky curls fanned around my face like a midnight halo. I looked into astonishingly green, feline eyes, exactly like my own. My mother's fingers gently combed through my mane of hair. The sensation was comforting, and I fought to keep my eyes open. This was, hands down, my favorite part of the day.

"Mama?" In my little girl's voice, I said, "Tell me a story." I felt my mother laugh and smiled. I loved how the quiet shaking reverberated through my entire body.

"Ava, my love, how many stories have I told you tonight?"

Like a small kitten seeking reassuring warmth, I snuggled closer to her and pleadingly asked, "Just one more? The one of the little girl that sailed around the world."

It was a part of our routine, and she never denied my requests for an extra story. My mama tucked me in close against her body and kissed the tip of my nose.

"Once upon a time. . ."

I was startled awake and felt the warm, wetness of tears upon my cheeks.

"Dammit," I muttered under my breath.

The memories were solace and torture simultaneously. It'd only been a year and a half since my parents' passing, but I already struggled to remember exactly what their voices had sounded like, what their precious faces looked like. It was only in dreams that they came to me so clearly. It struck me that it wouldn't be long before the same happened to my memories of Carri. She would be joining the ghosts that haunted my sleep.

I viciously scrubbed my face with my hands, trying to force myself to think of something else. The problem with the vast silence of the sea was that it allowed my mind too much time for reflection. Not a good scenario given the circumstances.

I slowly scanned the horizon, quadrant by quadrant. The sun was beginning its slow descent, painting the sky pearlescent blush, lavender, and apricot far above my head. The clouds were gorgeous, feathery swirls that gleamed silver and gold. The clouds. . . The clouds abruptly ruined my appreciation of the sunset. I knew the look of those barely there wispy clouds and knew they didn't bode well for the weather tomorrow. Years of experience told me that the weather was going to change for the worse, and soon.

"Sweet Jesus, let it hold off until I make it into port tomorrow," I prayed fervently. The thought of enduring another storm so soon made my stomach churn queasily.

The hours after the sun went down ticked by. The sea was relatively calm, and the breeze was consistent, which made for pleasant sailing. The evening was clear, and the Milky Way splashed its way across the sky in brilliant swirls of violet and gold. I vacillated between extreme calm and heart-pounding, crushing anxiety, sleeping fitfully in short spurts, interrupted by horizon scans and sweat-inducing dreams.

Morning dawned crimson. As the clouds began to move in, I watched them nervously. *How long until the next system moved through?*

The sky lightened and I judged that there were still several hours before the storm arrived. My hasty calculations told me that as long as I maintained my current speed I might just squeak into the protected anchorage of Brest before the worst of it. Based on my projections, the storm would be coinciding with nightfall again; something that any sailor can tell you, always seems to happen.

I spent the day in the same state of heightened anxiety that I'd spent the night. Exhaustion nipped at my heels and depression settled heavily on my shoulders. I counted down the hours until I made it to a safe harbor, but I dreaded the questions I knew I'd be answering.

I would have to report Carri's accident. The official report would be bad enough, but I was worried about explaining it all to my best friend's parents. How could I tell them that our grand adventure had ended in disaster? That they would never see their bubbly, beautiful daughter again? That somehow, I— Ava, the one that no one would have missed, was still alive, but their family would be torn apart forever? My stomach twisted in knots every time I thought about it.

Miraculously, the wind stayed with me throughout the day, and the boat's speed kept me on course to arrive around sunset. As the afternoon wore on, I watched the clouds as they scuttled across the sky, getting darker, ominously gathering all around me. A sudden gust made me look up apprehensively. How close of a call was it going to be?

I heaved a deep breath, strapped on my safety gear, and moved up to the mast to reef the sails. I couldn't risk leaving too much sail up as the wind increased, even though I knew I'd be sacrificing speed for safety. I figured I had about two hours left before I made it to Brest, and I was fervently hoping to beat both the dark and the storm. At that moment, a fat raindrop splashed against my cheek. Then another.

"Dammit." I cursed, to myself or at the sky as another drop splattered on the back of my hand. I cursed fluently as I moved below to put on my rain gear, still damp from the previous storm, before I headed back above deck.

As I approached the inlet that led to Brest, the boat was closer to land. It would take about an hour before I passed through *la Goulet de Brest*, a very narrow opening framed by *la Pointe du Petit Minou* on the north and *les Pointes des Capucins* on the south. The tide funneled through *la Goulet*, reaching four to five knots of current in either direction. It was best to traverse the skinny entrance at slack tide, but beggars couldn't be choosers. Thankfully, the tide should be with me, pushing me swiftly into *la Rade*. Once in the bay, I expected the sea state to improve dramatically since the bay was protected by land from nearly every direction.

In the rapidly dimming light, I could just make out the stark sandstone cliffs and headlands that made Brittany so picturesque. The sky lit up briefly beyond the cliffs. Lightning. Well, shit.

The situation was rapidly devolving. I would have to keep a close lookout for the rocks this area was known for, in addition to fighting the incoming storm. Honestly, the timing couldn't be worse. *If only the storm would hold out for a few more minutes.*

My hands were damp with sweat despite the cold rain and wind that were gaining strength by the minute. *It's incredible how time always seems to drag by in shitty situations.*

The visibility was steadily worsening as the rain came down in sheets. The hammering water struck the doghouse roof of the cockpit and created such a din that it made it difficult to think. It was nearly impossible to see. My knuckles were white as I gripped the wheel and strained my eyes in concentration. I could barely make out the rocks to my right. Based on the charts, they should be right there, and yet—

Boom!

I jumped and nearly slipped. There! Their jagged edges jutted up sharply out of the sea for a brief moment. The sound reverberated in my head like a cacophony of cymbals crashing, and the air sizzled with electricity. The hairs on my arms stood at attention and the back of my neck prickled uneasily. It was too damn close for comfort. The boat fought against the waves and current, but I could feel it sliding, getting inexorably closer to the rocks.

I reached down to turn on the engine. It would give me an extra little boost of maneuverability. I turned the key, pressed the ignition button, and waited for the dependable roar of the engine, but nothing happened. *What the hell?*

We had never had issues with the engine starting before, but of course, now, when I desperately needed it. . . I shook my head determined to dislodge that thought. My heart pounded as I swallowed down panic and tried again. Again. Another bright burst of lightning lit up the sky, just a bit further than where the last one struck.

I blinked hard, stars swimming before my vision, my eyesight dazed momentarily by the blinding, brightness of the light. In survival mode now; I turned the boat hard to port. *I have to get farther from the shore.*

My hands were slippery with sweat as I struggled to keep the boat in the center of the channel. The wind screamed past me, buffeting my little vessel. My brain looped in an endless refrain of curse words. I hadn't expected the storm to get so nasty so quickly.

I should be near the mouth of the inlet now, but I couldn't see anything past the driving rain and incessant wind. *Why is it so dark?*

The pounding of my heartbeat roared in my ears; my mouth was dry as dust. I couldn't see the cliffs at all, still— I could sense rather than see, that the yacht was inching closer to them, and disaster.

Suddenly, my senses were besieged by the most intense light I had ever seen. The overwhelming heat of it surrounded me and seared my skin. My ears buzzed loudly as if a swarm of furious bees surrounded me. Cocooned within my mind, I dimly heard a sudden clamor of voices.

"Jump!"

"Get away from the boat!"

"Ava!"

"Please God— get her off—"

Then, silence, sacred silence. I was enveloped in the frigid, tumultuous sea, floating freely. My mind wandered.

It felt so nice after the bright, red heat of the boat. Has the ship been struck? No, I must've run aground. No matter. The cool water was so soothing.

Then, the cold rushed in. I was immersed underwater. *Which way is up?*

Instinctively, I kicked hard, and my head broke the surface. I took an enormous breath and filled my lungs with salty air, just before a wave collapsed violently over me. My arms and legs worked furiously as I fought to keep my head above water.

The initial lethargy was gone. I was freezing now. My life jacket barely kept me afloat in the tumultuous sea. I tried to catch a glimpse of the boat, but all I could see was endless, crashing water. The rain pelted into my eyes.

Far above, the sky lit up briefly and horrifically, but I barely noticed. I was caught in a maelstrom of storm and sea, as the current and waves pushed me about mercilessly. I had no sense of space or direction. *Where is the shore?*

My mind was screaming. Maybe I was screaming. I opened my mouth to catch a breath and it filled with salt water. I choked and sputtered, closed my mouth, and fought to breathe through my nose instead. Time slowed to a crawl. I swam, without knowing which direction I should move in. The effort was taxing. I was freezing.

It was bone numbingly cold. I clenched my jaw, trying to stop shivering, and trembled regardless. The water shoved me viciously as another wave closed over my head. Searing pain shot through my arm and right side. A tiny part of my brain registered that I'd been rammed ruthlessly into a rock. The pain was white hot, and tears sprang to my eyes, mingling with the salt of the merciless ocean. My limbs were beginning to slow down. The frigid water was depleting my strength. *Swim!*

Relaxed numbness was spreading throughout my body. I moved my arms and legs halfheartedly, but the fight was being sapped out of me. The entire right side of my body was knotted in agony, and I could barely move my arm. Every moment that I stayed in this wretched, freezing water intent on killing me, I let go a bit more. I was getting drowsy. *Surely, it would be okay if I closed my eyes and rested for a moment. When did I last sleep soundly? Days... certainly.*

My body cried with exhaustion, but now— Now, I didn't feel cold anymore. Warmth slowly stole over me. A wave washed across me. It was gentler than the last, but I barely noticed as my lashes slowly swept down over my eyes.

THREE
WHAT IS SHE WEARING?

I was numb, limp, enveloped in the most exquisite feeling of warmth. The light was soft and golden, like a tender kiss against my skin. *This must be heaven.*

There was no pain. I could smell my mother's rose petal perfume and hear the unique cadence of my father's deep, soothing voice. *What was he saying?*

No matter, I snuggled into the downy warmth, content to stay here forever.

Someone shook me. Why would anyone do that?

There was my father's voice again. It was urgent and sounded worried. "Ava. Ava, you cannot stay here. Ava, you *must* wake up. It is not your time. You must go back."

Why would my papa say that to me? Didn't he want me to stay with them? It was so good to be reunited. Didn't he love me? Why would I want to go back?

"Dépêcher vous!! Ici! Il y a quelqu'un ici." — Hurry! Over here! There is someone here.

Someone shook me again, then dragged me across the most unpleasant, bumpy surface.

"Elle est vivante! Venez' ici!" — She is alive! Come here!

Dimly, I heard the words being shouted back and forth. It was like listening with my ear pressed against a thick wall, but I couldn't understand them. *What were they saying? Why was it so loud? Was that the wind?*

Abruptly, the enveloping warmth was gone. Tears wet my cheeks. "Come back!" I shouted. *Did I say it aloud? Or in my head?*

I was freezing, shaking uncontrollably with cold and shock. *Where am I?*

I tried to sit up, but the sudden pain was so fierce I fell back to the ground. It was wet and gritty. Sand. I was on a beach. My eyes opened and I winced at the starburst of light that flashed before me. I hastily closed them again, rolled over, and with a spasm, I retched violently, feeling my entire body heave repeatedly. Exhausted, I rolled onto my back, turned my head, and rested my face on the cool sand.

"*Qu'est qu'elle port?*" — What is she wearing?

"*Je ne sais pas.*"

My brain fuzzily thought the voice sounded soothing and simultaneously like its owner would broker no nonsense.

"She is wearing men's clothes!" came a scandalized whisper. "Have you found anyone else yet? She could not have been on the ship alone."

"There is time to worry about her clothes later. I haven't seen anyone else, check the beach for others." There was the soothing voice again. "Mademoiselle."

Large, warm hands gently took me by the shoulders and lifted me into a seated position. Gingerly, I opened my eyes, conscious of the swimming sensation in my stomach and the incessant pounding in my head. *Please don't be sick again.*

I raised my eyes and met a concerned stranger's gaze. The light had almost completely gone, but I caught a glimpse of dark gray framed by sooty, black lashes. Windswept, wavy hair, in the light of an old-fashioned lantern, completed the look. I could have sworn the lantern was an actual oil lamp, it seemed so realistic. *Weird.*

Strangely, I felt safe. I let myself go and my eyes fluttered shut.

FOUR
A WHORE AND A PRIEST

Dieu. She had the most stunning eyes Gabriel had ever seen. They were light, jade green in color, and shaped like a cat's. His body tensed in response. They were open only for a moment before they glazed over, and long, dark lashes closed over them again.

"Mathieu! Venez ici." He didn't have to yell the words. His voice rang with confidence and carried naturally over the wind. The storm was subsiding. "We need to get her help. Did you find anyone else on the beach?"

"Non." Mathieu shook his head negatively. Gabriel watched his friend's eyes flicker over the girl's body, as he appraised the situation. *"La Chapelle?"* Mathieu suggested.

Gabriel grunted his assent and knelt next to her prone body. He whipped his cloak off and gently wrapped it around her before he carefully lifted her. He handed her to his brother-in-law, swung his leg over his horse's back, leaned over, painstakingly arranging her in front of him, and clicking softly, turned his horse's head away from the beach and toward *La Chapelle.* He urged the horse forward, trying not to jostle her too much. She was injured and looked as though she'd swallowed half the sea.

Mathieu caught up to him, but he said nothing. In silence, they walked their horses up to *La Chapelle.* His brother-in-law swung down off his horse first, and Gabriel gently handed her down to him before dismounting his horse.

He knocked on the door as loudly as he could and called out. *"Père?"* — Father? Mathieu handed the woman back to Gabriel.

After several long moments, the large, red door opened with a creak, and a wizened, old priest peered out. He looked at Gabriel, then at the bundled woman in his arms, and back to him inquisitively.

"Oui, mon fils? Je ne peux pas prendre cette pute." — I cannot take that whore in, he said sharply, waving his hands around for emphasis.

"Je suis Gabriel Chabot, le Vicomte de Landévennec," replied Gabriel with quiet authority. He nodded his head back toward Mathieu. *"Et ici, mon beau-frère, Mathieu Gardin, le baron de Trégoudon."*

He motioned to the woman in his arms and said, "We need your help, *si vous plait*, there was a ship in the storm, struck by lightning. We found her on the beach. There is no one else that made it. I don't know who she is, but she is injured."

"Un bateau? In this weather? *Mon Dieu!"* The priest reluctantly held the door open wider and stepped aside.

Gabriel stepped over the threshold and inhaled the comforting aroma of incense and beeswax candles. "Which way, Father. . . ?"

"Boisot." The priest supplied and motioned that Gabriel follow along.

Gabriel walked behind *Père* Boisot. His footsteps echoed dully on the stone floor as he led the way to the rectory.

"Cette pièce n'est pas utilisée." — This room is not being used, the priest said, as he lit a few long tapers which cast the room into puddles of shadow and light.

He spotted a utilitarian bed in the corner and strode over, gently laying the girl on it. Her face looked as though it'd been carved in alabaster. Long, dark curls were plastered to her skin. He thought she looked like a fallen angel. He glanced back at the priest, who was watching him thoughtfully.

"Votre compagnon devrait se rendre au fort pour consulter un docteur." — Your companion should ride to the fort for a doctor, suggested *Père* Boisot.

Gabriel nodded. *"Oui Père, Il ne fait que s'occuper des chevaux."* — Aye Father, he is just tending to the horses, he replied.

Boot heels dimly struck the flagstones, and Mathieu's voice rang out in the quiet chapel.

"Back here," called Gabriel.

Mathieu surveyed the room at a glance and looked at Gabriel. "Shall I go find a healer?" he asked.

"*Père* Boisot suggested *la Forteresse Vauban.*"

"Right. I'll be right back then," replied Mathieu over his shoulder as he strode away.

Gabriel looked back at the priest. "Perhaps something to drink and a few blankets to get her warm, *Père*?"

Père Boisot nodded and disappeared into the hallway. He returned a few minutes later with his arms full.

"J'ai aussi apporté des vêtements. J'imagine que tout ce qu'elle porte est mouillé?" — I brought some clothes as well. I imagine everything she is wearing is wet, he said, as he laid old, but serviceable clothing across the chest at the foot of the bed.

He piled the blankets on a nearby chair and, holding up a finger to indicate he would return, walked back out of the room. He reappeared a moment later with a bottle of brandy and several goblets, which he set on the carved wood table next to the fireplace.

"Merci, Père."

He waved one hand toward the fireplace and said, "I will fetch someone to lay a fire." He pivoted on his heel, rather spryly for an elderly priest, and disappeared once more into the dark corridor.

Discomfited to find himself alone with the woman in the silence of the rectory, Gabriel sat in one of the chairs and, used his teeth to uncork the bottle of brandy. He poured himself a healthy serving and took a long, slow swig, feeling the warmth of it slide down his throat to his stomach. The tension drained from his body, and he willed himself to relax into the chair.

Had they missed their rendezvous in the storm? Ships were rarely on time, but they were expecting it within the coming days. Had she been aboard the ship carrying his point of contact? What in God's name had she been doing on a ship, to begin with, and what the hell was she wearing?

He rubbed one hand over his face and unwillingly looked back toward the bed. She hadn't stirred since he'd scooped her up onto his horse.

"Gabriel." Mathieu's voice cut into his reverie.

Gabriel looked up to see a young matron and her servant standing with Mathieu. They were each carrying a large, covered basket in their hands. He stood up, bowed to the women, and motioned that they should set their baskets on the table.

"Merci d'être venue Madame." —Thank you for coming, he said. He waved his hand toward the bed. "I don't know how badly she is injured. We found her on the rocks by the water." He took in the women's shocked expressions and nodded toward the clothes on the chest. *"Père* Boisot brought some dry things, perhaps you can change her?"

The healer stepped forward and curtseyed, her servant dropping into a deeper curtsey behind her.

"Je suis Madame Amelot. Docteur is away, but I often assist him. I will see what I can do for her."

Briskly, she stepped toward the bed and, removing small, silver scissors from her apron pocket, began gently and competently cutting away the girl's clothing. Madame glanced back over her shoulder and nodded her head toward the door. Gabriel and Mathieu looked at each other and wordlessly left the room, shutting the door behind them.

They stood in the hallway quietly for several moments until *Père* Boisot emerged from around the corner with a sleepy servant in tow, holding a bucket full of tinder.

With a glance at the closed door, Gabriel said, "Madame Amelot is with her now. I'm sure a fire would be useful, though."

Mathieu turned to the priest, "*Père* Boisot, is there perhaps another unused room where we might stay?"

"Bien sûr! S'il vous plaît, venez avec moi."

The men followed the priest around the corner to another door. As the priest opened the door and stepped inside, he apologized. "It's a bit dusty, I'm afraid. I'll send someone to bring you a few things to make you comfortable."

Gabriel took in the neat, small room, with two dormitory-style beds. It was sparse, but it was more than he expected. *"Merci beaucoup, Père Boisot. Ce sera bien."* — Thank you, Father, this will be fine.

Père Boisot nodded and bowed. "If there is nothing else I can provide you with, my day begins early. I will bid you a good night."

Five

"Où Sont les Toilettes?"

As I came awake slowly, I fought it off. I was warm and safe, cradled in softly diffused light. Despite my half-conscious wish to remain in the world of dreams, I gradually became aware of the noises growing around me. Gulls called in the distance, and I heard the quiet roar of waves as they retreated and returned ashore. Closer to me, telltale kitchen sounds, as pots and pans banged, and the occasional sound of footsteps as they rang in a sharp staccato against the stone floor. As my senses began to hone, the agony returned with a vengeance. My head throbbed, and the pain in my arm was searing and constant. I winced as I opened my eyes. They were gritty and scratchy, and I silently took in my surroundings.

The light that streamed in from the open shutters was dazzling, and the sky beyond the window was the cornflower blue of autumn. I slowly took in the rest of the room. The furniture was of superior quality, carved of dark wood, and somehow appeared old-fashioned and new, as though someone had taken great pains to replicate antiques. Next to the enormous stone fireplace, in which a cheery fire crackled, was a table with two chairs, upon which sat a bottle of wine and two elaborate goblets. A large candelabra adorned one corner of the room, next to a small, roll-top desk and another chair.

Curiously, I turned my gaze toward the arched wood door as I heard footsteps approaching. After a perfunctory knock and a brief pause, the door opened, and there appeared two women in floor-length dresses, complete with starched white aprons and kerchiefs on their heads.

They looked as though they'd walked out of the 1800s. The older woman noticed I was awake, curtseyed, and smiled at me.

"Je suis Madame Amelot. Je travaille avec le Docteur Hautefeuille. Comment vous sentez-vous ce matin?" — I am Madame Amelot. I collaborate with Doctor Hautefeuille. How are you feeling this morning?

She spoke as she busily set her basket on the table and approached the bed. The French threw me off. I hadn't spoken the language in over a year and my brain scrambled to translate.

After a moment, I smiled weakly at the woman and nervously replied, *"Mon bras me fait très mal, Madame."* I was in quite a lot of pain.

The healer— Nurse? Clicked her tongue sympathetically and helped me to sit up, propping pillows behind my back.

"Oui. The arm is broken in at least two places. It will take several weeks to heal. Your ribs are bruised as well, perhaps even broken, although it's not as easy to tell. You're lucky to be alive, though. Who knows what might have happened if the *Vicomte* hadn't found you?" She shook her head at the thought.

Le Vicomte? Did the nobility still exist in France?

Before I could pursue this train of thought, however, Madame Amelot industriously pulled back the quilted comforter to check the bindings and bandages covering the right side of my body. I looked down and realized I was wearing a prettily embroidered linen dress— what they would have called a shift, once upon a time— with another dress of soft blue wool worn on top. Someone must have changed me. It was an odd choice of clothing though. *Where am I?*

The hairs on my arms prickled. Certainly, this wasn't a modern hospital. In fact, it was very obviously *not* modern. I glanced around the room again.

Did this place even have electricity? Where did the men from the beach take me?

One of them must be this *Vicomte* that Madame had mentioned.

"Ah, Madame?" I asked hesitantly. *"Où est que je suis?"* — Where am I?

Madame Amelot blinked at me in surprise and then tutted to herself. "Oh! Of course, you don't know. *Le Vicomte de Landévennec et le Baron Trégoudon* brought you to *La Chapelle de Notre Dame de Rocamodour.*" She noticed my blank gaze and helpfully added, "In *Camaret-sur-mer.*"

Ah, of course. I remembered seeing the name *Camaret-sur-mer* on my charts. It'd been close to the mouth of the Bay of Brest. It didn't explain why on earth I was in a church instead of a hospital, but at least I recognized the name. I had read about this particular chapel, built on a tiny spit of land jutting into *La Rade.* If memory served— *Rocamodour* meant 'the rock in the middle of the waters'— an apt name, considering its location. I racked my brain and remembered reading that it shared this tiny strip of land with the Tower Vauban, which was part of an old fortress. I frowned in concentration. I couldn't remember anything else. It was like groping for memories that were hidden behind a dense fog. What exactly had happened to the boat?

Madame Amelot had been gently undressing me while these thoughts occupied me. It was awkward having a stranger undress me, although *Madame's* competent, business-like manner made it feel less intrusive. After all, I wasn't in any condition to dress and undress myself, particularly not with all these laces, ribbons, and ruffles. Most of my upper body was now exposed, and goosebumps rose on my skin in the chilly autumn air. The fire helped, but it still wasn't that warm in the chapel. I glanced down and was stunned to see how bad my injuries looked.

My arm had been carefully wrapped, but it was swollen rather grotesquely, and the fingers that protruded from the bottom of the bandages were tinged purple and blue. Madame removed the bandages wrapped around my torso, and starburst bruises ranging nearly every color of the rainbow covered most of my upper body. The barnacle-encrusted rocks I'd slammed against in the water had left long, angry, red welts and oozing scrapes on my arm and ribs.

Unable to hold it in, I hissed in pain as Madame gently applied a soothing, herbal-scented ointment from a glass jar to the various scrapes and contusions that decorated my otherwise white skin. This done, she pulled a new length of rolled bandage from her basket and began wrapping it around my ribs. I felt slightly better after she was finished, as though the bindings held my battered body together. I grimaced as Madame and her helper pulled my clothing back on and settled me against the fluffy pillows.

The urgent need to pee overcame me. "Madame," I began awkwardly. *"Où sont les toilettes?"*

Madame Amelot looked briefly around the room before she produced a small wooden chair with a lid. I watched her with a mixture of trepidation and fascination. She lifted the lid to reveal a ceramic pot nestled inside. She didn't mean for me to pee in a ceramic pot. . . did she?

"La voila," said Madame Amelot in a matter-of-fact manner.

She walked back toward the bed, helped me sit up, and beckoned toward the oddest-looking 'toilet' I had ever set my eyes upon. Intuitively, I knew this contraption was a chamber pot, but logically knowing this, and having to use it was a different story.

I completed the most embarrassing pee of my existence, settled back into bed, and Madame Amelot's helper began to untangle my salt and sand-encrusted hair. I winced as she gently brushed out the worst of it, and wished I could take a bath to properly get it clean. A long soak in a hot tub would go a long way in easing my sore muscles.

She set about braiding its long, gleaming length while I pondered how lovely a wash would be. Salt had made my skin feel dry and stretched out. When she finished, she pulled a cream-colored ribbon from her apron pocket and tied off the end of it. It was a strange choice of hair accruement, but there were more than a few curious things going on at the moment. I didn't feel particularly unsafe, but my sense of unease was beginning to grow. My chest was tight with anxiety, and my stomach churned. *Why am I not in a hospital? Why are the women dressed in such an old-fashioned manner?*

A knock sounded at the door and at Madame's nod, the other woman opened the door and curtseyed deeply. *What's with the curtsying?*

I looked beyond her and glimpsed someone that looked strangely familiar. I searched my mind and connected the dots. I'd seen the stranger briefly on the beach the night before. Dark, wavy hair was pulled away from a chiseled, aristocratic face. Silver-gray eyes took in the scene before they settled on me. With him, stood another man, similarly dressed. *Why are all these people in costume?*

There was also an older woman, dressed in attire similar to Madame's. The men stepped aside as she bobbed a curtsey and carried in a tray that she carefully arranged on my lap.

My mouth watered as I took in the spread before me. There was a steaming cup of hot tea accompanied by a small pot of cream and another pot that, upon inspection, proved to be honey. The plate held crisp, sliced apples, and a woven, covered basket revealed a small, crusty loaf of bread. The smell of the food made me realize I was famished.

I looked up at the angel who served the food and smiled warmly. "Thank you, this looks delicious."

The woman blushed and with eyes cast down, she bobbed another curtsey. She beat a quick retreat to the fire, which she stoked and added a log to, before excusing herself to the corner of the room.

I shrugged to myself at this odd behavior, but I was too hungry to pursue the thought. I turned my attention to the bread and sighed happily; it was still warm. Nothing is better than bread warm from the oven, with some whipped, salty butter and marmalade.

I awkwardly broke off a piece and began to eat it daintily, letting the delicious sourdough fill my mouth before I took a cautious sip of tea. I prefer mine without cream or honey. It was lovely, and its warmth quickly spread through my body. Madame Amelot excused herself, promising to check in with me the following morning. Abruptly left alone with the two men, save the maid who wouldn't speak; I looked at them and gestured clumsily with my left hand, toward the chairs by the fire.

"S'il vous plaît, asseyez-vous, messieurs"— Please, have a seat gentlemen. I'm told I have you to thank for saving me last night.

Both men bowed smartly. *"Je suis Gabriel Chabot, le Vicomte de Landévennec à votre service Mademoiselle —?"* There was a slight hesitation and a brow raised in question from the handsome, gray-eyed man.

"Et je suis Mathieu Gardin, le Baron Trégoudan à votre service," chimed in his companion.

The companion was not nearly as handsome as the *Vicomte*, nor did he have the commanding air that his friend emanated, but he did have a pleasant, friendly look about him that the *Vicomte* lacked.

"Je m'appelle Ava Martel." I supplied, in answer to *le Vicomte's* unspoken question.

"How are you feeling this morning, Mademoiselle Martel?" inquired *le Vicomte* solicitously.

"Grateful to be alive, sir. Very tired, sore, and unsure about what happened last night." My French sounded painfully rusty and awkward compared to the men, but at least I knew the language well enough to communicate.

"It was divine intervention that we were on the beach last night Mademoiselle," put in *le Baron.*

"Comment êtes-vous arrivé sur le navire qui a fait naufrage du Mademoiselle Martel?" — How did you come to be on the ship that wrecked Mademoiselle Martel, questioned *le Vicomte.*

I raised an eyebrow at his peremptory tone. *Who the heck did this guy think he was?*

"Why shouldn't I have been on the ship, *Monsieur le Vicomte*? It was my ship. Not that it's any of your concern."

Surprise flickered in his quicksilver eyes. Whatever he'd expected me to say, he obviously hadn't considered that I might be the owner of the boat. Truthfully, I couldn't see why not. Women sailors aren't exactly unusual, although it is still a pastime largely dominated by men.

"You are the owner of the boat, Mademoiselle?" asked the friendly-looking *Baron* cautiously. "You mean your family, no? We found no one else on the beach or the rocks, surely you had a crew on board with you?"

Tears welled in my eyes unbidden, and I quickly looked down, although likely not before the men noticed. I was not ready to talk about this yet, but I somehow managed to murmur a barely audible *"Oui"* in response.

There were several moments of awkward silence while I struggled to control my emotions. Thankfully, the men kept quiet, no doubt sensing that this was not the moment to push me too hard for answers.

Finally, after taking several long, deep breaths to relieve the tightness in my chest, I spoke. "I will have to make a report to the authorities about what occurred. Where might I do that?"

Le Vicomte spoke, "There is time yet for that Mademoiselle Martel. It is not necessary to rush. When you are feeling well enough to travel we will take you ourselves. *Le Baron* and I have already informed *le Commandant Leroux* at *la Forteresse Vauban* of your shipwreck. He will send the initial report to Nantes where you can follow up with the details."

"Oh! Thank you, but— there is no need, for you to wait for me. If you point me in the right direction, I will find my way, I'm sure."

The men exchanged a surprised, slightly horrified look.

Then *Baron Trégoudon* kindly said, "We cannot let you go off on your own Mademoiselle. Who knows what trouble you might encounter?"

"*Non,*" added the handsome *Vicomte* firmly. "We have business to address in the area. We will wait for you and safely escort you to your destination."

I was beginning to get annoyed, and what had started as a faint prickle of unease when I'd first awoken, was morphing into full-blown apprehension. *What on earth was going on here?*

"*Messieurs,* I am fully capable of making a report on my own. Why are you insisting on accompanying me? What nefarious plans are you hatching? And, come to think of it, why didn't you take me to a hospital? A church is an odd choice for a shipwrecked stranger, don't you think?"

Incredulity, shock, and a touch of anger reflected on *le Vicomte's* face momentarily before his face smoothed out. "*Je suis désole Mademoiselle.* Having found you, we are now responsible for you." He raised an eyebrow and added, "As for the *hôpital,* the closest city large enough is Nantes, a hard seven-day ride from here."

A chill penetrated my bones. My hackles rose like a wolf sensing danger. There was something very, very wrong here. These people were insane. My knowledge of French geography surely left something to be desired, but I knew Nantes couldn't be more than a few hours' drive from the coast.

In fact, there was no way in hell that it would take a week to get from any point in France to another.

I was in a strange place with exceedingly bizarre people who were obviously a part of some weird cult. Aha! Maybe they were a French version of the Amish. That would explain the lack of electricity and the old-fashioned clothing. *Are there Amish in France? How can I verify my theory without offending them?*

Panic threatened to engulf me.

"Messieurs, I cannot wait days to make my report. My friend fell overboard, and they must begin searching for her immediately. Time is of the essence, or there will be no chance of finding her alive." My throat felt tight and sore as I fought to quell the rising tide of tears.

"Mademoiselle, the Navy has already been made aware of your wreck. We reported it to *la Forteresse* last night when we recovered you from the beach. There is nothing more you can do in your condition," put in *le Vicomte* firmly.

I clenched my hand in the blankets, crushing the soft material in my fist as I fought to control my breathing. The entire ridiculous situation overwhelmed me, but fatigue began to roll over me in waves, and the room became incredibly cold. *I must still be in shock.*

Le Vicomte watched me in silence, no doubt taking in a multitude of clashing expressions as they flit across my face. Could he see what was going through my mind? I'd never been good at hiding my thoughts.

I squared my shoulders, determined to get the men out of there. I needed to think about what had just happened. *"Merci, Messieurs,* I am feeling quite tired. I think I will rest now." I motioned toward my tray and added, "Perhaps one of you might be so kind as to move this for me and close the shutters a bit? I'm feeling cold as well."

Gabriel was startled by the speed with which she changed the topic and mystified by her assumption that he and Mathieu would function as chambermaids but shrugged it off. She had just been in a horrifying shipwreck, after all.

He acted quickly, motioning to get the maid's attention. "Mademoiselle, the lady would like her tray removed and the shutters closed."

With a curtsey, the maid moved forward and removed the tray, placing it on the table by the fireplace. As she stoked the fire, Gabriel wordlessly turned and gave Mathieu a look that indicated he would catch up to him.

He turned his attention back to the girl, Ava, he thought to himself, testing her name out in his mind. He gently settled her back on her pillows. She truly did look tired, he thought to himself and felt an unexpected rush of tenderness move through him, as though he was putting a tiny child to bed.

"Rest and feel better, Mademoiselle. I shall come back after dîner to check on you." He turned, quietly walked to the door, bowed smartly, and left, closing the door behind him.

SIX

LA BITE DE BALEINE- A WHALE'S DICK INDEED

Gabriel strode outside, his long legs quickly eating up the distance as he caught up to Mathieu. In mute agreement, they aimed for the beach. It was the best place for a private conversation, and Gabriel wanted to thoroughly check the beach and rocks for signs of life by the light of day. *Her friend fell overboard.*

He hadn't known how to tell her that the odds of a rescue were minuscule. The hope reflected in her face had been wrenching to witness.

The gulls cried loudly as they circled overhead. Seabirds dove for their lunch in an ocean that was far more placid than it'd been the previous night. The beach was small and it took little time to scan it meticulously for bodies. It was clear that not another soul, living or deceased, had washed up on the shore.

"It is odd, isn't it?" commented Mathieu tentatively.

"Very," agreed Gabriel. "I see no sign of the crew, no sign of the boat, nothing." He had a vague sense that something was wrong with the entire situation.

Mathieu changed that topic and asked, "Have you ever had a lady eschew your offer to escort her? She's quite pretty. All alone in the world too, from the sounds of it. . . I reckon you might win her undying gratitude," he added, with a lascivious grin and waggling brows.

Anger flashed on Gabriel's face. "Do not talk about her like that!" He was startled by how viscerally he felt about protecting this slip of a woman he didn't even know, but he did not question it.

Surprised, Mathieu held up his hands in mock surrender. "I meant nothing by it, Gabriel. Relax! Just a little fun between us, eh?"

Gabriel frowned and shook his head. "What are the odds that nothing would have washed ashore other than the girl?" he mused, switching the subject back to the matter at hand.

Mathieu shrugged his shoulders, Gabriel knew he was still stung by his reaction. "Unlikely, unless everything else was swept away. I saw a shipwreck as a child once, and debris was strewn all over the beach."

Gabriel looked thoughtfully up toward the cliffs just beyond the narrow strip of sand they were standing on. He gestured. "Let us walk up that way. Perhaps we will have a better view from the top."

They climbed, sidestepping boulders and loose rocks. Slightly out of breath, the men reached the summit of the limestone bluffs. The wind was colder up here, as it rippled through the swaying goldenrod, gorse, and heather. Neither spoke as they intently surveyed the water and rocks below. Several long moments passed before Mathieu broke the silence.

"The tide is out. This area is shallow. We should see the remains of *le bateau* at a minimum, yet I see nothing. How can that be?" He scratched his head absently.

Gabriel spoke up. "Did you see the ship? Last night?"

"*Oui.*" There was no hesitation in Mathieu's reply. "Only for a moment, mind— when the lightning touched the tip of the mast and the entire thing lit up like a beacon."

Gabriel nodded, the hairs on his arms standing up. "That is exactly what I saw as well. Yet not before and not since. I suppose the entire thing might have sunk to the bottom?" he speculated aloud, but he did not sound convinced. "By the way," he added, "have you heard anything from your contact?"

"*Non.*" Mathieu shook his head negatively. *"J'ai l'intention de chasser le fils sournois d'un bâtard cet après-midi."* —I intend to hunt the sneaky son of a bastard down this afternoon.

Gabriel snorted. "Can he be trusted?"

"I doubt it," came the wry response. "We have no one else local to the area though. We have no choice."

"*Fils de pute.*" Gabriel cursed mildly in answer. Then, he turned away from the view and began walking back toward *La Chapelle*. His stomach growled as he waited for Mathieu to follow. "I could eat a horse. Let us see what there is for *dîner*. Perhaps we can solve both our mysteries when our bellies are full."

Gabriel had intended to check in on Ava after their lunch. He had compiled a complete list of questions he wanted to ask her about her family, where she came from, and where she'd been headed, but Mathieu had convinced him to accompany him to his contact's home. Their business was urgent and delicate, and since he was impatient to complete it he'd agreed. Perhaps if their informant realized who he was dealing with, he would be more inclined to be honest. Unfortunately, they hadn't been able to find the man, even though they'd spent the better part of the afternoon loitering outside his hovel, hoping that he would show up.

The man's wife hadn't been particularly helpful. She'd simply muttered something about *le poisson*, while vaguely waving her hand toward the sea. Then she'd turned away, yelling back at a few grubby children working in the small, fenced kitchen garden before she disappeared inside the stone hut.

She did not reappear and one by one, the children vanished inside, lugging their autumn harvest with them. Eventually, with the light failing, Gabriel and Mathieu gave up and began the walk back to *La Notre Dame*. At least, reflected Gabriel, they had a comfortable place to stay. They had planned to find an *auberge* nearby, but *La Chapelle* was far preferable to whatever the local inn boasted in terms of accommodation.

They arrived at *La Notre Dame,* and at last, Gabriel swung off his big bay. He ran his hand lovingly down the horse's shiny neck, turned, and led it toward the stables. After he handed the reins off to the stable lad and instructed him to give his horse fresh hay and water, he headed into the rectory to wash before his evening meal. He wondered how Ava was doing and found himself anxious to see her. Perhaps he could invite her to dine with *Père* Boisot, Mathieu, and himself. He walked into the rectory with this cheerful thought in mind and found himself nearly accosted by *Père* Boisot, who had evidently been lying in wait for his return.

"Ah, Monsieur le Vicomte!" exclaimed the little priest, wringing his hands. "I have been waiting for you. The lady has taken a turn for the worse. The maid was unable to wake her for her *dîner*, she is feverish. We have sent for Madame Amelot, but she is attending a birth. I do not know when she will be able to return."

"Merde. . . ah- je m'excuse Père." He cursed lightly before apologizing to the priest. "I will go check on her now. Please, let Mathieu know, and send the maid in when she has a moment." He bowed and turned away as he hurried toward the rectory.

He arrived at her door and paused to knock, but there came no response. He opened it slightly and peered in. She was asleep. He strode inside, leaving the door wide open, and crossed the short space to the bed in seconds. He was surprised at the sense of panic he felt.

Her skin, normally marble white was flushed with fever. Her breath was rapid and shallow, and her lips were chapped, and cracking. Tendrils of hair had eluded her braid and curled gently against her face, sticking in places to her damp, feverish skin. He hesitated for a moment before he reached out and pressed his hand against her cheek to measure how hot she was. He snatched his hand back quickly. The heat emanated from her in waves.

The customary practice for fevered patients called for heaping blankets on them and stoking the already roaring fire. But the *Docteur* he'd known as a boy had once divulged that this was not in fact, the secret to breaking a fever.

'Pour faire baisser la fièvre, mon fils, vous avez besoin d'air frais, d'eau fraîche où des deux. Enlevez les couvertures, ouvrez la fenêtre, une débarbouillette trempée dans de l'eau sur le front - n'importe laquelle de ces méthodes est de loin préférable.' To bring a fever down, my son, you need cool air, cool water, or both. Remove the blankets, open the window, and a washcloth dipped in water on the forehead. Any of these methods are far preferable. He closed his eyes and could hear *Docteur* Henri's voice in his mind.

Galvanized into action, his mind made up, he strode to the window and flung open the shutters. The cool autumn air flowed in, immediately lowering the room's ambient temperature. The sun had set, and the salty breeze was already cooler than just an hour prior. He moved back to the bed and carefully peeled the top coverlet back, leaving just the thinner quilt over her for the time being. Although he was confident in his actions, he found himself pacing the floor anxiously as he waited.

There was a sound in the corridor, and he spun toward the door to find the housekeeper and Mathieu standing at the threshold.

He addressed the housekeeper first. *"Madame Carel, s'il vous plaît,* fetch clean water and a washcloth."

She curtseyed. *"Certainement. Y a-t-il autre chose Monsieur le Vicomte?"* Certainly. Is there anything else?

Gabriel thought briefly before asking, "Have you any oils or herbs? Lavender perhaps?"

"Oui bien sûr Monsieur le Vicomte." With another curtsey, Madame quietly left.

He turned his attention to Mathieu. "She is burning hot. Do you suppose there is anyone else in the area with knowledge as a healer?"

"I will check with *Père* Boisot. I can walk over to the fort as well and inquire there?" Mathieu suggested.

Gabriel glanced down at the bed, where Ava tossed and turned restlessly. There was a fine sheen of perspiration on her face, and she was muttering in her sleep. It sounded as though she was pleading with someone, but she was speaking in strangely accented English and his grasp of English was poor.

He suspected that the fever was worsening and nodded in agreement with Mathieu. "Thank you, my friend."

Mathieu dispatched as well; Gabriel set about rearranging the furniture in the room. He moved the small washstand from the far wall to the space just next to the head of the bed and moved one of the chairs as well. He sat down and quietly watched as she thrashed about.

Her voice alternated between barely audible, broken whispers to agonized shouts. He caught the word or name 'Carri' several times and wondered who this Carri had been to her. He detested the feeling of helplessness he felt as he sat beside her; it reminded him of how he'd felt when his father had been ill.

He remembered sitting on the edge of his father's bed and wondering how such a great man could be reduced to skin and bones, in mere weeks. He'd felt powerless then, relying on doctors to heal his father, something that ultimately had not been in the cards. His father had quietly passed from a mystery ailment just a brief time later, leaving Gabriel as head of the household shortly after his twelfth birthday. The usual feelings of anger and sadness at the unjustness of it welled up inside him, gathering in a familiar, tight knot in his chest.

Memories of his father were always bittersweet. He'd been unusually close to his sire, revered him, and learned so much from him, and he always asked himself what his papa would have done in difficult situations. His father had been known for his patience, forbearance, and wise level-headedness. What would he have said about the predicament Gabriel found himself in now?

The sound of footsteps in the corridor heralded the maid's return, and he firmly pushed memories of his father's final days aside as he turned his attention to utilizing the materials he had asked her for. The basin of cool water was placed carefully on the washstand. Beside it was a tiny, glass amber bottle, tightly corked. He uncorked the bottle and carefully passed it beneath his nose.

The refreshing and calming scent of lavender greeted him, and he felt the knot under his ribs ease slightly. He counted drops under his breath, adding several to the water before he dipped the washcloth in and swirled it about. Pleased with the soothing scent wafting up from the basin, he wrung out the washcloth and lightly placed it across Ava's forehead.

"Mathieu and I will take our supper here tonight, I want someone to stay here with her overnight, in case she gets worse. Please make arrangements with the household," Gabriel informed the housekeeper. As an afterthought, he added, "Does the rectory have a large tub for bathing?"

"*Oui, Monsieur le Vicomte.* Shall I have a bath drawn for you after your meal?" Madame Carel inquired.

"*Non,* not for me. It may help break the lady's fever. Could you assist her after we eat?"

"*Certainement.*" She bobbed a curtsey and left quickly, passing Mathieu at the door.

Gabriel looked at Mathieu, one eyebrow raised in question.

Mathieu walked over to the remaining chair by the fire and sat before speaking. "*Père* Boisot says there is no other healer in the area. The fort does not know when to expect *Docteur* Hautefeuille or Madame Amelot. They assured me they would pass the message along as soon as one of them returned. I can ride back to *Trégoudon* and bring my local healer, or I can ask Amélie to come?"

Gabriel thought for a moment. It was tempting to have Mathieu ride back to his home, and return with help. He would love to see Amélie, his younger sister, and Mathieu's wife. She did have some skill with the herbs as well. But they had a young son and Amélie was expecting their second child soon.

"*Non, merci mon ami.*" Gabriel shook his head. "You deserve some rest. Let us see what the evening brings. Perhaps tomorrow if help doesn't arrive by then."

They fell silent as the supper cart rattled its way down the corridor.

The maid bustled into the room and immediately busied herself as she set out steaming bowls of stew and a large, covered basket of crusty, country bread. She filled their cups with wine and backed away with a curtsey. "Should Mademoiselle awaken, I have brought her a bowl of soup as well," she said.

Gabriel smiled at her. *"Merci Madame."*

He raised his cup to his lips and he slowly sipped the wine. It was an excellent quality *Chinon*, made from the cabernet franc grapes grown locally Hungrily, the men spent the first few minutes heartily eating.

Gabriel wiped his mouth on his napkin before he sat back and queried, "Shall we head to the beach this evening?"

Mathieu carefully spooned up the last of his stew and sat back, unconsciously mimicking Gabriel. *"Oui,"* he responded slowly. "I am concerned that we were not able to meet with *la bite de baleine...*" he added, referring to the contact they had tried to meet earlier that day.

"La bite de baleine?" chuckled Gabriel. "He fancies himself to be that well-endowed?"

Mathieu shrugged a shoulder. "Better *la bite de baleine,* then *la bite d'un hippocampe,*" he chortled crudely. He yawned and stood up. "We should go. The moon is not out tonight. It's the perfect night for a rendezvous."

Gabriel got to his feet and placed both hands on the small of his back as he stretched. "I'll meet you in the stable in a moment."

He turned and walked back to the bed where Ava lay. He stood and looked down at the way her dark lashes lay against the curve of her cheek. She still looked flushed and the cloth on her forehead felt warm to the touch when he lifted it off her skin. He soaked the cloth in the basin of lavender water and wrung it out before tenderly placing it back on her head. He loathed to leave her but knew he had to deal with business. Hopefully, the ship they were meeting would arrive tonight. He let his fingertips linger against her skin for a minute before he forced himself to walk away.

"Should the lady awaken, or take a turn for the worse, please inform me," he said to Madame.

"Oui, Monsieur le Vicomte," she replied with a curtsey.

He gave her a brief smile of thanks and made himself leave the room.

SEVEN
CAINA

I shivered as I traveled over a desert of snow. In the distance, I could make out human forms, sculptures carved into the eerily blue-tinted ice. Frost decorated the hair of the heads that stuck out of a lake that appeared to have frozen in an instant; choppy waves and frothy bubbles forever encased in ice. Expressions of horror and malice were permanently etched on their faces, eyes wide, white, and unseeing.

I stumbled closer and realized in dawning terror that they were not statues, but real people; their faces preserved in twisted grimaces of pain. Fear skittered up my spine and twisted my stomach into knots. I recognized Cain, which could only mean one thing. I was in the company of traitors to their families and loved ones. The cold permeated my bones and froze deep within my soul.

I was in Dante's nine circles of hell.

From a distance, I heard my voice repeating desperately, "It was an accident, I never meant for Carri to die."

I looked around in desperation, willing them to believe me, but they all laughed, mouths agape, as they shook their heads and pointed their fingers at me. The fierce, freezing wind blew across the tundra and drove splinters of ice into my eyes and exposed skin.

Tears froze to my cheeks, as I screamed, "It was an accident, I swear. I would do anything to bring her back!"

I tried to turn, fully intending to run away, but my limbs wouldn't respond. My body was paralyzed, and as I looked down, my heart hammering in fear and horror, I realized I was encased in the ice as well.

I opened my mouth to scream in protest, but my throat was frozen, and no sound emerged.

It was dark, and I floated in a scathing midnight sea. My lungs burned as I struggled to come to the surface and break free of the dream. Bells tolled nearby, the sound clanging discordantly like crashing cymbals in my head, reverberating endlessly. I opened my eyes. My cheeks were drenched in scalding tears. They ran down my temples, soaking my hair and pillow. I tasted the salt of them on my lips.

I awoke disoriented, my limbs weighed down with lead. I tried to lift my head, but my muscles wouldn't cooperate. My skin burned as if fire ants crawled over my body, marching from head to toe. *Why was it so excruciatingly cold?*

I shivered uncontrollably. Every inch of my body ached. I struggled to clear my mind, but my thoughts were disjointed, and the exhaustion overwhelmed me.

I closed my eyes for a second and tried to gather strength. I opened them again and wordlessly took in the dark, empty room. A single candle's flame danced on the washstand beside my bed. Images of the past few days flickered across my mind's eye, memories of Carri's beautiful, laughing face, and long, golden hair streaming behind her in the wind. Memories of terror and death, playing like a cruel slideshow. I was drowning in pain, fear, and heartbreak. My chest ached, and every breath was painful. The weariness was too much. Black scampered its way into the edges of my vision, before finally overtaking it entirely.

My eyelashes slowly lifted again; it was daylight. I had escaped dreams of hell to arrive back in this confused, French-Amish world. Honestly, I wasn't sure which was worse. My stomach churned with hunger, and I desperately needed to pee.

I gasped in agony as I struggled to sit up. My head swam with the effort and black dots pranced before my eyes. I closed them briefly and took several long, slow breaths to stem the tide of pain. When my head had cleared slightly, I awkwardly pushed the blankets off my body and shimmied my way to the edge of the bed.

I had accomplished this much but, I had to pause again as I breathed deeply through my nose and out through my mouth. In this fashion with frequent stops to calm my swimming head, I managed to swing my legs over the side of the bed and make my way to 'la toilet.' Each step across the room and back to the bed proved arduous. I was weak and shaky when I sat back down on the edge of the bed. My heart thundered in my chest, and I closed my eyes and listened as it slowed to an acceptable speed.

Quiet footfalls approached down the hall, and I unconsciously straightened my back and lifted my chin. I desperately wanted out of this odd place. It made me determined not to show an ounce of weakness in front of anyone. I smiled wryly as I heard my father's voice joking about my fierce, stubborn streak. *Just like your mother. . .'*

A brief knock at the door broke my reminiscence.

"Entrez," I called out, surprised by how strong my voice sounded.

The door opened immediately, and I registered the fleeting look of relief and surprise on *le Vicomte's* handsome, chiseled face before his customary mask settled over his features.

He bowed smartly, peeked into the corridor, waved a maid into the room, strode closer to the bed, and gestured to the chair beside the wash-stand. "May I sit?"

"Yes, of course." I forced a gracious smile, even though I could feel my body stiffening with increasing pain by the second. I am *definitely* not well yet.

"I am relieved to see you looking so much better today, Mademoiselle," said Gabriel in his deep, commanding voice.

Frankly, I was surprised by the warmth I heard in his voice. This was only the second time we were speaking and I wouldn't say that the first time went exceptionally smoothly. I met his piercing gaze and felt myself suffused in a warm, golden glow. The expression of tenderness in his quicksilver eyes was startling.

I looked down at my lap in confusion. *What is happening?*

"I am feeling better this morning, though I am hungry. Is it possible to get something to eat?"

"Ah, of course, you are hungry, Mademoiselle," he exclaimed. "You have taken no sustenance in days! I will fetch Madame Carel immediately—"

"Wait! *Monsieur le Vicomte. . .* How long did I sleep?"

"Mademoiselle Ava, you were asleep for three days. You had a terrible fever. We were all concerned."

"I didn't know." My voice was weak and startled. *Three days? No wonder I'm shaky.*

I slowly sank back against the pillows, suddenly feeling exceptionally tired. In a flash, he was back beside me gently guiding me and propping the pillows against the wrought iron headboard. *"Merci beaucoup,"* I murmured.

"Of course, Mademoiselle. I will be right back," he promised.

He bowed and left, the maid following him out before he closed the heavy door quietly. I sagged back against the headboard in shock. There was no need to pretend I felt better than I did now that he was gone. I closed my eyes. Three days… it was hard to believe, but my empty, gnawing stomach seemed to indicate that he was being truthful.

I opened my eyes tiredly and my gaze landed on a newspaper that had been left on the washstand by my bed. Curious, I picked it up. Perhaps some light reading would help me while away the hours. I had to admit that I felt utterly wretched, and I was truthfully in no condition to travel yet, even though you would never hear me say so aloud.

My eyes idly scanned the front page of *le Journal de Paris.* There was an interesting-looking historical article about '*le Affaire du collier de la Reine'* — The Affair of the Queen's Necklace. I perused the article hungrily, eager to get my mind off my current situation. The tone of anger and accusation in the writer's words was shocking. It didn't seem like an objectively written, historical piece. *Who was reading this trash?*

I glanced back at the top of the newspaper and my eyes fell on the date at the top, just above the name of the publisher, I blinked, rubbed my eyes, and blinked again.

23 Octobre 1787

My mind raced in its search for an explanation. Perhaps these French-Amish people enjoyed reading newspapers from two hundred years ago. It was in line with their clothing, and lack of electricity. The journal was in perfect condition though. The paper was thick, and the crease was sharp. A newspaper this old probably belonged in a museum. The paper would be worn and fragile. Did they print and recirculate old papers in France? A perfunctory knock at the door interrupted me before it swung open.

"Mademoiselle," came the maid's timid voice. "I am glad to see you awake." She busied herself, settling the breakfast tray on my lap, fussing with the linen napkin, and rearranging the plates and cups.

"*Merci, Madame.* This all looks lovely." I looked beyond the maid and saw that the *Vicomte* had returned. Drat!

He sat back down in the chair beside the bed and noting the newspaper on the bed beside me, he gestured toward it. "Quite a nasty business, with that necklace."

I didn't know what to say. Obviously, he'd read the paper too. I settled for nodding noncommittally and took a fortifying sip of my tea. "I've been wondering, have you been back to the beach since the night my boat wrecked?"

"*Oui,*" he answered simply. "Mathieu and I have walked the beach and the cliffs looking for signs of crew or wreckage every day." He looked perplexed, and added, "It is quite odd, I think. We have found nothing."

"The ship is not on the rocks? I thought perhaps it could be salvaged—"

"*Non,*" asserted Gabriel. "The boat did not run aground, she was struck by lightning."

I was stunned into silence. I felt like someone had punched me in the stomach. It was worse than I'd expected. If the boat was struck by lightning, it had likely sunk. I was surprised to hear that none of it was visible though. Based on what I remembered from the charts, it wasn't deep in the area where I wrecked. I expected some of it to be visible at low tide at least.

"I did not know— that is, I had not realized that the ship was struck by lightning. In the chaos of the storm. . . I thought the boat was pushed onto the rocks by the current and wind. Are you sure it was struck?"

"*Oui,*" came the instant answer. "I am deeply sorry Mademoiselle Ava, but there is no doubt she was struck. Mathieu and I agree about what we saw. Lightning hit the mast. To be honest, I am amazed you survived. It was a spectacularly large bolt. The odd thing is that neither of us saw your boat at all, until the moment it was hit by lightning. One would think we would have seen it sooner."

The wheels in my mind spun like a hamster in a race for its life. If he was correct, then I truly had nothing left. With the boat being unsalvageable, I couldn't even continue my journey. Not that I even wanted to imagine continuing without Carri anyway, but the boat had been my home as well. All of my possessions had been on it, other than a few boxes of things I'd left in Carri's parents' attic. I felt like I was going to vomit.

I had no family, no best friend, no boat, no home, and no adventure. Nothing. Truly, nothing. I bit my lip until I tasted coppery blood. I knew I was spiraling, but I couldn't seem to stop myself. *What could possibly lie ahead for me now?*

Eight
Transportation Troubles

Even though my head was bowed, I could feel Gabriel's eyes on me. I sensed he was patiently waiting for me to look up, but I couldn't stand to see the sympathy in his dark eyes. Somehow, I knew it would only make me feel worse.

He said nothing, silently lying in wait. He reminded me of a great cat, crouched in the tall grass, watching, and planning his next move.

I lifted my teacup to my mouth and paused, allowing the fragrant steam to waft over me comfortingly. I wished I could walk into an enormous sauna filled with it. I looked down and noticed dispassionately that my hands were shaking. Deliberately, I carefully wrapped both hands around my cup and willed them to stop trembling.

I took a deep breath, squared my shoulders, and lifted my eyes to his. He wasn't going to disappear simply because I ignored him. "Perhaps, in a day or two I will feel well enough to visit the beach and see for myself."

"*Oui*, of course, Mademoiselle Ava. I would be honored to accompany you— if I may?" Gabriel hastily added. He seemed to remember my earlier refusal and how I'd reacted when he'd insisted on escorting me to the authorities.

"*Merci*," I replied simply. "There is much I don't remember about that night."

Gabriel inclined his head. I caught a brief glimpse of pleasure at my acquiescence on his face before he ruthlessly smothered it. Then, he pushed his luck rather recklessly and added, "I would still very much like to escort you when you feel well enough to Nantes, so that you may make your report to the Navy. Was the ship carrying cargo?"

Although he posed the question in a deliberately nonchalant voice, as though he didn't care one way or the other what my answer might be, I sensed that he was burning to know. I paused, furrowing my brows before replying. Why would he care about cargo? Would the Navy be asking me this question as well? Regardless, there could only be one response.

The truth.

"Cargo? No," I answered decisively.

I took a moment to observe while Gabriel hid his obvious surprise. Was that a hint of disappointment I caught as well? In a Gaelic manner, he shrugged, as if resolving some inner argument.

I hastily added, "I appreciate your insistence in accompanying me to the authorities. Perhaps we can set out in a few more days?"

Inwardly I scrambled to make plans. Surely, I reckoned, he would be easy to get rid of once I was out of this village of people stuck in the 1700s. I could catch a cab— but then my thoughts derailed. I was utterly dependent on him to get me to Nantes. It suddenly occurred to me that I had no cash and no identification. I would never be able to get a taxi to take me anywhere. Shit!

"You have made me very happy," he said deferentially. "I shall begin to prepare. I hope to have everything ready by the time you are well enough to make the journey."

I couldn't think of anything else to say, my mind was in turmoil. I nodded. "*Merci.*"

Gabriel made to leave but hesitated at the threshold. "Where are you from? Shall I send word ahead to your family about what happened? Perhaps someone could meet you in Nantes?"

I sat still as a rabbit being hunted. Frozen. For a moment I considered ignoring his question, but it seemed pointless. I would need to get used to answering such queries. "My family has all died," I said as simply as I could, but my voice still wavered, betraying my inner anguish.

I watched in fascination as his face underwent a rapid variety of expressions before he settled on regret. "I am so deeply sorry for the loss of your family, Mademoiselle. I too have lost most of my family. For many years it was only my sister and myself. I know the agony all too well."

I looked up at this unexpected admission and briefly caught a glimpse of longstanding grief in his eyes. It reminded me of an old break that had knit but still aches when it is cold or stormy. He quickly looked away, hiding his pain the same way I attempted to hide mine. It was soothing to know that he understood the agony I was in.

After a moment, Gabriel glanced back at me, but I was lost in my thoughts and barely noticed as he bowed smartly before he quietly closed the door and left.

My mind was in turmoil, and my breakfast, forgotten now, sat mostly uneaten on my tray. The morning's revelations had completely dried up my hunger, as though it had never existed. I sat in the quiet room as I gazed sightlessly into the flickering flames of the fire, and wondered what on earth I was going to do after I made my report to the authorities.

I supposed Carri's parents would forward me money for a return flight home once they were notified. I had money in an account that they could access. Their cooperation would hinge on how they felt about me after hearing the news, of course. *I have always been like a second daughter to them. . . but how will they feel about me now?*

I would have to find the local American consulate. I had no documents. *How will I get a new passport to return to the States? How will I prove I am who I say I am?*

As I thought about it, I realized that the entire process might take weeks or longer. The minutes ticked by and turned into hours as I sat and thought about how things had gone wrong. I was so lost in my thoughts, that I barely noticed when the maid returned and exchanged my uneaten breakfast tray for lunch.

Nine
Incense and Petticoats

On the morning of our proposed departure, I shivered as I climbed out of bed. Ice frosted the window, but there wasn't a cloud in sight. The priest had kindly provided me with an old, wool, fleece-lined traveling cloak to keep me warm. It was itchy against my neck but smelled comfortingly of incense. I wrapped a shawl around myself, creating a protective layer between the cloak and my skin.

I wore the extra ridiculous layers that Madame Amelot and Madame Carel had insisted I wear, *'for both modesty and warmth,'* I had been sternly told. I smiled thinking of how the two of them had cornered me; Madame Amelot holding up a long warm petticoat, Madame Carel holding stays, and a shorter petticoat. I had balked at the stays in particular, but the two women working together were formidable.

Madame Amelot told me plainly that my ribs and the bruising had healed enough to wear them, and I, unequal to the challenge, had finally given in. I had to admit that I was pleasantly surprised to learn that the stays weren't extraordinarily tight. I'd expected them to feel like a corset, but they didn't impede my breathing the way I thought they would.

Gabriel had suggested the night before that we take a look at the beach on our way out of *Camaret-sur-mer* and I nodded my head vigorously as I inhaled the delicious stew Madame Carel had served. I was eager to see the beach for myself and finally answer any lingering questions and doubts. I had worked hard at building my strength and health back over the past week. The bruises across my ribs had faded to a putrid green. My arm was still immobilized and would be for weeks, but I was learning how to manage the injury, carefully stretching it multiple times each day, and becoming more adept at accomplishing tasks single-handed. Overall, I felt ready. My chest tightened at the thought of what lay ahead, but there was also a kernel of excitement at finally escaping the little chapel and getting back to the modern world.

I ate my customary breakfast of warm, crusty bread, slathered in creamy butter and raspberry marmalade at dawn, and managed to fully dress with minimal help from Madame Carel. We had struck a tentative kind of friendship, and I was going to miss her no-nonsense attitude, and witty remarks, as well as her incredible mutton stew.

I strode out the picturesque, red door of the chapel for the first time since I'd arrived and closed my eyes, lifting my face to the cold, bright, autumn sunlight. I took a deep breath and a tiny smile tugged at the corners of my mouth. Its warmth felt delicious against my skin and it infused me with a golden moment of optimism.

A small, well-tended, garden faced the sea, and there I found a cozy, wooden bench where I sat in the warm sun impatiently awaiting my self-appointed 'escorts.' Anxiety at the long trip ahead swirled in my stomach. *How uncomfortable is it going to be?*

Le Vicomte and I had struck a tentative kind of friendship, though his natural reticence and my shyness made it awkward at best. Within a few moments, the men appeared, leading glossy, well-cared-for horses. Honestly, I didn't know whether to laugh or cry at the absurdity of traveling in this manner but I had resigned myself to it.

A small smile played at the corners of my mouth as *le Vicomte's* long-legged stride ate up the distance between us. The quizzical look on his usually aloof, chiseled face indicated that he was wondering what had brought a smile to my face, but I couldn't bring myself to care. Being outside after so many days cooped up felt glorious.

He bowed low over my hand, "Good morning Mademoiselle Ava. I trust you slept well?"

"I did, thank you," I murmured, "I hope you did as well?"

"Aye," he replied simply, and indicated toward the larger of the two horses, with a lovely chestnut coat. "This is Automne," he said, introducing his horse, holding the reins in one hand, as he ran his other hand lovingly down the horse's neck.

"He's lovely," I breathed as I moved closer to the horse's head and gazed into his beautiful eyes. Quiet intelligence gleamed in their depths as the horse gazed at me.

"What a charming, gorgeous, smart boy you are," I murmured.

Automne blinked ridiculously long eyelashes at me and pressed his nose against my hand.

"Do you enjoy a nice scratch back here?" I whispered as I rubbed behind his ears. "My old dog Bella used to love this."

Automne just watched me steadily. Something in his eyes made me feel like he was plumbing the depths of my soul. Like he was intuitively picking up the sadness I carried within me. It was simultaneously comforting and disquieting.

I glanced up to see Gabriel watching my exchange with Automne in amusement.

Finally, noticing how *le Baron* was anxiously shifting from one foot to the other, I patted his neck. "Perhaps traveling the old-fashioned way won't be so bad after all."

I caught the look of confused laughter on Gabriel's face. He shook his head, but wisely kept his mouth shut when I cocked a brow at him.

Stepping back from Automne, I watched Gabriel mount the horse and felt a flutter in my stomach at the way his body moved in one fluid motion.

Suddenly Madame Carel hurried out of the chapel and ran toward me. She thrust a small glass bottle into my hands. "*Huile de roses*, I know you love the scent."

My hands were trembling as I carefully took the precious bottle and wrapped my good arm around the housekeeper, blinking back tears of gratitude. It was my mother's favorite scent, and it made me feel close to her whenever I smelled it. A single tear escaped as I swallowed down the lump in my throat. "*Merci, Madame.* I will think of you every time I wear it."

Madame Carel's kind, old face smiled at me shakily. I felt sadness well up from somewhere deep inside. *Why am I always leaving people behind?*

She patted my cheek and stepped back as a teenage boy appeared behind the men with a little step stool which he placed next to Automne. I tucked the little bottle carefully in my pocket.

The stable lad offered me his hand as I mounted the stool and scrambled awkwardly, one-handed onto the horse behind Gabriel. My balance was severely off without the use of both arms and for a moment I envisioned myself falling off the horse and landing in a heap at his feet. Miraculously, I managed to avert extreme embarrassment and stay on the horse as I gingerly arranged my skirts and cloak around myself.

It felt odd to be holding onto *le Vicomte*, but I knew I had to, or risk slipping off. His proper, standoffish nature didn't invite personal touch, and I hadn't been this close to a man, or anyone really, in at least as long as my parents had been gone. There was no help for it though. I nervously placed my good arm around him, whilst scrupulously maintaining space between our bodies. I felt him stiffen momentarily, and despite the frigid temperature, my palms began to sweat. Up close in the bright sunlight, I could see lovely glints of gold and fire in his dark wavy hair.

He turned his face slightly toward mine. "Ready, Mademoiselle Ava?"

I involuntarily caught my breath as I felt something shift inside me. I nodded mutely.

"Let's go then."

The horses moved forward as one, jostling me as we began walking toward the beach. I turned slightly in the saddle as we moved away and raised my hand in silent farewell to Madame Carel and *Père* Boisot. It was bittersweet leaving the chapel. *Always, on the move. I was forever, saying goodbye.*

Automne stumbled over a shifting boulder, and I hurriedly turned my attention back to the horse. I hadn't ridden since I was a child and it took me a while to accustom myself to the rolling gait.

Within a few short minutes, we were walking on the sand. I had virtually no recollection of the beach from the night I had washed ashore and I viewed it eagerly with fresh eyes. It was tiny and it wouldn't take long to search the entire thing.

It curved gently in a half-moon shape. To the right, the land extended into *la Goulet de Brest* in a narrow strip of rocks which housed *La Chapel Notre Dame de Rocamodour*, where I had spent the last two weeks, and beyond that *La Tour Dorée*— the Golden Tower, and the ancient stone *Forteresse Vauban*. To our left, the land rose precipitously into the steep, gilded, sandstone cliffs that the area was famous for.

The men had been right, there were no signs of wreckage along the beach. I knew of course, that no one had been on the boat other than me, but for some reason, I had decided not to divulge that information to them. I couldn't quite put my finger on the reason for my reticence, but a little niggle in the back of my mind had cautioned against telling them the full story. I took a deep, fortifying breath, salty air filling my lungs, and sat up straighter in the saddle, feeling slightly restored.

Gabriel glanced over his shoulder at me. "Shall we head up to the cliffs?"

I nodded and the horses began picking their way up the narrow, winding path. The lane was not well-worn; it was littered with rocks and boulders. The sweet scent of heather and gorse swaying in the salt-kissed breeze tickled my nose. The chill of the early morning was beginning to lift slightly as the sun warmed the air and closing my eyes, I lifted my face to the sky and breathed deeply. My practiced eye recognized at a glance that we had perfectly timed our visit with low tide, and a little seed of hope stirred in my chest. Maybe, I would catch a glimpse of my boat.

We crested the summit, and the horses stood side by side a few feet from the abrupt precipice down to the water. I ignored the leap of nerves in my belly and forced myself to look down. Numerous sharp rocks protruded from the exposed tidal pools and continued well beyond, into deeper water. The sun glinted off the dark blue depths that lay deceptively still at slack tide. There was barely any movement. A few seabirds picked over the shallows for their breakfast.

After several long minutes, I was forced to concede that there was no sign of the boat. My shoulders sagged and I rapidly blinked back tears. It would appear that the men had been honest when they'd claimed that there was no sign of the wreckage. Further, down the coast, I could see the old remains of a wooden shipwreck, but my boat must be lying at the bottom of the ocean.

I gave a quick prayer of thanks that I'd made it out of the storm and wreckage relatively unscathed. It was the first time since Carri had fallen overboard that I had felt even a glimmer of appreciation for being alive. For weeks I'd been consumed with guilt and misery, my chest so tight it physically hurt, my eyes raw, scratchy, and swollen from the constant tears. I had often found myself wishing that I had simply drowned in the deep blue with Carri. The moment of thankfulness was fleeting, but I found myself clinging to the gossamer thread of gratitude, and it carried me through the following days.

By unspoken agreement, the men turned the horses away from the cliffs and began traveling away from the coast. I knew, from looking at the charts on the boat, that we were on a peninsula of sorts, and the first order of business would be to get further inland.

"You mentioned last night that we will stop at *le Baron's château* in *Trégoudan* first?" I asked tentatively.

"*Oui*. Mathieu's wife, my sister— Amelie— is expecting another *bebe*. Mathieu is anxious to get home to them." I could feel his quiet voice rumble through his chest as he spoke. It was an oddly soothing sensation.

"How far is it from here?"

"Not too far. We should arrive late this afternoon."

I silently absorbed this information. It would mean many hours on horseback, and if I were completely honest, my butt and legs were already feeling sore.

"We'll be leaving this evening then?"

Gabriel didn't answer immediately, and I sensed his hesitation in committing to a plan. Finally, after a lengthy pause, he replied, "I think we will wait to see what time we arrive, and whether we will be able to continue onto our next stopping point and arrive before sunset."

"Haven't you traveled this way many times?" I asked, my brow furrowed.

"*Oui*, our business often takes us this way."

"Then why wouldn't you know if we will have sufficient time to continue today?" I could tell there was something I was missing and it was annoying me that I couldn't piece it together.

He glanced back at me, a faint smile crinkling the skin around his eyes at my badgering. "You're still injured, aye? We're taking it a fair bit slower than we would if it were just Mathieu and myself."

I opened my mouth and shut it again without saying anything. Well, that burned.

But I couldn't blame him for laying it out that way. His thought process was reasonable, and I had to admit inwardly that I didn't think I was in any condition to travel at a faster speed.

I felt Gabriel rummaging, and after a moment he held his hand out to me, palm up. "Lemon candy?" he offered. His eyes twinkled as he smiled over his shoulder at me. My stomach flipped as I carefully took the proffered treat.

"Thank you." I popped the candy in my mouth savoring the sweet and tart burst of flavor on my tongue.

After a period of companionable silence, while I digested this unexpected bit of chivalry, I began again. "You mentioned we would be traveling with more men after we stop at your sister's?"

Overhearing my query, *le Baron* answered, "It is always wiser to travel in a large party, my lady."

"We'll need supplies for the journey," added Gabriel, "And a chaperone for you."

I rolled my eyes, suppressing the urge to snort in laughter at the word chaperone. It had come up in conversation multiple times over the last few weeks, and I had lost the argument— if you could call it that— every time. It seemed that the men were committed to protecting my virtue, and I had decided there was nothing to be gained by arguing with their old-fashioned ways. Instead, I planned to immerse myself, and pretend I lived in eighteenth-century France until we made it to Nantes. I wondered how they would interact with modern Frenchmen and women. At a minimum, it was going to be an interesting week, and I figured I would leave with a greater appreciation of modern amenities. The history lover in me was excited to watch it all play out.

We ambled through small towns and along rutted lanes, past pastures, dotted with farmhouses. I was quiet as we passed through the picturesque landscape. Gabriel's taciturn personality and his simple, to-the-point answers didn't exactly invite conversation, and I was absorbed in watching the land change around us. We wound our way slowly along the coast, keeping it always on our left. The further we went, the more the pit in my stomach grew. I had never doubted for a moment that the world outside of the chapel was modern. I had fully latched onto my explanation of all the weird things around me as proof that French-Amish living must be a thing. To be honest, it had sustained me for at least the last week.

As we made our way toward *le château de Trégoudan*, however, I began to anxiously search for signs of modern life, with an increasing sense of panic. My stomach twisted upon itself, and my chest felt tight. I hadn't caught a glimpse of a properly paved road; I hadn't seen a single car. The farms we passed showed no signs of advanced farming implements. The handful of people I saw on the road were dressed in long gowns and stockings, sturdy boots, or in some instances, uncomfortable-looking wooden shoes, old-fashioned waistcoats, and coats worn over what appeared to be hand-sewn linen shirts, breeches, and cloaks. They were all traveling on foot, on horseback, and on one occasion, they ambled past us in a rickety, wooden wagon.

As the miles gradually melted by, I found myself looking, with desperation, for signs of electricity. After about two hours, I noticed our direction had changed, and we were now headed north.

Gabriel passed me a heel of bread and a chunk of hard cheese for lunch. I forced myself to munch on the crusty bread as I carefully watched the countryside. The food settled like a rock in my stomach, but I knew I had to eat something. We passed two more unstable-looking wagons led by tired horses. The villages we passed through had cobbled streets and charmingly hand-painted signs, but I didn't catch a single glimpse of a person dressed in modern clothing. There was no way that this entire region of France was dedicated to living in the past.

I had devoted years of my life to learning about France and its history, surely, I would know if this was a thing. *Wouldn't I?*

Gabriel must have noticed how quiet I was because as we put more distance between *Camaret-sur-mer* and us, he began to uncharacteristically point things of interest out to me along the way. For the most part, I did nothing to keep the flow of conversation going, other than the occasional nod. I felt overwhelmed by how the day had unraveled. None of my expectations prior to leaving the chapel had come to fruition.

As we entered the small town of *Trégoudan*, he turned partially in the saddle toward me. "We are quite close now; *le château* is just up that crest." He gestured toward a gently sloping hill beyond the edge of town where I could barely make out a handsome stone house with a turret in one corner. "How are you feeling?"

"A bit tired," I admitted grudgingly.

In fact, I was feeling quite sore. The ride had jostled my ribs and injured arm quite a bit, even though the pace had been considerately slow. I felt a stab of guilt at the knowledge that the men could have traveled a good deal faster without me. As we approached the summit, the charming *château* came fully into view; the limestone shining in the last golden rays of light. I watched as a heavily, pregnant young woman walked out the front door to stand on the wide, stone steps.

"Mathieu! Gabriel!" she called gaily, waving one hand at them.

The men quickly alighted their horses, and Mathieu strode swiftly toward her and kissed her passionately.

This pretty young woman must be his wife.

Her golden blonde hair was sleekly pulled away from a heart-shaped face that was eerily similar to Carri's. From a distance, I might have mistaken her for my friend. I swallowed down the instant lump in my throat and hastily blinked back tears. This was not the time to start crying about Carri.

Gabriel dismounted, and turned immediately toward me, gently helping me down from Automne. My legs wobbled and Gabriel held me steady until I felt stable on my feet. My stomach fluttered unexpectedly as he kept one hand supportively under my elbow and turned to his sister, warmly hugging her with his other arm.

"Amélie, may I present Mademoiselle Ava Martel. Mademoiselle Ava, this is my dear sister Amélie, *la Baroness Trégoudan.*"

I awkwardly curtsied to Gabriel's sister and smiled warmly. I looked up into glacial, assessing, light blue eyes that did not smile back at me. Mild disapproval was clear on Amélie's face. My heart sank.

Why would she take such an obvious and immediate dislike to me?

Amélie raised a blonde brow questioningly at her husband and Gabriel, but serenely stepped aside and said, "Welcome to *le château de Trégoudan,* Mademoiselle Martel."

"*Merci beaucoup,*" I murmured.

I quietly followed the men into a neat, stone entrance hall, hung with tapestries. I glanced back over my shoulder to see two stable lads leading the horses away. For a moment, I wished I were back on Automne being jostled and jolted across the country. I squirmed uncomfortably under Amélie's scrutinizing stare and meekly followed everyone into a bright sitting room, with a large cheery fire and several tall, mullioned windows that overlooked the gardens. It was a beautiful room that I ordinarily would have loved exploring, but not today. I sat quietly, straight-backed in, what I would bet my life on was, a Louis XVI chair with heavily carved, delicate arms.

I let the conversation swirl around me. Mathieu and Amélie were looking at each other tenderly, obviously, a match made in love. I felt a little stab of envy at the way Mathieu held his wife's hand. I forced myself to look away and my mind drifted as I busily turned over Amélie's obvious aversion to me. The potential implications of the utter lack of modernism viewed thus far on my journey to Nantes swirled dizzily in my head.

"Mademoiselle Ava, where is your journey taking you?" Amelie's voice cut into my reverie.

I glanced up in surprise, my gaze caught in the glittering brightness of her eyes. "*Le Vicomte* has promised to help me get to Nantes," I murmured, feeling my cheeks flush.

She raised a perfectly plucked brow and I thought again of how much she favored Carri. I glanced away, blinking my eyes furiously against the prickle of oncoming tears.

"What awaits you in Nantes?" she asked, forcing me to look back at her.

Gabriel and Mathieu were in the midst of their own conversation, and catching the words *'La Reine,'* I glanced toward Gabriel, scrunching my brow in interest. The double doors were suddenly flung open and the most adorable, tow-head little boy ran gleefully into the room, followed by a harassed-looking nanny.

"Papa!" he cried joyfully. He ran toward Mathieu, who knelt to receive the enthusiastic hug. Turning, the little boy launched himself into Gabriel's arms next, who laughingly swung him up in the air, before gently depositing him safely back on the ground.

"Comment vas-tu, Étienne?"

"Très bien, mon oncle. Comment vas-tu?" Came the piping reply.

"Je vais très bien," replied Gabriel, ruffling his nephew's blonde hair.

"Avez-vous des bonbons pour moi?"

Gabriel laughed and reached into his pocket, producing one of the hard lemon candies he always seemed to have on him, and held it out to the boy.

Gabriel's easy exchange with his nephew squeezed my heart.

"Merci." He quickly unwrapped the candy and popped it into his mouth. *"C'est qui?"* he asked, glancing inquisitively at me.

I smiled warmly at his serious expression and leaned forward in my chair to be at eye level with him. I looked into eyes exactly like his mother's, with the difference that he was looking at me warmly and openly. His little boy's face was alight with excitement and curiosity.

"Je suis Mademoiselle Ava Martel, mais vous pouvez m'appeler Ava." My name is Ava Martel, but you may call me Ava, I said in a conspiratorial whisper.

Étienne smiled at me and gently reached out to touch my arm, which I was now keeping in a sling that Madame Amelot had fashioned for me.

"How did you get hurt?" he asked earnestly. The innocent sweetness of the gesture and the obvious concern on his small face touched my heart.

"My boat was caught in a storm, and it wrecked. I hurt my arm on the rocks," I answered simply.

Out of the corner of my eye, I caught a look of surprised horror on Amélie's face, but I disregarded it and focused on Étienne's wide, shocked eyes inches from my own.

"Were you being chased by pirates?" came his eager response. His blue eyes twinkled with excitement.

I laughed out loud. "Thankfully, no," I answered honestly, "But I am not sure I would have survived if your papa and uncle had not saved me."

"My papa and my uncle are heroes!" Étienne bellowed exuberantly.

"They truly are," I replied warmly. I glanced up and caught Gabriel watching me intensely. I looked away, flustered, goosebumps stippling my arms.

"That's enough of bothering Mademoiselle Ava," interjected Amélie, gently herding Étienne back toward the nanny. She glanced back over her shoulder and addressed me. "I've had a room made ready for you. I'll show you up now so that you may rest before supper."

I stood up nervously and Gabriel and Mathieu stood up as well. *I suppose that means we'll be staying the night.*

My shoulders slumped a bit at the thought.

"I will come to see you shortly, if I may?" asked Gabriel in his proper manner.

"Yes, of course." I looked down, hiding my confusion.

I followed Amélie out of the open doors and up the wide, gleaming wood front stairs. At the top of the stairs, we turned to the left.

"You have a lovely little boy, Baroness Amélie. He must bring you so much joy."

Amélie glanced at me sharply, but her face softened dramatically when she realized that I was being sincere. "He truly does Mademoiselle. He makes every day better." She stopped at a door halfway down the corridor. "I will have one of the girls bring up whatever you might need." She paused and fidgeted with her skirt. "Were you truly injured in a shipwreck?"

I nodded grimly and bit my lip hard. "I was caught in a terrible storm and the ship was struck by lightning. I cannot remember everything that happened, but there is no doubt that your brother and your husband saved my life. I don't know what they were doing on the beach in that storm," I added in afterthought. "But I thank God that they were there." I hid my hand in my voluminous skirt, pleating the soft fabric nervously between my fingers.

Amélie crossed herself solemnly. "Thank God indeed." With a ghost of a real smile, she turned to go.

I quietly closed the door behind her and sank onto the edge of the bed. The room was delightfully pretty and serene. Assuming that Gabriel's sister had overseen the decoration of it, it gave me a little insight into the young woman. The colors of the tapestries on the walls were the soft, muted blues, grays, and greens of a misty forest. The pretty quilt spread across the bed echoed the same soothing palette. The room was warm and comfortable, the pillows looked soft and inviting. I thought that Amélie was probably usually a kind, warm, and generous person. The puzzle was why she had taken such an instant dislike to me. A knock sounded quietly at the door.

"Come in," I called.

The door opened to reveal Gabriel— *le Vicomte*— I corrected myself.

"I thought we might stay here for the night," Gabriel began as he hovered at the door. "If that's amenable with you?"

"I don't think your sister wants me here." The words were out of my mouth before I could bite my tongue. *Why did I say that aloud?*

It didn't matter what his sister thought. Except— I was surprised to hear a small internal voice pipe in— except, it *did* matter to me.

Ruefully, Gabriel chuckled. "I am sorry she didn't give you a warm welcome. Amélie is one of the kindest people you will ever meet, but she is extremely protective of her family. No doubt she is thinking right now that you are a hussy that will spirit me away. . . I will speak to her."

I grinned at the image he painted. The thought of spiriting this serious man anywhere was positively laughable. "I don't think she needs to worry about that!" I laughed. My mirth was cut short by the heartfelt expression on his face.

"I do believe you could spirit me away quite easily if you wished it," Gabriel said quietly. My face must have reflected my surprise because he hastened to add, "But do not worry, I am sure you will win over my sister. You have already won over little Étienne, and that is half the battle!"

I smiled easily at the thought of Gabriel's nephew, "He is such a sweet little boy."

Gabriel smiled indulgently. "Our family is small, but we all rather dote on him." Then he changed the subject. "So, will we stay tonight? I am sure a good, warm meal and a real bed will be restorative after today's journey. You are still not fully recovered."

I gave in. The thought of a satisfying meal was enough to sway me. I was in no rush to get back on Automne's back, no matter how much of a beauty he was. Anyway, it would give me some time to digest what I had, or rather, what I hadn't seen today, and what it might mean.

TEN
MINEFIELD

I awoke in the morning to the steady, unmistakable sound of rain, and I stood, my bare feet cold against the floor, looking out the window at the muddy puddles below, and beyond that, at the angry, windswept ocean. I rested my forehead against the cool glass and closed my eyes. Surely, we wouldn't be leaving today. I just wasn't sure if I was relieved or frustrated with the delay.

There was no help for it though, I might as well make the best of it. On the bright side, perhaps I could spend some time with little Étienne, who was well on his way to stealing my heart.

An hour later, I made my way downstairs. I was getting tired of wearing the same clothes day after day, but I had nothing else. I should be grateful that the church gave me this gown— I told myself— even if it did smell of horse from yesterday's ride.

I longed for a broken-in pair of jeans and one of my favorite, soft, cozy sweaters. *Will I ever get to wear them again?*

I ruthlessly tamped down the thought. It wouldn't serve me to get caught up in missing things. Possessions, after all, could be replaced. Unlike people.

I rapidly blinked back the sting of oncoming tears at *that* thought and ambled my way slowly toward the dining room where we had eaten the night before. I paused to admire the tapestries on the walls. The colors were more brilliant than any I had seen in the *châteaux* I had visited in

France a few years ago. It occurred to me that the silk threads used must be newer, and therefore brighter, but I quickly shook that thought away, as it threatened to derail my sanity entirely.

I felt rather like I was picking my careful way through a minefield that promised to blow me to oblivion with a single misstep, and I stopped just outside the dining room doors which stood ajar, to peer at a posed portrait of a man and woman with three young children.

The painter had done a beautiful job of capturing the family. I instantly recognized a young Gabriel and a sweet, blonde toddler that had to be Amélie. There was an older boy who bore a striking resemblance to Gabriel, obviously a brother. The gentleman must be their father; his eyes were the same molten silver as Gabriel's and the woman was stunningly pretty in a quiet, unassuming way. Soft voices floated out of the room.

"Was there no trouble with the shipment then?" asked Amélie.

"None," came Gabriel's barely audible reply. ". . . the storm. . . "

I strained my ears to hear what he was saying. Shipment? Was that what he and Mathieu had been doing on the beach the night of my wreck? I'd been thinking that it was extremely odd that the men would have been out in such a storm.

"We were able to hand off the cargo. . . "

I heard footsteps as they approached on the parquet floor and my heart was pounding as I turned to see *le Baron* walking toward me.

He smiled kindly. "Have you had breakfast yet?"

"Ah—no. Not yet," I stammered. "I was just looking at this painting." I gestured lamely toward the portrait. It wasn't a lie. I *had* been looking at it before I had been distracted by Gabriel and Amélie's conversation.

"It's a beautiful painting, isn't it?" commented Mathieu. "I believe Gabriel was six and Amélie was three when this was commissioned."

Thank God he didn't seem to suspect I had been trying to listen in on his wife's conversation with her brother. "This is their older brother?" I pointed at the older boy; his smile suggested a hint of mischief.

"*Oui*. His name was Pierre." He offered me his arm and added, "Shall we?"

I caught the past tense and wondered at it, but Mathieu was obviously done with the conversation, and I didn't see that I had a choice, so I took his arm as graciously as I could and walked into the dining room with him. Gabriel, who was facing the doors, noticed our entrance immediately. His eyes found mine and he smiled warmly as he scraped his chair back and stood.

"Good morning, I hope you slept well?" he asked solicitously, inclining his head toward me as I sat down.

A maid appeared, seemingly out of nowhere to place a plate in front of me and pour me a steaming cup of chocolate.

"Very well, thank you," I murmured. *When did he become so chatty?*

I glanced at the streaming windows. "I suppose we will be delaying our departure with this weather?"

"*Oui*," came Gabriel's rueful reply. "Although it is a blessing in disguise. It will give you an extra day to recover before we begin the longer part of our journey in earnest, and it gives me an additional day to visit with my little sister." He gave Amélie a teasing, brotherly look at this, then winced as she kicked him under the table. He redirected his attention toward me. "We plan to set out early tomorrow morning. It should take us about six days to arrive in Nantes."

I still couldn't get over the fact that I was going to be traveling through France by horseback, but I merely nodded at Gabriel and concentrated on my breakfast. The *chocolat* was incredibly rich and satisfying, the bread fresh and crusty, and the butter, light and creamy. My *déjeuner* was delightful, and if I had to be stuck anywhere, I mused, at least it was France, where the food was incredible.

With nothing to do after breakfast, I wandered around the maze of corridors and found the library. In keeping with the theme of rejecting anything modern, it was exactly what I would imagine an eighteenth-century, private library should be. The ceiling soared above my head, and the walls bore shelf after shelf of books. One wall was dominated by a large fireplace and another had the same tall, mullioned windows the parlor had. As a lover of books, it was fascinating to sort through hundreds of leather-bound, gilt, embossed, and stamped books. I carefully opened them, one after another, and inhaled the old, musty, comforting aroma.

Eventually, I found a French history book that looked promising, and brought it up to my room with me. I curled up cozily on the window seat and listened to the rain beat incessantly outside. As fascinated as I had always been with French history, I found myself unable to concentrate on the book. My mind wandered as I stared sightlessly out the window. I rested my cheek against the cool, wavy, glass and let my mind drift over the past weeks. I was beginning to question my French-Amish narrative, but the alternative was simply too crazy to give credence to.

What if— just what if it was true though? Was it possible that I had somehow fallen back through time? Could it truly be 1787?

From the moment I washed ashore on that rocky beach, there was absolutely nothing I could remember from the twentieth century. *If I did time travel though... when did it happen? How did it happen?*

My mind sifted through the days before the shipwreck. I had certainly still been in the twentieth century when Carri and I left Britain. By my calculations, that had been about three weeks ago now. It had to have been 1987, during the storm when Carri had fallen overboard. I closed my eyes against the sudden pain brought on by the thought of Carri and a silent tear squeezed out from beneath my down-swept lashes to make its solitary way down my cheek. I tasted the saltiness of it on my lips and it made me think of the sea.

Our ship's radio had been working just prior to the storm. We had been in communication with a nearby boat discussing the impending weather and potential route changes. After the first storm, the radio no longer worked. Had I time-traveled during that storm? Or had it happened a few days later, when I encountered the second storm and took a direct strike of lightning to the mast? Was lightning the catalyst? Was I losing my grip on my sanity by even mulling this over? My thoughts were interrupted by a knock at the door.

"Entrez."

I expected it to be Gabriel and was surprised and disappointed to see his sister and another young woman who I'd seen briefly at breakfast; both with their arms laden with clothes instead. Her full, pregnant belly protruding ahead of her, Amélie walked briskly into the room and unceremoniously dropped several dresses and petticoats on the bed. She motioned for the girl to do the same.

"I thought you might need a few more dresses, as I'm sure you lost everything in the storm," she said conversationally. My mouth opened in shock and then snapped closed again, without uttering a word. Amélie continued, unperturbed, "I'm a bit taller than you, but I think with Esme's help we can adjust a few of these for you before you leave. She's going to be traveling with you. Gabriel wants a chaperone, so she can help with the others on the road. She's usually one of my companions, but she's eager to do a bit of traveling."

"I. . . thank you, thank you so much," I stammered in response. "Truly, this is more than I need though. Surely, you would rather keep some of these for yourself?" I asked, fingering a gorgeous, soft, green velvet. It was almost the exact color of my eyes, and I knew I would turn heads in it. Not that *that* was my intention.

"Not at all!" replied Amelie airily. "I have plenty, and honestly, this green one here will suit you so much better than it ever did me. Let's try it on now to see how it fits."

The next hour flew by as I was deftly buttoned and laced into one gown, after another. Esme possessed a good eye for fashion and made adjustments, carefully pinning the changes we discussed to each dress. By the time one of the maids appeared, to inform us that lunch was served, Amélie, Esme, and I were smiling and laughing, as though the animosity I had felt from her the previous afternoon had been a figment of my imagination.

Eleven
1787

The following morning, I awoke to more dreary, wet weather. Rain pattered unceasingly against the thick stone walls of the *château*, steady as a heartbeat. The wind howled around the eaves and rattled the shutters at the windows eerily, making the hairs on my arms and neck prickle. One peek out of the pretty, wavy glass, at the roiling, steely ocean, told me we certainly would not be leaving today either.

The miserable, stormy weather continued for the next several days before feeble sunshine finally broke through the clouds, late on the fourth day. Eager to set out, my stomach tight with anticipation, I found myself up uncharacteristically early the next morning. The garden and grass were slippery with iced-over puddles, and I picked my way carefully to where the horses were waiting. *The last thing I need is to slip on ice and break my other arm.*

The frigid wind bit through my layers of clothes and I shivered. The temperature had dropped precipitously overnight and never a fan of the cold, I was fervently hoping that the bright sunshine would warm us on the long ride ahead.

I had dressed as warmly as I could in a lovely dark emerald wool gown. I was loathe to admit it, but the additional petticoats helped me keep warm on the first day's ride, and I donned them without a murmur of complaint this morning. I shivered again, as a particularly strong gust whipped across the garden.

Amélie, Esme, and I had spent a great deal of time over the last few days taking in and hemming the clothing Amélie gave me. I was excruciatingly self-conscious during our sewing hours; my seamstress skills left a lot to be desired compared to Amélie's neat, consistent stitches, particularly with my arm in a sling. I couldn't think of a way to explain my obvious ineptitude with a needle and thread though, without coming across as stark, raving mad.

I chuckled as I thought of trying to explain where I came from, needlework was an unnecessary skill. Instead, I focused my energy on improving my eighteenth-century talents and tried to get to know Amélie and Esme better. I had been pleasantly surprised by how lovely it was to sit cozily in peace with them while the rain poured outside. It'd been equally delightful taking breaks to read to and play with little Étienne. I was going to miss Amelie. It was ironic considering how we'd begun, less than a week ago, but her dry sense of humor had Esme and me rolling with laughter during our sewing sessions.

It was wonderful to wear a new-to-me dress, and I knew the color and cut were flattering on me. Amélie also thoughtfully gifted me several pairs of stockings, a pair of warm, fleece-lined gloves, and another cloak. I walked out the front door that morning with a flutter of anticipation, knowing I looked radiant, and secretly looking forward to Gabriel's reaction when he saw me. Something about the way he quietly watched me made the blood race in my veins. Amélie followed me out onto the cobbled path with little Étienne in tow.

"Thank you so much for everything. It's been lovely spending the last few days with your family." I felt an unexpected catch in my throat as I affectionately hugged Amélie and froze mid-squeeze as images cartwheeled through my mind.

Amélie paced her chamber in a long, white night rail. Her hair was coming loose from its plait and the strands straggled over her shoulders and down her back. Her face, usually so serene wore a grimace of pain, and sweat made her nightgown stick damply to her skin in places.

Her endless walking suddenly halted, and she doubled up over her belly, clutching it tightly, and moaned. After what seemed like an eternity, she straightened up and resumed her frenzied pacing.

A moment later she was on the floor, curled in the fetal position, tears streaming down her face.

The scene faded before being replaced with a new scene.

Amelie handed a baby swaddled in linen and lace to Gabriel.

"This is my beautiful Thérèse," she said, her eyes shining with love.

His eyes crinkled at the corners as he smiled down at the sweet face.

"Ava—Ava! Is everything all right?"

I blinked and pulled away from Amélie's concerned grasp. *What the hell just happened?*

"I'm fine," I muttered. But I didn't feel fine. My pulse was hammering, I felt sweaty and chilled to the bone. My head was throbbing. I forced a smile. "I just remembered something I thought I had forgotten."

Amélie looked at me doubtfully but nodded. "Have a safe trip." She hugged me again and I held my breath, bracing myself for visions, and carefully let it out when nothing happened.

"I'm sure we will be fine." I gave her huge belly a gentle pat. "Have a smooth and safe delivery," I added fervently, the images of the vision fresh in my mind.

She smiled serenely. "Everything will be fine. I had no problems with Étienne, thank God." She crossed herself reflexively.

I crouched down to receive Étienne's enthusiastic hug and closed my eyes briefly to inhale the sweet, warm, little boy's scent of him. I opened my eyes and met Gabriel's eyes watching me with an inscrutable expression. Feeling the telltale heat of embarrassment creeping up my neck, I looked away. *How did I allow myself to grow so attached to Gabriel's family in just a few days?*

I knew why though— I was clinging to his family because I had none of my own. I probably wouldn't see any of them again. Getting attached was an exercise in futility. The knowledge was a punch in the stomach, leaving me feeling hollow and empty.

There were questions in Gabriel's eyes as one of the stable lads helped me onto Automne behind him. "Are you all right, Ava?" He searched my face for clues.

"Yes, thank you," I lied, acid churning in my stomach.

His gaze met mine and held it for a long moment. He seemed to be saying that he knew I wasn't being honest, but he didn't push me, he simply tucked my free arm under the layers of his cloak and fur and clicked softly to Automne.

As we rode away, with a much larger entourage this time, but missing Mathieu, who had opted to stay behind for his second child's impending birth, I looked back at the neat, stone *château* overlooking the water, and felt a pang of longing. They all seemed so content. They all belonged here, and I did not belong anywhere, although I had fooled myself for a few brief moments that I might belong here. *As always, I am saying goodbye.*

I sat quietly behind Gabriel and felt the sadness swell inside me as I watched the hills and bluffs roll slowly by. I could only assume that Gabriel was lost in thoughts of his own, or sensed my mood because he was quiet for the first hour we were on the road. For the majority of the morning, we rode within sight of the coast, as it wound its way south and east.

Gabriel finally broke the silence. "We'll be stopping in Quimper this evening. There's a little *auberge* there that I know. The food is excellent."

"Will we just be stopping for one night?"

He studied the wide, blue expanse of sky before replying. "Aye, unless the weather turns. I don't think it will though."

I had to agree. This part of France was considered a microclimate, but the signs all indicated we were in an area of high pressure. The weather should be clear for the next few days, at least.

"I'm sorry to have dragged you away from your sister. I'm sure you would have preferred to stay longer?"

He shrugged and threw a glance over his shoulder at me. "I don't particularly relish the thought of sticking around for childbirth if that's what you mean?" he raised an eyebrow at me, and I blushed. I hadn't thought of that. He passed one of his lemon candies back to me. A peace offering.

"Thank you." I plucked it out of his palm and dropped it in my mouth. "How many of these do you carry around with you?"

The grin transformed his face, making my stomach flutter. "Aren't they delicious? I was running low, but luckily Amelie keeps some for me at *Trégoudan* and I was able to replenish my supply."

I let out a soft laugh at this. "They're like a drop of sunshine," I admitted, and it was the truth. I could feel the citrus pulling me out of my funk.

"A drop of sunshine," he mused. "That's an excellent description.

We fell into an easy, companionable silence as we left the rocky, dramatic bluffs behind. As the miles passed, I noticed dispassionately that I was no longer searching avidly for signs of modern living. The part of me that had been clinging to the idea that the party of people I was with were all crazy, had silently given up. I wordlessly took in the passing terrain, the muddy lanes, the stone and wood houses and farms that we passed, with a sinking feeling in my gut. *Am I stuck in the eighteenth century for good?*

The hours crept by, and I felt increasingly cold and uncomfortable. The warm clothes Amélie gave me helped immensely the first few hours of the journey, but as the autumn sun began its leisurely descent across the sky, I grew colder. My toes and fingers were numb and tingly by the time we made the final turn toward Quimper, and the pretty town came into view. It was growing dark, as we made our way past picturesque, half-timbered houses that faced the river Odet, which bisected the town.

I watched as shopkeepers and residents came out onto the cobblestone lane to light the oil lanterns. After a few minutes, our horses turned off the main street. We passed a charming stone church and arrived outside an *auberge* bearing the name *'Le Coq Danseur.'* I chuckled to myself as a rooster danced in my over-tired brain. I slid off Automne and rested against him as my trembling legs accustomed themselves to being back on solid ground. I had never ridden a horse for so many hours, and I felt stiff and sore from my head to my frozen toes.

Gabriel offered me his arm and I took it gratefully. We were followed into the warm *auberge* by Esme and Luc; one of the men who had traveled from *Trégoudan* with us. I took a deep breath as we entered the old, half-timbered inn. It smelled strongly of woodsmoke, which brought back comforting memories of nights around the bonfire with my parents. I also caught a whiff of freshly baked bread, which was quickly becoming one of my favorite things about France, and the mouthwatering aroma of whatever the kitchen was preparing for supper.

Along one wall was a roaring fire, and after the long, cold trip, I was drawn to it, like a moth. It wasn't long before our entire entourage was gathered by the hearth, warming outstretched fingers, and basking in its glow. A long wood bar lined the back of the room, and I watched as the buxom barmaid hurried over to greet us.

While Gabriel secured two rooms for the night and other accommodations for the rest of the men, I busied myself by looking around the inn; internally verifying that there were still no signs of electricity. My stomach was a knot of anxiety and I felt like I couldn't get a full breath of air in. It was becoming harder to ignore the mountain of evidence staring me in the face.

Somehow, I am no longer in 1987.

The men brought our belongings up the creaky wooden stairs and Gabriel opened the second door in the corridor, motioning for Esme and me to enter. It was sparsely furnished but looked clean and cozy.

"I will be in the room right next to yours should you need anything." Gabriel pulled a gold pocket watch out wand glanced at the time. "The *auberge* is serving supper downstairs in about thirty minutes. Will you come down? Or shall I have them bring it up for you?" He looked at me expectantly as he slid the watch back into his pocket.

I leaned against the door frame. I was tired down to my bones, but I did not feel like sitting alone in the room with only Esme, my chaperone, for company, even if she was genuinely nice. "I will see you downstairs for supper," I decided.

Gabriel let out a breath and smiled at me. I couldn't help but smile back. "I will see you soon then." Gabriel bowed deeply and left, pulling the door shut behind him.

As soon as the door closed, Esme sighed dramatically. "Ava, did you see how he looked at you? He's so handsome."

I looked at Esme curiously. "He is very good-looking," I conceded. "Have you been with the family for long?" Somehow, Esme's history hadn't come up during our sewing sessions. Now that I thought about it, it was a bit odd.

"*Oui,*" Esme responded, adding, "After my father passed away, we were left nearly destitute. He gambled away all his inheritance. . . and mine, I suppose. Thank the Lord that my mother and Gabriel's *maman* grew up on neighboring estates. We moved in with them and my mother became Gabriel and Amélie's governess. Now she looks after little Étienne."

"You grew up with them?" I asked, surprise making me raise my brows.

"I did. They are a lovely family, very generous. Of course, it could have gone very wrong with Gabriel coming into his own at such an early age, without many older people around to guide him— or so my mother always says," divulged Esme chattily. "You know, I do believe he has been caught up by you," she added slyly with a sidelong glance at me.

"Oh. . . I don't think so," I murmured. *What game is she up to? Pushing Gabriel and I together.*

I wanted to ask more about his childhood, and what Esme meant by her cryptic remark about coming into his own, but I was distracted by her last comment. Could it be true? My heart leaped at the thought. He had been exceedingly kind to me and even teased me a few times, but generally speaking, he was very reserved. As far as I could tell, that was just his personality though.

As if reading my mind, Esme said, "He is not the type to be obvious, or flamboyant, mind. He is incredibly quiet about his feelings. Even after his father and brother died, he only disclosed his grief to a few close friends. But anyone with eyes could see the way he looks at you. I would kill for a man to look at me like that."

I blushed furiously, feeling the heat creep up my neck. I had never been as boy-crazy as some of my friends had been growing up; as a teenager, or in college. Very few boys, or men for that matter, had ever stirred my interest, and those that had, had all been so self-absorbed that I'd quickly lost interest myself.

The things that ignited my passion were rarely shared with others. There were few people that I'd met that had loved sailing and the sea, as much as Carri and I had. Even fewer had an interest in French history, reading, gardening, or traveling the world. Those who enjoyed traveling were limited in the places they wanted to see. They certainly didn't want to circumnavigate the world. As for sailing, even growing up in Annapolis, commonly considered a sailing mecca, I hadn't met many people who did it more than recreationally. The fact that Carri had loved the same things, had created a bubble around us where only the two of us existed.

Although I hadn't spoken a great deal with Gabriel over the few weeks since he and Mathieu had rescued me, I felt a quiet connection with him, which was inexplicable. I also had to admit to myself, even if I didn't reveal it to the lively Esme; that he was unquestionably handsome. I would probably have to be dead at the bottom of the ocean; to not feel the jump in the pit of my stomach every time we made eye contact. It wasn't the kind of feeling I could ignore.

Thankfully, Esme dropped the subject then. "Shall I fix your hair? It's a bit windblown."

Twelve
Breathing in Unison

I was significantly warmer and reasonably spruced up when Esme and I made our way downstairs a brief time later. Gabriel and some of the others sat at a table and several of the men were clustered around the bar. It was loud, dimly lit, and it was clear that a few of the men had already begun to drink heavily.

Relief swept through me as I spied an empty seat next to Gabriel. I walked toward him when he waved me over and I sat beside him. My stomach clutched as he smiled radiantly at me and leaned in close to be heard above the din. It was obvious that he'd had a drink or two as well. It had loosened his natural reserve considerably.

"Wine?" he offered, pouring a glass, and sliding it over to me.

"*Merci*." I took a cautious drink and was pleasantly surprised by its smooth finish.

I felt the warming and relaxing effects of it almost instantly. I took another sip and gingerly settled back in my chair. My legs, bottom, and back were sore from riding Automne all day. I had vastly underestimated how many muscles were needed for riding horseback. I grimaced slightly, unaware that Gabriel was watching my expression avidly.

"Are you all right?" His face displayed a moment's hesitation before he dove in. "Am I correct in assuming you are not accustomed to riding?"

My obvious unease and stiffness in the saddle had evidently not gone unnoticed by him. For one wild moment, I envisioned myself telling him exactly why I was unaccustomed to riding, but I settled for nodding instead. "I'm all right, just a little sore. I imagine I will get used to it soon."

A steaming bowl of *cotriade*— fish stew arrived just then, and I hungrily turned my attention to the food. It was surprisingly well seasoned, and garlicky, and they hadn't skimped on the serving of mackerel, potatoes, and leeks. I ate my fill until I was satiated from the food and the effects of the wine, which I was beginning to realize was stronger than I initially thought. I sat back and relaxed, observing what was going on around me.

Gabriel was deep in conversation with Luc, and Esme had excused herself to go to bed immediately after we ate. As tired and sore as I was, I did not feel ready to sleep. I had never been in an *auberge* in eighteenth-century France, and I was excited to watch the people interact.

For a while, I observed a few upper-crust patrons, as they argued heatedly at a table in the corner. They must be talking politics if their avid expressions were anything to go by. My attention wandered to a group of rough-looking men clustered around the bar. The barmaid flirted with one of them; leaning over suggestively as she displayed cleavage. *Some things have not changed much in the last two hundred years.*

As the hour grew late, I noticed most of the well-dressed people retired, and the ones left were getting increasingly drunk and belligerent. A fight over a woman of questionable repute broke out in one corner. I looked on, impressed, as the owner, obviously not the type to put up with rowdiness, threw the men out of the *auberge* to continue their fight in the street.

I scanned the room and unintentionally met the eye of a tall, hulking man with a huge, greasy mustache at the bar. I recognized him as one of the men who had come with us from the château. He leered at me, and I hastily looked away.

I could feel his eyes on me, making the hairs on my arms stand at attention. *It's time for me to go.*

I stood, pushing my chair back, and Gabriel immediately stood up as well. It was silly, I was a fully capable twentieth-century woman after all, but I felt a rush of relief when he offered me his arm.

As we made our way through the throng of people crowded around the bar, I was forced to press my body close to his arm. The back of my neck and arms prickled, and I glanced over my shoulder to see the same sleazy man watching me. I shuddered slightly and moved marginally closer to Gabriel. I could feel his strength and comforting warmth through both our clothes. I allowed myself a small sigh of relief when we reached the stairs and began the ascent.

Gabriel noticed when Ava pressed more closely against him. He'd have to be dead not to notice. Her slim figure was closer than strictly necessary, though he would never dare to complain. His skin was on fire where her slender body leaned against his.

He was suffused with a sense of hyperawareness, of where his body ended and hers began, of every minute inch of his coat brushing against her gown. He was equally aware of the space between them, where they weren't touching, and the air flowed between them.

He felt a slight release of tension in her as they approached the stairs, and as he looked down at her gleaming, dark hair, he felt an inexplicable rush of tenderness. No other woman had ever affected him this way. They arrived at the door of the room she shared with Esme far too quickly to suit him, and she turned to face him.

"Thank you. . . Gabriel." She hesitated briefly over the use of his Christian name, her brow furrowed as though she were unsure if she had overstepped.

Gabriel relished the way his name sounded in her lilting voice. He could hear his heartbeat thundering in his ears. He swallowed; his mouth as dry as a young boy's lusting after his first girl.

Get ahold of yourself Chabot, he told himself sternly. He bowed low over her hand and brushed his mouth over her knuckles, daring to linger a moment longer than he knew he ought.

I felt the heat of his breath on my skin and felt a golden, pulsating glow infuse my entire body.

He straightened up, took a step back from me, and said in a slightly rough, gravelly voice, "*Bonne nuit* Ava, please. . . make sure to lock the door behind me."

The loss of warmth was instantaneous as he stepped away and I stood still for a moment, feeling bereft. Then I stepped back as well, quietly closed the door, and slid the bolt home.

I leaned my hot forehead against the polished wood of the door and closed my eyes. *Did Gabriel feel the heat between us?*

I let out an unsteady breath and heard the echo of another shaky breath being released in the corridor. A small smile touched the corners of my mouth.

He definitely felt it too.

Thirteen
Game Time

The days slid by as we plodded on toward Nantes. As we traveled to the south and east, an icy blast dogged our footsteps. The steadily increasing elevation made it hard to get a full breath in and in the distance, some mountain peaks were already capped in snow. Esme mentioned chattily that we were now in the *Sillon de Bretagne*, a small mountain range that Esme had never been to and that I had never heard of.

It was clear that the men were used to long trips on horseback as they seemed unaffected by the wearying days. They talked genially amongst themselves, and I often heard them joking, laughing, and cheerfully singing bawdy songs on the road.

I was used to periods spent with little sleep on passages on the boat, but I found myself exhausted traveling the countryside by horseback. By day, I froze, huddling as closely as I dared against Gabriel for warmth. At night, my muscles cramped painfully, and I tossed, and turned, unable to sleep, as Esme snored quietly beside me.

The few hours of sleep I managed to snatch, were spent fitfully dreaming of Carri and my parents. A relaxing drink after supper would help me sleep better, but after the first night in Quimper, I had avoided lingering downstairs after supper.

As the days dragged on, I became aware that the dark, heavily mustached man was still watching me. It was disquieting to see the look in his eyes as they followed me, everywhere. The other men called him Cifarelli and they nearly all gave him a wide berth. I deduced that Cifarelli had been with the group for only a few months based on fragments of conversation I picked up and a few tidbits of information, Esme shared.

He was known to drink too much and seemed to enjoy picking fights. Although I suspected that Gabriel tried for nonchalance, he was noticeably stiffer and more guarded around Cifarelli. The clipped, proper voice he used to speak to him, was at odds with the friendly, relaxed attitude he displayed around the other men. Esme and I scrupulously avoided his company.

By midmorning on the fifth day, the air was bitter and the clouds that rolled slowly across the sky were heavy with approaching snow. When we stopped for lunch, Esme and I sat huddled under a giant chestnut tree, our backs against the wide trunk, and slowly ate our customary bread and cheese. I watched Gabriel furtively under my lashes as he stood talking to some of the men several feet away. The first fat, lazy flakes had just begun to fall.

Esme nudged me and barely nodded her head toward Cifarelli. He stood a little way off, leaning negligently against a fence post. She barely moved her lips as she said, "I don't like the way he's been watching you."

"He scares me," I muttered quietly under my breath. "I wasn't sure if I was imagining it."

"You are not imagining it. I have seen men like him before. Please do not go anywhere alone from now on."

I was touched by Esme's concern and nodded. "How did he come to be with *le Vicomte et le Baron*? He does not seem to fit in with the other men."

"He does not," asserted Esme. "He showed up with Friloux." She nodded toward a weathered, old seadog with a kindly face. "Friloux met him on a trip a few months ago. I heard he was let go when they arrived at the port. He felt he deserved another chance." She shrugged, but her eyes were skeptical. "I know that Amélie has not taken to him. . . he is one of the few things I have ever seen Amélie, and *le Baron* argue over. I suspect that's why he was sent along with us, instead of staying at *le château*."

I let this bit of information sink in. It wasn't surprising that Amélie hadn't wanted him around. Something about Cifarelli was sinister, and it wasn't just his dark, slimy appearance. The feeling of being watched made my skin prickle. I looked up to find him staring boldly at me. When our eyes locked, he licked his lips lasciviously and grinned like a jack-o-lantern, revealing brown, rotting teeth, and a missing eyetooth.

I looked away in disgust and my gaze collided with Gabriel's who was studying me in his usual pensive way. As soon as my eyes met his, he straightened up from the tree he was leaning against and walked purposefully toward me, without breaking eye contact. Luc was talking to him, but Gabriel didn't seem to hear as he walked away.

He moved with an innate, quiet grace that made my pulse race and my mouth dry. I swallowed compulsively. Esme hurriedly excused herself, leaving me alone before I could protest. *So much for being my chaperone.*

He knelt in front of me, pulled a flask out of his coat pocket, and offered it to me. I took it but made no move to drink.

"It looks like the weather is done cooperating with us," he said quietly. "We still have many miles to cover today before we make it into Savenay for the night." He glanced up at the sky and frowned. "Snow is unusual at this time of year, but the weather is always unpredictable in these mountain passes." He nodded his head toward the flask that I was still holding in my hand, and added, "The brandy will help keep you warm, please drink a little."

His eyes looked concerned, so I obediently took a small sip. Its warmth spread down my throat, across my chest, and into my belly almost immediately. I took another tiny mouthful and the knot that had lived in my heart for days loosened. Emboldened by the brandy, I licked my chapped lips and met his eyes.

"Thank you."

His gaze lingered on my face like a caress. I could feel the telltale flush creeping up my neck, and my face was hot under his steady stare. I was inexplicably embarrassed and self-conscious, and my eyes slid away from his, to look over his shoulder. Cifarelli was watching us with an angry, dark expression on his face. I shuddered and glanced back at Gabriel.

Gabriel quickly looked behind him. He was scowling as he turned back toward me. "Has he been bothering you?" he demanded.

"Not exactly," I admitted in a whisper. I was surprised by the threat of violence in his usually calm voice. "He hasn't spoken to me at all. . . but it feels like he is always watching me. It makes me uncomfortable."

Cifarelli hadn't done anything threatening. Many people would argue that I was being dramatic. It didn't sound important when I verbalized it, but my intuition screamed not to let my guard down. I made it a point to listen to my inner voice, it hadn't failed me yet.

"Esme noticed as well, she told me not to go anywhere alone," I added.

Gabriel's eyes narrowed and darkened as he listened. "Esme is quite right," he said shortly. "Let me know if he says anything to you."

I felt slightly foolish for saying something about Cifarelli, but I was relieved that he took me seriously, and didn't brush me off. I took a deep breath, feeling calmed by his reaction.

Gabriel stood up and held his hand out to me. I took it gratefully. I still struggled with small, daily tasks and it was much easier to rise from the ground with help. He stayed uncharacteristically near me, nearly hovering, as he instructed the men quietly. Luc helped me onto Automne behind Gabriel before he mounted his horse. Esme, well-practiced at riding, swung up behind Luc effortlessly.

As the horses turned down the lane, I noticed tension and a sense of urgency in the men. I shifted behind Gabriel and leaned in closer to him. "Will we make it to Savenay before nightfall?"

Gabriel turned toward me. "We should have, but with the storm approaching, I'm not sure if we still will." He took out his flask and took a long swig before handing it back to me. "Are you cold? You should have a bit more."

I took another small swallow and returned it to Gabriel. The brandy was stronger than the wine I'd been drinking the last several weeks, and I was beginning to feel effects other than warmth. I closed my eyes and let it dance like fire through my veins. Emboldened by the brandy, I gave in to what I wanted to do all week and leaned against Gabriel, resting my cheek against the rough wool weave of his cloak.

The muscles in his back tightened for a second as the weight of my body pressed against his. A moment later, I felt the release of tension and breath as he relaxed. The stiffness was so fleeting that if I hadn't been so attuned to his response, I might have thought I imagined it.

The snow was falling thickly now, and the wind swirled it around in little eddies across green fields that quickly turned white. We followed along the rutted lane, passing the occasional farmhouse before we eventually turned off the main road onto a narrow path, which led to the entrance of a dense pine forest. We plowed onward as evergreens towered magnificently overhead, blocking out most of the light and making it appear later than it was.

The pine needles below the horse's hooves were already invisible under a thick, soft carpet of snow. I looked up to see boughs heavily frosted in sparkling white. I was startled as a shower of snow cascaded down from a branch that suddenly snapped under its weight.

I briefly glimpsed a doe as she leaped gracefully and soundlessly between the tree trunks and took a deep breath, holding it as I absorbed the serenity around us. I cupped the beauty of the moment close to my heart and it eased the loneliness that lived inside me. We were walking through a real-life enchanted forest.

As we continued through the pines, the intensity of the wind gradually strengthened as the storm ramped up in earnest. It whistled and howled through the branches, and blew the snow into ever higher drifts. The horses put their heads down and determinedly pressed on. The men mimicked the horses, their heads down, the hoods of their cloaks pulled high, and wrapped their scarves around their faces, leaving only their eyes visible.

It grew steadily darker. By the time we broke through the forest into the foot of the next mountain pass, the terrain around us was unrecognizable. Everywhere I looked, all I could see was white. The horses and men stayed close together. With visibility this poor, it would be easy to lose someone in the bleached landscape.

Ice began to mix in with the snow, and the wind pelted frozen shards into my exposed skin mercilessly. I hid my face against Gabriel's back and wrapped my free arm tightly around him. He took his thick fur and wrapped it more snuggly around us both before he tucked my arm and hand under his.

"Are you alright, Ava?" his voice was muffled against his scarf.

"Aye," I answered, burrowing as close to him as I dared. Despite the sheer misery of the blizzard, I felt cocooned in a blanket of safety and warmth. *I almost don't care if we never make it to Savenay.*

We traversed the narrow pass between the mountains, and the snow changed completely to ice before switching back to snow. It was fully dark by the time we arrived in the outskirts of the small town, and I, no longer as cozy as I'd been several hours before, was thrilled to see the church steeple come into view.

We found the only *auberge* in town, conveniently next to a stable. After we settled the horses in, Gabriel procured rooms for the night. The inn was modest, dimly lit, and smelled strongly of yeasty beer and unwashed bodies. It was the type of place I suspected might be swarming with fleas, but I was grateful to be indoors at last.

I sat with my back to the meager fire as my cloak dripped melted snow and ice onto the murky, stained floorboards. Esme and I ate our supper of pork sausage, slathered in mustard, and wrapped in a *crêpe* quickly. Paired with a dark beer, it made a surprisingly tasty meal. It reminded me of a good old American hotdog. A wave of nostalgia crashed over me.

I bit into a ballpark hotdog the explosion of juices filling my mouth. The unseasonably warm April heat made tendrils of hair stick to my neck and cheeks. The fans roared as Brooks Robinson struck a walk-off homer, clinching the Orioles victory. My dad and I held hands as we jumped up and down in excitement.

The images of that day and so many others like it played like a movie in my overtired brain. *I wish I had one more opportunity— one more memory with my father.*

The impossibility of it made my eyes grow hot with the threat of tears and my throat seized up. I missed the quiet strength of my dad fiercely.

Fourteen
A Flicker in the Night

Exhausted from the long day, Esme and I tiredly climbed the dark stairs. The fire in our room was a slight improvement over the one downstairs, and we hung our clothing and cloaks over the two chairs in front of the hearth. I wearily sat to remove my leather boots and placed them by the fire.

"Hopefully our things will dry by the morning," said Esme as she placed her boots by the fire.

I looked at the meager fire skeptically. "Probably not."

Esme helped me put on my night dress and gently detangled my hair before she plaited it for the night. "Today was difficult, but at least there is only one more day of travel until we arrive in Nantes," she observed.

I nodded sleepily. "At least we're almost there."

Several days after I accepted the idea that I had somehow fallen back through time, I realized my errand to the authorities no longer made sense. I'd been lying sleeplessly in bed, listening to the sounds of the inn, when it occurred to me that the authorities wouldn't care much about my wreck. There was nothing to be gained by informing them that Carri had fallen overboard. They could never notify Carri's parents; at this point, a month had passed since the accident. There was no chance of a sea rescue. That ship had sailed.

I was beginning to wonder if it wasn't a mistake to speak to the authorities altogether. It would only raise more questions about me, where I was
from, and how my boat had wrecked. Questions that I couldn't answer.
Ever since that night, these thoughts, questions, and different possible
scenarios plagued my every waking moment.

I couldn't come up with a plausible explanation for no longer wishing to
make a report to the Navy though, particularly since I had been adamant
and insistent on making a report, to begin with. *How could I tell Gabriel,
after he had taken me and an entire group of men on a weeklong journey—
at great expense to himself— that now that we were on the cusp of arriving
in Nantes, I no longer wanted to speak to the Navy?*

An urgent pounding suddenly made the door shake in its frame. I
frowned, my stomach tense with anxiety, and my eyes met Esme's, in
concern.

Esme was up and was sliding back the bolt when I yelled, "Wait!"

I was too late. The door swung open and slammed against the stone wall
with a loud thud. Cifarelli stood in the ill-lit doorway, swaying drunkenly.
His black gaze landed on me as I jumped from the chair in alarm. He
roughly shoved Esme out of his way as he pushed his way into the room
and made a beeline toward me. Esme staggered into the doorway before
she fell heavily on the dirty, wide-planked floor.

"Esme!" I cried as I moved toward her to help her up.

"Come here!" leered Cifarelli's heavily accented voice, grabbing me with
a brutal grasp.

I gasped in pain as he jerked me toward him. "No!" I screamed.

I raised my left arm to fend him off, but he easily grabbed it and bent
it viciously behind my back. I blinked back tears at the intense pain as I
twisted and turned desperately in his harsh grasp. He leaned his face down

toward mine, and I gagged involuntarily at the rank, unwashed smell of him.

It was a mistake to show my disgust.

I knew it as soon as it happened. He grinned cruelly and twisted my good arm harder behind me as he licked the skin below my ear. My skin crawled as his saliva dripped down my neck, and my gorge rose in my throat. I turned my face away to see Esme quietly sneaking toward the door he'd left ajar. I closed my eyes briefly. *Please God, please God, please.*

Cifarelli let go of my injured arm and grabbed my face. He squeezed it cruelly between his large, blunt fingers, and wrenched it toward him. I gritted my teeth and elbowed him as sharply as I could in the gut with my broken arm. He doubled over and I raised my knee fiercely toward his groin. I missed my mark. *Fuck.*

He laughed maniacally. "I can give it to you rough, if that's what you like, *petite pute.*"

He grabbed my braid in one hand and yanked so hard my teeth snapped together. Then he slapped me brutally across the face. My mouth filled with the hot, metallic taste of blood. Cifarelli walked me backward farther into the room as panic surged through my veins. The backs of my legs hit the edge of the bed a second before he shoved me down. I filled my lungs to scream, but one massive, filthy hand crammed down over my mouth, crushing my lips against my teeth. My eyes filled with tears, but it only seemed to urge him on. His forearm pressed down on my throat. I closed my eyes in terror and kicked out wildly. I was no longer trying to aim my blows, just trying to land as many as possible.

His weight pressed down on me, compressing my lungs. It was becoming difficult to get a full breath in. Desperate, I bit down on his hand as hard as I could. The bones and tendons in his fingers ground sickeningly against my teeth.

Screaming, Cifarelli yanked his hand away from my mouth. I spat the taste of him out and took the moment to breathe as deeply as I could. Then I screamed at the top of my lungs. His hand connected harshly with my cheek. My ears rang and my vision blurred. He was using his forearm again, squeezing my windpipe. Black dots twirled before my eyes, and my vision grew dim. He was going to crush me beneath him. *I survived a freaking shipwreck, just for it to end like this.*

I closed my eyes to offer up one final, desperate prayer when his weight was abruptly lifted off.

I heard a sickening crunch and opened my eyes. I gasped for breath as I sat up. My hand went automatically to my neck and rubbed it as I panted, trying to suck air into my lungs. Every attempt burned painfully. My gaze landed on Esme. She was plastered against the wall of the room and her wide eyes were fixed on Gabriel who was crouched over the crumpled form of Cifarelli, systematically punching him. Several of the other men were clustered around the door watching impassively, but no one made a move to stop Gabriel.

Esme made a beeline for me, and hugged me, crying. "I ran for help as quickly as I could. He didn't. . . "

I hugged her back as fiercely as I could. "No, he didn't. Thank you, my friend. Without you, I don't know if—" I didn't finish. It was too horrific to contemplate.

"I am so sorry I opened the door! I don't know why I did that!" Esme sobbed.

I squeezed Esme again, tighter. "It's not your fault. Please don't blame yourself. I'm all right."

Esme embraced me back gratefully before we turned our attention to the men on the floor.

The room was utterly silent other than the merciless sound of Gabriel's fists making contact with Cifarelli's body. Despite myself, I winced in sympathy. After several tense minutes, Gabriel stood up. He was panting heavily and absentmindedly wiped his bloody hands on his breeches. Other than the steady rise and fall of his chest, Cifarelli lay motionless on the floor. Still alive then.

Gabriel's eyes sought out mine and slowly ran over my body, taking in my cut and bruised cheek, the bruises that were probably already darkening on my neck, and the blood I knew trickled out of the corner of my mouth. My nightgown hung off one shoulder, tattered, torn, and covered in blood. *I'm sure I look like hell.*

"*Putain de merde.*" He swore softly under his breath.

Luc stepped forward; he was the only one willing to approach Gabriel. He put one hand on his shoulder, leaned in, and quietly said something in his ear. Gabriel nodded once, barely taking his gaze off me before he stepped in my direction.

The ferocity in his eyes was scarcely repressed. I shivered and sought out Esme's hand, hidden in our skirts. Gabriel stopped a few feet short of the bed, noting our linked hands. His gray eyes were opaque with worry and regret. He opened his mouth to say something, but shut it abruptly, evidently rethinking whatever he meant to say.

Behind him, Luc gave quiet orders to the rest of the men. Two of them picked up Cifarelli's limp body and carried him out of the room. The rest of the men filed out so quietly, that I barely heard the shuffle of their boots on the floor.

Gabriel took another tentative step forward before he fell to his knees in front of us. He stared down at the grimy floorboards and gruffly said, "I am so sorry this happened, I take full responsibility. I should have taken the threat that scum presented more seriously. I never thought—" He broke off and raised eyes full of self-castigation and misery to meet mine. "You were under my protection, and I failed you."

I didn't expect Gabriel to blame himself for how Cifarelli had acted. Overwhelmed and confused, I looked away and stared at a knot on the wood floor, tracing the pattern it made with my eyes. Esme squeezed my hand lightly and I looked up to meet her gaze. Wordlessly she managed to convey that this was meant to be a private conversation. I nodded imperceptibly as she gently extricated her hand from my death grasp, stood up, and made her way to the door.

"I will be downstairs if you need me." She left the bedchamber door open as her feet pattered quietly down the hallway.

I watched her go before I turned my eyes back on Gabriel. His head was bent, studying the floor. I watched in detachment as my hand tremblingly reached out and settled on his thick, wavy hair. Its texture felt simultaneously soft and rough, and it flooded me with a feeling I couldn't name. Unconsciously I rubbed it between my fingertips and marveled at how the ends of it curled against the palm of my hand.

A fine tremor ran through his body, reverberating through us both. When he looked up at me, his expression was naked and vulnerable. I couldn't face what was written there and closed my eyes against it.

He swallowed hard. The way I swallow when I'm trying to push down bitterness and regret, but I can still taste it in the back of my throat. There were so many things I wanted to say, to ask, but I couldn't form the words. He let out a shuddering breath and took my hand in his, tenderly cradling it against his cheek.

I kept my eyes closed, imprinting the rough, prickly texture of his day-old beard in my memory, and the warm, smooth skin of his cheek under my fingers. My hand was trembling when he turned his head and pressed his lips fervently against my palm. His warm, moist breath fluttered against my hand and an answering quiver of longing thrummed in the deepest part of me.

I inhaled deeply and found my voice. "It's not your fault. No one could have known what he intended to do."

Gabriel opened his eyes and gazed at me. "Thank you for saying that, but I should have guessed. You entrusted me with your safety; I should have had a dependable man standing guard outside your room. I knew you had qualms about him. . . I had misgivings myself. I should have taken them more seriously. He will never bother you again." His voice sounded broken at his failure. I felt rather broken myself.

He noticed I was shaking before I did. He rose gracefully, removed his cloak, and gently placed it around my shoulders. Then he sat next to me, the bed creaking slightly and lowering under his added weight. The urge to lean my head against his shoulder and cry was crushing. *That wouldn't be acceptable, Ava.*

The enormity of my narrow escape was beginning to set in. Now that Cifarelli was gone, I began to shake uncontrollably as my rush of adrenaline crashed. Tears sprang to my eyes, and I blinked them back mercilessly.

Gabriel watched as I struggled to ingest the events of the last half hour. I turned imploring eyes on him, unshed tears threatening to gush like Niagara Falls. He cupped my face with one hand and gently rubbed his thumb over my cheek. It was tender and bruised, and I winced before I could check my reaction. Scarcely suppressed fury flashed in his eyes before he deliberately masked his expression. His hands trembled before he clenched them and sat as still as a big cat on a hunt, listening to an internal voice known only to himself.

After a moment, he stood swiftly and strode to the washstand in the corner of the room. He stood with his back to me, shoulders slumped for an interminable minute, then broke the thin film of ice in the basin, and carefully dipped his handkerchief in the freezing water.

He knelt before me and gently washed the blood away from the corner of my trembling mouth and then applied the cloth delicately to my swollen cheek. There was a quiet shuffling sound, and we both looked toward the door where Esme and Luc stood. Gabriel waved them in.

Esme carried a cup of hot tea to me immediately. "I had her add some brandy to it."

I shakily raised the cup to my lips and took a fortifying sip. My eyes met Esme's concerned, blue gaze and the corners of my mouth tilted up slightly. "Thank you. . . for everything."

Esme smiled back at me. I glanced at Gabriel and Luc, who were talking quietly by the door. Their voices were so low, I couldn't hear them over the general din of the bar downstairs. After a few moments, Gabriel turned to face Esme and me.

"If you are all right. . ." He sought my eyes out questioningly. "I will leave you to get some rest now. Luc and I will be taking it in turns to watch your door tonight."

We both nodded, and Gabriel and Luc bowed before they closed the door. Esme immediately jumped up to latch it behind them.

She began to rummage through my trunk before she pulled out a clean, spare, linen shift. She clucked to herself as she carefully removed the *Vicomte's* cloak from around my shoulders and helped me into the clean gown. She settled me under the covers like a small child, before she doused all but one candle and climbed in next to me.

"*Bonne nuit*, Ava," she said softly.

"Good night, Esme," I replied.

I closed my eyes and silent tears slipped down my cheeks, wetting my pillow. I needed to sleep tonight. *Please, no dreams.*

My body ached everywhere; my arm, in particular, throbbed. It'd been feeling so much better over the last week, really beginning to heal, but I had injured it anew tonight. I thought of Cifarelli and was unable to stifle the shiver that flowed through me.

Unbidden, I remembered the first conversation I had ever had with Gabriel and Mathieu and their horror at the idea that I might travel alone. In light of everything that had happened in the weeks since that conversation, I was overcome by intense gratitude that they insisted on accompanying me. It was shocking to think how much my perception of my self-reliance had changed in the last month. *They were right, dammit.*

I thought of Gabriel keeping watch outside my door, foregoing sleep himself, to keep me safe. A small flame flickered to life inside me, a single candle warding against the dark of night.

Will I ever get home to my own time? Do I even want to? There is nothing for me there, and here... Well, maybe there is something for me here.

Fifteen
Mirror, Mirror

I clawed my way out of sleep, gasping. My heart was galloping, and my face was streaked with tears. I glanced over to see Esme sleeping serenely next to me. The dim, gray light in the room heralded the break of dawn, but there would be no more sleep for me tonight. As quietly as I could, I slid out of bed and pattered, barefoot to curl up on one of the chairs by the fire. It had burned down to embers and the room had grown frigidly cold overnight, but some meager warmth still emanated from it.

I wrapped the cloak Gabriel left around me, snuggling into the softness of the fleece-lined wool, tucked my icy feet up underneath me, and inhaled his familiar scent. I stared sightlessly into the hearth, my mind full of disjointed images from my dreams while the room gradually lightened around me. I heard Esme stir behind me and glanced over my shoulder at her.

"How are you feeling?" she asked, pattering over to me.

I grimaced. "Sore, everything hurts."

She tsked. "Let's get you dressed and packed so we can leave, aye?" She rummaged through my trunk and pulled out stockings, petticoats, a shift, two shawls, and the warmest gown I had; a soft, thick, blue wool.

"Please," I murmured. I couldn't wait to leave this town and Cifarelli behind.

I winced as she helped me into the layers of clothing. Hopefully, with some movement, the soreness would ease a bit. She gently detangled my hair, pinned it up, and handed me a small, handheld mirror. I inspected my bruised, cut cheek and the impressive array of colors on my neck and collarbone. It was worse than I imagined. I closed my eyes, instantly re-living the pressure of Cifarelli's forearm pressing on my throat. I swallowed hard and reopened my eyes to meet Esme's sympathetic gaze.

"It will heal," she said softly.

"Yes, I expect it will. Thank you, Esme."

She smiled at me and busied herself changing, as I gingerly packed our belongings in the trunk.

"Ready?" she asked.

I nodded, and she slid the bolt back, opening the heavy, wood door. Luc leaned against the wall.

"Good morning, *mesdames.*" He straightened as soon as he saw us. Esme smiled up at him coquettishly. He blushed— inasmuch as a grown man can blush, and offered us each an arm as we made our way down the stairs.

The mood was muted while we sat down to the customary bread, butter, and raspberry marmalade. I sipped at my tea while I scanned the room for Gabriel. Luc walked a few feet away from us and quietly gave some of the men instructions to bring the trunks downstairs, after which he hovered over us like a dark thundercloud while we ate. I was taking my last bite of bread, when the door to the *auberge* opened with an icy blast, and Gabriel and Friloux walked in. My mouth suddenly dry, I tried to chew and swallow as Gabriel made a beeline for us. His eyes lingered over my bruised cheek, and I could see residual anger in his expression.

He nodded at Luc before he turned back to me. "If you feel well enough to travel, we will continue onto Nantes today. With any luck, we will arrive by nightfall, and we should be able to find accommodations finer than these." He spared a glance at the interior of the dark, dank inn.

I was ready to put as much distance between us, and this God-forsaken town as possible. "I am ready to go." I hesitated, "What will we do with Cifarelli?" I didn't know what the plan was, but it wasn't going to involve me if he would be traveling with us. If I had to look at him again, I suspect I would end up being tried for murder.

Gabriel's face hardened and his gray eyes grew flinty. "Friloux and I took him to the constable last night and made a report. No doubt they will let him out in a few days; however, I have made it clear to Cifarelli that if I ever set eyes on him again, he will not live to tell of it."

A sense of relief came over me like a wave and I felt my shoulders relax. I took a deep, steadying breath and simply said, "Thank you."

The relief in her voice was evident, and it gave Gabriel a queer feeling in the pit of his stomach to hear it. The fervent way she thanked him, it was as though she'd thought he might have considered doing anything less than this.

Gabriel wanted to do far more. He'd been tempted to call him out, but reason, and cooler heads, prevailed. He typically considered himself to be calm and levelheaded. It was out of character for him to require someone else to help him compose himself. That was the role he usually fulfilled for others.

Thankfully, Luc had been there and stepped in. A man abusing a woman, or a child, topped the list of injustices he couldn't tolerate. Having it happen to Ava was affecting him more than he cared to admit, particularly since she was under his protection. For that matter, everything that concerned Ava seemed to affect him more than he was used to. *Merde.*

Was it a passing thing? He didn't think so, and although it was tempting to continue to live his life in the blithe, uncomplicated, comfortable manner he had thus far, he knew it wasn't what he wanted. He wanted what his sister seemed to have found with Mathieu and what he felt sure his parents had shared.

He had never been interested in the paltry, dramatic affairs, or in the quick release of tension and lust with a whore, that so many of his friends routinely engaged in. They'd ribbed him about his disinterest in satisfying his basic needs in the brothels to no end when he'd visited them at the *université* in Paris.

He shrugged his shoulders at the thought now. It wasn't that he felt he had higher morals, or that he thought himself better than them. He'd always known that he wanted a deeper and more satisfying connection. Was he crazy to think she might be the one he would find that with?

His chest felt tight as he thought again about what might have happened if he'd been a moment later the previous night. Thank God Esme had moved as quickly as she had. He crossed himself reflexively and forced himself to unclench his hands.

Cifarelli was an unscrupulous beast. No one would have offered to serve as his second. . . Firmly, Gabriel put the thought from his mind. But the question of Ava lingered stubbornly.

He glanced at her covertly from across the room as he oversaw the men load the wagon outside the door. There was something about the way she held herself apart that made him want to tear down the barricades she'd built around her heart. She was warm and caring—he'd seen the evidence of it in some of her exchanges with Étienne, Amélie, and Esme. . . even with the housekeeper from the chapel, Madame Carel.

But she rarely let her guard down. Her smiles were magical because she didn't bestow them freely. He remembered the few easy exchanges they'd shared when her eyes had been full of light and laughter and knew he wanted to feel that effortless joy from her again.

The sound of chairs scraping across the dirty floor interrupted his thoughts. Reluctantly he moved toward the women and Luc. It was time to get back to their journey. He could admit only to himself that he quite looked forward to their time spent on the road. Even if it was largely spent in solitary thoughts, the warm, weight of Ava riding behind him had become one of his favorite sensations; he often found himself unbearably aroused by the innocent press of her slim body against his back. He'd had several internal arguments with himself that she would only be so close to him because she was freezing, but his cock was certain he was wrong.

Gabriel, Luc, Esme, and I donned cloaks, furs, and gloves as we walked to the door. The horses and wagon were ready to go. I stepped outside and instantly froze. The wind howled down the narrow alleys, whipped through the tree branches, and cut right through every layer of clothing I wore. I shivered and wrapped my cloak more firmly around my body as we stepped onto the cobblestone street to mount the horses.

Luc handed me up behind Gabriel. He held the reins firmly in one hand as he turned in the saddle to face me.

"Best put this one on as well," he said as he handed another cloak back to me, his gray eyes serious on mine.

I felt a blush stain my cheeks crimson. "Thank you," I murmured as I struggled to wrap it around myself.

"Here," he said softly, dropping the reins and carefully settling the heavy cloak around my shoulders. His gloved fingers brushed my neck as he fumbled to hook the closure shut and my breath hitched as his touch rushed through my veins. His gaze lingered on me as he draped his fur over my shoulders and wrapped us both in it.

Firmly wedged behind Gabriel, trussed up in my extra layers, I settled into Automne's rhythm. I was glad to leave Savenay and its horrors behind and I relaxed as Automne steadily put distance between Cifarelli and me. It heartened me enough that I didn't mind the way the wind cut like a knife through our clothing, at least for the moment. *Thank God we will finally arrive in Nantes tonight. With any luck, Gabriel will decide to stay for a few days.*

To say that I was weary of the constant travel would be an understatement. Worry niggled the back of my mind. A reminder that I don't know what will happen after I speak to the Navy about the shipwreck.

I've come to realize that I can't avoid it, since Gabriel and Mathieu sent word of the wreck ahead, via the *commandant* at *la Forteresse Vauban*.

For the last several days I have put off thinking about it, but I suspect that Gabriel will expect me to return to my family. I told him that my family is gone; which is true after all; but he probably thinks that I have some distant family or relatives to call on. He doesn't know that I have no family at all, in France, or anywhere for that matter. I also have no means to support myself. No friends to call upon for help. No home.

Will it be odd or suspicious to him and the rest of the men when I'm forced to reveal that I have nowhere to go from here?

I know that my father's side of the family originally immigrated from France. I loved digging into my family history while I was in college. I spent countless hours poring over books and family trees, meticulously tracing my family back to Roussillon. According to my research, they were there for centuries. I even visited Roussillon once, a gorgeous little village on an elevated ridge. It'd been thrilling to look through the church register and find my family's name there; as well as in the little, old cemetery full of ochre mausoleums.

The houses were built of clay in the varied hues of a desert sunset and sometimes were even carved directly into the ochre rock. At one point, my family had been nobility and lived in the valley just below the ridge. Over the years, through a series of poor investments, and reckless spending, they had become impoverished and slowly lost their land, or so the story went. I suppose I could tell them that my family was from Roussillon, it was unlikely that anyone would ever think to check, and after all, it wasn't untrue.

What will happen if I make my way to the Martels of Roussillon and claim to be a distant relation? Will they take me in? How hard could it be to find them?

I sighed deeply as my temples began to throb. The truth is, I can't think of another option open to me. I'm unmarried, and in the eighteenth century, I know I cannot continue to travel across the country with men unrelated to me. Nantes is very much the end of the road.

The mystery of what the future holds used to excite me. I loved not knowing what lay around the next bend. But right now, the unknown yawned before me like a pit of dangerous uncertainty.

I rubbed my hand hard over my face, wishing I could scrub my problems away. The big, bay horse plodded onward beneath me, bringing me closer to an uncertain future with every step. I rested my forehead tiredly against Gabriel's back and closed my eyes.

Hours later we entered the outskirts of Nantes. We followed the curving, flat, silver ribbon of the Loire past the bustling seaport *Saint-Nazaire*, into the heart of the city. After having spent the last month in quaint, rural villages, Nantes is a culture shock to me. Once within the old city walls, the town sprawls in a maze of canals, quays, and footbridges that meander off the river.

Here, the pristine, white snow of the previous day is mottled shades of gray and brown, slushy, and slippery. The canals and cobblestone streets are littered with refuse, rotten food, and I have no doubt— raw sewage, both of the animal and human variety. I wrinkle my nose as I catch a whiff of something noxious. I can only imagine how much more overwhelming the smells must be during the hot, summer months.

We pass a huge ship unloading crates onto the quay as men scramble on the docks tossing lines from the boat to the cleats.

"What are they importing?"

Gabriel frowned, lines appearing between his eyes. "Sugar, from the French West Indies," he answered stiffly. I shudder, our lunch curdling in my stomach. He glanced back over his shoulder at me, one eyebrow quirked in question. "You know what that means, aye?"

"Slavery." I blinked my eyes to clear the sudden blurriness.

"Aye," he said softly.

I completely forgot that Nantes was at the center of the French-Atlantic slave trade. It hit differently, knowing it was currently happening. The word 'slavery' reverberated in my mind, as we snaked our way down the streets, carefully picking our path between rushing people, wandering animals, farm wagons, carts of goods, and opulent carriages.

I heard a shout and glanced down a side street. Three men brawled in the middle of the lane while a group of residents looked on. A few men jostled and shoved each other, jockeying for position. A mother pushed two young children behind her, shielding them with her body. Most of the people, however, simply looked away in boredom, shuffling their feet in the slushy snow as they inched forward in line.

"What's going on over there?"

Gabriel looked over his shoulder as we passed the street. "Bread line," he answered tersely, his expression inscrutable.

Of course. The infamous bread lines. I should have known. History was a different beast when it was lived than when it was learned two hundred years after the fact. Our steady passage down the streets slowed to a crawl as the crowd pressed close. A street urchin dressed in rags darted in front of Automne and Gabriel pulled back on the reins just in time.

"*Merde,*" he muttered.

I huddled closer to Gabriel as my breaths became short and shallow. I was beginning to feel claustrophobic. We passed the stately old castle of the Dukes of Brittany— now the Breton seat of the French monarchy and turned down a small, quiet, side street. The hustle and noise of the river receded into the distance, and we finally came to a stop in front of a large building made of light-colored stone. The street immediately outside the *auberge* was freshly swept. The arched, wood door gleamed with oil, and the diamond-paned windows sparkled. The difference in wealth between this part of town, and just a few streets away was striking.

I grimaced in pain as I slid down Automne's side and my feet touched solid ground again. We stopped today only to water the horses, and I felt extra achy and sore. Gabriel lingered beside me, patting his horse's neck, scratching his ears, and lovingly running one hand down his forehead and muzzle. Intuitively, I knew he was killing time, waiting for me to feel steady on my feet, but I couldn't protest. He offered me his arm and handed Automne's reins off to Friloux with precise timing.

I found myself letting him support me, more heavily than I would have liked. The bell above the door jangled as we entered the *auberge*, attracting the attention of the proprietor. A portly, cheerful man, dressed impeccably in a peacock blue waistcoat bustled over to help us.

A glance around assured me that the interior was as scrupulously clean as the outside had been. The wide, polished floorboards gleamed as brightly as the proprietor's balding head. I imagined I might see my reflection in the shiny dome, and smothered a bubble of laughter in my throat, turning it quickly into a strangled-sounding cough. Gabriel looked at me suspiciously, but I smiled innocently at him, and he returned his attention to the owner.

A large stone fireplace dominated one wall of the room, with wooden tables and chairs clustered cozily around it. Several wall sconces and candelabras cast light brilliantly across the room and the entire place smelled pleasantly of woodsmoke.

"Madame, Monsieur, please allow me to introduce myself. I am Monsieur Auguste Kergoat. How may I assist you?" gushed the proprietor. His gaze roved over us in a quick, measuring glance, lingering over my bruised face, before deliberately looking away.

"Monsieur, I am Gabriel Chabot, *le Vicomte de Landévennec* and this is Mademoiselle Martel. Do you have rooms available?"

"Of course, of course! How many rooms do you require?"

"Four. We are traveling with several people."

"Certainly, certainly! If you would follow me?" I watched in amusement as Monsieur Kergoat veritably scampered like an overeager puppy, to his office in the back. He reappeared in a moment and waved us forward enthusiastically. "Follow me, follow me. Right this way!"

Esme, Luc, and the others had gathered near the door, and Gabriel waved them over. Everyone wearily followed Monsieur Kergoat, climbing the stairs to the third floor. The proprietor waved his hand grandly down the corridor.

"This entire floor is all yours!" he exclaimed, as he quickly and methodically opened each door; handing the keys out.

"*Merci, Monsieur,*" said Gabriel. "We will be down for supper shortly."

"Take your time. Please, settle in! Let me know if there is anything I can assist with to make your stay more comfortable. I'll have the fires lit immediately!" Monsieur Kergoat bowed smartly before he disappeared down the stairs.

Gabriel indicated that Esme and I take the room next to his and Luc's; Friloux, Michel, Armand, and Phillipe split up into the two rooms across the hall. Gabriel turned to us. "Luc and I will wait to escort you downstairs," he said quietly.

"*Merci,* Gabriel. We won't be long." I turned, immediately entering our room, but I noticed that Esme lingered by the door, talking quietly with Luc. After a few minutes, she shut the door, carefully latching it.

"What?" she asked.

"Oh, nothing," I replied, a smile hovering around my lips. "I was just noticing that Luc seems to be rather taken with you."

"Oh! Do you think so?" Esme's bright blue eyes looked at me with a mixture of hope and trepidation.

"I do. Why wouldn't he be? He would be lucky to have you. Do you fancy him?"

"I have for years. Ever since I went to *Trégoudan* with Amélie, and he visited with Gabriel. But I never thought he saw me in that light."

"Well, if he didn't before, I think he does now," I said encouragingly. "You should speak to him more often."

Esme threw her arms around me and nearly knocked me over in the process. "Thank you for saying that." She stepped back, her eyes looking misty. "Now sit down so I can make you beautiful for Gabriel!"

"Don't fuss too much. I look terrible with all this. . . " I motioned to the bruises on my face and neck.

"Not at all!" asserted Esme loyally. "You have the most stunning hair, your skin is flawless, and your eyes are to die for." Esme airily chef kissed her fingers. "You are gorgeous, and Gabriel knows it. He will see past those bruises. Believe me. Anyway, they will be gone before you know it!"

I grinned at Esme; rather doubting the truth of her words, but I had to admit that she did an excellent job of lifting my spirits. I sat quietly while she busied herself with my hair, curling the loose tendrils around my face with her fingers to make them more pronounced. Then she set to work smoothing out her chestnut hair.

"I wish I could help you do yours," I said, gesturing helplessly toward my injured arm.

"No need!" Esme replied with a quick smile. "I'm used to it. It's rather more boring than yours, but I suppose that makes it easier to take care of."

"Everyone wants curls, but my hair looks like a bird's nest half the time. It's always so messy and your hair is the most beautiful color!"

"Thank you," demurred Esme, making the final changes to her updo. "Now let's go eat. I'm starving!"

Sixteen
When Pigs Fly

I awoke with a pounding headache and a feeling of dread in the pit of my stomach. We spent a few days relaxing in Nantes, recovering from the long trip, which I enjoyed immensely. Today, was the day I was making my report to the Navy. *I don't want to relive Carri's death; I don't want to relive the shipwreck, and I definitely don't want to think about what will happen next.*

Where will I go? How soon will Gabriel expect me to leave?

I wished I could close my eyes and wake up in my own time, with Carri still alive. That was a child's fantasy though. *I have to put on my big girl pants, or in this case, my multiple petticoats, and face the music.*

Preoccupied with my thoughts, I didn't offer much in the way of conversation that morning as we got dressed. Esme must have noticed but wisely didn't press me after a failed attempt to draw me in. I let Esme's gay chatter swirl around me, cheerful as bird song at the break of dawn, as I went over what lay ahead for the millionth time.

She wasn't eating. Maybe she fooled the others by pushing her bread and marmalade around on her plate, but Gabriel paid more attention than most people.

"Are you ready to go?" he asked finally.

She offered him a wan smile, lifted her napkin to her lips, and stood up in response.

He suspected that she must be nervous, and he cast around for something to say that might ease her anxiety as they rode to the naval base, but she answered all his questions and comments with one-word answers. Clearly, she was not in the mood to be drawn out of her shell. He felt a sympathetic flutter of nervousness in his stomach.

As they approached the gates, Gabriel called up to the officers patrolling the entrance, "*Vicomte de Landévennec avec la Mademoiselle Martel.* Here to see *le Commandant des Rochefort.*"

The wrought iron gate swung open slowly.

"Please dismount Monsieur, Mademoiselle. I will take your horse if you please. Second Lieutenant Du Campe de Rosamel will escort you to *le Commandant des Rochefort,*" said a naval officer who looked like he hadn't reached puberty yet. He was smartly dressed in white breeches and a shirt, with a beautifully cut, blue waistcoat piped in gold; but that didn't disguise the fact that he didn't yet have hair growing above his lip.

We followed Du Campe de Rosamel across the wide open courtyard up the stone steps and into the echoing, stone entrance of the base. I was shocked at how young many of the officers looked and reminded myself that it hadn't been unusual for boys to join the Navy at the age of twelve, or sooner. It was one thing to know intellectually, and another thing entirely to see what amounted to young boys, a part of the Royal Navy. We followed Rosamel up the stairs and into a spacious office.

"*Le Commandant* should be with you shortly." Without another word, he left us alone and shut the door with a snap.

I could feel Gabriel's eyes on me; no doubt wondering why I was avoiding him, but I couldn't manage conversation when I felt so nervous. Instead, I silently took in the stunning, crimson, and gold Turkish rug that dominated the parquet floor, and the enormous, heavily carved, wood desk which was perfectly situated in front of floor-to-ceiling windows that allowed the sunlight to stream in.

The walls were covered in immense, marvelously detailed maps, complete with sea monsters, and mermaids. Intrigued by what amounted to ancient charts, I stared up at one after another. I slowly made my way down the wall and stopped in front of each one. I was familiar with some of these coastlines, and it was fascinating to see how much the maps had changed over two centuries.

I knew Gabriel was watching me as I pretended to be immersed in the map of North America. My eyes traced the familiar coastline around the

Chesapeake, my home waters. But in my mind, I replayed my memories of the storms, and Carri falling overboard.

Sometime over the last few days, it dawned on me that I would have to be largely dishonest about the crew on my boat, and what Carri and I had been doing. I *hated* the idea of lying. It went against every fiber of my being. But the cold realist in me whispered that they would never buy the idea of two women sailing solo. It was unequivocally not something that would happen in the eighteenth century. I settled on a loose idea of what I intended to say and hoped to stick as close to the truth as I possibly could. I knew lying any more than necessary would trip me up.

The door opened behind me, and panic fluttered in my stomach. This was it. I turned to face the newcomer with what I hoped was a calm expression. Out of the corner of my eye, I could see that Gabriel had made himself at home in one of the chairs by the fireplace.

"Commandant des Rochefort, à votre service."

Des Rochefort looked like he was in his forties, ate a bit too rich, and when he removed his hat with a flourish, I could see his black hair was thinning on top. His eyes were long, almond-shaped, and glittered black as onyx. He ran them lazily down my body, before returning to my face. His lips smiled, but they had a cruel twist to them. He was dressed sharply in his Navy uniform, but it didn't disguise the menacing air about him that reminded me vaguely of Cifarelli. My instincts told me to run. But of course, that was not an option.

Gabriel stood up and made his way over to the *Commandant*. He bowed and introduced us. *"Commandant des Rochefort,* I am Gabriel Chabot, *le Vicomte de Landévennec.* My brother-in-law and I found Mademoiselle Martel washed up on the beach in *Camaret-sur-mer* several weeks ago. We reported her shipwreck to *la Forteresse Vauban,* I believe *Commandant*

Leroux was going to inform you. Mademoiselle Martel is now here to answer any additional questions you may have."

Gabriel walked over to stand beside me and gently took my arm, guiding me to sit in a chair, as *le Commandant* moved to sit behind the desk.

He said nothing for the first several moments, as he poured himself, Gabriel, and me a round of brandies. He waited until Gabriel sat in one of the chairs in front of the desk before he toasted us, tossed his entire brandy back in one gulp, and promptly refilled his glass.

It seemed he was inclined to drink this one more slowly, as he sat back in his chair languidly, and looked at me. "I read the report that *Commandant* Leroux sent. It was rather short on details. What took so long for you to arrive in Nantes?"

"She was gravely injured—" Gabriel began, but des Rochefort lifted his hand to stop him and then motioned to me.

"I would like her to answer the questions, *Monsieur le Vicomte*."

I sat up a bit straighter in my chair. A muscle twitched in Gabriel's jaw. It seemed that *le Commandant* was going to give us a hard time.

"I'm sorry for the delay, *Commandant des Rochefort*," I said softly. "Unfortunately, I was in no condition to travel for several weeks. I was injured during the wreck." I gestured to my arm, still wrapped and in a sling. "After that, I suffered a fever for several days, and then we encountered bad weather."

Des Rochefort said nothing, watching me over his glass for several long moments. "I see," he said finally. "How exactly did the ship carrying you wreck?"

"I am told she was struck by lightning, *Commandant*, although I cannot say for certain. We were in a terrible storm coming into *la Rade de Brest*. I thought perhaps the vessel might have run aground on the rocks, but *le Vicomte* witnessed the ship getting struck."

Des Rochefort's eyes cut briefly away to assess Gabriel. "You were on the beach during the storm?" His raised eyebrow and thin smile suggested this might bear further looking into. Without waiting for a response from Gabriel, however, he addressed me. "How many other souls were on board with you, Mademoiselle? You were the only survivor?"

This was one of the questions that I had been dreading. I had no idea what the appropriate answer was and prayed that my response would be believable.

"There were six of us on board, Monsieur, three crew members, myself, my cousin, and our maid. I— I was the only survivor. *Le Vicomte* and *le Baron* searched the shore for others, but—" My voice cracked. "But we believe they sank with the ship." I took a bracing sip of my brandy and closed my eyes briefly. I opened them to find Gabriel looking at me encouragingly.

Des Rochefort was not smiling though. "I find it odd, that you would be the only survivor. The shipwreck was close to shore, was it not?" He narrowed his eyes at me as though he knew I was lying.

"It was," I answered quietly.

The compulsion to squirm was intense. I was overcome by the sudden extreme need to pee. I tried to shift in my chair unobtrusively and wondered how much longer the questioning would continue. I sensed he didn't believe my story, but I desperately needed him to accept it.

Des Rochefort took a long, slow sip of his brandy, and nonchalantly topped off his glass. "What was the vessel carrying in terms of cargo?" He switched his line of questioning on me swiftly.

My mind was sluggish to respond to the sudden shift. Cargo. . . I hadn't thought of cargo, although—dammit! I should have. After all, Gabriel had also asked me about cargo. Why hadn't I prepared for this? As my mind raced, des Rochefort's eyes seemed to focus on me. I broke out in a fine sheen of perspiration, my underarms and temples were getting damp, and my heart galloped like a runaway horse. The urge to pee was overwhelming now, making it difficult to concentrate. *Fuck it, tell him the truth. Tell him what you told Gabriel.*

"There was no cargo on board, that I was aware, *Commandant* des Rochefort," I answered, consciously addressing him by his title.

"No cargo?" He raised a brow. "Surely you know this is most irregular, Mademoiselle."

I forced myself to be calm and relaxed. I lifted one shoulder in a shrug before letting it fall. I cocked my head slightly to the side and offered him a small smile. "To be honest, *Commandant. . .* I do not know. *Le Capitaine* would be the best person to answer your question, but of course, he cannot. It was not a large vessel though; I cannot think of where the cargo would have been stowed. Certainly, I never saw evidence of any."

He did not seem pleased by my answer. "Who did the vessel belong to, Mademoiselle?"

"It was mine," I answered steadily. I had rehearsed this part. "I inherited it from my parents—"

"You inherited?" The incredulous tone in *le Commandant's* voice immediately alerted me that I had made a grave error.

Shit. Women could rarely inherit anything before the Revolution; which of course, hasn't happened yet. With a jolt, I realized that the Revolution would begin in two short years and that it would change everything. How could I have made such a mistake? I knew better, dammit. This was my area of expertise. There was no way I could backpedal now though, I had to plow ahead.

"*Oui,*" I answered steadily. "I am the only surviving member in my family. I should have inherited everything, as I am not yet married, but—" I began to wildly, make things up. "My uncle, my father's younger brother, felt he should have inherited the estate. He kicked me out. My maid and I took one of my family's ships to visit my cousin on my mother's side of the family in England. We were returning to France when the ship was destroyed."

The *Commandant* sat back. He had been packing his pipe with tobacco as I concocted my story and now he lit it and contemplatively puffed on it. I shot a glance in Gabriel's direction and saw that he also seemed surprised by the details I just provided. Clearly, my story was not as believable as I hoped it might be.

Finally, *le Commandant* spoke again. "Your family name is Martel, and. . . pardon me, Mademoiselle Martel, from which part of France does your family hail?"

"Roussillon."

"Roussillon. And you stole one of your uncle's ships for this trip to see your mother's family in England. And then *le Capitaine* that you hired, sank the ship. Do you know what that ship was worth Mademoiselle? How do you intend to repay your uncle for his loss of property?" Des Rochefort suddenly stood up, braced his hands on the desk, and leaned forward menacingly.

I wanted to shrink back in my chair but instead, I lifted my chin. "I stole nothing, *Commandant*. That ship was rightfully mine. If anything, you might say that my uncle stole the rest of my family's ships from me, as well as my home and my lands. I see that you are not of the opinion that women should own property, and I suppose that doesn't surprise me. You do not strike me as the forward-thinking type." I stood up, pushing my chair back aggressively. I was now trembling, in anger. The rage surged through me and obliterated any fear I might have felt at *le Commandant's* threatening words. *How dare he?* "I believe I am done here, Monsieur."

Without waiting for Des Rochefort to say a word, or to see if Gabriel was coming with me, I marched to the heavy double doors and yanked one open. The young officer who had been leaning against the wall outside of the room jumped to attention.

"Ah, Mademoiselle?" he asked, sounding unsure.

"I am ready to leave. Please show me out," I replied haughtily.

Gabriel materialized beside me. "Ava. . . " he said quietly, "I don't know if this is the best way—"

"I am leaving right now. I do not intend to stay here and listen to that pig insult me and treat me like I am lesser simply because I am a woman. I have lost everything in the world dear to me. He has no right—" My voice cracked, "NO right to speak to me in such a manner. Are you coming with me? Or are you staying with him?" I spat the last sentence out.

Something I couldn't identify flickered in his expression. "I am coming with you, of course."

My chest was heaving with indignation, but a tiny part of me had doubted he would take my side, and I felt deeply relieved that I wouldn't be walking out of the base alone. Still seething, I acquiesced to taking the arm he offered me. The young lieutenant was still hesitating over what he should do, but no order came forth from *le Commandant's* office, and he finally made up his mind to escort us out.

We walked out of the building and into the sunshine in silence. As soon as we mounted Automne, and passed through the imposing gates I let out a sigh, and let my body sag against Gabriel. The rush of adrenaline that had accompanied me out of Des Rochefort's office, was gone.

"Ava?" asked Gabriel tentatively.

"Can we please hurry back? I need to use a chamber pot."

"Of course," he murmured, a burble of laughter smothered beneath his smooth voice.

He clicked to Automne and dug his heels in a bit. The beautiful chestnut responded immediately, moving into a trot that jostled my bladder. I gritted my teeth. *Please let me make it to the auberge in time.*

SEVENTEEN
DRUNKEN ANTS

I spent the rest of the day working on my sewing. Esme tried to cajole me into going to the market with her, wanting to shop for ribbons and lace, but after the morning I'd had, I was adamant about not going, and she eventually gave up and set out alone. I sat by the window and concentrated until my eyes swam with the effort of trying to make my stitches small and even.

I sighed and stopped, resting my flushed, frustrated face against the freezing window. My head throbbed, and my stitches marched like drunken ants down the hem I'd been trying to take in. It had been a mistake to lose my temper with des Rochefort. He did not seem like the type of man who would allow a woman to call the shots and get away with it. How much power did he wield? Could he call me back to answer further questions, force me to pay my fictitious uncle, or imprison me over this? The thoughts chased themselves around and around in my head until I thought I was going to lose my mind.

The only solution that presented itself to me, was if I disappeared. If des Rochefort couldn't find me, he would eventually give up the search. *If* he was going to search for me at all. Perhaps, I was not important enough for him to bother with pursuing me. That brought me back to the question of where I would go. *Where can I possibly go?*

Esme returned late in the afternoon, her basket full of beautiful lace and ribbons that she excitedly showed me. I forced my bleak thoughts to the back burner and turned my attention to her.

"This one," she said, pulling forth a gorgeous, hand-worked, length of lace. "I'm going to add it to the edge of my pale blue velvet." She smiled shyly. "I thought it might make for a lovely wedding dress."

I nodded, examining the creamy lace. "It would be beautiful with your coloring," I murmured. "Does that mean that—"

"Well, nay. Not yet," interjected Esme. "He hasn't said anything about that. But I *do* think he might like me." Her cheeks blushed rosily at her admission.

I looked at my friend and noted the sparkle in her bright blue eyes and the exuberance in her voice. I smiled at her.

"Esme, I am quite certain that he likes you. In fact, I will make it my mission to see you happily married to Luc, if that is your heart's desire." I wasn't sure if I would *actually* see her married, I would probably be long gone by then. But I could certainly set the wheels in motion.

Esme seemed to suspect I wasn't being entirely truthful. "You will stand witness?"

"Ah, well—" I stuttered. "Of course, if I am still around, I would be honored to stand witness."

Esme narrowed her eyes at me. "Why wouldn't you be around? Where would you be?"

I looked down at my hands and fiddled nervously with my sewing. "I don't know. But I cannot stay here. Things did not go well with *le Commandant*. I am afraid to stay in Nantes, and I cannot keep traveling with *le Vicomte* either. He escorted me to the Navy as he promised. Any duty he thought he might have to me has been fulfilled."

"I do not understand you, Ava. I am sure that Gabriel would never consider his obligation to you fulfilled. He will take you back to his home if you have nowhere to go, he'll offer you his protection, if you need it. I do not think *le Commandant* would go against *le Vicomte* if that were the case. Surely you know this too?"

I shrugged one shoulder. "I do not know that Gabriel would do that, and anyway, I am not interested in being under his or any other man's *protection*. I know what that means."

"What that means. . . What do you think it means, Ava? I am talking about marriage. He is not the type to keep you as his whore."

I said nothing and the silence stretched out between us. I had not been thinking of marriage. It truthfully hadn't occurred to me. But now that Esme said it, I wasn't sure it was something I wanted anyway. The mere idea that I needed a man's protection rankled me. Even more so because I knew deep down that I probably *did* need it. Women in the 1700s had no rights, would have no rights, for several years yet. My exchange with des Rochefort today reminded me of this fact. Furthermore, with the French Revolution staring me down, like the lights of an oncoming train in a tunnel; having a man's protection would be paramount.

Where did Gabriel's family stand in the oncoming war? How many people have I met in the last month who will die in the next few years?

I knew the statistics, of course, but the number of people who met their end at the guillotine's blade had always been a part of the distant past. I was going to be living out the nightmare, right here in France. *Have I survived everything life has thrown at me the last few years, only to die in the Revolution?*

I shuddered. "I do not think that Gabriel would wish to marry someone like me," I finally said.

And I am not sure, that I would wish to marry him.

After all, we just met. I barely knew him. What I did know. . . Sure, he seemed like a stand-up guy. Certainly, he was the silent, noble type. I couldn't even deny that he made me feel safe and simultaneously hot and bothered. But that was not a strong basis for a marriage. I certainly would never consider marrying under such circumstances in my other life.

"I wouldn't be so sure. . ." replied Esme with a sly smile.

When Esme and I left our room that evening to head to dinner the men were waiting for us. I watched the way Luc looked at Esme and caught how Esme blushed prettily as she took Luc's arm. Something was brewing between the two of them and it warmed my heart. I dawdled at the top of the stairs, letting them go ahead of Gabriel and myself. Gabriel looked at me inquisitively and I found myself blushing as well.

"They make a nice couple, don't you think?" I whispered.

Gabriel raised an eyebrow at me. "I suppose they do. I hadn't noticed before, but now that you mention it I do think Luc may be harboring some hopes regarding Esme."

"Well, I do believe she may be harboring some hopes as well," I shot back. "Maybe you ought to give him a bit of a nudge."

"Are you playing matchmaker?" he asked, grinning.

"So, what if I am? They deserve to be happy," I replied tartly, feeling heat creep up my neck.

"They do," he murmured in agreement as he pulled a chair out for me. I sat down, nodding my thanks as he sat next to me. Gabriel leaned in close.

"What about you? You deserve to be happy too," he said so quietly I had to strain my ears to hear him.

My eyes collided with Gabriel's molten silver ones. The heat in them made my insides feel like melted molasses and the moment stretched out as the sounds around us faded. After an eternity, I forced myself to look away. I studied my hands resting quietly on my lap. The magnitude of everything that happened over the last few years crashed over me. Most days, I stuffed the feelings and sadness down and locked them up. But today, it kept bubbling up refusing to be corked and put away.

Finally, in a raw voice so low that it was almost inaudible I answered him. "I don't know if I will ever be happy again."

There was no response. I closed my eyes and fought back tears. *Why did I say that aloud?*

It was true that I felt that way, but opening myself up and being vulnerable in front of this man I barely knew. . . It was the height of stupidity.

His warm, slightly rough hand took mine and squeezed gently. I let out a slow, shaky breath, squared my shoulders, lifted my head, and opened my eyes to meet his.

"Ever?" he repeated. "Surely, you will be happy again one day. I would make you happy— if I could. I would live to see your bright, beautiful smile, every day."

I shook my head. "I don't think you would genuinely want that. You do not know me. I would not make you happy." I looked back down at my lap and fiddled with my skirt, my heart breaking a little bit. "I've been thinking, it is probably time we part ways. You have done everything you promised by bringing me to Nantes."

Gabriel stared at me, "So, you have a plan? Somewhere safe to go?" He sounded angry and I was surprised to hear the trace of it in his voice.

"Ah, no. I thought I might try to track down some extended family and see if I could stay with them," I muttered. It was a weak plan, I knew it.

"Not the uncle that disinherited you from your parent's estate?"

"No, not him." I twisted my linen napkin between my hands.

"Who then? Do you know where any of them live? How do you intend to find them? How will you get there?" His voice rose in volume with every question.

I looked at him, my eyes blurry with unshed tears.

Gabriel gazed at me, a pained expression on his face. "Ava," he began and then paused, hesitating. "If it's truly what you want to do then I will take you. I cannot just walk away from you though. Particularly not after what happened this afternoon with *le Commandant*. He will be looking for you within a few days, I have no doubt."

"I do not know where they live," I whispered. "I do not know any of their names. I do not even know. . . if they exist." I let out a shuddering breath. "But I don't see any other options open to me. I am afraid of des Rochefort. I know he will come looking for me and I am terrified of what will happen if he finds me."

"Why are you set on this course of finding family that may not exist, Ava? Why not come to my home with me?" His hand brushed a tendril of hair back gently sending shivers down my spine.

"I do not want to burden you with my problems," I answered honestly. "We barely know each other. I am used to being independent. I cannot explain it all to you, but this is not the life I am used to. I will never fit into yours."

"Please think about it, Ava. I will keep you safe; from des Rochefort and everyone else. I am not asking it lightly. I would ask you to be my wife."

I stared at him. *Wife. . .*

He continued speaking, his voice sounding stronger, as he hit his stride. "I know that we do not know each other well. But— we can learn, can we not? I want to know everything about you. I want to uncover all your secrets and know what is going on behind your eyes when you are quiet. Surely, you feel there is something between us? The room feels different to me when you are in it, I feel it here—" He held my hand against his chest. "Like a punch in my stomach when you look at me. When I look at you, it feels impossible to imagine walking away. It cannot all be in my head." He took a deep breath. "But most of all, I want you to be happy. I believe that is a stronger basis for marriage than most."

Goosebumps covered my arms. It sounded too much like the kind of love I had always longed for, but never really expected I'd find. Despite what Esme said I hadn't believed that he would ever actually consider marrying me. I knew that marriage was treated differently in the 1700s and he wasn't offering to marry me for any of the acceptable, typical reasons for forming a union in his time. What he was proposing sounded a lot like the idea of two people pledging lifelong love and loyalty. Not quite a twentieth-century partnership, but certainly closer to one than most contemporary marriages. I scrambled to find all the reasons why this was a terrible idea.

Gabriel gently lifted my chin, forcing me to meet his eyes. "You feel it too, *ma belle* Ava."

I couldn't deny it.

He was so close, I could see the flecks of lighter silver in his dark gray eyes. His thumb traced over my bruised cheekbone, as soft as a butterfly's wings. His other hand came up to frame my face and I leaned into his touch. *Ava, what are you doing?*

I ignored the logical voice in my head. My skin craved his touch and my lips parted; I was dizzy with desire and rapidly losing all sense of time and place. His breath was warm against my lips a moment before his mouth met mine. My eyes fluttered shut. The blood raced through my veins like a song. I was exuberantly drunk on the taste of him. Time slowed to a crawl. I was content to stay, with my lips fused to his forever.

It was over too soon.

"*Dieu.* I've been wanting to do that since I met you." His voice was rough with unspent passion.

I opened my eyes, feeling bereft. Gabriel was staring at me with so much longing in his face that I was tempted to take his hand and lead him up the stairs right then.

His voice broke into my thoughts. "Please say you'll marry me."

I opened my mouth and knew I couldn't say no. "Okay," I answered.

He looked quizzical. "Okay? Is that English?"

I giggled, and his face lit up at the sound.

"Aye, I will marry you."

When I told Esme that night in our room, she squealed and threw her arms around me.

"I knew it!" she exclaimed. "I saw that kiss! Oh, I am so happy for you! And that means that you will not be leaving us. Has he said when the marriage will take place? Of course, they will have to call the banns. Are you going to his *château*? Or will we be returning to *Trégoudan* to have the wedding there?"

I laughed at the jumble of questions pouring forth. "I don't know! We haven't spoken about any of that."

"Well then, we can at least decide upon which gown you will wear! I think you should wear the green brocade. . . The one that matches your eyes. I have some lace we can add to it. Oh! And flowers. It's a shame it'll be a winter wedding. But perhaps we can use some things from Amélie's glass house. Evergreen and orange blossoms would look gorgeous. . ." She trailed off at the look on my face. "What?"

I shook my head, sending my dark curls flying, and smiled. "Nothing. Thank you for being so excited about this. I was never really the type of girl to fantasize about my wedding, but I also never imagined I'd be getting married under these circumstances. . . It's nice to have someone to plan with."

Esme waved her hand. "I love weddings. I am thrilled to be able to help you plan this. What do you think of my ideas?"

"I think they are perfect. Which lace were you thinking of using?"

Esme grabbed her basket off the floor and enthusiastically pawed through it, looking for the lace she had in mind. "This one," she announced, holding out a long rolled length of stunning, wide, cream-colored lace.

"Oh," I breathed. "That will be beautiful with the brocade."

I was suddenly overwhelmed by emotions and felt a bit tearful. I was grateful Esme was here but I missed my mother, father, and Carri fiercely. I never imagined I would be going through the milestone experiences of my life without them.

"We'll start working on it tomorrow," decided Esme.

Long after Esme fell asleep, I lay awake, watching the feeble candlelight flicker, listening to the distant sounds of the bar downstairs, and the creaking sounds of the *auberge* settling in for the night around me. I never found sleep easily anymore. My thoughts were haunted by the ghosts of my former life, particularly at night when there were no distractions to keep them at bay. With some effort, I turned my thoughts to the matter at hand.

Marriage. I didn't love Gabriel. Was I deeply and inexplicably attracted to him? Yes. He was kind, thoughtful, and honorable. I added these qualities to the running list of pros in my head. He was going above and beyond to protect me. Perhaps, there was a chance that what existed between us could grow into love.

But— I had secrets. Most of what Gabriel thought he knew about me was untrue. I couldn't, in good conscience, go into this marriage without coming clean, and giving him a chance to change his mind. The foundation of a good relationship had to be trust and respect.

How could I tell him I traveled through time? He would think I was insane. I tried to imagine how such a conversation might go. . . and laughed shortly. I might be able to prove I had knowledge of what was to come— particularly since I studied French history so extensively— I paused mid-thought. Prophesizing though. . . that was frowned upon in the 1700s. And. . . would he recognize that I was warning him about the Revolution because I studied it some two hundred years after it occurred, or would he think I was being prophetic?

Had prophets over the years *all* been time travelers? After all, if I had time traveled, it stood to reason that there were others out there, somewhere that had as well. It was comforting to think that I wasn't alone and also disquieting. It made sense though. How many inadvertent time travelers like myself, had been seeking to warn others about tragedies to come, only to find themselves persecuted, imprisoned, or burnt as witches?

Someone pounded at the heavy wood door. It shook in its frame under the force of a brute's fist. I winced and shrank away from the deafening sound. There was a pause, and I let out my breath in relief. Perhaps he was gone?

A boom sounded, and I jumped in alarm as the wood showed signs of splintering. Cifarelli kicked it open, slamming it back against the wall. He sauntered in with a sickening smirk.

I froze in terror, unable to do or say anything as he moved closer and closer.

"You've been waiting for me, petite pute, haven't you?" Cifarelli grabbed my long braid, yanking it back so hard my teeth snapped together, and roughly pushed me down onto the bed.

I opened my mouth to scream., but no sound emerged.

I was being shaken, urgently.

My lashes lifted groggily. Someone was pounding on the door. My eyes met Esme's worried blue ones.

"Mademoiselle Martel! Open this door immediately! In the name of his majesty, King Louis XVI, I command you to open this door!"

"Ava, Esme, do NOT open the door."

The quiet, authoritarian voice was unmistakably Gabriel's.

"Monsieur—"

"Gabriel Chabot, *le Vicomte de Landévennec, Monsieur.*"

I could almost picture Gabriel executing a bow with a flourish and had to bite back the urge to giggle. We pressed our ears to the door.

"Ah, *Vicomte de Landévennec. . . le Commandant des Rochefor*t has requested that Mademoiselle Martel report to his office, to answer questions regarding her ah. . . involvement in a possible theft. He requires her presence at the Naval base immediately."

"Please relay to *Commandant* des Rochefort my regret that Mademoiselle Martel will be unable to meet his request."

"But Monsieur—"

"*Vicomte,*" cut in Gabriel, his voice deceptively soft.

"Ah, aye, of course, *Vicomte. . .* I apologize. Unfortunately, I must insist—"

"I think you misunderstand. Mademoiselle Martel is my betrothed. Please let des Rochefort know that she is not to be bothered again. She has fulfilled her duty by reporting the shipwreck, and he can expect no further cooperation from either of us on this matter." His voice made it clear he would broker no further argument.

If I could have, I would have kissed him on the spot.

"Ah, I will inform *le Commandant* des Rochefort, Vicomte. Thank you for your time."

I envisioned the poor lieutenant des Rochefort had sent, wringing his hands in apology for insulting a standing member of the nobility.

The quiet click of his bootheels receded into the distance, followed by several moments of silence.

"Ava? It's me. You can open the door now."

My hand shook as I tried to unbolt the latch. After a moment of fumbling, Esme gently pushed my hand away and smoothly slid the bolt back, stepping back so I could open the door. I smiled at her in thanks.

Gabriel and Luc both stood in the hallway. Gabriel must have been dressing when he heard the commotion in the corridor and ran out of his room. His linen shirt was untucked, his sun-kissed hair, unkempt. I took several steps toward him, hands outstretched, and Gabriel took them unhesitatingly. He held me at arm's length and ran his eyes over my face, before pulling me in close.

I was excruciatingly aware of the way my body fit against his. My cheek settled against his chest, and I felt him lower his head to the top of mine and kiss my hair. The sweetness of the gesture, combined with the morning's scare had me swallowing down sudden tears. After a moment, Gabriel seemed to realize we were standing in the middle of the corridor, and he pulled away slightly. His eyes were dark on my face. I was suddenly acutely aware that I was still dressed in my nightdress, my feet were bare, and the plait Esme had put my hair in the night before, had completely unraveled, leaving curls, tumbling around my face and down my back. Gently, Gabriel tucked a stray curl behind my ear.

"*Dieu*, you are beautiful," he murmured. "I promised I would keep you safe but considering how quickly des Rochefort sent someone looking for you, I do believe we should not linger in Nantes. I suspect he will not give up so easily and send a larger contingent of men next time." The frown lines between his eyes gave away his concern, though he kept his voice light.

"I thought I was dreaming when I heard the knocking at the door. . ."

Gabriel shook his head. "Can you be ready to leave after breakfast?"

"Yes, of course. Esme and I will begin packing right away."

He bowed low over our linked hands and brushed my knuckles with the whisper of a kiss.

Eighteen
You Had me at Tacos

"How old are you?"

"Hmm?" I glanced sideways at Gabriel with an eyebrow quirked, his voice drawing me out of my reverie.

We were back in Savenay, in the same grimy accommodations we'd stayed at the first time— there were no other options in the tiny town. The tension had been building in me all day. Every step Automne took, led us closer and made me withdraw further into myself.

"Your age, how many years do you have?" He ran his thumb over the back of my hand as we sat in the *auberge*, the remnants of our supper pushed away from us on the table. He was trying to distract me from my thoughts; I was strung as tight as a bowstring and his gray eyes told me he knew it.

"I'm twenty-three, how old are you?"

He raised his eyebrows. "I thought you were younger." Surprise tinged his deep voice. "I'm twenty-four."

I raised one shoulder in a quasi-shrug, and let it fall negligently. "I never met a man that interested me enough to get married," I replied, answering his unspoken question.

"Lucky me," he whispered gruffly, tracing a finger over the veins on the palm of my hand. It shot tingles up my arm and straight into the pit of my stomach, making it hard to concentrate on his words. "What's your favorite food?"

I laughed shortly. "Mexican," I answered automatically and truthfully without thinking. "What's with the questions?"

"You're going to be my wife, shouldn't we get to know one another?" He raised a dark brow at me.

"Well, I suppose when you put it that way," I answered sulkily.

He grinned at my annoyance, flashing strong white teeth at me. "Now, what is Mexican?"

I paused, the remembered taste of Tex-Mex flooding my tastebuds. The crunch of a taco, the perfect combination of meat and cheese, how the cold, tangy sour cream, and the crisp, clean taste of lettuce blended into the perfect, mouthwatering meal. I missed the tartness of lime against the creamy texture of avocado. I shook my head slightly, trying to think of a way to explain to him something that likely didn't exist yet. Mexico as a formal country wasn't even a thing.

"It's more a manner of cooking, using certain spices and ingredients," I answered finally. "I'll have to see if I can gather what I need to make it for you one day."

"You can cook?"

"Of course. At least a few things, though I wouldn't call myself a culinary genius."

He laughed. "You're full of surprises. It's a bit unorthodox, but my favorite food is *chocolat*," he confessed.

"Mmm, that is a close second for me, you have good taste."

"Favorite color?" he shot out.

"Green, yours?" I replied.

"Twas always blue, but I've changed my mind. It's the color of your eyes," he said softly.

I blushed at the compliment; I always feel awkward when someone says something like that.

He seemed to sense my unease and continued his line of questioning to divert me. "Do you have brothers or sisters?"

"No."

"I already know you can read and speak French and English, Any other languages?"

"A bit of Spanish and Latin, though it's not very fluent."

"My English is not good, but my German, Spanish, and Latin are decent," he replied.

"My turn," I said, getting into the spirit of things. "What is your favorite season?"

"*Automne*, I love the colors, the crisp feeling in the air, bringing in the harvest, and knowing that winter's deep sleep is coming." His answer was surprisingly poetic.

"Is that why your horse is named Automne?"

"Aye, his coloring is perfect for it, no?"

"It is. I struggle with choosing a favorite." I admitted. "Each season appeals to me for different reasons, but I think I love summer best."

He nodded, "Do you prefer the country or the city?"

"Country," I answered immediately. "The city has amenities, but I love being surrounded by nature."

"The air is clean. . . you can breathe, you can walk thousands of fathoms and never see another person, it's free," he said approvingly, putting my feelings into words.

"It is free." I agreed. We fell silent for a moment, appreciating that we were in tune with each other in this. "Do you prefer the beach, the mountains, or the forest?" I asked finally.

Gabriel was quiet for a moment, his expression thoughtful as he turned my hand over in his. "I love them all. They're all beautiful in their own right. But I feel most alive when the ocean air is in my face, and I can hear the sea crashing on the shore."

I let out a quiet breath, I have always felt an inexplicable kinship with the ocean. It has pulled me into its mysterious embrace for the entirety of my life, but it stole Carri from me and catapulted me into a time and place not my own. Its beguiling promise has turned out to be the most traitorous of lies.

After a moment I shook the clouds from my mind and forced myself to smile at the unasked question in his eyes. "I always loved the sea the most. After the shipwreck though. . . I'm not sure how I feel. I suppose time will tell."

"Who was Carri?"

Startled, I looked up into questioning silver eyes.

"You spoke their name when you were in the depths of fevered dreams at *Camaret-sur-mer*," he responded to my unspoken query.

"She was my best friend from the time I was a child." I paused trying to get my bearings before continuing. I could feel the threat of tears burning in my throat. "We were inseparable. She was on the ship with me. . . " I choked, but there was no need to say more.

Gabriel gathered me against him comfortingly as I pressed my hot face against his chest. I sniffled, barely suppressing the urge to sob. His heart beat a steady, reassuring tattoo, calming me. One hand gently smoothed my hair away from my face before settling against the small of my back.

I wrapped my arms around him and squeezed him in wordless thanks before moving back slightly. He placed two fingers under my chin and tipped my face up to meet his. It was filled with regret.

"I'm sorry for asking. I thought perhaps that it was an old love. My mind was filled with jealous possibilities. I didn't intend to make you relive her loss."

"Other than my parents, she was the person I loved the most. But, it wasn't the type of love you were thinking of," I sniffed with a watery smile.

He smiled into my eyes, the heat in the depths of his making my toes curl inside my boots. He bowed his head until his forehead gently bumped against mine and I could feel his warm breath on my skin.

"I'm glad," he murmured huskily. "I'm glad that it wasn't that kind of love. I'm glad you never met a man that interested you enough to marry."

His lips pressed against mine for the barest of moments, but the promise in them settled in my bones.

NINETEEN
MATCHMAKER, MATCHMAKER

It'd been three days… or four? I couldn't remember anymore. The time and the landscape blurred as we trudged along, leaving Nantes behind. I was overwhelmed with anxiety when we stopped on the first night in Savenay; my hyperactive imagination envisioned Cifarelli lurking around every corner. The tension in Gabriel and the other men was palpable, as was the sense of relief I think we all felt when we left the small town of horrors behind once more. *It will be too soon if I never have to pass through Savenay again.*

I shifted in the saddle, trying to find a more comfortable position. My butt was numb and sore, my thighs exhausted, and my back ached with every bump we encountered on the road. At least the weather had warmed slightly. The unseasonable snow melted, and the temperature was more like early December than the dead of winter. *Perhaps, I feel a bit warmer on the return trip north because of the growing ease between myself and my travel mates.*

There was a raised brow or two when Gabriel made our betrothal known, but the men had warmed considerably toward me over the last few days.

I thought of Gabriel and unconsciously tightened my arms around him, reveling in the new sensation. Today was the first day I'd gone without the arm sling, and I would never again take for granted how lovely it was to use both arms. I rested my cheek against his back and breathed deeply.

He smelled of musk, horse, woodsmoke, the rosemary in his soap, and the lemon candies he liked to chew. The combination had become intoxicating to me.

We passed the long hours in the saddle talking about ourselves. I introduced him to 'this or that?' and it was an instant hit, both of us laughing at the absurdity of the questions we asked once we exhausted the normal ones.

"Ava?" I felt his voice rumble through his chest under my ear.

"Mmm?"

"I wanted to bring you to *Landévennec*, to my home. . . " He sounded wistful. "But I think we should stop in *Trégoudan* first. We can get married in the chapel there. It's quite beautiful. Amélie and Mathieu can stand witness. It'll be more of a celebration if they are there. And it will be nice to meet the new *bebe* as well."

It occurred to me that he was asking what I thought, in a roundabout way, enumerating all the reasons why he thought we should go to *Trégoudan* instead.

"I would love to see your sister and their new baby. We can go to *Landévennec* after? Is it where you usually stay?"

"Aye, although my work—" he hesitated, "means I travel along the coast quite a bit. But I'm eager to take you to *Landévennec*. It's truly magnificent there. I think you will love it."

"It's where you and Amélie were born?"

"*Oui*. We grew up there. It was a happy childhood, even with the loss of our parents. . . and my brother. I cannot imagine living anywhere else. I went to the *université* in Paris— it's where I met Mathieu, you know? But I always knew I would go back home." His voice was full of affection at the thought of his birthplace.

"What happened to your parents and brother?" I hesitate to ask, knowing how hard it is for me to think about mine.

"My mother passed when I was eight. After Amélie was born, there was another child, but neither my *maman* nor the *bebe* survived. My father. . . " His voice broke. "Well, we don't know. He got sick, and it took him very quickly. I was twelve when it happened." Gabriel let out a deep sigh, as if a weight had been lifted, simply by letting me sit and share in his grief. He took in a shuddering breath. "My brother Pierre passed away a few months after my father. He was thrown from his horse during a hunt. He broke his neck."

"I'm sorry," I whispered. "How old was your brother?"

"He was two years older than me. . . Just fourteen. It was a dark time for Amélie and me."

I nodded, trying to imagine what it must have been like. "You must miss them all terribly."

I swallowed down the ache in my throat that thinking about the loss of my parents and Carri always brought and hid my face against his shoulder so he wouldn't see the tears that sprang to my eyes.

Gabriel was quiet, probably remembering his own feelings of fresh loss. Only those who have navigated deep grief intuitively understand that nothing can be said to take away the anguish. He covered my hands with his and squeezed gently, then turned his face, and rested his cheek against the top of my head, rubbing it across my hair as though marking his territory, like a big cat.

"Would you like to spend Christmas at *Trégoudan*, or would you prefer to spend it at *Landévennec*?" he asked, attempting to redirect the conversation.

"Mmm. I don't know. Can we see how things are at your sister's before we decide?"

"*Oui*. They may want some time as a family," he answered thoughtfully.

"So, you met Mathieu when you went to university?"

"We boarded together when I first went to Paris. We were both ten at the time. Of course, I came back early after Pierre passed away to manage the estate. Mathieu stayed in Paris, but we kept in touch, and he met Amélie when he visited me over the summer a few years later. The two of them were inseparable almost from the beginning. . . He treats her very well."

"You sound relieved."

"There are many unscrupulous men. From the moment our father and brother died, I worried about her eventual marriage. For years I had night-mares about how she might be treated. There was no one other than myself to ensure that she not be dishonored or treated poorly. I was partial to Mathieu. . . I knew he was a good man—"

"You played Cupid!" I gasped, laughing.

"Well. . . I did harbor hopes that they would strike it off. It worked out better than I could have hoped though."

"Then what do you think about Luc and Esme? Have you spoken about it?"

"A bit. They're well-matched, and the interest seems to be mutual. I suspect that Luc is working himself up to ask for her hand. He's a bit older than her, but she doesn't seem to mind?" he asked glancing back at me.

I shook my head. "She's quite taken with him. I know she is embellishing her favorite gown in the hopes it will serve as a wedding dress."

"Oh, it's gone that far, has it? In that case, I will speak to him about it tonight."

I squeezed my arms around him in thanks. "Esme will be thrilled."

"You seem to be very close with her."

"She's been wonderful. I know she is meant to be my chaperone, but I consider her a friend."

Gabriel was quiet for several moments. He pulled two lemon candies out of his pocket, handed one back to me, and popped the other in his mouth as he thought.

Finally, he said, "If you like, and if Esme is open to it, I could see if Amélie and Mathieu will let Esme go. Esme has been Amélie's companion for years, but Luc has a small house of his own on my land. If they marry, I can see about providing a dowry for her. Esme and her mother were left nearly penniless when her father passed away."

"Oh, I would love that. Would Esme be a companion to me then?"

"Of course, if you wish." Gabriel hesitated for a moment. "It will mean leaving her mother. Margaret will stay with Amélie's children."

"But when we visit or when they visit us, can we bring them with us?"

"Certainly."

I held our secret plan close to my heart for the rest of our trip to *Trégoudan*. It filled me with warmth to know that Gabriel cared about Luc, and Esme enough to help broker their marriage and that he would go out of his way to bring Esme back to *Landévennec*.

The only thing that still weighed on me was whether or not I should tell Gabriel my real story. There wasn't a day that went by that I didn't play out different possible scenarios in my mind. It worried me, what he would think, whether he would believe me, what would change between us.

I treasured the newfound warmth and openness between us and I hated the idea of losing it. The enormity of the secret kept me up most nights. Telling him the truth would be a relief, but what if it all went wrong?

TWENTY
Déjà Vu

I was still mulling over my options when the *château* came into view.

Mathieu walked out the door as the horses and wagon pulled to the front steps. "Gabriel! I wasn't expecting to see you so soon." Mathieu was positively beaming. "Come in and meet your niece."

Niece.

So, my vision, or whatever it was, had been right. They'd had a girl. I would have to mull over that revelation later.

"How is Amélie?" asked Gabriel as he swung off Automne and turned to help me.

"She is doing well. Already wanting to be up and about, even though I keep telling her to stay in bed and rest." Mathieu shook his head ruefully. "But you know your sister. Stubborn as a mule when she wants to be."

Gabriel laughed. "Aye, I know."

The rueful tone in his voice suggested he was well acquainted with his sister's stubborn streak. Gabriel tossed the reins to Luc, and cupping my elbow in his hand moved to follow Mathieu into the front hall.

Mathieu glanced over his shoulder at me. "Did your errand with the Navy go well?"

I laughed shortly. "No, I wouldn't say so. But it is hopefully behind me now."

He raised an eyebrow in question. "The two of you will have to fill Amélie and me in over supper."

"We have quite a bit to tell you about later. The last few weeks have been eventful," added Gabriel with a wink at me.

"Amélie and Étienne will both be excited to see the two of you. We weren't sure if we would see you again Mademoiselle Martel."

"I'm excited to see them as well. What have you named the baby?"

"I'll let Amélie tell you if she's awake." Mathieu opened the heavy, wood door to their room and peered inside, then waved us forward. "I have a surprise for you, *ma chérie*."

Amélie sat in a brocade chair by the windows but stood as soon as she saw Gabriel and me.

Gabriel strode over to hug her delicately. "How are you? And how is my little niece?"

"We're both well, you big worrier. Come and meet my beautiful Thérèse." Amélie walked over to the cradle and gently picked up the swaddled bundle.

She cooed into the little face before handing her over to her uncle. *Déjà vu* struck. I had seen that exact handoff when I'd said goodbye to Amélie.

Gabriel stared at the baby lovingly, not noticing my stunned reaction.

"She's perfect. I think she looks like you. . . but maybe she got your eyes, Mathieu," he joked. He beckoned to me. "Come look at *la petite* Thérèse."

I moved forward to stand next to Gabriel, still shocked at the preciseness of my vision. He shifted Thérèse to his left arm and casually wrapped his other arm around my waist. I was surprised by how easily he seemed to hold such a tiny baby. I leaned in close, peering into the diminutive, rosy-cheeked face.

"Hello, sweetheart," I murmured, running the tip of my finger along the baby's smooth, downy skin. She opened cornflower blue eyes, pinning me in her curious gaze. I looked at Amélie with a smile. "She's gorgeous. I'm so glad I got to come back and meet her."

Amélie was assessing the way Gabriel's arm was wrapped possessively around my waist, but she smiled easily at me. "I'm glad too. I hoped we might see you again." She looked from Gabriel to me, and back to her brother again. "Do the two of you have any news to share?"

"Plenty, but it can wait until supper." The teasing light in Gabriel's eyes showed he knew exactly what Amélie was hinting at. He'd caught how she watched us, but he enjoyed giving his sister a hard time. Typical brother.

I watched as her face fell a teensy bit before Gabriel gave in. I was glad that Amélie and I became friends and I hoped she would react to our announcement with happiness.

He nudged me. "Would you like to tell them?"

"Me? N-nooo," I replied, flustered. I felt the heat creeping up my neck and knew I was blushing furiously.

Amélie turned her gaze to Gabriel expectantly. Mathieu looked perplexed, as though he hadn't picked up on the undercurrent in the room.

Gabriel shrugged and grinned broadly. "Ava has agreed to marry me. We thought we might do it here. . . soon. If the two of you don't mind?"

Amélie squealed and clapped her hands together, before throwing them around Gabriel's neck. "I knew it!" she crowed triumphantly. "Oh, I am so glad. Of course, you can marry here. I wouldn't want to miss it and it will be so much easier for us to attend with the little ones. How soon were you thinking?"

Mathieu hugged Gabriel, slapping his back, and then lifted my hand for a kiss. "Welcome to the family," he said heartily. "I've waited years for my friend here to take the fall." A quick grin flashed across his face.

Gabriel laughed. "Amélie has you wrapped around her finger. I'm in no rush to join you in your predicament." He turned to Amélie and added, "As soon as we can make the arrangements. Nothing lavish, mind. We just want to celebrate with family. Can we do it before Christmas?"

Mathieu shook his head and chuckled gleefully. "If my eyes do not deceive me, it is too late for that *mon beau-frère*."

"I'm sure we can. We can have Esme, Margaret, and the others begin preparations tomorrow. You'll stay for Christmas?" Amélie looked at Gabriel and me for confirmation.

"Possibly," hedged Gabriel.

"We have time enough to decide that later," ruled Amélie. "In the meantime, why don't the two of you rest for a bit and settle in before supper? The rest of the news can wait, aye?" She turned to me. "You must be clamoring for a proper wash. I'll have them bring the tub up for you, shall I?"

"That would be lovely. Thank you."

Gabriel gently deposited the sleeping Thérèse in her cradle before returning to my side. "I'll walk you up." He turned to look at Mathieu. "I need to speak to you. . . if you'll meet me in the stables in a few minutes?"

Mathieu nodded, "I need to check in with the men anyway. I will see you there."

"We will see you at supper," tossed Gabriel over his shoulder at Amélie, as he led me out of the room.

We walked down the corridor in silence, lost in our thoughts. As we approached the door to the room I stayed in previously, Gabriel slowed. We were utterly alone in the hallway, and I was suddenly aware that we had rarely ever been left alone for more than a moment.

Gabriel turned toward me at the door and gently lifted my face to his. "I have to tell Mathieu what occurred with Cifarelli."

My heart sank. I hated even thinking about what happened in Savenay. "Aye, of course. I imagine they need to know. . . " I murmured.

"I have to warn them, should he ever show up here."

I nodded quietly.

"Ava, please look at me."

I forced my eyes up to his, noting the concern and care in them that was plain to see. "I intend to tell Mathieu quietly. I see no reason to make you relive what happened, or make you answer questions about it, however well-meaning they might be."

"Thank you. I do not want to have to speak about it. I wish to put it behind me, as best I can." My stomach churned at the thought of Cifarelli.

He searched my face shrewdly for a minute before nodding slightly to himself, apparently satisfied with whatever he read in my expression. His hand cupped my face as he ran his thumb tenderly over my bottom lip. I was suffused in heat so intense I tried to look away, but I was mesmerized by the raw desire in his eyes. My insides felt like warm honey. He moved slowly, his face questioning, silently allowing me to back away. Instead, I threw caution to the wind and boldly closed the distance between us.

Her body was a hairsbreadth from his, Gabriel felt her heat through both their clothes. His other hand came up and he tilted her head back, his fingers tunneling into the hair at the nape of her neck, anchoring her, as his mouth came down to meet hers. The kiss was tentative, exploratory; he intended to just brush his lips softly over hers.

His world tilted on its axis as Ava sank against him, pliant, wordlessly asking for more. She tasted like his favorite lemon candies, bright and citrusy, and Gabriel drowned in it, and the intoxicating rose scent she always wore. His hand ran down the buttons along her spine, settling at the small of her back. The moment spun out timelessly. He pulled away from her regretfully, in physical pain. Her responsiveness had stoked his hunger instead of satiating it. The blood pounded through his veins, slow and thick.

Her lashes lifted slowly, revealing eyes the color of new spring leaves. Her face, delicate as a cameo, hovered inches from his. He read the raw yearning writ on it, as her body swayed against his, and he felt the tremble in her legs as she stood on her toes to take his mouth back. He groaned and crushed her to him, relishing the way her slender body fit against him.

Her lips were urgent against his, fueling the fire between them to burn hotter and brighter. Gabriel felt his self-control slipping. It took a Herculean effort to force himself away from her.

"Ava." His voice was rough with longing.

He ran his hands down her arms, lacing his fingers through hers, shocked to realize they were shaking. She looked at him, her gaze glazed with desire. He let out a shuddering breath and closed his eyes, struggling to master himself.

I said nothing. My thoughts were muddled, and I couldn't have strung words together into a comprehensible sentence if I tried. *He's being honorable*, said the tiny voice in my head. *But I want to kiss him again*, I argued against myself. *It's just a few more weeks*, said the voice, *you've waited this long...*

Gabriel opened his eyes, leaned in, and pressed a kiss to the top of my head, then took a step back, and raised our linked hands to his lips. "I am counting the minutes until we are married, and you are truly mine," he murmured, his deep voice raspy.

I gave him a dazzling smile. "I am counting the seconds," I replied pertly, and ducked under his arm into the open bedroom. I gently closed the door on his bemused face and leaned against it, letting my knees buckle.

Lust does not equal love, but holy hell. I have never felt so overcome with desire for someone. I don't consider myself a prude, although I haven't gone all the way with anyone. *It isn't because I wouldn't have been willing to, given the right person. I've just never found a man I cared about enough to go down that road with.*

The way I felt when Gabriel touched me, I was a flower opening to the sun for the first time. As if I found a piece of myself that I never knew existed, and I was giving that secret part of myself to him immediately upon its discovery. It was intimidating to realize how much power I was handing to Gabriel. *Did I wield the same control over him? Maybe, although he exercised more self-discipline today than I did.*

Twenty-One
Zippers

A knock sounded at my back. I straightened and opened the heavy door, stepping out of the way so the wooden tub could be carried into the room. I waited until they finished filling it with buckets of steaming water and everyone left the chamber except for one of the maids.

I smiled at the young girl, eager to put her at ease. "Hello, I'm Ava. What's your name?"

"Jeanne," she answered softly with a curtsey.

"Thank you for your help today, Jeanne." I turned to give her quick, deft fingers access to the long row of buttons along the back of my gown.

As she helped with the endless laces, fastenings, and ties that kept the layers of garments on, I reminisced about the ease of zippers. *God, I miss them. When exactly had that little game-changer been invented?*

I stepped out of my stockings, petticoats, and gown, and Jeanne wrapped a warm, thick cloth around my body while I kept up an easy chatter.

"Are you from *Trégoudan* Jeanne?" I asked, trying to draw the shy girl out of her shell.

"Aye, my lady." She presented me with a box of scented oils to choose from.

I dithered for a moment, trying to decide if I should stick with my signature rose scent, or try something new, then settled on my favorite, dropped my towel, and stepped into the bath as Jeanne poured oil into the water.

"This is lovely," I murmured, half to myself as I sank into the hot water gratefully. It was delightful against my skin, melting away the days of accumulated soreness in my muscles. I relaxed into the scented water and closed my eyes. It was downright heavenly to take a proper bath.

Chalk that up as another thing I missed about the twentieth century. The ability to bathe daily was a luxury I vastly undervalued. You would think life on a boat would have prepared me for the inconvenience of rare baths, but one never really gets used to it.

I shrugged mentally, determined to enjoy this one to the hilt, as Jeanne gently detangled my long hair and washed it. It was strange to bathe in front of someone else, even though I'd had to do it several times now. Once my arm was completely healed, I vowed the first thing I would do was take a bath without spectators. I laughed a bit at myself. In life, it truly was the little things.

I stiffened, my back ramrod straight, my warm bath suddenly frigid, as my vision went as black as a moonless night.

Images rolled through my mind like an old, silent movie.

A slightly older Jeanne cowered in the corner of one of the small tenant huts I had seen dotted across the landscape. The only light in the one-room cabin came from the open door. Jeanne's hair was lank and dirty, revealing a bruised face when she lifted it. She raised imploring hands as a large, blonde man advanced on her. I caught a glimpse of his face as he moved through the sunlight streaming in through the door.

It would have been a handsome face if it weren't twisted in the same angry, sinister expression that I'd seen on Cifarelli's. It bore the look of a man who enjoyed inflicting pain on those he controlled. His eyes glinted in the half-light, crazed, relishing in his power, delighting in her terror.

He towered over Jeanne, raising a meaty fist as he yelled at her. I wished I could hear what he was saying, but my ears were filled with a strange buzzing sound; like I was being swarmed by a hive full of bees. He drew back a booted foot to kick Jeanne, and she fell to the side, curled in the fetal position, desperately protecting her rounded belly.

"—Mademoiselle. . . Mademoiselle Ava! Are you all right?"

With difficulty, I focused my gaze on Jeanne's small, unblemished, and concerned face.

Fuck. Who the hell would do that to this sweet girl?

My stomach clenched.

"Fine— I'm fine." I lied, forcing what I hoped passed as a believable smile on my face. "I'm feeling a bit cold. I think I will come out now."

"Of course," whispered Jeanne. "Which gown would you like to wear for supper?"

"The blue brocade please," I answered, distractedly.

My mind raced. *So far, only one of my 'visions' has come true. . . If that was even what they were.* I felt nauseated and my head throbbed.

How could someone mistreat this child?

The premonitions— or whatever they were— were meant to be a warning. The question was, did I have the power to change what I saw? Were they a guide? A peek at what could be?

Or were the visions etched in stone?

TWENTY-TWO
WOMEN'S INTUITION

Gabriel stepped out of the cold sunshine and into the warm, dark stables. He breathed deeply, taking in the comforting scents of hay, horse, leather, sweat, and manure. His long, unhurried strides quickly took him past the row of stalls until he arrived at Automne's. He fished into his pocket, pulled out the apple he'd swiped from the kitchen, and offered it on his palm. The horse delicately lipped the proffered fruit out of his hand, crunching it appreciatively, then interrogatively bumped him with his nose, checking for more treats.

Gabriel chuckled and affectionately rubbed the bay's head. "I have nothing more for you, you big brute."

Automne looked at him in obvious disappointment, blinking his ridiculously long eyelashes as if to point out that he'd carried Gabriel and Ava halfway across the country in recent weeks, and didn't he deserve more than a measly apple in thanks?

Gabriel turned out his pockets. "I promise to bring you more tomorrow, and maybe some carrots as well. That will be nice, eh? I'll have the stable lad give you a nice bucket of oats tonight."

Gabriel walked away, singing softly under his breath. 'Gentlemen, would you like to hear, the song of famous *la Palisse*? You may indeed enjoy it. . .'

He found Mathieu in the tack room, cleaning his favorite saddle. He took Automne's saddle off the wall, grabbed a rag, pulled up a stool, and began to polish his as well. They worked in companionable silence for a few minutes.

Mathieu waited patiently, no doubt sensing that Gabriel was working out what he wanted to say. Gabriel had long since found that it was easier to have difficult conversations when his hands were busy, and this was a discussion he wasn't particularly looking forward to.

He took a deep breath, and dove right in. "You might have noticed that Cifarelli did not return with us."

Mathieu raised an eyebrow in question, but Gabriel did not expect him to answer. Of course, Mathieu would have noticed the absence, but he also would have known that an explanation would be forthcoming.

"He attacked the women in one of the *auberges* one night. Ava in particular. Had Esme not been able to get away and fetch me. . ." He spread his hands out as if to say he didn't know what would have happened. A muscle ticked in his jaw, and he swallowed hard. He looked his brother-in-law in the eye. "I was tempted to kill him."

There was a momentary silence, and Gabriel could see his desire for murder reflected in Mathieu's eyes. He relaxed his shoulders a bit, realizing that he had foolishly worried about Mathieu's reaction.

"Why didn't you?" Mathieu finally responded quietly.

"Cooler heads prevailed," he admitted. "We took him to the constable. He knows that I will not be so reserved should he ever have the misfortune of meeting me again."

"Amélie will be glad to hear it." Mathieu ran a hand through his hair. "I don't look forward to telling her. . . I should have listened to her women's intuition about him. I thought she was being foolish and unfair, projecting her prejudices against him, but it seems she was right."

Gabriel shook his head. "Ava and Esme sensed something from him as well. I didn't dismiss their fear out of hand, but I may not have taken it as seriously as I should have. It seems we should both listen to our women a bit more."

Mathieu grinned, "Do not let Amélie hear you say that. I will never hear the end of it!"

Gabriel laughed, but his face became serious again. "There is more—"

"More?"

"*Oui.* We ran into problems with *le commandant* in Nantes as well."

"Ava mentioned something about that. What happened?"

"The short of it is that he did not like Ava's explanation of what happened. He took extreme offense to the idea that she might have inherited anything after her parents' death. They argued… " He smiled as he recalled how she stood up and yelled at des Rochefort. She'd been magnificent, like a tigress defending her cub. He shook his head. "*Le commandant* sent a man after her the next day. I essentially told him he could shove his order up his ass."

Mathieu sat back, ruminating on the story. "You must admit it is unusual for a girl to inherit," he put in diplomatically.

"Of course. But it is not entirely unheard of."

"Perhaps not. Remind me where her family is from?"

"Roussillon. Though she mentioned that her mother has family in England somewhere."

Mathieu stood up, arching his back in a stretch, before placing his saddle back on its hook. "So, I suppose that *le commandant* in Nantes is now considered an enemy. What did you say his name is?"

"Des Rochefort," replied Gabriel, standing up as well. "That's the other thing I wanted to mention, he was asking her questions about cargo."

The easy, relaxed look on Mathieu's face changed to interest. "Oh?"

"She had no idea. But it was the way he asked it. I couldn't say for sure, but the feeling I got was that he would not be a friend to our endeavors."

Mathieu absorbed this in silence and nodded once to himself. "It's good to be aware. It's doubtful that we would ever run into him, Nantes is some distance from here, but the information is always valuable. One never knows."

Gabriel nodded, replacing Automne's saddle on the wall. He felt relieved now that he had unburdened himself to Mathieu. There was some lingering disquiet over the recent events, but he was confident that everything would reveal itself in time. They began to walk past the stalls toward the open door of the stable. Sunlight streamed in, temporarily blinding him with its brightness.

"I need to speak to you about Luc and Esme as well."

Mathieu looked at him. "Oh aye? Do I hear more wedding bells chiming?"

"You knew?"

"Aye, Amélie and I have suspected it for some time. Does that mean it's official?"

"Nay, not that I'm aware. But it's certainly moving in that direction. Does that mean you and Amélie would be willing to let Esme go?"

Mathieu rolled his shoulders and hunched them briefly as they walked out of the warmth of the stable and into the brisk, autumn air. "I suppose so. Amélie and I haven't discussed that part of it, but of course, we wouldn't stand in their way if they wish to marry." He gave Gabriel a sidelong glance, "I assume you will find something for Esme?"

"*Oui*. Ava will be glad of it. She and Esme seem to have struck up a friendship."

"Amélie and Margaret will be sorry to see her go, but baby birds must fly the nest eventually."

Gabriel grinned at the imagery. "Aye well, in that case, I will speak to Luc about it, and we will see what happens."

Twenty-Three
Silence and Scented Sunsets

I avoided intruding in the kitchen during my first stay at *Trégoudan*, but my growling stomach insisted it be fed before supper. I followed the enticing scent of stew, finding my way into the bustling room, and paused at the threshold, uncertain of my welcome. The heat from the huge fire and ovens made it feel like I stood at the entrance of a sauna.

Herbs hung in bunches from the rafters, there was a substantial, bubbling cauldron of stew at the hearth and a smaller pot of cooked, sweet apples cooling. The cook's back was turned to me as she rhythmically kneaded and pounded dough on the massive, floury work surface. Her helper noticed me awkwardly hovering by the door and waved me in, wiping her hands on her apron as she approached me.

"Ah, Mademoiselle Martel! You must be hungry after your long journey. Shall I make you a plate?" She smiled pleasantly revealing a missing eyetooth.

"I don't want to put you to any trouble," I began hesitantly. "I thought I might just have a bit of bread or an apple. . . "

"Nonsense!" She flapped a hand in my direction as she busily began filling a plate with cheese, bread, and walnuts before heading to the apple pot and spooning a hearty serving onto the plate. She stood in the middle of the kitchen with the heaping platter in one hand, the other hand on her hip, and surveyed the room. Her eyes alighted on the ham sitting on the table and she started toward it purposefully.

"Oh please! This is quite enough, I assure you. Thank you so much, but if I have ham too, I will never have room for supper," I protested with a laugh.

She eyed me skeptically. "You could do with some fattening," she muttered, reluctantly placing the plate on the heavy wood table.

I sat as she poured me a glass of wine.

"I hope you don't mind if I eat in here," I asked, cocking a glance at the head cook apprehensively.

"Ah, nay, of course not! We enjoy having visitors, as long as they don't get underfoot. It's nice to see people appreciate the food we spend all day making." She poured herself a glass of wine and hefted her not-inconsiderable weight onto the bench across from mine. "I hear we'll be busy with your wedding feast soon."

I had just taken a bite of bread spread with apples and cheese and choked. I gulped wine and hastily swiped at my streaming eyes with the back of my hand. It shouldn't have surprised me that the news would travel quickly, particularly since the preparations would affect the kitchen, but I'd been taken off guard by the abrupt change in subject.

My throat still scratchy, I managed to say, "I apologize for the extra work. . . I'm sorry, what is your name?"

She downed half her glass in one swallow. "*Je m'appelle* Madame Frenault, and don't you worry one bit about the wedding supper. Madame le Roux," she waved her hand nonchalantly at the head cook, "and I live for these occasions. We've already begun working on the menu." With this, she rose laboriously to her feet, using the table to leverage herself up. "Enjoy your *petite déjeuner.*"

She left me to mull things over in silence while I munched on my snack. I watched in considerable interest as Madame le Roux shoveled risen dough into one of the ovens built into the side of the great stone hearth. She stirred the stew, paused to taste it, shook her head to herself, reached for a little ceramic jar, and added something to it. Probably salt. I watched her move to one of the monstrous work counters and begin chopping an onion.

I caught a glimpse of the setting sun through one of the large windows and vainly trying to roll the tension out of my shoulders, decided I could do with a little air to clear my head. I abandoned what was left on my plate, crumbs mostly, and made for the kitchen door.

As the frigid air hit my skin, I inhaled sharply. After the warmth of the kitchen, the wind felt like hundreds of tiny penetrating needles, and I immediately wished I'd brought my cloak. The initial shock wore off quickly, and I began walking amidst the dark rows of wintering plants, moving briskly in an attempt to stay warm. When I came across cabbages lining one edge, I realized this must be the kitchen garden.

The frigid air had its intended consequence, and I began to feel clear-eyed for the first time since that afternoon's vision of Jeanne. I crossed myself reflexively, something I've never been in the habit of doing, but given the circumstances, it was a good time to become more devout.

I sat on a bench against the rough stone wall of the house. It was perfectly situated to catch the last warm rays of sunlight, and I closed my eyes basking in it, trying to absorb every drop of golden warmth. A sense of peace settled over me, and I exhaled, trying to force the general unease that lived in my chest out with my breath.

It didn't quite work. My hands were clenched in my skirts, and I consciously straightened my fingers, spreading them over the soft, warm fabric. I concentrated on the texture of the weave under my fingertips and let out another long slow exhalation. Slightly better. I opened my eyes and emitted a muffled screech.

Gabriel breathed deeply of the salty air and listened to the cry of the gulls as he meandered back toward *le château*. He felt deeply contented as he pondered the events of the last few months. Sure, there had been difficulties, as there always were in life, but meeting Ava and everything that had transpired since cast a rosy glow on the current state of his affairs.

He stepped lightly for a tall man; his footsteps were nearly soundless as he approached the gate to the kitchen garden and quietly unlatched it, swinging it on well-greased hinges. He'd taken a piece of cheese for himself when he grabbed the apple for Automne earlier, but it barely put a dent in his appetite. He was famished. Humming to himself, he rounded the corner of the garden and stopped in his tracks.

Ava sat in the final dying rays of light, suffused in shades of rose and gold. At first, she looked peaceful, eyes closed, inhaling deeply and slowly, but then he noticed the tension in the set of her shoulders. His feet began moving toward her before he realized he'd made up his mind to approach her. She must be deep in thought if she hadn't heard him he thought, as he stood looking down at her. Suddenly, she opened her eyes and screamed making Gabriel jump in surprise.

"*Dieu*!" He took a step back reflexively but recovered quickly. "I thought you would hear me walking. I didn't mean to startle you *ma chérie*."

My hand was on my chest, feeling the galloping beat of my heart. I certainly hadn't heard him. The man could move as silently as a cat. At least he had the grace to look sheepish about sneaking up on me.

I huffed out a little breath and patted the bench, inviting him to sit beside me, which he did promptly, wrapping his arm around me and drawing me close.

"Aren't you cold?"

"Aye," I answered truthfully. "But I don't want to miss the sunset," I added, nodding toward the magnificent sky painted in sorbet hues.

Gabriel nodded and drew me closer, wrapping his cloak around us both. I rested my cheek against his shoulder, some of my anxiety ebbing away.

Gabriel pressed his lips against my hair and inhaled deeply. Is he committing my scent to memory? I am foolishly glad I decided on rose oil. Given enough time maybe he will think of me whenever he smells roses. My lips tilted up at the corners. *I am becoming a romantic fool.*

We watched the sun sink below the horizon in companionable silence.

Twenty-Four
Forsaking All Others

On the date Amélie and Esme appointed for the wedding. . . a Sunday, the favored day for weddings I'd been informed; a full moon for prosperity and happiness, Esme inserted knowledgeably, the sun dawned cold and clear. I stood by my window looking at the bright, bluebird sky. Fresh snow sparkled in the sunlight as if a fairy flew overhead, waving her wand overnight, strewing tiny diamonds over the landscape.

Nervousness fluttered deep in my stomach, reminding me of a bird I once saw in a pet store, beating its wings against the bars of its cage in a futile attempt to escape its enclosure. I was scared. I could admit this as I stood alone in my shift, bare feet frozen on the wood floor, in the early morning light. Before I could venture further down the rabbit hole my mind had lately become, I heard a perfunctory knock at the door. Hastily I turned and pasted a welcoming smile on my face just in time to see Esme's face peek in. My shoulders relaxed immediately, and my smile became genuine.

"Oh good, you're awake," exclaimed Esme, bustling into the room, swiping my dressing gown off the chair, and handing it to me efficiently.

"I couldn't sleep," I admitted, shrugging into the flowing silk garment, and belting it around my waist.

"Understandable," murmured Esme as she industriously hustled me to the table and chair by the fire. "Jeanne should be here with your breakfast in a moment. After you eat, I am having them draw a bath for you and

Amélie should be here shortly to make sure we have everything you need to get ready." She ticked each item off on her fingers, mentally keeping track of what needed to be done before the ceremony.

Jeanne entered, carefully balancing a heavily laden tray that she placed in front of me. She curtseyed and backed out of the room so quickly, that I scarcely had a chance to thank her. Over the last few weeks, I often found myself ruminating on the vision of Jeanne. It hadn't happened again, but that hadn't stopped me from wondering if and when it would become her reality.

Esme meaningfully pushed my tray closer to me, bringing me back to the matter at hand.

Marriage.

They told me that custom required the wedding to take place at high noon. Until I'd been accosted with a flurry of well-intentioned folklore, I hadn't fully appreciated how much wedding traditions changed over the last two hundred years. Thankfully, I was able to leave the bulk of the planning to Amélie and Esme, who had exuberantly taken over.

The two weeks since our arrival had flown by and I was apprehensive; partly because I still hadn't figured out how to reveal to Gabriel any of the things, I wanted to tell him, and partly because I knew I was entering a binding, lifelong commitment today. While I don't mind being spontaneous about most things, diving headlong into my nuptials was never something I imagined myself doing. The romantic in me always believed marriage was a sacrament, not something to be entered lightly.

Esme interrupted my thoughts impatiently. "Ava! You must eat something; they are preparing the bath already."

Two men were hauling the washtub into the room, followed by Jeanne with buckets of steaming water. I rapidly spread butter and marmalade on my toast and took a healthy bite, followed by a sip of tea. From the looks of it, I was going to be on a tight schedule and would have to save my daydreaming for another time.

The morning passed in a flurry of activity that saw me bathed, scented, powdered, and plucked. Noon found me dressed in my best gown, borrowed shoes pinching my feet uncomfortably, hair cascading unadorned down my back to signify virginity, with a circlet made of spruce, holly, and orange blossoms from the hot house perched atop my head.

I walked decorously under the dazzling, azure sky to the chapel, clutching my matching posy in my trembling hands. On the stone steps I paused, trying to remember to breathe, as Esme made minute adjustments to my hair and dress. I closed my eyes and inhaled deeply from my little bouquet, the sharp resin of the evergreens mingling with the sweetly scented white blossoms, an oddly relaxing combination.

"It's time," whispered Esme, with a gentle shove.

I took a breath and stepped forward, blindly stopping at the threshold, waiting for my eyes to acclimate to the dim recesses of the modest chapel. Candlelight flickered and the comforting scent of incense rose around me. Dust motes danced in the colorful light shining through the stained glass windows. The entire small town and most of *Trégoudan's* tenants must have turned out to witness the wedding, cramming like sardines into the tiny, stone church.

My vision swam as dozens of faces turned expectantly toward me. *Oh God, I can't breathe.*

I was going to fall on my face in front of all these people I didn't know. My blurry eyes found Gabriel's face and focused on it. He was illuminated by the light streaming in through the window behind me. He stood tall, taller than most of the men in the room. His face wore its customary serious expression, but his eyes were glued to mine, beckoning me toward him like a moth to a flame. Suddenly my feet were moving forward, and I found myself standing before him, my hands gripping his like a lifeline.

Ava stood at the entrance of the chapel, silhouetted against the sunshine pouring through the open doors. Gabriel stared, committing the moment to memory, tracing the curve of her cheek, the fullness of her mouth, and her dark curls backlit in the golden light. She seemed to hesitate there, eyes sweeping over the room before finally locking on his. He swallowed down the lump in his throat as she slowly walked down the aisle separating the rows of simple wood benches.

Uncertainty and apprehension were written in every line of her expression, and he felt a trickle of cold sweat run down his spine. He reached out, took both of her icy, shaking hands in his, and squeezed soothingly, trying to convey that it would be all right. He was surprised by the strength in her hands as she squeezed back, reminding him she was stronger than she looked.

Her green eyes looked into his with confidence, but he caught a glimpse of anxiety underlying it. He raised their linked hands and kissed hers tenderly, his eyes never leaving her face. Gabriel waited until he felt some of her tension melt away, before turning his attention to the minister.

I barely heard a word the Reverend said, I have no idea how long he droned on, or how I responded to his queries. The afternoon had the fuzzy quality of dreams half-remembered. Gabriel's hands tightened on mine, seeming to recognize that I wasn't fully present. I concentrated on his face, tracing his features with my gaze, and etching the fierceness of his expression in my mind's eye. His gray eyes blazed with purpose, and I found I couldn't look away. Later, I would recall nothing from the mass and precious little of the ceremony, but this moment would be clear in my memory.

"I, Gabriel Henri Michel Chabot, 7th *Vicomte de Landévennec*," I blinked at this litany of names, and a fleeting smile touched his mouth, as if he read my mind, "Take thee, Ava Martel, to be my wedded Wife, to have and to hold from this day forward, for better, for worse, for richer, for poorer, in sickness and in health, to love and to cherish you all the days of my life, forsaking all others, till death us depart, according to God's holy ordinance. And thereto I plight thee my troth."

"I, Ava Celina Martel, take thee Gabriel Chabot. . . " I got the words out through numb lips and parched tongue. Gabriel's eyes never left my face.

"May I have the rings?"

Mathieu smoothly deposited the wedding bands into the priest's out-stretched hand, who promptly placed the smaller of the two shining, gold bands in Gabriel's open palm.

Gabriel raised the ring to his lips, kissing it solemnly. "With this ring, I thee wed, with my body I thee worship, and with all my worldly goods I thee endow. In the name of the Father, and of the Son, and of the Holy Ghost. Amen." He gently slid it onto my fourth finger, wrapping his hand around mine, as if to keep it in place.

My turn, I echoed his words, somberly sliding the proffered gleaming, gold ring onto Gabriel's hand.

Impatient, Gabriel didn't wait for the priest's final pronouncement, cupping my face in his hands, he bent his face to mine and brushed my mouth with his.

"Ava, breathe," he whispered, his lips rubbing softly against mine as he stepped forward, closing the distance between us. I had a fraction of a second to laugh against his mouth before he obliterated every thought from my mind.

"Enough!" We broke apart as Mathieu playfully clapped a hand on Gabriel's back. "Save it for tonight, eh?" He waggled his brows lasciviously, making me giggle.

The pastor frowned disapprovingly at our kiss, likely a bit more enthusiastic than what the Catholic church would endorse, but I caught the hint of a smile in his eyes as he muttered a final blessing over us.

The crowd surged forward in effusive congratulations. My hand stayed securely in Gabriel's firm grip as we were jostled down the aisle and out onto the steps. The brilliant sun was warm on my face, the air bracingly cold and refreshing. I hadn't realized how close and uncomfortably warm the chapel had been with so many sweating bodies nearby.

I expected a small family gathering for the wedding, and I was surprised by the number of well-wishers who accompanied us back to the house and stayed to eat, drink, and dance. Amélie's housekeeper and army of maids and cooks outdid themselves, bedecking the *château* with evergreen boughs and creating more delectable dishes and desserts to eat than I thought possible. The revelry lasted late into the night, continuing long after Gabriel appeared by my side to lead me upstairs.

I leaned against him tiredly as we made our way up the lengthy, curving staircase, followed by catcalls and a few ribald jokes contributed by some of the more boisterously, drunk merrymakers. My stomach, which had been uneasy for the greater part of the day, churned, and my heartbeat hammered away like a drum solo. The culmination of the wedding day was rapidly approaching, and I was suddenly excited, nervous, and a little sick.

Esme told me they would be moving my things into Gabriel's chamber that afternoon, so it didn't come as a surprise when he quietly led me past the door of the room I'd stayed in up until now. The door swung open silently on its hinges. Someone had already been in here, several tall tapers were lit, casting little golden pools of light throughout the room, and the table boasted two goblets, a few bottles of wine, and several baskets and plates of food.

I wavered at the threshold, but Gabriel gently tugged my hand, drawing me into the room and shutting the door behind me. He let out a deep sigh, stretching his back and rolling his head to loosen the stiff muscles in his neck and shoulders.

"I've barely spoken to you today," he said, his eyes soft on mine.

"I didn't realize there would be so many people."

"Amélie loves an excuse for a party," he answered ruefully.

"It was nice," I admitted. "Just a bit overwhelming and tiring."

"Aye, did you have a chance to eat?" He was gradually but persistently pulling me closer to him, and I had the distinct feeling he wasn't particularly interested in my answer. His eyes darkened and took on the look of a man hungry for something other than food.

I didn't bother responding. Instead, I raised myself on my toes and closed the distance between us. His hands settled on my shoulders as he kissed me slowly, brushing his mouth back and forth over mine until I thought my knees would buckle. I wanted to lose myself, my fears, and my trepidations in the heat that always seemed to be lurking just beneath the surface between us, and I pressed my body against him.

His fingers tightened briefly on my shoulders in response, before gradually moving up under my hair, twisting the strands between them, tenderly massaging my neck and shoulders until the soreness and stiffness I hadn't realized I was carrying, began to melt away. I arched in pleasure against him like a cat, seeking more, as his hands methodically kneaded their way down my arms, and he laced his fingers between mine.

"*Dieu.*" He drew away slightly, resting his forehead against mine, his breathing ragged. "Ava—"

The words died in his throat as I looked at him. I knew my desire was evident in the way my body strained unconsciously against his, in the thoughts he must read clearly in my face. Tentatively I placed my hands on his chest undoing the first button on his waistcoat. He inhaled sharply but stood stock still as I systematically moved down the row. Time seemed to be suspended as my trembling fingers freed the final button. I pushed the garment off his shoulders, and he shrugged out of it, letting it fall to the floor. Taking a tiny step closer, I purposefully began tugging his shirt free of his breeches.

Gabriel's hands settled on my waist, and he spun me smoothly away from him. He ran his fingers leisurely down the line of buttons at the back of my gown before unhurriedly getting to work. He paused to gently brush my hair away, and I scooped it over one shoulder, allowing him easier access. His lips pressed against the newly exposed skin on my neck, and I shivered at the sensation. Feeling my response, he rained kisses along my shoulder, neck, and collarbone as he lingered over every button and lace, stopping to pay homage to each additional inch of skin revealed.

By the time my dress and stays fell away, the room was spinning. He carried me to the large four-poster effortlessly and laced his fingers between mine, solemnly slowing the pace, deliberately anchoring me to the bed. I poured myself into his searing kiss, reveling in the weight and warmth of his body against mine. I wanted to lose myself in a frenzy of feeling, to drive him to the brink, and I desperately wanted to feel him come apart at the seams and lose his self-control. I ran my hands down his back, urging him closer. His muscles were taut with restraint, holding back, determined to savor every moment.

"Gabriel, please. . . " My voice broke. Wordlessly, I implored him, using everything at my disposal. My body was flooded with inexpressible urgency. I applied my lips, tongue, and teeth to every inch of skin I could reach until he couldn't hold back anymore, and we lost ourselves in ecstasy.

I came back to myself gradually, relishing the fact I roused such a reaction in him, secretly surprised and thrilled by the depth of my response. I stretched languidly; my skin was pliant and satisfyingly damp against Gabriel, but the exposed skin was rapidly cooling in the chilly air. I shifted slightly, curling against him, and pulling the coverlet over me for warmth. Gabriel's hand was warm on my hip. He drew the quilt over us both, cocooning us. His fingers trailed up and down my spine lazily, bringing a rash of goosebumps to my skin. I snuggled closer to him.

"Is it always like that?" I mused out loud.

He stirred beneath me, and I felt his voice rumble through his chest. "What? Making love?"

"Yes," I answered, apprehensively. Suddenly, I worried what his response would be.

He stroked my hair. "Mmph, I wouldn't know."

Astounded, I raised my head slightly to look at him in the dim candle-light. Sensing my surprise, he shrugged one-shouldered. "I won't say I've never been tempted to lie with a woman before, aye? But it never felt quite right— going through with the act, I mean."

Shocked, I let my head drop back onto his chest and silently ingested this information. While I knew it was presumed that a woman would maintain her virginity until marriage; I also knew that men were not judged by the same measure of expectation.

"Why are you so surprised? Let marriage be held in honor among all and let the marriage bed be undefiled. . . " he quoted.

"I know, I just assumed. . . that is. . . I didn't expect to be the first."

He shifted, gently rolling me onto my back, and raised himself on his elbows to look properly into my face. His eyes looked black in the dim light, but they blazed with heat and purpose. "I didn't know what it would be like, nor what I was waiting for, but I am glad I waited for you. I only want to belong to you. '*Forsaking all others*'." He quoted softly, reminding me of the vows that we'd solemnly spoken not twelve hours before.

I placed a hand on either side of his serious, aristocratic face and pulled his mouth down to mine. "Forsaking all others," I echoed.

The second time was slower. I relished the feel of his skin, rough in some places, soft in others, against my fingertips. I delighted in exploring and finding what made him catch his breath sharply, I thrilled in my power when he groaned my name, and I dragged him over the precipice with me.

Twenty-Five
A Pirate's Life

Gabriel studied her face, open and innocent as a child's in sleep. The early dawn light gilded her tumbled hair and caught the edge of her profile. Her beauty often took him off guard, making it feel like he couldn't quite catch his breath. The thought of leaving her, even only for a day or two, squeezed his heart and twisted his stomach, leaving him with a hollow ache. He had a rendezvous that he had to make in the next few days, and he'd delayed telling her about it, preferring to soak in every moment together, and secretly worrying about her reaction.

The last few weeks were nothing short of blissful. They left Amélie and Mathieu's *château* a week after the wedding and traveled back to *Landévennec* to celebrate the Christmas season at home. Gabriel was surprised at how thoroughly he enjoyed introducing Ava to his household and tenants.

They had fallen into an easy routine, the highlight of which was ensconcing themselves in their shared chamber every evening. The lengthy, cold, dark winter nights were spent in quiet conversation and a satisfyingly thorough exploration of Ava's body. The joy of falling asleep and waking up wrapped in her pliant warmth was a newfound one. One he wasn't looking forward to giving up. He couldn't put it off any longer though.

Tenderly, he brushed a lock of hair off her face. She shifted in her sleep, stretching languidly before her eyelashes lifted. Her jade eyes were muddled with sleep, but her lips curved in a smile for him as her body pressed sleepily against his. *Dieu*, the response she roused in him with a simple, innocent look. . . he was never satiated for long. He rolled over, bringing her with him, and slipped inside before she was fully awake.

She let out a breathless little moan and lifted her mouth to his with abandon. He moved slowly, savoring every sensation, the suppleness of her skin, the mingled, musky scent of their entwined bodies, how she moved, mutely urging him on until he gave himself to her.

I felt cozy and pliable, my skin warm against Gabriel's, sleepily listening to the reassuring thump of his heart as he stroked my hair. The last weeks had flown by like a beautiful fantasy, calling to mind the dreamy quality of Monet's Water Lilies. I had resolutely set all negativity, sadness, and heart-rending memories from my waking mind, choosing happiness, and succeeded in banishing them fairly effectively, although they still haunted my dreams.

The hopeless romantic in me reached out and embraced Gabriel with both hands, refusing to let go, even when I felt a hint of unease prodding the edges of my newfound happiness, searching for a crack it might squeeze into.

Gabriel let out a long sigh. "Ava," he began tentatively.

A little pebble of unease found an entrance, opening the crack a bit wider.

"Mmph?" I responded, hoping it was my overactive imagination hearing nonexistent apprehension in his voice.

"I have to leave to meet a ship tomorrow. I'll be gone for two or three days." His reluctance was obvious when I lifted my head to look into his face.

"Can you send someone to go for you?"

He shook his head slowly before answering, "*Non*, Mathieu and I need to be there to receive the goods. Our operation is. . . delicate. . . I cannot risk losing the trust we have established by sending someone else. Perhaps in time," he mused aloud. "I have been bringing Luc along and some of the other men." He shrugged as if to say time would tell.

"You and Mathieu are importing? Is that why you were on the beach the night of my shipwreck?"

I sensed his hesitation, and the pebble became a small rock, insistently widening the crack.

"*Oui*," he answered finally. "That is the simplest explanation, though it's a bit more complicated."

"Oh?" I was careful not to let my anxiety show on my face.

"We are not quite importing in the traditional sense. *Le Roi* would look down on it," he said, choosing his words cautiously.

"Smuggling then?" I didn't beat around the bush. I knew enough about the early days of the Revolution to know a great many nobles, particularly in Brittany, had been involved in subversively ending the three-estate system. Inwardly I sang the chorus to the *Pirates of the Caribbean* ride at Disney. I felt him start at my bluntness, but he nodded. "What are you bringing in?" I asked succinctly.

"Coffee, mainly."

I took a deep breath. I often wondered to what extent we might be able to stay out of the oncoming war, but it was obvious to me now, that was a child's fantasy. The small pebble was now a full-sized rock, settled firmly in the pit of my stomach. I stepped out of the beautiful dream I immersed myself in for the last few weeks and walked, eyes wide open, into reality.

"Tell me what I can do to help."

Gabriel's eyes softened. "I would prefer not to involve you if I can. I do not wish to risk you." Reaching up he tucked a stray curl behind my ear.

"If you are involved, then I am involved," I said simply.

His gray gaze was serious on mine for the space of several heartbeats before he acknowledged the truth of my words with a small nod. "I will think on it."

Gabriel was taken aback by Ava's matter-of-fact acceptance of his smuggling, and he wondered not for the first time, where her own family's politics and loyalties had lain. He'd meant to question her about it before he had to take his leave of her, but the day escaped him in a frenzy of preparations.

He was unexpectedly called away to tend to a broken fence in the corral, and then one of his new tenants, Jules Gautier, fell off his roof while replacing shingles. Thankfully, the man only suffered a broken arm. Between one thing and another, he found himself unable to ask her before he had to leave.

As far as he could tell, if she had any further qualms about his business, she squashed them, choosing to present him with a calm and cheerful disposition instead.

"We plan to bring Esme home with us." He stood before me; both of my hands clasped securely in his.

"I'm glad to hear that. Will the wedding be soon then?"

"I believe they plan on doing it in March, so Amélie, Mathieu, and their entourage can come to celebrate. . . Margaret too of course."

I pushed a stray tendril of windblown hair back. "When do you expect to be home?"

"If all goes well, the day after tomorrow."

"And if it doesn't?"

"I can't imagine that it would take more than five days at the most. If the ship doesn't arrive or has met with poor weather, it could be delayed a day or two." He knew I was well acquainted with severe weather on a boat.

My face blanched. "What are the odds that you would meet with trouble?"

"Unlikely," he answered truthfully. "Please do not worry for my safety *mon cœur*. Most of the time they look the other way or can be persuaded with a bit of gold."

Gabriel rested his forehead against hers and looked into her clear, steady eyes. She believed him, but he could still see a hint of uncertainty lurking behind her smile.

He rested his hands on her hips and pulled her close, kissing her until he felt her body straining against his, and he was satisfied that she would miss him while he was gone. He wanted to take the taste of her on the road with him.

Luc cleared his throat with a loud, impatient, "Ahem."

Gabriel heard it but deliberately ignored him.

"Will you pray for our success and that I return to you quickly?"

"You know that I will." She took his face in her hands and kissed him one more time. "Go now, before Luc leaves without you," she added teasingly.

"Aye." He swung up onto Automne, who'd been patiently waiting. With a click of his tongue and a gentle nudge of his booted heels, they started on their way.

At the end of the lane, he turned back for a moment and raised his hand in farewell. His stomach felt hollow as he looked back at her rapidly shrinking figure. He never imagined he might one day be so infatuated with his wife that he would regret the need to leave her for a few short days. Ruefully, he shook his head.

"We haven't even stepped foot off our land, yet I miss her already. How is that possible?" he asked Automne under his breath.

The big bay snorted and tossed his head, sending his chestnut mane flying; as if to say he'd never yet met a mare that held his attention for more than a day. Clearly, this was Gabriel's problem, not Automne's.

TWENTY-SIX
A STORM'S A BREWIN'

I stood outside and watched until the speck that was Gabriel disappeared from view. Suddenly chilled, I turned away and walked back in, eager to warm up before the fire.

I wandered the *château* aimlessly, it felt odd to be left behind. All of Gabriel's household welcomed me with open arms. I supposed it was my household now too. . . something I wasn't yet accustomed to. I quickly discovered Gabriel was no idle, land-owning noble. He was intimately involved in the daily running of his land and tenants. Most days he left the *château* after breakfast, to hunt, oversee the repairs, mediate squabbles between tenants, or help Pierre Gustave, whose wife had suddenly died, leaving behind three young children. It was illuminating to see this softer, hardworking side of him.

On the flip side, I was feeling extremely indolent. I was unused to spending my days in leisure, and I felt compelled to find a way to contribute to the running of the *château*, or at least, to participate in some other way. I was at a loss as to how I might accomplish this, as I was grossly unprepared for rural life in the eighteenth century. To add insult to injury, the *château* ran like the well-oiled gears of a clock, needing absolutely no assistance from me. Every individual in the household knew their part and executed it flawlessly. It stung to realize I was redundant.

Nonetheless, I was determined to find a way to be of service, to find my place. Not just as the *'lady of the château.'* Honestly, I was tempted to look behind me to see who they were talking about each time someone said it. I felt rather like an imposter. I wasn't even skilled at the conventional, accepted, ladylike talents women from this era were expected to have mastered.

My sewing lacked proficiency, although it *had* improved since I'd regained the use of my right hand. My knowledge of running a household, hosting a party, or even properly entertaining a guest for an afternoon, was sorely lacking. Despite my knowledge of French history, which came in handy a time or two, I knew virtually nothing about an embarrassing number of items and customs.

Tired of my aimless existence, I walked to the kitchen and hovered at the door, before resolutely barging in. After all, I owned the place— in a manner of speaking. The head cook, Mademoiselle Ollivier and her helper Madame Bleuzen were both busily working with their backs turned to me.

"*Bonjour*!" I said merrily, alerting them to my presence.

Mademoiselle Ollivier and Madame Bleuzen whirled around and dropped deep curtseys in perfect unison.

"*Madame la Vicomtesse*! How may we be of service?" asked Mademoiselle Ollivier.

I smiled and resisted the urge to fiddle with my skirt. "I was wondering how I might be of service to you."

The cooks shared a look.

"Ahh, I am not sure I understand, my lady," Mademoiselle Ollivier answered warily.

"Do you have a few minutes? I know you are exceedingly busy." Without waiting for an answer, I sat at the table and waved my hand toward the other seats. "Please, sit with me for a moment, perhaps we can share a glass of ale. I have a few questions for you."

Madame Bleuzen grabbed a pitcher and cups from the pantry, while Mademoiselle Ollivier sat, wiping her hands on her apron nervously. I poured us each a cup and tried to smile reassuringly at them.

"I wanted to first, thank you for the warm welcome as the new lady of the house. I appreciate all the hard work and the lovely meals you have made for *le Vicomte* and me thus far." I paused, and drank deeply of my beer, while the cooks shared another apprehensive look. They looked slightly comforted by my compliment, but it was clear they were wondering where their crazy new mistress was going with this.

Madame Bleuzen spoke up, "It's been our honor, my lady."

"I aim to make *Landévennec* a place everyone loves working and living at. Thus, I would like to enlist your help, with what I might do to better things here." I smiled brightly and awkwardly waited for one of them to speak up, but neither woman answered. "For example, perhaps there is something you feel is lacking in the living arrangements?" I put in delicately, "Or perhaps there is something that would improve the working conditions? Is there anything that you feel would lighten your workload, or. . . " I cast around for another example, trying not to wilt under the two cooks' carefully composed faces. "Do you have trouble sourcing any ingredients?"

The silence that followed was deafening. I lifted my cup and drank thirstily to fill the uncomfortable moment.

Finally, Mademoiselle Ollivier spoke deferentially. "*Madame la Vicomtesse,* would you please give us leave to think upon this matter for a few days? I'm certain some things could stand improvement, but I should like to give the list some serious thought and consult with the other women if I may."

I beamed in relief. "Yes of course! I intend to ask the rest of the household as well." I hesitated briefly and then threw the rest of my cards on the table. "I was not raised to run a household of this magnitude," an understatement if there ever was one, "I realize it may seem backward, but I would appreciate it if you would be so kind as to let me know *discretely* if I do something blatantly wrong. . . "

Madame and Mademoiselle's eyebrows rose so high they nearly disappeared into their respective hairlines. After a brief pause, however, they both nodded, and Madame Bleuzen offered me a trace of a smile.

I smiled back and rose from my chair, relieved. While not a roaring success, the interview had certainly cemented the beginnings of what I hoped would be a solid working relationship. I was about to leave when sudden inspiration struck.

"May I inquire as to who manages the kitchen garden?" I loved gardening and knew I would enjoy spending time amongst the dirt and quiet peace of growing plants, provided I wasn't stepping on any proverbial toes by doing so.

"We do, although it is an area that could stand improvement. We used to have someone dedicated to the garden during the growing season, but it has been four years since she left," admitted Mademoiselle Ollivier.

"We do what we can, but it's not as tidy, or well-kept as we would like," added Madame Bleuzen.

"The head gardener, Monsieur Marec, will usually lend us a lad to help with the heavy work, but he's quite busy with the management of the other gardens and the orchard." Mademoiselle Ollivier finished her tankard of ale, and belching softly, replaced it on the table.

"Wonderful. So, no one would be opposed to it if I took over the management of the kitchen garden? Perhaps I could hire a girl or two to help out. . . " I glanced at them calculatingly. "Might either of you know of a young lady who would be interested in such a position?"

"My niece is looking for a position. I may mention it to her. She's a hardworking lass." Mademoiselle Ollivier acted nonchalant, but the sudden gleam in her eye told me that she wanted the job for her niece.

Not to be outdone, Madame Bleuzen interjected, "I believe my daughter would be interested as well."

I nodded in satisfaction. "Send them both to see me in the next week." I glanced out the window at the sparkling snow. "It doesn't feel like it now, but the planting season is just around the corner, I would like to begin planning soon."

"Your aunt tells me you have an interest in plants." I poured two steaming cups of tea and offered one to the young girl who took it from me nervously.

Her aunt, Mademoiselle Ollivier, had wasted no time getting word to her niece. Nor had Madame Bleuzen, whose daughter, Éloise, had shown up a mere hour before Isabelle. She had just left, promising to return in one week to take her place within the household, when I'd been informed that Mademoiselle Ollivier's niece was here to see me.

"I do, my lady."

Judging by her clear, freshly scrubbed face, and earnest expression, the girl couldn't be more than fifteen.

I nodded, "How old are you, Isabelle?"

"I turned fourteen just before the winter solstice." She carefully took a sip of her tea, her young face pink with nervousness.

"Do you have experience working in the garden?" I asked gently, "Perhaps at home?"

"*Oui*," she nodded enthusiastically. "My mother—" She paused, and a shadow passed over her face. "I used to help her in our garden. She taught me the uses of many plants and showed me which plants grow well together."

I gathered from her response that her mother had gone to her heavenly reward. "Do they not need your expertise at home?"

Isabelle looked down at her hands, neatly folded in her lap. "No, my lady. My younger brother died of smallpox with my *maman*, three years past. My papa has remarried, and my stepmother. . . just had a *bebe*. They are a complete family now, they have no need of me."

Isabelle said this resolutely; with a slight shrug as though it was no skin off her. But I caught a slight wobble in her voice that betrayed her true feelings on the matter. My heart ached for her.

"Well, we have a great need of you," I said emphatically. "I look forward to learning everything I can from you, Isabelle, I hope you won't mind sharing your secrets."

She smiled shyly in response.

"Do you know Éloise Bleuzen? I believe you are both of a similar age."

"We have met on a few occasions. . . but I do not know her well."

"Well, I imagine you will get to know her quite well soon. You will be working together. She will be starting a week from today; you shall start at the same time if it suits you. I will inform the maids to have a room made ready for you upstairs. I imagine it'll be too far for you to make the journey daily from town."

"Oh yes, thank you *Madame la Vicomtesse*," she gushed effusively.

I smiled warmly at her. "No, thank you."

I sat at the small writing desk in Gabriel's study, staring at the list before me.

Pole Beans
Snow Peas
Turnips
Onions
Garlic
Potatoes
Tomatoes
Peppers
Squash
Aubergine
Carrots
Pumpkin

Thyme
Rosemary
Tarragon
Marjoram
Lavender
Parsley
Coriander
Strawberries
Raspberries
Blueberries
Blackberries
Melon

I nibbled on the end of my quill thoughtfully as I worked on writing what would hopefully be an exhaustive list of all the vegetables and herbs I proposed to grow in the new kitchen garden. Now I needed to cross-reference my list against my cooks and garden helpers' knowledge, figure out which plants we already had seeds for, harvested from the prior year's garden, and source where I might obtain the balance of the seeds I hoped to grow. I was eager to start on the project since the list was becoming dauntingly long. Luckily, it was keeping my mind busy, off of missing Gabriel, or wondering when he would be back, and if he was okay.

He'd been gone for four days now and he had said he'd be back yesterday if everything went smoothly. The weather had been calm the last few days, which hopefully meant he was on his way home. No one knew better than I, how the ship could have been delayed, though. I forced my mind back to my list, refusing to go down the dark and thorny path of worst-case scenarios. Gabriel *was* fine. I knew it.

I got up from his plush, comfy seat, and stretched my back, feeling the vertebrae pop in relief, then walked to the large, leaded window overlooking the hills and woods that stretched behind the *château*. I hadn't noticed the lack of light until now. The sky had darkened considerably while I'd been working. The clouds looked heavy and ominous, and the air held the calm, quiet feeling that precludes treacherous weather. The hairs on the back of my neck prickled with unease.

Suddenly nervous, I strode toward the door, grabbed my new fur-lined cloak, and stepped outside. A few feet into the garden, I stopped and lifted my face to the heavens. Snow was coming. I could smell it.

Dry leaves, remnants from autumn, crackled and rustled as a whiff of breeze spun them lazily across the path before me. In the distance, I heard a stronger gust moving through the trees, whistling among the branches. The odds of Gabriel making it home before the storm broke were slim. I hoped he, the men, and Esme— if she was with them— were dry and warm somewhere. I hugged myself as goosebumps rose on my skin and turned back toward the *château*.

TWENTY-SEVEN
THUNDER SNOW

I didn't sleep, attempting, and failing miserably at the impossible task of not worrying. The blizzard began shortly after supper; large, perfect snowflakes quickly covered the bare spots in the garden where the sun melted the previous snow down to dark earth. I stood by the window watching it accumulate. It always amazes me how deeply and intensely quiet falling snow is.

I forced myself to work on my plans for the garden before changing for bed and cozied up with a copy of *Robinson Crusoe* I found in the library, trying valiantly to lose myself in the story. It didn't work. As the storm gathered intensity, and the wind began to howl, I anxiously stared out the window, the book lying forgotten on my lap. The wind drove the snow in a blinding curtain. My parents would have called it white-out conditions. I wonder if that term exists now.

Then nature's fireworks show began. Growing up in the northeast I was no stranger to thunder snow, even though it is an unusual phenomenon. The first distant rumble caught me off guard. A few minutes later, I caught a diffused flash of gold and violet light followed by a distinctly closer, muted boom. The lightning made the hairs on my arms stand up.

Before the storm that stole Carri from me and the one that tossed me back in time, I had never minded Mother Nature's occasional violent tantrums. I enjoyed sitting out on the porch and watching the rain fall. The sound of rain pattering on the roof of my house or the boat deck lulled me to sleep. Thunder and lightning gave me a surge of adrenaline, a thrill that raced through my veins.

Tonight, though, for the first time, it made ice flow along the corridors of my body, making its way through my arteries and settling around my frozen heart. Each flash of light made my skin prickle. I felt nauseous, faint, sweaty, and my ears buzzed unpleasantly. I paced, I watched the window, I got down on my knees, and uncharacteristically prayed, I tried in vain to sleep. Nothing kept my mind from playing out terrible scenarios.

By daybreak, I was back in my chair, exhausted, and fighting to keep my eyes open, but the blizzard hadn't abated. The sky was the flat, heavy, gray of snowstorms, stretching out in every direction. The dim, hazy sunlight made everything blindingly bright as it reflected off the endless, sparkling white. The snow had been blown into drifts several feet deep and still came down at an impressive rate. *How much longer will it last?*

My eyelids were heavy, and the urge to abandon my fear to sleep was beginning to overpower me. I nodded off, and jerked awake, looking around blearily.

The dream, when it came, was unpleasant.

I was alone in the frozen silence, forcing my way through impossibly high drifts. How long had I been outside, walking steadily through the icy terrain? It must have been a while because my fingers and toes were numb with cold. Somehow, I had lost all sense of where I was. No matter which direction I looked in, all I saw were pine trees, peppered with groves of bare oak and

beech; their naked branches scraping the colorless sky like angry, outstretched fingernails. The landscape was a sea of glittering white.

A crash sounded in the undergrowth behind me, and I spun around wildly, searching. My foot caught on a branch, invisible beneath the layers of ice and snow, and I stumbled, throwing my hands out to stop my fall.

Down on my knees, I struggled to catch my breath, my stays pinching uncomfortably; before I unsteadily pushed myself back up. I felt unwieldy, the ice clinging to the layers of my skirts and petticoats, weighing them down. I glanced over my shoulder, toward the sound I heard, squinting into the dense underbrush, but nothing was there. I turned my attention back to a shadow I could see ahead, marring the perfection of the fleecy ground. As I approached, I realized with dawning horror that it wasn't a shadow at all.

Bright, crimson blood was streaked across the otherwise flawless, frosty, earth. The ground was churned up and there was a deep indentation where it looked like someone or something had fallen, before being dragged away. I scanned my surroundings slowly, feeling spooked, noticing for the first time that branches in the area were snapped, lying like broken matchsticks strewn about haphazardly. Blood was splattered across the pristine snow.

Never one to handle bodily fluids or gore well; I felt my stomach muscles tightening and tasted bile in my throat. A branch cracked somewhere behind me, and I whirled in a neat semi-circle, miraculously managing to keep my feet beneath me this time.

My breath backed up in my lungs. Small, malicious, red eyes stared out of the gloom at me. I froze, my feet planted on the ground as though I'd rooted there. It was huge, tusks gleaming wickedly in the dim light of the forest.

'Fuck.' I thought, 'Don't move. No sudden movements. . . Pretend you're a statue.'

My heartbeat thundered in my ears like galloping hooves. The pig pawed at the ground; beady eyes fixed malignantly on me. I let out an unsteady

breath, trying to calculate how far it was, and how fast it could conceivably
move. . . could I make it up a tree before it got to me?

I was quickly considering my options, and just as rapidly discarding them
when the boar decided for me and charged.

I gasped for breath as my eyes sprang open. My heart pounded uncontrollably, I was sweaty, shaky, and sick. The dream had felt stunningly real.

"*Bonjour Madame la Vicomtesse*!" sang out my lady's maid, Mademoiselle Adrienne. She bustled into the room, balancing my breakfast tray in one hand, and holding a fresh bucket of tinder for the fire in the other.

"*Bonjour Mademoiselle*," I replied, trying to sound cheerful and failing miserably.

My eyes were scratchy and dry, and my throat was hoarse. . . *did I scream in my sleep?*

It felt as though I had. Adrienne glanced at me, worry written on her face. I probably looked like hell. I certainly felt like it.

"Ah, my lady," she began hesitantly, concern for me and reticence at overstepping her position, warring for control in her expression. "Are you feeling quite well this morning?"

I managed a weak smile. "Thank you, Mademoiselle Adrienne, I'm fine. I slept poorly last night."

"Ah, yes, the wind was extraordinarily loud, was it not?" The relief that it wasn't anything more serious than a sleepless night was plain to hear in her voice.

"Nothing a good breakfast can't fix," I replied gaily.

She smiled at me and busied herself with rekindling the fire. When she was done, she stood up and wiped her hands on a rag that she stuffed into her apron pocket. "I will be back shortly to help you dress if that suits you?"

"That would be lovely. Thank you, Adrienne."

As soon as she left, quietly shutting the door behind her, I let out a shaky breath and slumped back into my chair. After spending the night under heightened stress, every inch of my body ached. I stood and raised my arms over my head, reveling in the satisfying burn of stretching muscles.

I glanced out the window, the storm appeared to be abating. Then I looked briefly at my reflection in the mirror and recoiled slightly at what I saw. No wonder Mademoiselle Adrienne was worried. The raccoon circles under my eyes told the story of my sleepless night.

I picked up the pot of my favorite cream, made with soothing lavender, and gently dabbed a bit under each eye. I shrugged, there was only so much I could do to combat the effects of the prior evening. I let the details of the nightmare drift back to me as I sat to eat.

I have always been a vivid dreamer. I remember the shock when at the age of ten, I learned that Carri rarely remembered her dreams. We'd argued because she'd been adamant that no visions visited her in the dead of night, although she eventually acquiesced that she simply might not recall them.

What just occurred, however, was different. This was not merely an intense dream. I wasn't one for grandstanding, but it felt like a fucking prophecy, and it left me feeling uneasy and nauseous. I lifted my cup of tea and cradled it between my hands, soaking in the comforting warmth it radiated into my skin, lowering my face, and letting the steam wash over me, cleansing my mind of the chilling images. Breathing deeply, I focused on my breakfast, allowing the heat of the food to warm my body and soul, and basking in the restorative effects of the tea. By the time I finished, I felt better. Not immensely, but more settled within myself, nonetheless.

Adrienne cheerily bustled into the room. "Would you like a bath drawn this morning before you dress?"

"That would be lovely, thank you."

A hot bath would kill some time and hopefully banish the dream from my mind entirely. . . To the pits of hell, where it belonged.

TWENTY-EIGHT
BLOODY BOAR

A rash of goosebumps rose on my skin and the tiny hairs on the back of my neck stood at attention, minutes before I could hear or see the commotion of the returning party. I stood by the parlor window looking out at the empty road leading to the *château*, straining my eyes to catch movement in the sea of white.

I thought I'd caught a glimpse of something a moment ago, but it disappeared behind the hills and trees before I could get a proper look. The steady ticking of the clock in the hallway compounded my ominous feelings, impassively counting down the seconds to tragedy. A heavy sense of oppression and despair settled over my shoulders like a cloak. Something was wrong. I knew it the moment I awoke this morning. The dream had been an omen.

From a distance I saw a lone horseman galloping over the crest of the summit, making a mad dash for the *château*. The chill in my bones intensified and my breakfast congealed in my stomach. I strained my eyes for a minute that felt like an eternity, before I recognized Luc, riding hell for leather toward the entrance.

I rushed to the large double doors, ignoring Madame Pichon, our housekeeper, and Mademoiselle Noemi's startled looks. Swearing under my breath, I fumbled with the latch and yanked the door open. Luc was dismounting, his face white with strain, and fear. I could now see the rest of the party of men straggling behind him.

"Gabriel? Where is Gabriel?" I asked urgently.

He was gasping for breath but managed to shake his head. I sagged against the doorframe in momentary relief. It was not him. *Thank you, God.*

"Who? Who is injured?"

While I waited for his response I called over my shoulder to Mademoiselle Noemi, one of the housemaids, who still stood in the hallway looking dumbfounded. "Tell Mademoiselle Ollivier to start boiling water and to get fresh bandages ready. Have Madame Bleuzen get food and drinks for the men and Mademoiselle Esme, I'm sure they will need nourishment after the trip. Let Madame Pichon know that *le Vicomte* has returned." Without waiting for a response, I turned back to Luc with an eyebrow raised.

"It's Denis Bleuzen. A boar got him early this morning."

Every hair on my head was prickling, and my stomach felt like a washing machine full of acid on the agitation cycle—first visions, now premonitory dreams.

"Fetch Madame Bleuzen, inform her that Monsieur Bleuzen has been injured, and have her meet us in the surgery," I said to Mademoiselle Adrienne, who had just appeared at the foot of the stairs.

I looked beyond Luc and could now recognize Gabriel and Esme among the group on horseback. I clattered down the front steps and ran toward Gabriel, slipping on the ice and snow, and skidding to a stop in front of Automne.

I muffled my gasp as I took in the grisly scene. Automne's chestnut coat was crimson, and the snow beneath his hooves was turning red with the steady drip of fresh blood. Georges Madec and Maurice Prigent had already handed the reins of their mounts to Timothée Seznec who was leading the horses down the path toward the stables. Jean-Paul Le Gall, one of the stable lads who had accompanied the men was unloading items from the wagon.

I watched as Gabriel grimly and painstakingly handed Denis down to Georges and Maurice, being careful not to jostle him overtly. Denis's eyes were closed, and his face was ashen. For a moment, I thought he was dead already, but then I saw his chest rise ever so slightly. *God, the amount of blood.*

I caught Gabriel's eye for a brief moment and nodded mutely at what he managed to convey during that minute connection. His face was tired and etched with grief, but he was whole, and the blood covering him was not his, as far as I could tell. There was time enough for anything else later. For now, the only thing of consequence was trying to save Denis.

I turned away, skirting the blood stains on the cobbled walk as I followed the men into the *château* and waved Georges and Maurice into the still-room, behind the kitchen. They carefully placed Denis on the raised bed in the center of the room. Someone had made a fire in the large hearth, and Madame Bleuzen was waiting in the corner, her hands clasped nervously in front of her. The moment the men stepped away from the bed she moved toward her husband.

To give Madame Bleuzen a moment of privacy with her husband, I turned away and addressed Maurice Prigent first. He was one of Gabriel's youngest tenants, having moved out of his parents' cabin a few years prior.

He looked green; carefully keeping his eyes averted from Denis, and taking shallow, panicky breaths, so I sent him out of the room before he fainted.

It reminded me of the story my aunt and mother loved to tell at Christmas every year; of my uncle passing out in the delivery room, when my aunt was giving birth to my cousin Beatrice. They'd retell the tale; belly laughing, tears of mirth rolling down their cheeks, while my Uncle Paul would shrug sheepishly. I shook my head quickly, we didn't need to contend with men giving themselves concussions because they couldn't manage a little blood.

"Maurice, can you please find Mademoiselle Esme, and send her here?"

"Yes of course, *Madame la Vicomtesse.*" The relief on his face at escaping the surgery was evident.

"Thank you, Maurice. After that, you may find Mademoiselle Éloise Bleuzen. Please inform her that her father is here. . . gently if you can. And then find *le Vicomte* and see if he requires further assistance from you."

I set my sights on Georges Madec next. A middle-aged man, with a weathered, friendly face, it was obvious he was no stranger to blood and gore, and he struck me as being impressively stoic at the gruesome sight of his eviscerated friend. I waved him forward to stand beside me. Madame Bleuzen stood by her unconscious husband's head, smoothing the hair back off his forehead tenderly. Tears clung to her lashes, but she'd held them at bay so far.

In an undertone, I asked Georges what happened while I began to tentatively explore the site of the injury.

"We set out early this morning, 'twas still dark out. We were forced to seek shelter close to Lomergat last night because of the snow, aye? It was still snowing, but we were all eager to make it home. One of the horses picked up a stone in his shoe, so we stopped, and Denis took the opportunity to take a piss in the bushes in the clearing just ahead." Georges took a deep breath. "I heard the pig squeal first but I didn't react quickly enough. *Le fils d'une putain de pute*— begging your pardon Madame— already got Denis by the time I got him with my spear."

I looked up at this, waving away his apology. "You killed the boar?" I asked in affirmation.

"*Oui.*"

I nodded in relief. "*Bonne*," I said succinctly.

I worked to expose the wound, admitting inwardly that I was entirely out of my depth. Carri and I both took a survival first aid course before we left in case either of us should fall ill or were injured days away from help. The class focused on injuries likely to occur in a marine environment however, covering what to do if someone was essentially disemboweled by a wild boar had not been included.

Which was exactly what it looked like happened to Denis. My gorge rose as I cut away the layers of blood-soaked clothing and hasty bandaging that they had applied in a futile attempt to stem the flow of blood. With most of the tattered cloth pulled away from his abdomen and groin area, I could see the ragged edges of skin with bits of glistening entrails and mangled muscle showing through. I gritted my teeth, picked up a clean rag, and dipped it in the boiled water, assessing the temperature to ensure it cooled sufficiently. I was worried about introducing infection, although it was likely too late.

I carefully began to clean the area around the wound, hoping to get a better look at the damage. His entire torso was covered in blood, and it had begun to crust over, making some of his clothing stick to his skin.

I turned to Georges. "Could you fetch some whiskey and brandy?"

"*Oui, Madame.*" He bowed hastily and walked out, passing Esme at the door.

At the sight of her, I felt some of the tension in my body seep out. Although I knew more about bacteria, infections, and sterilizing, concepts that were foreign in the eighteenth century— Esme knew far more about the uses of herbs and contemporary medicine than I could ever hope to.

"I'm glad you're here," I said.

Esme smiled faintly in return, she looked exhausted.

The quick patter of footsteps interrupted whatever she'd been about to say. Éloise skidded into the room, stopping in her tracks at the sight of her father on the bed. Instinctively, I moved to shield the worst of it from her view.

She looked wildly at her mother and then at Esme and me. She took a few stumbling steps forward, and collapsed on her knees next to the bed, grabbed her father's hand like a lifeline, and pressed it desperately to her cheek.

"Papa! Papa! Please, Papa, you must say something. Your Éloise, *votre petite fée* is here. Papa, you must be strong and wake up now!" The despair in her young, broken voice was wrenching. I felt tears prick the back of my eyes and looked helplessly at Esme. Her gaze mirrored my powerless sorrow.

Madame Bleuzen knelt next to Éloise and gathered her in her arms. They sat on the cold stone floor, wrapped around each other, rocking, and sobbing for several long minutes. I felt like an intruder witnessing their shared grief. Madame Bleuzen straightened up first, wiping her face on her apron.

"Come, *ma petite fée*, your Papa would not want you to cry. We must be strong for him. Sit with me, and we will keep watch over him."

She stood, helping her daughter up, and with an arm wrapped around her waist, led Éloise to two chairs that Esme moved to the head of the bed. Éloise rubbed her hands over her pale, drawn face, scrubbing away the tear tracks, and took a shaky breath, sitting beside her mother.

I looked at Esme. "Tell me what you need me to do."

She took in the situation in a sweeping glance. The room was thick with the hot, metallic scent of blood, but Esme seemed undeterred by it. The animal's tusk appeared to have entered the left side of Denis's groin, near his hip, and ripped up at an angle, severing through intestines, muscle, tissue, countless vessels, and some organs, no doubt.

Esme bit her lip and glanced up, her grave gaze catching on Madame Bleuzen's.

Madame stood and took a step forward, her trembling hands outstretched beseechingly. "Please, *Madame la Vicomtesse*, Mademoiselle Esme, can he be saved?"

There was a stifled little wail from Éloise at this.

I looked at Esme in consternation. I wanted desperately to tell her that all would be well, but I knew that abdominal wounds carried a substantial risk of infection. One glance at Esme's face, and I knew she was thinking the same thing.

"Madame Bleuzen, I cannot say yet what may happen. . . it is in God's hands. But *la Vicomtesse* and I will do the best we can."

Madame Bleuzen sank into the chair and buried her face in her hands.

Esme motioned that I join her at the washstand, and we took turns washing our hands. She quickly surveyed the neatly stocked shelves of the room that functioned as both surgery and still room for the *château*. She moved economically and precisely as she took down several labeled jars of herbs, premade balms, creams, small cautery irons, and a jar of suturing needles, the curved metal glinting wickedly in a ray of light.

"No laudanum," she murmured, looking worried.

"Are we out?"

She nodded her head in a quick, jerky movement. "I suppose whiskey will have to do."

Georges reappeared with a bottle in each hand, followed closely by Gabriel. He must have changed into clean clothes and washed hurriedly since he was no longer covered in Denis's blood. He looked warmly into my eyes, holding my gaze for a moment, before looking at Denis.

Esme was carefully cleaning the laceration. She indicated wordlessly that I hold the torn skin away from the opening of the injury so she could pour saline into the open wound, washing away the worst of the blood, dirt, and grit.

"Are any of his organs punctured, other than his intestines?" I asked Esme under my breath.

She nodded her head slightly. "It's just missed his spleen here," she indicated, "And it's missed his pancreas as well, but the stomach is punctured, and the intestines. . ." she gestured, "They're quite mangled."

I focused on what Esme was showing me, trying to view it dispassionately and reminding myself to breathe, even though I had never handled blood well. Out of the corner of my eye, I saw Gabriel move another chair, sitting beside Madame Bleuzen, picking up Denis's limp hand and cradling it in his own.

He squeezed it gently and leaned forward. "You're in good hands, Denis. Stay with us, man."

Denis's eyelids flickered as if in answer to Gabriel's words, but he showed no other sign of consciousness.

"We need to clean the wound with the whiskey and suture what we can. If he wakes up, he should drink some as well."

Esme looked at me doubtfully. "Clean it with whiskey?"

"Yes," I said firmly. "It's the closest thing we have to a disinfectant."

"Disinfectant? What is that?"

My mind stalled, scrambling for the words I needed, and then I explained, "An infection is more likely to happen when something isn't clean.

When a wound has pus?" I paused, hoping she knew what I meant. She nodded, and I continued. "That is an infection. It prevents a wound from healing properly, and if it gets into the blood and it becomes gangrene, it can kill the patient."

"Aye, I've seen that, I suppose." She was still looking at me skeptically but held out the whiskey bottle.

I had no idea how much whiskey to use. Should I pour it into the wound like I'd seen Esme pour the saline? Should I apply it to a rag and dab it on? How much was too much? Could I give him alcohol poisoning?

Esme's blue eyes were looking at me expectantly. With an internal sigh, I poured a measure of whiskey into a cup first and then very carefully poured a small amount into the cavity where his intestines lay.

"You should suture those first, and then I can pour a little more on."

Esme already had a needle threaded and began the painstaking job of suturing the small intestines. I carefully took a needle from the jar, threaded it, and began to sew the tear closest to me. We worked in silence, falling into a rhythm of knotting thread, sewing, knotting again, and snipping the excess.

The world slowed and contracted to this small, stone room. I could hear the steady pounding of my heart in my ears and feel every breath expand my lungs in my chest, a brutal reminder that I was alive; but that Denis may not be for much longer. My view narrowed down to focus solely on the section of the intestine I was suturing, watching the flash of the needle as it worked its way slowly and methodically through his innards.

My hands were stained crimson to the wrists, but I refused to dwell on that. If I did, I would surely unravel. We finished the intestines and moved steadily onto the puncture in his stomach, barely speaking, working in a silent dance, balancing on the edge of life and death. We grimaced mutely at the state of his torn muscles and then did the best we could with them.

Esme cauterized the blood vessels that were torn. I was sure we missed some— there were so many. We paused to irrigate everything with more whiskey before finally closing the wound.

I have no idea how much time passed by the time we finished bandaging him. The angle of the meager sunlight coming in through the windows indicated it was late afternoon. It'd been hours, surely. Madame Bleuzen and young Éloise had wordlessly sat at the head of the bed, their hands clasped through it all. Gabriel hadn't stirred from his position. For his part, our patient hadn't moved a muscle or regained consciousness.

Considering how much blood he lost, I wasn't surprised. It was probably a blessing. We had nothing to offer in the way of pain management other than alcohol, and I rather doubted it would be sufficient.

I washed my hands slowly and thoroughly, trying not to focus on how low Denis's odds of survival likely were. We had done the best we could for him with the limited resources we had. Would he have fared better in more skilled hands? Someone with formal training?

Since I was from the twentieth century, I regarded most doctors and surgeons from the eighteenth century as little more than butchers. The idea of germs, bacteria, and infection, or the sterilization of instruments, was nebulous, at best, and mostly nonexistent.

My hands dry, I pressed them to the small of my back and tried to stretch the sore muscles. Hours of standing hunched over poor Denis left my muscles so cramped it hurt to walk. I turned to see Esme in whispered conference with Madame Bleuzen. Young Éloise had fallen asleep in her chair, head nodding against her chest.

Madame Bleuzen left the surgery, and Esme walked over to me.

"What do we do now?"

Esme shook her head. "Someone needs to stay with him, in case he wakes up or worsens. I will set a watch schedule." She waved Gabriel over. My eyes tiredly met his as he gently laid Denis's hand on the bed and stood, walking toward us. "Is there anyone else that has knowledge of the herbs? A midwife perhaps?" she asked Gabriel.

His brow furrowed for a moment, then cleared. "*Oui*," he answered slowly. "Many tenants call upon Madame Cariou when they are near their time."

"We should send for her. She may be able to help in some way. *Le Château* doesn't have laudanum in stock. Perhaps she has some."

Gabriel nodded, "I will send someone for her." He glanced over his shoulder at the sleeping Éloise and lowering his voice, asked, "In your opinion, how likely is he to live?"

Esme frowned. "Not likely," she admitted. "The amount of blood he lost…" She shook her head sadly. "We did the best we could. But you know how it is with these wounds."

Gabriel nodded quietly. "Thank you, Esme. You may see to your watch schedule with the staff. My lady Ava and I will wait here until someone returns. Please inform Madame Pichon that Madame and Mademoiselle Bleuzen will be staying here for the time being and to have a room made for them." He paused, "If you happen across any of the men, ask them to send for Madame Cariou."

With a curtsey, Esme left.

Twenty-Nine
Philosophy in Death

I turned to Gabriel, and he wordlessly wrapped his arms around me as I rested my head against his chest, listening to the comforting thump of his heart, and realized, with some detachment, that I was trembling. Now that I was no longer riding high on the adrenaline of focusing on what was likely a futile rescue operation, I was crashing. The strain, terror, and blood of the afternoon ricocheted in my mind like a ping-pong ball.

Gabriel's hands moved up and down my arms soothingly before stepping back and reaching for my hand. "Come," he said quietly, leading me closer to the fire. "You were incredible today. Did you train with herbs at home?"

I shook my head tiredly. "I had no idea what I was doing. I just followed Esme's lead and used common sense I suppose. I hope I didn't do more harm than good."

Dark gray eyes regarded me skeptically. "Considering the condition he was in. . . I don't think it's possible, Ava. He would certainly be dead by now if it weren't for you and Esme. Perhaps this way his family will have the opportunity to say goodbye to him if he doesn't survive."

"Is that truly better? Or are we drawing out his suffering?"

"*Oui*, if he doesn't survive, he will go with the peace of knowing that his family was with him at the end, and his wife and daughter will be able to carry that with them, to soften their grief as well. It's no small thing, aye?"

I rested my forehead tiredly against his chest. "I suppose I hadn't thought of it in that way." I hesitated briefly, before blurting out the thought I'd been hearing like a refrain all day. "It feels as though I am cursed lately, like death has followed me the last few years."

"And the dust returns to the earth as it was, and the spirit returns to God who gave it." Gabriel quoted softly. "It follows us all Ava," he added gently.

"I know that. . . of course. I suppose I'm letting the stress of the last day get to me. First, there was the storm." I looked up at him. "I couldn't sleep, I had the most ominous feeling that something was wrong. I prayed all night that you weren't caught in it. Then, when I finally fell asleep for a bit this morning, I had the most awful dream. . ." I stopped, suddenly unsure if I wanted to go down this path. If I wasn't exhausted, I wouldn't have mentioned the dream.

Gabriel raised one eyebrow at me. "*Oui*? What was the dream about?"

I sighed and buried my face in my hands before throwing some of my chips on the table. "I dreamt I was walking through the forest; it was winter, and everything was covered in snow. Rather like I imagine it is now. Something was following me, stalking me through the woods. I came to a clearing, and the snow was scarlet with blood. Truly, Gabriel, I've never seen so much. . . until this afternoon."

He watched me in silence, sensing my story wasn't complete. I took a deep breath. "I looked around, I heard a noise, I think. . . Then I saw it, the boar. It charged at me and then I woke up. It felt like a premonition. I think I saw what happened to Denis."

Gabriel said nothing for a long moment, as though he was waiting for me to say more. When I didn't, he reached for my hand and laced his fingers through mine before speaking.

"I can see why you feel like you saw what happened to Denis before it happened, the timing is certainly odd. But, is there a reason why you don't think this was just a dream? Merely a coincidence with truly atrocious timing?"

I raised one shoulder in a shrug before letting it fall. "From the moment I woke up, it just felt different. I've never had a dream like that before, except. . ."

"Except?" he prompted.

"Well, it wasn't a dream." I began. Shit, I hadn't intended to talk about this, I wasn't even sure if it were something I would ever tell him, but I couldn't think of a way to gracefully, backpedal. "I knew that your sister's baby would be a girl."

"It wasn't a dream? How did you know?" There was no disbelief in his voice, just curiosity.

"Before we left the first time— when we were going to Nantes, I hugged her goodbye. I saw. It was a vision, I suppose, although I never had one before."

"What did you see, exactly?"

"I saw her handing you the baby, and you showed her to me. When we returned to *Trégoudan*, do you remember how we went in to see your sister and little Thérèse right away?" He raised a brow imperceptibly, but the look in his eyes urged me on. "It was precisely like that, the vision. When it happened in real life, I couldn't believe it."

Gabriel nodded his head thoughtfully. "Has anything like that happened to you before?"

"No. I did have what I think was another vision, but it hasn't come true yet. Or rather, I don't think it has."

"I don't know if your dream was a premonition Ava, but I don't think there is anything you could have done to prevent it or change it if that is what you are thinking."

My shoulders slumped slightly. "You're right. I just can't shake the feeling that I could have done something. What is the point of knowing something ahead of time, if there is nothing you can do to change the outcome?"

It occurred to me again, that there was so much more that I knew would happen. But, I wasn't ready to take Gabriel down that rabbit hole with me yet.

Gabriel took both my hands and pulled me close to him bending his face down until his forehead rested against mine.

"I don't know. We will figure it out together, aye?"

I smiled wanly in response, and he dropped a kiss on my nose.

Footsteps in the corridor made us turn toward the door in unison. Madame Bleuzen and Mademoiselle Noemi walked in.

Mademoiselle Noemi dropped a curtsey. "Begging your pardon, my lord, my lady. I'm to show Madame Bleuzen and Mademoiselle Éloise to their room."

Gabriel smiled gently. "Please go ahead, Noemi." He glanced at Madame Bleuzen. "Do you want to wake her?" he asked, gesturing at Éloise. "Or shall I carry her up?"

"Oh please, my lord. You needn't bother. I'll wake her. She should have a bite to eat, she'll need her strength."

"It's no bother," Gabriel assured her.

Esme walked in and saw Madame Bleuzen and Mademoiselle Noemi. "Oh! You're here. Madame Pichon said the room for you is ready."

"Aye, thank you. We've just come to fetch Éloise," Madame Bleuzen replied.

"Can I help with anything?" Esme questioned.

"You've done so much already Esme. Thank you for watching over my husband. Noemi will help me get Éloise upstairs should I need it."

"It's the least I can do." Esme turned to Gabriel and me. "I've sent Georges Madec to fetch Madame Cariou and set a watch for this evening. I'll sit with him for now, you rest a bit. You look fatigued my lady."

"Thank you, Esme." Gabriel smoothly led me away.

I looked back over my shoulder and met Esme's eyes. She nodded her head imperceptibly at my unspoken question. Confident that Denis was in the best hands we had; Gabriel and I headed to our chamber.

Thirty
Death's Tender Caress

My stomach grumbled, and I felt Gabriel chuckle. My cheeks colored slightly in embarrassment; I was famished, but couldn't muster the energy to lift my head off his shoulder. We were lying in our large four-poster bed in silence. The day's emotional, psychological, and physical fatigue had culminated with us lying fully clothed in bed; each of us lost in our thoughts. The stillness that settled over us had been complete. Until that moment, I assumed he was asleep and had been on the brink of slumber myself.

"Your stomach sounds discontent." I detected a suggestion of laughter in his voice.

"Mmph," I answered, my eyes still closed.

"Shall we go down for supper?"

"I'm more tired than hungry. The thought of changing into fresh clothing to go downstairs. . . " I shuddered.

He made a noise between a snort and a laugh. "You've earned your supper in bed if you like. I'll have them send some sustenance for us."

"That would be lovely. I don't think I can move from this position." I opened one eye and craned my head back to look at him. "Do you suppose you might feed me as well?"

"Aye," he replied softly and seriously.

The momentary levity vanished like smoke in the breeze. I sighed and wrapped my arms fiercely around him.

"I am so relieved and glad that you came back safely to me," I said honestly. There was a telltale tremor in my voice, as I thought about Denis, who had *not* made it home safely.

He looked at me and smoothed my hair away from my face. "If you mean it, then I am glad as well."

"Why wouldn't I mean it?" I asked. I meant it with every fiber of my being, something I was only slightly discomfited to discover within myself.

"Well, I didn't quite intend it that way. . . It's only that, I know feelings exist between us, and passion, aye? It's a tangible thing. But I also know that you had reservations about our marriage." He fell silent for a moment. "I've sometimes wondered if you had regrets." There was a surprisingly raw, vulnerable quality to his voice, that made me lift my head to look at him properly.

"I would not take back our marriage, Gabriel." I felt my way painstakingly for my words, aware that the ones I chose were important. "It's early days yet. But I awaken every morning grateful to have you beside me. I was terrified of losing you last night and this morning."

His arms tightened and he held me crushingly close for the space of several heartbeats, then he shifted, pulling me up so that we were eye to eye, and our breaths mingled.

"I'm sorry for making you fret. I wouldn't cause you a moment's grief, if I could prevent it." He reached out and tucked an errant curl behind my ear solemnly. "I meant it when I said I would make you happy if I could and that I would protect you. I don't—I will never take the vows I made to you lightly."

Then his mouth was warm and insistent on mine, telling me with his body, what he couldn't properly convey with his words. My exhaustion vanished replaced with a visceral need to illustrate my total lack of regret concerning him or regarding the promises I had made to him.

He moved slowly, deliberately, every touch feather-light, intense with emotion. There was a poignant sweetness to our lovemaking underscored by an unspoken urgency. Death had brushed its skeletal fingers through our lives. Surely only for the first, of what would be many times. Each caress was rendered more tender, every moment made sweeter by the reminder that life is fleeting.

Gabriel played with the ends of Ava's hair, careful not to wake her, as he replayed the day in his mind. He loved how the silky strands coiled around his fingers as if her hair had a life of its own. Her skin was warm against his, her weight reassuring. He closed his eyes and savored how she sleepily rubbed her cheek against his chest. A lump rose in his throat as he recalled how she'd admitted that she'd feared for his safety.

'What is the point of knowing something ahead of time, if there is nothing you can do to change the outcome?' Her words came back to him, and he thoughtfully turned them over in his mind. Aye, she was right, although he was damned if he knew the answer to her question. She'd been honest about the visions and the dream. Of that, he had no doubt.

The expression in her eyes when she told him had been earnest, though there'd been a fair bit of trepidation mixed in as well. He imagined it hadn't been a simple thing for her to tell him. Most people either wouldn't believe her or would accuse her of witchcraft. The hairs at the back of his neck prickled. She would have to tread carefully. No doubt she already knew;

she was no fool, but there was a real danger to her premonitions, and it squeezed his heart to think of it.

He sighed, turning his mind to other concerns. He would have to follow up with Timothée and the others to make sure that the boar was being butchered and smoked. By rights, the Bleuzens' should get the meat. Which brought to mind the matter of Denis. Knowing as he did, how slim the man's chances at a full recovery were, he would have to make arrangements to ensure that Madame Bleuzen and their daughter were taken care of.

His body ached with the strain of the day but he knew his mind would not allow him to fall asleep until he took care of the issues at hand. He carefully disentangled himself from Ava sliding out from beneath her slowly to not disturb her. She rolled over and mumbled in her sleep. He froze, waiting as she snuggled beneath the blankets like a sleeping cherub. After a long minute, he let out a slow breath and dressed quietly.

Gabriel opened their bed-chamber door soundlessly, just as Mademoiselle Noemi walked down the corridor.

"Noemi, please have Mademoiselle Ollivier send supper up to my chamber. My lady and I will be dining in our room this evening."

"Yes, of course, my lord," she murmured, hurrying down the hallway toward the back stairs.

Gabriel made his way down the stairs and headed toward the stillroom first. As he walked he went over his mental list of things to see to. Checking on Denis topped the list.

The door to the surgery stood ajar, candlelight spilling out onto the smooth stone floor. He pushed the door open, his eyes sweeping the room at a glance. Madame Cariou and Esme stood at the long worktable, speaking in quiet undertones as Madame Cariou industriously ground something with a pestle. They must not have heard him, neither of them turned around.

Denis Bleuzen hadn't been moved. He was covered in several warm blankets, but his face had an unhealthy, waxy, color, as though he'd been carved of the finest Carrara marble. Gabriel cleared his throat to alert the women of his arrival. They turned to face him, Madame Cariou still holding the pestle in one hand and the mortar in the other as she curtseyed.

He inclined his head, "Thank you for coming, I have heard that you are very skilled with the herbs Madame."

Madame smiled prettily, displaying a dimple in one cheek. "I do my best, *Monsieur le Vicomte.*"

"How is our patient faring? Has he awoken yet?"

"He has not awoken, and he is feverish, my lord. Mademoiselle Esme has just finished explaining the situation to me. His blood loss was tremendous. As to his survival, I cannot say with certainty, but I believe we will know fairly quickly how the matter lies with Monsieur Bleuzen. Every day that he lives, his chances at recovery will increase."

"Thank you, Madame Cariou." Gabriel turned to Esme. "You must be exhausted. It is well past time that you ate and recuperated from the journey and today's events."

Esme placed both hands against the small of her back, stretching. "I was just leaving Gabriel. Madame Cariou will stay with Monsieur Bleuzen until the next person on watch relieves her."

Gabriel held the door open for Esme. "I'll walk with you. Do you happen to know if Timothée has gone home?"

"In truth, I do not. He fetched Madame Cariou and escorted her back. He may still be here."

I'll leave you here then." He stopped at the kitchen door. "If you see Timothée, let him know I was looking for him. . . Oh, and Esme? Should you run into Luc, please ask him to find me as well." Gabriel turned to leave but pivoted neatly as he remembered something. "Has anyone shown you your room yet?"

"Yes, a little while ago."

"Excellent. Thank you, Esme."

I awoke but couldn't immediately locate what had interrupted my sleep. The disorienting fog of the deep, dreamless sleep I'd been in, took several moments to clear, as I blinked owlishly. The darkness in the room was absolute— save for the light of the fire, and the candles by our bed. Dawn was still hours away.

Gabriel was already awake and in his normal fashion did not appear to be groggy in the least. He had the annoying habit of waking up clear-eyed and alert. Earlier, I awoke from a short nap, and we'd supped in our room, Gabriel exchanging news from Amélie and the children. I shared with Gabriel my plans for the gardens, and how I enlisted the help of Éloise and Isabelle. We talked late into the night, relishing each other's company, and it felt like we had just fallen asleep.

"What is it?" I whispered.

Gabriel shook his head, listening intently.

Goosebumps rose on my skin, and I briskly rubbed my hands down my arms. I felt a chill run down my spine and a nameless feeling of dread settled in the pit of my stomach. My hand reached out, groping in the dark until I found Gabriel's. Wordlessly, he laced his fingers through mine. He squeezed my hand comfortingly before letting go and sliding soundlessly out of bed.

I tied my wrapper over my night dress, Gabriel pulled his breeches on and lit the big candelabra, and within seconds we both heard the rapid patter of footsteps coming down the corridor.

We looked at each other. "Denis," I said, as Gabriel reached for the door.

He pulled it open, just as Mademoiselle Noemi reached the entrance to our room.

"Is he alright?" I asked.

She shook her head in bewilderment. "My lord, my lady, Monsieur Bleuzen has awoken, his fever is extremely high, and he is incoherent, but he asked for you, my lord."

"Thank you, Noemi."

I had already pushed into the hallway and started for the stairs when Gabriel caught up to me.

"Careful on the steps," he murmured, taking my elbow.

We walked in silence the rest of the way to the stillroom. I could hear Denis's shouting before we made it to the main floor. I looked at Gabriel, my eyes wide with concern, hoping to glimpse reassurance in the gray depths, only to find that his expression mirrored my thoughts.

The room was lit as bright as the noonday sun. Madame Bleuzen was already there, her husband's hand embraced in hers, trying vainly to calm him. He seemed utterly unaware of her presence, his gaze roved wildly about the room, and his skin, shiny with perspiration, reflected the light of a dozen candles.

Gabriel immediately moved to the opposite side of the bed and took Denis' other hand. He leaned over the sick man's head. "Denis, man, I am here with you. You are safe."

As he quietly and unobtrusively worked to calm him, I took in the rest of the room's occupants. Esme was tucked into the far corner of the room conferring quietly with Éloise. The poor child's face was streaked with tears, her eyes red and swollen. Esme's blue gaze met mine for the space of a heartbeat, as she wordlessly conveyed the despair that had steeped into the fabric of the room. A young woman I didn't recognize stood by the worktable; her face turned away from me. This must be Madame Cariou, the midwife and healer.

I faltered for a moment, feeling superfluous. I didn't want to take Esme's attention from Éloise, who surely needed her more than I did. Madame Cariou had a competent air about her, but something about the vibe she gave off, made me feel she wouldn't welcome whatever help I might be able to offer.

I made my mind up and walked over to stand beside Gabriel. I felt eyes boring a hole in my back and had the disconcerting feeling that Madame Cariou was looking at me in a most hostile manner, but I ignored it. Gabriel looked up briefly, his eyes smiling into mine warmly before he returned his attention to Denis.

The poor man was now writhing in agony on the bed, muttering brokenly, and groaning. Blood frothed on his lips. What little I could make out, was disjointed and nonsensical.

"*Éloise, ma petite fée.*"

Éloise materialized next to her mother, as I frantically waved Esme over. Her eyes followed my gaze and instantly met mine reflecting my grim horror.

"I'm here, Papa."

His eyes rolled blindly around the room, trying to pinpoint the source of his daughter's voice.

"*Ma Chérie?*" he gasped.

"Right here, *mon cœur*," came Madame Bleuzen's steady soothing reply.

"He must calm down," came Madame Cariou's voice from behind me. "He is going to reopen his wound."

Esme shook her head sadly and motioned to his crimson mouth while Madame Bleuzen directed such a scathing look of intense dislike at Madame Cariou that I was taken aback.

"Thank you, Madame Cariou," she replied icily. She turned her attention back to her husband, and her face transformed back into one of loving adoration.

"Silouane?" he whispered, his voice weak and gurgling.

She clasped his hand between both of hers and lowered her head close to his. She murmured something, but I couldn't catch it.

Denis' eyes cleared and he suddenly appeared cognizant. "*Je t'aime, mon cœur. Je t'aime. . . ma petite fée.* Take care of each other, my loves."

Tears soundlessly streamed down Madame Bleuzens' face, wetting her husband's dark hair. "You stay with us— you take care of us. We need you. . . " she choked the words out, weeping.

"Papa! Do not say that. You will get better," gasped Éloise, her face awash.

"*Non, ma petite.*" He took a struggling breath, and I heard the ominous gurgle again.

I watched as comprehension dawned that he was drowning in his blood.

"I will look down on you. . . from heaven. . . I will always be with you." His words were so quiet that I could scarcely hear them as they passed through his chapped, cracked lips.

His brilliantly blue eyes closed.

"*Non*! Papa!" screamed Éloise.

His chest rose ever so slowly one last time, and he let out a long sigh, a bubble of blood bursting upon his lips in his final breath.

I took a deep breath of my own, and turned my face against Gabriel's shoulder, surprised to find that my cheeks were wet with tears. I shook my head in silent refusal. I could not accept another death, even though I knew he was gone already. I leaned against Gabriel, absorbing his quiet strength, before straightening my shoulders.

Several long minutes passed in a surreal outpouring of grief. Eventually, in unspoken agreement, Esme gently pulled a sobbing Éloise off her father's chest, and I moved to Madame Bleuzen and took her unresisting hand in mine. She walked with me without protest, submissively, the fight gone out of her.

I didn't say a word as we followed Esme and Éloise up the stairs to their room. The words I sought to comfort her escaped me entirely. But, I don't think she noticed. She moved like an eighty-year-old woman, stiff and rheumatic in her shock.

We saw them safely tucked into their room and walked together back down to the surgery, where Madame Cariou bustled about Monsieur Bleuzen, preparing him to be laid out.

Gabriel looked relieved to see me, taking my arm and leading me into the corridor as though he couldn't escape the surgery quickly enough. There was an odd frisson in the room that made my hackles rise. Madame Cariou's behavior made me feel as though I'd walked into a private and uncomfortable conversation without knowing. I looked at Gabriel questioningly but kept my peace. He would tell me when he was ready.

Thirty-One
Gardening Therapy

The week following the burial of Monsieur Bleuzen passed in a haze. Everyone walked around muted, conversations were quiet and somber, and laughter was suppressed, as though someone turned down the volume dial on the radio. Madame Bleuzen and Éloise opted to return to their cabin after they stayed in the *château* for three days, and their cottage became a revolving door of tenants bringing them food, sympathy, and offering them help.

Gabriel gave them leave to grieve in private until they were ready to return to their positions at the *château*. Although I couldn't imagine that anyone would force someone to work under the circumstances, I gathered based on Esme's reaction to the news, that it was unusual for a lord to be so gracious.

A week after we laid her father to rest, Éloise showed up ready to work. Her face still showed signs of grief and strain, her eyes seemed permanently swollen, and there were lines of pain bracketed around her young mouth. My heart ached for her.

"Come sit," I said gently, patting the chair beside mine in the parlor.

"I'll stand, thank you *Madame la Vicomtesse*," she answered in a quiet, but clear voice.

"Éloise dear, if you truly feel ready to get to work, then I am thrilled to have you, but I don't want you to feel like you must begin immediately.

There is time yet, before we must begin planning the spring planting in earnest."

"Please Madame, I am ready to get to work." Her voice wavered. "I need something to do, I cannot spend another day sitting at home, seeing reminders of my papa everywhere. I cannot stop crying when I am there. My *maman*— she is broken. I have never seen her this way, not even when my little sister died. I don't know how to help her, and I cannot sit and listen to her cry anymore." Tears streaked her cheeks as she spoke, and her lower lip trembled.

"I understand," I said in quiet sympathy.

I did. I knew exactly what she meant and I knew that the distraction of work would be a welcome one. Grief takes every person differently. This was her way of coping, and I wouldn't deny her. Working in a garden was particularly therapeutic, or at least, I had found it to be so after I lost my parents. I hoped it would prove to be beneficial for Éloise as well.

"Thank you, Madame."

"Come," I said, rising. "Esme and Isabelle are in the surgery creating their proposed lists. You can join them."

I stood and stretched my aching back, dusted my hands off on my apron and I smiled wearily at the women.

"I feel really good about our plans for the garden ladies. We have an excellent strategy in place, and I thank you all for your help."

"Isabelle, Éloise, and I have been working in the stillroom as well," piped up Esme. "It's been wonderful collaborating with them. We are bringing all our knowledge together and I think it will benefit everyone at *Landévennec.*"

I beamed. "I love that we are all working so well together. I know I've missed many of the meetings you've held, but I'm truly looking forward to learning from all of you, there are so many holes in my knowledge of the herbs."

Esme waved a hand airily at me. "Please! You are *la Vicomtesse*! You have many duties and items to oversee. We are lucky you spend so much time with us as it is."

Éloise and Isabelle both nodded solemnly, and I blushed a bit.

"Nonsense! I consider this to be my project. I'm excited to get my hands in the dirt alongside all of you." I meant what I said, but I wondered if I was stepping out of the bounds of proper protocol for a lady. I shrugged my shoulders to myself and gave them all a final smile. "I'll see all of you in the stillroom tomorrow morning."

The younger girls nodded and curtseyed as I turned away and began walking out of the garden back into the *château*.

"Ava!" called Esme, catching up to me at the door. "I wanted to talk to you about something."

Her expression looked uncertain and even nervous, which was out of character.

I frowned slightly and shifted from one foot to the other. "What's wrong Esme?"

She looked over her shoulder as if to ensure that no one was nearby before she spoke. When she began talking, her voice was so low I could barely hear her.

"The other day, I rode out to Madame Cariou's cabin." She must have seen the confusion on my face because she specified, "You know, the healer."

Ah, yes. I was terrible with names, but I remembered her now. I ignored the little frisson of disquiet, I felt at the reminder of the midwife and nodded at her to continue.

She let her breath out in a rush. "I thought it might be wise to collaborate with her. Perhaps she would be willing to instruct the girls and me in healing. She has so much knowledge that we lack, it seemed like a clever idea at the time. . . "

I nodded again but raised an eyebrow quizzically, something had clearly gone wrong, and I wondered what the problem could be.

"When I arrived, I thought she might be out because she didn't answer when I knocked, but the door was ajar and I peeked in, thinking perhaps she was busy and simply didn't hear me."

I looked at her encouragingly. "What happened, Esme? Whatever it is, you can tell me."

"She came out of the back room with a man, handed him something and he left." Esme hunched one shoulder. "I wouldn't have thought anything of it if it hadn't been for her reaction when she saw me. I figured she gave him a posset or a tea. Maybe whatever he was there for was embarrassing. . . but I cannot see that would be cause for acting the way she did."

"How did she act?"

"Angry. Guilty. As though I had caught her doing something wrong."

I absorbed this in silence, the fingers of my hand tapping against my thigh as I thought. "Did you recognize the man she was with?"

She shook her head. "I know many of the local people, but I have been gone for four years. He must be new to the area."

"Would you recognize him if you saw him again?"

"*Oui.*"

"*Bonne.* So, tell me what happened next? What did you say to her and how did she reply?"

"She asked me what I was doing there, I could tell she was angry by how she said it. I asked her if she would be interested in collaborating and teaching us some of her knowledge. Her answer was unnecessarily rude."

I frowned and my stomach clenched. "What was her response?"

"She said, 'If you haven't gained the skills and knowledge by now, then I am far too busy to waste my time sharing my art and my secrets with you.'"

My mouth hung open and then snapped shut comically.

"That was my thought as well," responded Esme wryly.

"What makes her think she is above collaborating with you? Or with me, for that matter?" I sputtered indignantly.

Esme shook her head. "I honestly don't know. But truthfully what bothers me more is how upset she was that I saw her with that man. I've been thinking about it for the last two days, and I can't seem to let it go. What is she hiding? What is she afraid we will find out?"

"Damned if I know," I muttered under my breath. Then I thought of something else that nagged at me after Bleuzen's death. "I sensed that Madame Bleuzen did not like her, the one time I met her. Do you happen to know why?"

"*Non.* But I will find out, you can rest assured."

"Madame Cariou is not married. . . is she widowed?"

"*Oui.* But I do not know the circumstances surrounding her husband's death."

"Ah. Well, let us investigate a bit, shall we?"

Esme smiled at me in obvious relief. "It may be nothing, but it's been weighing on me, I had to tell you."

I gave her a quick hug. "I'm glad you did. We will get it sorted out."

Thirty-Two
Honeyed Lies

Little by little, life returned to normal, or close to it, as winter reached its peak and began to show signs of spring's arrival. Things with Éloise's mother came to a head when the poor child desperately enlisted the help of her mother's friends to get Madame Bleuzen back on her feet. Having lost her father at such a tender age already, she'd been terrified that her *maman* would follow him to an early grave with a broken heart.

Madame Bleuzen returned to the kitchen after the tenants rallied around her, dragging her out of bed and reminding her that Monsieur Bleuzen's last wish had been that Éloise and Silouane take care of each other.

After the conversation I had with Esme about Madame Cariou, I decided to visit her myself. The look of fear on Esme's face seemed to be out of proportion with the exchange she'd had with the healer, although I wasn't one to dismiss a person's intuition, and I had also felt that something was off with the midwife when I met her.

I hadn't been able to put my finger on it, and in the aftershock of Bleuzen's death, I forgot about it entirely. As the lady of the *château*, I decided it was my responsibility to put misgivings about any of our tenants to rest. I also thought I should make it a point to get to know everyone who lived on our land. After I came to that conclusion, it took me several additional days to produce a believable excuse for making the trek to her cabin.

As I walked, I thought about how nice it was to see Madame Bleuzen back to work in the *château* and smiled. She'd even had a bit of her old spunk when we'd spoken about Amélie and her family's upcoming visit yesterday. Shadows of grief still showed in her blue eyes, and she looked like she'd aged ten years in the last two months, but I had walked away from our conversation feeling that she had already hit bottom and was now clawing her way out of despair.

I shifted my basket from one arm to the other and directed my mind back to today's errand. I was bringing some herbs, garlic, and two jars of precious honey with me; items that would be useful and welcome to her. My mother had always been interested in herbal remedies and had tried valiantly to teach me what she learned.

I had preferred to be outside, exploring and sailing, and I never paid much attention to those conversations, something I now wished I'd done differently. I would give anything for just one more opportunity to sit in the warm kitchen of my childhood with my mom, watching her mix oils as she explained the medicinal properties of each to me. I'd retained precious little from those lessons, although I'd been pleasantly surprised by the random golden nuggets of wisdom that popped into my brain at unexpected moments. Some of it had stuck with me.

I rolled my shoulders to ease the strain, humming a few verses of Bob Seger's 'Turn the Page', and felt a pang of longing for the music I had grown up with. I shifted my basket again and wondered why there wasn't a better method for carrying goods about the vast property. At least that was something I could change. I would talk to Esme about helping me recreate a modern backpack. Surely, we could put our heads together and produce something more comfortable. This damn basket was killing my arms.

As I approached Madame Cariou's cabin, I stopped momentarily, absorbing the details of the place. It looked sturdily built, the stone fireplace smoking cheerily, a small, covered porch in front of the door, with wood stacked neatly on one side. There were two sparkling windows with glass set in them, a real luxury for a widowed healer.

I wondered again about her deceased husband. To the left of the small house was a decent-sized garden with a fence around the perimeter to keep out hungry critters. In spite of the generally warm, clean feeling of the cabin, I felt an inexplicable wave of apprehension wash over me as I stepped onto the porch. I raised my hand to knock, but the door whipped open before I had a chance, startling me.

Up close, I realized that she was quite pretty. Sexuality oozed off her in waves, even though she was dressed demurely. There was something about how she held herself, a knowing, hidden flash in her eyes that I imagined excited men of all ages. Dark hair was pulled back primly from a clear-skinned, heart-shaped face. She had a severe widow's peak, but it didn't detract from her beauty. Dark, intelligent eyes accessed me.

"My lady," she murmured in a calm voice, curtseying. "To what do I owe the pleasure?"

"Good morning, Madame, I've been making the rounds, trying to get to know everyone," I said with an easy smile. "I couldn't leave you out. I also wanted to thank you for everything you did for Denis Bleuzen. I meant to come sooner. . . I brought a few things I thought might be useful to you."

I held out my basket of offerings, hoping she would invite me inside. For several long seconds, she looked at me, as if trying to decide how much she could afford to offend me. I was beginning to think she must be on the verge of showing me the door; when she surprised me by instead stepping back and saying, "Won't you please come in out of the cold? I was just making some tea."

I smiled, hoping my trepidation wasn't obvious. *"Merci Madame.* I would love some tea."

She busied herself at the hearth, pouring the boiling water and letting the tea steep while I tried to look around the cabin unobtrusively. I was disappointed that nothing jumped out at me to satisfy my lingering feeling of disquiet. Everything looked neat, befitting a young widow living alone. She gracefully moved back to the table with the pot of tea and cups before she peeked into the basket I'd brought.

"Oh, my lady, this is lovely, thank you!" she exclaimed, real pleasure evident in her voice, as she unearthed the jars of honey and herbs. "I am always running out of such things by the end of winter. These will go to good use."

"I'm so glad," I replied sincerely. "I tried to think of what might be useful to you. I have a trip planned into town next week, if there is anything I can get you from the apothecary, please let me know."

"Thank you, my lady. I will go through my stores and make a list— if that would be all right?" She glanced over her shoulder as she quickly emptied the basket, placing the items on her shelves, before she sat across the table from me and poured the tea.

"Of course. Have someone bring the list to the *château* once it's complete."

"I will, thank you. How are you enjoying life in *Landévennec*?" she asked conversationally.

"I'm settling in bit by bit. It's beautiful here, so different from where I grew up."

"Ah yes, it's even prettier once spring truly arrives, and everything begins to bloom. Where are you from?"

"I'm looking forward to everything turning green," I answered wistfully. "I'm from the south. Roussillon."

"Mmm. I've never been."

"Have you always lived here?" I asked, trying to probe delicately.

"I was born not far from here. My mother was a healer, I learned most of what I know from her. Sadly, she passed away when I was sixteen. My husband and I moved here after we got married, two years ago." She smiled nostalgically as if remembering happier days.

"You are so young to be widowed," I said softly, feeling for her despite myself. "I'm so sorry you've been dealt such tremendous loss. You must miss him and your mother terribly."

She sat across from me, staring down at her cup of tea. When she finally raised her eyes, they were filled with tears. "I do."

"Is there anything *le Vicomte* and I can do to help you? Are you quite able to manage on your own?" I asked gently.

"That's exceedingly kind of you, my lady, but I get on all right. My work keeps me busy, and it keeps me fed and clothed. I imagine I will remarry one day, but I cannot quite come to terms with the idea right now. Not after watching what my dear Tomas went through." She smiled tremulously.

I wondered again how her husband had died.

As if she read my mind, she added, "It was very difficult; knowing as much as I do about the herbs and not being able to save him."

I nodded sympathetically. "What happened to him?" I hastened to add, "If you feel up to telling me about it, of course."

She closed her eyes and took a deep breath, before reopening them and staring disconcertingly right into mine. "I haven't really spoken about it with anyone, but he fell ill and just wasted away before my eyes. In a matter of weeks. He went so quickly. Nothing I tried seemed to help him in the least." She closed her eyes for a moment, and I felt relieved that her dark piercing eyes weren't staring at me. When she spoke, her voice was so low I had to strain to hear her. "The worst of it was that he was in so much pain."

I reached across the table and took her hands in my own. "I am so sorry."

She smiled at me, though it didn't quite reach the depths of her eyes. "Thank you, my lady."

Thirty-Three
Clocks and a Campfire

I walked back toward the *château* turning over the details of our meeting and feeling deeply conflicted. Either Madame Cariou was an excellent actress or she had gone through hell over the last few years. She'd been kind and gracious to me during my visit. . . after she'd chosen to let me in, and I wondered if my intuition had misled me. My skin prickled uneasily as I remembered the intense, unsettling way she stared at me during our conversation.

I was so lost in my thoughts that I didn't notice the gathering gray clouds that scuttled quickly across the sky or how the wind rushed through the trees. The first icy drop splashed against my cheek, surprising me.

I looked up at the broody sky, cursing my lack of observation, and quickened my steps. *Will I make it back before the rain begins in earnest?*

I glanced around for a familiar landmark and calculated I was still quite far from the *château*. Perhaps I could duck into one of the other tenant's cabins along the way.

A few more drops pattered on the dusty path before me and I ducked my head under the hood of my cloak and hastened along. On the walk out I leisurely took in the tender, green shoots of budding gorse, and I stopped to admire the snowdrops that littered the countryside, nodding their sweet, white heads in fields that were mostly still a muddy brown. There was no time for me to appreciate the signs of spring's approach now. I needed to get back before I arrived looking like a drowned rat.

As if nature sought to mock the thought; the sky chose that moment to open in a sudden downpour. *Shit!*

I broke out in an unladylike run, even though I was already thoroughly wet. I was so focused on getting back to the *château*, that I didn't hear Automne's approach behind me over the steady sound of the falling rain.

"Ava!"

Startled, I stepped off the path to the side and looked up into the driving rain.

"Ava!" Gabriel said again, reaching a hand to help pull me onto the horse behind him. Relieved, I wrapped my arms around his waist and realized that he was just as soaked as I was. "Hold on tight!" He raised his voice over the sound of the pouring rain.

His legs squeezed Automne's sides, and the horse responded immediately, taking off in a canter. The wind rushed past us, and the pelting rain stung as it collided with my skin. I huddled against Gabriel's back, grateful that he'd happened upon me.

I didn't peek up until Automne's gait slowed and the rain became a soft patter. I expected it to take longer to get back but realized that the deluge hadn't abated. We had entered a thick copse of trees that sheltered us from the worst of it.

Gabriel pulled back on the reins, waited for Automne to a stop, and swung lithely down off his back. He tied him loosely to a thick tree branch and reached up to help me dismount. In the distance, I heard a low rumble of thunder, like the growl of a hungry belly. I shuddered involuntarily, the hairs on my arms prickling.

He took my hand. "There's a small cave just ahead, where we can wait out the storm."

He led me further into the thicket. I strained my eyes in the gloom as leaves crunched under our feet. *How did he know that there was a cave here?*

Gabriel found it unerringly though, clearing overhanging branches away from its mouth and revealing its hidden opening. He tugged my hand gently and we ducked our heads, walking into the dark recess of the cavern. I paused, letting my eyes adjust to the lack of light.

Once inside, the ceiling of the cave opened up. It was large enough for Gabriel to stand without hunching, although I estimated it was only about fifteen feet deep.

"How did you know this was here?"

"My brother and I used to roam these woods when we were younger. We kept some branches and kindling for a fire. Ah yes, it's still here!" he exclaimed with pleasure.

I watched in the dim light as he quickly gathered the wood and twigs into a pile, stacking them just so. He pulled a flint out of his pocket and quickly started a small fire. I hadn't realized how prepared he was, even on his own property. It made me rethink the foolhardiness of my venture today. I shivered as I sat by the fire, holding my hands toward the warmth. Another crack of thunder rent the air, making me jump.

Gabriel sat behind me, his backside against the stone wall of the cave, and pulled me back to lean against him, wrapping his arms around me. I leaned my head against his shoulder.

"Thank God I came upon you when I did," he said. "Where were you going?"

"I was heading back home. I went to visit Madame Cariou."

I couldn't see his face, but I felt his body tense against mine, surprising me.

"Why were you seeing her?" His voice was carefully neutral.

My stomach dropped in apprehension, and the cave felt colder. There was a dangerous undercurrent in his voice.

I tilted my head sideways to look up at him. The glow of the fire threw golden light and dancing shadows onto the chiseled angles and planes of his face. His eyes were dark and inscrutable.

"Esme went to see her last week. She thought Madame Cariou might be willing to teach her and the girls and myself as well, I suppose, some of what she knows. She thought it'd be helpful if we all improved our skills and knowledge."

Gabriel narrowed his eyes slightly but nodded. "I take it Madame Cariou wasn't enthusiastic about Esme's proposal?"

"That's putting it mildly. But what bothered Esme was the feeling she got that she inadvertently caught her doing something wrong. She said she acted guilty and angry. I decided to visit her to see if I got the same feeling from her."

He let out a long sigh and sat quietly for a bit. "Ava, *mon cœur*, there are several things I want to say about what happened today, the first being that if you are going to visit tenants, I would like to know your plans before you go. . . and perhaps have someone go with you."

I looked at him in surprise, a bit miffed that he was going to concentrate on that of all things.

He held up a hand, obviously sensing I was about to protest.

"I know how independent you are. But, you know that danger is all around us, even on our land. If anything happened to you, and I didn't know where you were, or where to even begin looking for you. . . " He shook his head. "It was sheer luck that I happened to come upon you when I did today."

I sighed. He wasn't wrong, even though I hated to admit it. The fire popped and I tensed, startled.

His arms tightened around me, and he brushed his lips against my cheek and buried his nose in my hair, inhaling my scent. "I cannot lose you, Ava." His voice was gruff and slightly strangled.

I swallowed down the lump in my throat and leaned back against him, turning my face to find his mouth with mine. "You won't," I replied quietly.

He rested his forehead against my cheek for a long moment, before speaking again.

"As for Madame Cariou. . . I do not know her well. Less than most of my tenants, and although she has never done anything overt to make me mistrust her, I must tell you in all honesty, that I do not. There is something about her that makes my skin crawl."

I silently digested his words.

"Can you pinpoint anything she has done or said to give you that feeling? I ask because I felt the same way about her the first time we met. . . when Denis—" I took a deep breath. "When Denis passed. But when I spoke to her today, I felt that perhaps I misjudged her. She spoke about her husband's passing, and she seemed so sincerely distraught. It made me wonder if I imagined my initial dislike of her."

Gabriel shook his head. "The circumstances around her husband's passing contribute to how I feel about her."

"Why?" I asked in shock.

He sat quietly, choosing his words carefully. "She and her husband came to me as newlyweds wanting to settle here. They were both young, he was a skilled carpenter, and she was a healer. . . both useful professions in high demand. He built their cabin, perhaps you noticed that the workmanship is superior to many of the other cabins?"

I nodded but didn't speak, he wasn't done telling his story.

"Aye, so they moved in about two years ago, and within perhaps six months, her husband fell ill. I did not know the man well, but a few of the men had become rather friendly with him. Luc was one. So, I heard quite a lot about how quickly the poor man went downhill." He took a deep breath here, pausing and closing his eyes tightly. When he opened them again, they were swimming with sadness. "Everything Luc described to me about his illness was like recounting my father's malaise. I never came across another person who experienced quite the same symptoms, or who deteriorated so quickly before succumbing to death."

The misery of reliving his father's death radiated off Gabriel in waves. I closed my eyes and took his hands in mine, squeezing them tightly. He breathed out through his nose and gently squeezed my fingers back.

"We were never able to explain either death. It never sat right with me. But then, the way she behaved after her husband was gone. . . " He shook his head, baffled. "She picked up and moved on with her life as though he'd never been a part of it. I've heard a few rumors about her since. Questionable morals. . . if you get my meaning?" He cocked a brow at me, and I nodded. "Aye and selling potions to men and women that are useless and may even do some harm. Nothing concrete, of course."

"I see."

"In any event, I'll not forbid you from visiting with her, or anything of the like. I just ask that you be vigilant around her. Don't let your guard down and please, bring someone along when you see her."

I swallowed and shifted, turning to face him. He straightened his legs out toward the fire and pulled me onto him, so I sat straddling him.

"I will." I brushed back a damp lock of chestnut hair that had come free of its binding.

He caught my hand with his and brought it to his mouth, gently brushing his lips over my knuckles. The warmth of his breath against my skin brought a surge of desire deep within me. The rising tide of heat and need had become familiar over the last few months, though it still surprised me with its ability to appear suddenly and intensely.

"*Merci*, Ava. I need to know you are safe. I cannot stand to even think about anything happening to you. I need you." His voice was low and strained.

I lacked the words to soothe him at that moment, so I pressed my body against him, showing him with my desire, what I couldn't voice. A low groan came from deep in his throat. His hands settled on my hips, positioning me more firmly against him, the evidence of his arousal hard against me. I lifted my face to meet his kiss and tasted a hint of desperation in the way his mouth devoured mine.

I threaded my fingers through his hair, anchoring him closer to me, my hunger for him refusing to be satiated with just one kiss. His lips were fused to mine, his arms locked me in a frantic embrace; the always present embers between us being stoked to red-hot flames. One of my hands wandered down his back and crept to the laces of his breeches where I fumbled, trying to yank them free one-handed.

Gabriel moved his lips away from mine and slowly trailed soft kisses down my cheek and along my jaw. The hands that had gripped my hips, slackened as he deliberately changed the tempo of our lovemaking. One hand moved to the small of my back, gently tugging at the laces on my bodice, while his other hand traveled up my spine, sending delicious tingles up until he tunneled his fingers into the hair at the nape of my neck.

He worked to loosen the pins holding my hair until it fell in a cascade of wet curls and waves down my back, pins scattering all over the floor of the cave. He gently massaged my neck and head, and I moaned a little. I hadn't even realized how sore my scalp was and how much tension I carried there. I moved my head to give him better access and he pressed his mouth against my neck, moving to my collarbone, trailing fire as he went. I closed my eyes, reveling in the swirling sensations as they engulfed my body.

The world shifted and I opened my eyes, dimly realizing that Gabriel had somehow moved us so that I lay sprawled out on my cloak, his lean body warm and comforting over mine. He didn't stop raining kisses on every inch of exposed skin he could reach, pulling the bodice of my gown down with one hand, and rucking up my skirts with the other. With every touch, he wove magic. My limbs were heavy and my mind was disconnected from everything but the feeling of his mouth, and his skin, against mine.

I strained toward Gabriel, urging him on, needing him desperately. He braceleted my wrists in one hand, pinning my arms above my head.

"I mean to take my time with you, Ava." His breath tickled my ear as he growled the words.

He brushed his lips across my face as he moved, excruciatingly slowly, exquisitely, and determinedly pushing me to the brink. There was a new element to our lovemaking, an emotion I thought I recognized but couldn't name. In the end, I begged and screamed before he tumbled over the cliff with me.

We lay cocooned together in the aftermath, my body tingling as little aftershocks still erupted over my skin. Despite the frigid temperature, I felt deliciously warm and content. I could roast a gooey, sweet marshmallow over the heat that emanated from his body. *God, I could kill for a 'smore right now.*

Gabriel raised himself on one elbow and gently brushed my hair off my forehead. His fingertips traced the contours of my face as if committing it to memory. "I don't believe I can live without you Ava. The thought of it steals the breath from my lungs."

I reached up and placed my palm against the side of his handsome face, feeling the slight stubble against my skin. "You don't have to. I'm right here."

His thumb caressed my bottom lip as he stared down at me, his eyes opaque in the flickering light, his face serious. I felt like he was plumbing the depths of my being. "I love you," he murmured.

My heart stopped. My stomach churned. My ears buzzed. For a moment, the world ground to a halt.

Then everything clicked quietly into place, and it started again, like a clock that had just been rewound.

I looked up into his beautiful, dear face with certainty and said, "I love you."

THIRTY-FOUR
MENUS AND MISCHIEF

Gabriel lay in bed, Ava's warmth comforting against him, listening to the patter of rain against the shutters, and held her words in his heart, turning them over and over again. He'd known that he had fallen in love with this stubborn, gorgeous woman for months. It struck him the minute he'd seen her, standing in silhouette, hesitating at the chapel door on the day they'd married. He'd been overcome with such an intense onslaught of emotion in that moment, that it felt like all the air was being squeezed from his lungs.

He knew she hadn't loved him then, but he'd been determined to do everything he could to change that. He'd chipped away at her uncertainty, trying to prove he would be there for her. He was unwavering in his determination to show her how much he cherished her. Gabriel had felt certain that with time their marriage would develop into love.

'I am my beloved's and my beloved is mine,' he thought, recalling a line from the *Song of Solomon* he'd read years ago. He'd thought the simplicity of the verse was beautiful then, but it took on more meaning now. He absorbed how her hair lay strewn across the pillows and how her long lashes cast shadows upon her cheeks. The feeling swelled within his chest until he felt like he couldn't breathe.

He was bone tired; they'd begun planting the fields this week, and although he knew he didn't need to be so involved in the process, he found that he couldn't help himself. He reveled in being a part of turning the brown, muddy hills into verdant, growing crops. Each year brought new challenges, it was never quite the same. Too much rain or devastating drought; insects, unseasonable heat, cold, wet springs, the list went on and on.

He enjoyed implementing innovative ideas and producing solutions to the inevitable problems they faced. He felt the heartbeat of the land strumming deep within his body. It was tied to him in a way he couldn't explain. He knew it wasn't the same for most men, but to him, it was about so much more than simply being a landlord.

Despite his exhaustion though, he found that he couldn't fall asleep. He lay awake thinking about how the firelight had glowed on her flawless skin and how her eyes had gleamed with tenderness for him when she finally told him she loved him.

Dieu, he loved her so much.

It brought a sense of wonder every time he replayed the moment in his head. He felt the slow, steady rise and fall of her chest against his body, and it lulled him to sleep.

Things changed between us in some minute, indefinable way since that day in the cave. I pondered on it as I looked over the menu that Mademoiselle Ollivier and I prepared for Amélie's arrival and Esme and Luc's upcoming nuptials. We were expecting them within the next few days, and the *château* had been a flurry of activity, preparing, in addition to the spring planting mania I was told was normal for this time of year.

I set the menu aside, stood up from the desk, and stretched. It was midday, and my stomach was rumbling in discontent. I'd felt queasy and unable to eat the last few mornings and was consequently starving by the time we had lunch. Gabriel was making a big deal out of my lack of appetite, but I was sure it was nerves. I was juggling all my newfound duties successfully for the moment, and I was terrified I would drop one of the balls I had in the air, inadvertently causing a minor catastrophe of some sort.

I glanced at the grandiose clock in the hall as I made my way toward the dining room. Thank God it was time to eat.

I found Gabriel and Luc standing by the double doors discussing the repairs being done to some of the fencing that had been destroyed during the winter storms when Madame Pichon approached with a quick patter of her feet.

"*Madame et Monsieur*, the Gardin family has arrived! They are making their way up the road now."

"*Merci*, Madame Pichon, they can join us for dîner. Are their rooms ready?" I asked.

"*Oui*, my lady."

"*Le Vicomte* and I will meet them at the door. Please let Mademoiselle Ollivier know they have arrived and will be joining us for lunch and send Monsieur Dubois to bring their things up."

Gabriel finished speaking to Luc adding, "Find me this evening, aye?"

Luc nodded and bowed quickly to me, making his way toward the kitchen.

Gabriel turned to me with a smile, bowing over my hand and setting off a flurry of butterflies in my stomach. Will this feeling ever cease? Will he always set off a secret thrill of passion and desire in me?

I took the arm he offered with a smile and we walked together toward the entry.

Leaning close to me, with a mischievous glint in his eyes; he whispered, "You look delicious today."

I elbowed him and he laughed quietly.

Monsieur Dubois, our butler, appeared as was his custom, seemingly out of thin air. He opened the front door just as Gabriel and I made our way into the foyer. Amélie was already standing on the steps with Étienne while Mathieu stood by the carriage holding petite Thérèse in his arms and waiting for Esme's mother, Margaret, to step down. Amélie turned with a smile to greet us and Étienne, spotting his favorite uncle, let out a whoop and gleefully launched himself into Gabriel's arms.

Thirty-Five
Visions of Sugar Plums

I sipped my wine, letting the rich, sweet flavor fill my senses, and felt my shoulders relax in the enjoyment of Esme and Luc's wedding. *Le Vicomte de Argol*, a rather frail man from the neighboring *château*, had decided to confide the sudden onset of his digestive troubles to me. As he described, with a bit too much detail, the nature of his illness, I listened with half an ear while I let my mind wander. I had lost sight of Gabriel in the crush of guests and wondered where he was and whether I might be able to steal him away for a few minutes of fresh air outside.

"... the nausea has been truly terrible my dear."

"I am so sorry to hear that. Have you seen your *docteur* about it?"

As he raised his wine glass to his mouth, I noticed the skin on the back of his hand was covered in dark lesions and I frowned, as it tickled something in the back of my mind.

"*Non*, not yet. He is supposed to come to me in a few days. I've seen our local healer though. Useless girl, that one." He shook his head. "My wife knows more about the herbs than she does."

I tutted in sympathy, scanning the room for Gabriel. I desperately needed to get some air. I was feeling rather nauseous myself in the oppressive heat of the room.

"Ah, my dear, I was just singing your praises!" he exclaimed as a handsome blonde woman in what I judged to be her late thirties, dressed in a stunning, crimson, brocade gown joined us.

"*Madame la Vicomtesse de Landévennec*, may I present my beautiful wife, *la Vicomtesse de Argol*."

We inclined our heads to each other, and I smiled tentatively.

"Your husband was just telling me of your skill with the herbs and how you are nursing him back to health."

La Vicomtesse de Argol tossed her head coquettishly, gave her husband a tender look, and patted his hand.

"I do my best to help," she said humbly, though something about her words rang false.

Gabriel appeared beside me, sliding his arm around my waist. I looked up at him gratefully, and he raised a questioning brow at my expression. "Have you met already?" he asked. He turned to *la Vicomtesse de Argol*. "It's been so long since I've seen you, it must be strange to be back?" He smiled at her, but it didn't reach his eyes.

"I have happy memories here, although I'm glad to be back under more joyful circumstances than when I saw you last," she replied with a sad smile.

My brow furrowed in confusion, there was a history here to which I wasn't privy. I took another sip of my wine in a bid to calm my stomach and now, my aching head. The stress of the last few weeks must be getting to me.

Gabriel turned to me. "*La Vicomtesse de Argol* was my stepmother, for a brief time before my father passed," he said.

Ah. He had never mentioned having a stepmother. She must not have been around for long.

"It must be lovely to catch up after so many years."

They both smiled noncommittally.

Le Vicomte de Argol cleared his throat. "It was wonderful meeting you, my dear," he said with a smile at me. "*Mon chou*, won't you dance with me?" he asked his wife.

"Of course, my love," she said sweetly. She tossed a smile at me over her shoulder. "It was nice to meet you."

I smiled back at her though I had to grit my teeth not to wince at the pain in my head. Her skirt brushed against mine as she turned to go, and a ripple of unease crawled up my spine at the contact. My vision blackened briefly around the edges.

"Ava. . . Ava!"

I blinked and focused on Gabriel's face. His eyes were dark with concern. His arm was wrapped tightly around me, half supporting me. I shook my head slightly, trying to clear my mind.

"Let's get you out of here. . . " he muttered under his breath. "Excuse us, please." He smiled charmingly at several people as he steered me unerringly out the doors onto a terrace.

I shivered in the frosty night air, the sudden quiet a sharp contrast to the ballroom. Without a word, Gabriel removed his evening jacket and placed it over my shoulders. I sagged against him in relief.

"What's wrong, *mon cœur*?" he asked, worry creeping into his voice.

I turned toward him and stepped into his embrace, wrapping my arms around his body, and closing my eyes, taking in the familiar, comforting scent of him. I rested my cheek against his chest and listened to the reassuring thump of his heart, letting it calm me.

"It was just too hot in there, I think. I felt a bit faint."

"You scared me," he admitted. "The look on your face. . . "

"I felt quite odd, for a moment."

He reached into his pocket and pulled out a lemon candy.

"Have this, it will help if you're still feeling unsteady."

I popped it in my mouth and let the bright, citrusy flavor flood my senses.

His arms tightened around me. "Better now?" he asked.

I nodded. "Slightly. You never mentioned having a stepmother before."

He grimaced. "She married my father six months before he passed. He thought that we needed a maternal figure around, but she was never that. As soon as my father was gone, she moved into our house in Paris. I haven't seen her or heard from her, except to send her money each quarter since then. She wrote to tell me she was getting remarried and was moving to her new husband's *château* about eight months ago."

"Why get remarried now? It's been years since your father's death."

Gabriel rolled his shoulders to ease the tension in them and frowned thoughtfully before answering.

"She was rather young when she married my father; younger than we are now, if memory serves. I heard that *le Vicomte de Argol* is hoping for an heir, but he's getting up in his years. Although she is no longer in her prime childbearing years either." He shrugged. "Perhaps there's affection between them? *Le Vicomte* is not looking very well."

"He was telling me that he's been feeling ill lately. Stomach problems and the like."

A small frown appeared between Gabriel's eyebrows. "He told you that?"

"Yes. Shouldn't he have?"

"It's just odd. . . " He shook his head. "I'm sure it's merely a coincidence," he muttered.

"What is a coincidence?"

"Before my father fell ill, he also complained of stomach problems. In the beginning, it wasn't bad, but it slowly worsened, and then quite suddenly he became violently sick. From there it was over within a few weeks. It shocked all of us with the suddenness of it, but now I wonder if the stomach was an early symptom, a warning sign of sorts."

"Well, if the same fate awaits *le Vicomte de Argol*, then I'd say it isn't a coincidence at all."

He raised a brow at me. "Are you suggesting what I think you are, Ava? Should I warn the man?"

"And say what? I suspect your wife is poisoning you?" I shook my head. "Unfortunately, I don't think there is anything you can do without proof, Gabriel. We will have to see what happens with *le Vicomte*."

"*Merde.*"

"That's succinct," I murmured.

The doors opened and the sound of music, conversation, and laughter spilled out, interrupting us.

"Ah, the two of you are sneaking a moment away, eh?" Luc asked with a laugh.

His arm was around Esme's waist, and it was obvious from the looks on both of their faces, that they'd intended to find a private moment themselves.

I grinned at Esme's exuberant expression. She was positively glowing.

"We were just leaving," I said. "Enjoy your stolen moment together." I winked at them, and they smiled guiltily. Shrugging Gabriel's jacket off, I waited for him to put it back on and hugged Esme.

"I'm so happy for you," I whispered in her ear.

"Thank you, Ava."

I took Gabriel's arm and promptly tripped over my full skirt, accidentally bumping into Luc. The world immediately went black.

"How can I help?" I asked Esme.

It was a golden day, the sky bright, blue through the window, but the mood inside was somber. She shook her head, her eyes were red and swollen from crying, and fresh tears spilled down her cheeks.

"I don't know what to do, Ava. I don't know what is wrong with him. The tea that Madame Cariou is making isn't helping."

She sat on the edge of the bed she shared with Luc, holding his hand in desperation, and looked up at me.

"I'm afraid. What if he doesn't get better, Ava?"

No. No, no, no. This couldn't be happening again. I did not want this. I didn't want to see terrible things happening to the people I loved. This was a curse.

"Ava! *Mon cœur*!" Gabriel's voice cut into the vision, interrupting it.

I fought back against the current that threatened to drag me under, and his face swam blurrily into view. My head slipped back beneath the surface, and my hearing and vision were murky. As if from a great distance I heard voices raised in panic and argument. My head felt like it was being split in two, and I felt my stomach revolting. *Oh God, I'm going to be sick.*

Then I heard the deep, soothing, and commanding sound of Gabriel's voice break through the cacophony. I concentrated on it, using it as my anchor, and opened my eyes blearily. Gabriel was holding me against his chest, and several faces peered at me in concern.

"Ava! Thank God. Are you all right?" exclaimed Esme.

I closed my eyes temporarily in response and felt Gabriel clasp my hand reassuringly. I squeezed back, grateful for the silent support, and reopened my eyes with a strained smile.

"I'm fine, too much wine and not enough food I think," I lied glibly.

Esme gave me a narrow look to let me know she didn't buy what I was selling for a minute.

"Not to worry, I'll see to it that she eats something," said Gabriel lightly.

I gave Esme and Luc a little wave and clinging to Gabriel's arm, made a beeline for the doors.

As soon as we were out of earshot, Gabriel muttered under his breath, "You will eat something right now, although I think we both know there is more going on than meets the eye."

If I felt better, I might have argued with him merely on the principle that he couldn't order me around, but in truth, I felt terrible. Perhaps eating something would help. He deftly navigated me to a table, and waving down one of our maids, ordered us a plate.

"We'll talk later, aye?" He eyed me with blatant concern.

It wasn't a question and we both knew it. I nodded in silence, deeply alarmed by what appeared to be another vision and what it meant for Esme and Luc's future.

Our food arrived, and my mouth watered when the scent of the roast in plum sauce wafted toward me. I focused on eating and was surprised to realize that I was famished. Gabriel hovered over me, like a nervous mother hen. I snorted to myself as I imagined Gabriel trussed up like a chicken.

"What are you laughing at?" he asked, but I could see the relief in his gray eyes, and I felt a pang of regret for worrying him.

I swallowed and shook my head, grinning at him. "Nothing, just a silly thought."

I saw Amélie weaving her way through the crowd toward us and smiled at her. She arrived at the table breathlessly and plopped down in one of the chairs.

"What a crush!" she exclaimed. She waved down one of the maids and grabbed a glass of wine off the tray, taking a long sip. "You don't mind if I sit with you for a bit, Ava? I haven't danced so much since your wedding!"

I smiled at her with genuine affection. "Please stay. I am worn out myself, and Gabriel still has to finish making the rounds. I hear things are getting worse in the cities?"

Gabriel narrowed his eyes at me. "Aye, that's true." He glanced at Amélie and cocked a brow. "You are staying?"

She smiled brightly at her brother. "*Oui.*"

He nodded, and bending down, brushed his lips against my cheek. "Find me if you need me."

"I will."

THIRTY-SIX
ROYAL RUMORS

I rolled over and snuggled underneath the pile of blankets and furs, trying to drown out the morning light that seemed to be joyfully shouting, 'Get up!' I had been particularly tired lately, my energy level a fraction of its former self. I chalked it up to stress, but we were now sneaking up on April and I felt no improvement.

The days were getting longer, Esme and Luc's wedding had gone without a hitch, and Amélie's family would be setting off to return home in another couple of days. I yawned hugely and promised myself I would slow down, relax a bit this week, and get caught up on sleep.

Although Gabriel was likely running on a bigger sleep deficit than I was, he was already up and out of bed, his side no longer retaining the warmth of his body. I let my hand rest on his pillow and wished he were still beside me so that I could snuggle up next to him. We'd gone to bed so late last night that we'd both fallen asleep immediately, forgoing our routine talk at the end of the day. I stretched and sat up, suddenly remembering that Gabriel had been planning on gathering news during the wedding.

Tucked away in the country like we were, it took days or weeks, sometimes even longer during the winter months, to hear reports about what was happening with the monarchy, and the third estate. Considering the food shortages that had already been a problem before winter set in, I imagined things had likely worsened over the interminably long, cold months.

I found him at his desk, bent over a letter, tapping his quill thoughtfully against his cheek, no doubt debating, or deciding what to write next. He looked up at me and smiled tiredly as I approached. Placing his quill in its pot, he stood up and wrapped his arms around me.

"How did you sleep, my love?" he murmured, brushing a kiss across my forehead.

"Fine. I missed waking beside you this morning."

He pulled away slightly and cupping my face, brought his mouth down to mine. I tightened my arms around him, not letting him go when he would have moved away. He groaned deep in his throat and yanked me up against him until I was standing on my toes, my body pressed against the length of his. Breathing raggedly, he dragged himself away, sat on his chair, and tugged me onto his lap. He rested his forehead against mine, eyes closed for a moment that stretched out.

"I missed you this morning too."

I chuckled and gave him a quick peck on the lips. "So, how did last night go?" I nodded my head toward the letter he was working on. "Who are you writing?"

He sighed deeply. "I didn't learn a great deal that I didn't already suspect or didn't already hear. Rumors are circulating that the royal treasury is empty, but no one seems to know if it's true. *Le Roi et La Reine* continue to spend lavishly as though there is no bottom to the monarchy's coffers. The people are starving. . . it is worse now, after the winter, of course."

"So, the news is not good."

He shook his head and ran a hand through his hair in frustration. "*Le Vicomte de Argol* told me that when he was in Paris a few months ago the situation was rapidly devolving. The royal's greed seems to know no bounds, and discontent among the people is mounting. I am writing to Phillipe. I should have written to him sooner. He will be able to tell me how things are in the city."

I bit my lip and nodded. *Is now the time to tell Gabriel what I know about the Revolution?*

His friend Phillipe Girard, *le Comte de Saint-Denis*, lived just outside the city and would be able to give Gabriel unique insight. Not just into the circumstances in Paris as far as the third estate went, but he would also be able to tell him about what was going on in the inner circles of Louis XVI.

"I fear things are going to worsen a great deal further before they improve," I said sadly.

"I suspect the same." He sighed, tucking a stray curl that had fallen free of its pins back behind my ear. "But enough about that, what happened to you last night? It was more than being overheated or not eating enough."

He looked at me sternly. My stomach churned and my mouth felt dry. I knew that telling him about the vision was inevitable, but that didn't mean I was looking forward to it. I looked down, plucking the fabric of my skirt between my fingers, pleating it, as I thought about where best to begin. He raised a brow at me but waited patiently otherwise.

"I wasn't feeling very well, to begin with, a bit overtired I suppose. Then I met *le Vicomte* and *la Vicomtesse de Argol*, which put me in a strange frame of mind. . . I know we spoke about it a bit, but it's been going round and round in my head since, and I honestly think something odd is happening there." I glanced at Gabriel, his eyes had narrowed and darkened substantially at the mention of the de Argols, but he said nothing, so I continued. "When they walked away from us, *la Vicomtesse* brushed against me, just slightly, aye? My vision went dark the way it does when I'm about to see something, but I saw nothing." I shrugged. "I may have truly just been a bit faint, it starts out feeling rather the same, so I can't say for certain."

He nodded thoughtfully. "I did wonder about that, but then, on the terrace. You did have a vision then."

I noticed that he didn't word it as a question. *How did he know?*

"Yes, when I bumped into Luc. I saw that he was terribly ill, and Esme was distraught. I don't know what was wrong with him, but he was lying in bed. One odd thing I noticed, Esme told me that the *'tea that Madame Cariou is making him isn't helping.'* It's been stuck in my mind ever since, though I don't quite know why. It feels like a clue of some sort."

"Was that the entire vision?"

"Yes, it was quite short. Just a preview of what's to come, I suppose."

He tapped the fingers of his hand thoughtfully on his leg. "Did you get a feel for what season it was?"

It was a good question. As I paused to recall the details of the scene, my brow furrowed. The light streaming in had been bright, and based on how we'd all been dressed, I would guess it wasn't cold.

"Summer, I think. Maybe late spring."

"*Merde.* Likely within the next few months then," he muttered.

I leaned my head against his shoulder, feeling drained and defeated. "I'm sorry to be the bearer of bad news."

He rubbed his hand soothingly up and down my back, pausing to massage the tension out of my neck.

"I prefer to think of it as forewarning," Gabriel said thoughtfully. "We can use the information from what you see, glean clues from it, perhaps we can change the outcome."

I lifted my head to look at him in wonder. He had the habit of keeping his composure and staying positive, which helped me see the bright side in a variety of situations. Although I wouldn't call myself negative, I did tend to have more dramatic reactions than he did.

"Thank you."

Gabriel quirked a brow in question.

"You always seem to calm me down," I explained. "I feel better, now that we've spoken. Should I tell Esme and Luc what I've seen?"

He kissed me lightly. "No need to thank me. I'm glad your mind has been eased a bit. As for Esme and Luc. . . I don't know. Does Esme know about any of the other premonitions you've had?"

I shook my head. "No."

"Aye, that's probably for the best. I believe they can be trusted, but it wouldn't be wise to make it common knowledge that you have visions. It can raise too many dangerous questions. Let's think on it. Perhaps there is a way to warn them without letting too much on."

"All right. As for Madame Cariou—I keep circling back to what Esme said. . . about the tea in the vision, but also about how she wouldn't help when Esme asked her to. Do you think I'm making something out of nothing?"

Gabriel rubbed his hand over his face before answering. "I think for the time being, there is nothing to be done, other than to be watchful. Perhaps she is negligent, or there may be a more sinister intention to her actions, but we have extraordinarily little to go on at the moment."

"Always the voice of reason," I said teasingly.

"Aye, well one of us has to be," he replied with a snicker.

Recognizing that I was about to elbow him in retaliation for the gibe, he laced his fingers through mine and pinned my hands down by my sides. He flashed a wicked grin at me before covering my mouth with his, effectively cutting me off mid-protest. I struggled against him halfheartedly, before giving myself over to the kiss and sinking into him.

As if he sensed my capitulation, he changed the angle from playful to slow and sweet, letting go of my hands and running his gently up my waist and ribs, grazing the sides of my breasts. My skin tingled with need, and I arched against him, seeking more. I threaded my fingers through his hair, until my hands cupped the back of his head, and I pulled him closer to me.

He growled low in his throat and pulled back briefly, rearranging me on his lap so I sat straddling him. I pulled his mouth back to mine and slid my tongue against his. I could feel the evidence of his desire hard against me and I pressed myself provocatively against it. I ran my palms down his body until I found the buttons of his breeches and I deftly freed him from the constraints of his clothing.

He leaned back into the chair, maneuvering my voluminous skirts out of our way, rucking them up until I felt the heat of him pressing urgently against me, filling me, stretching me. I muffled my moan against his shoulder, and he rubbed his face against the side of my neck, pressing his lips on my collarbone. He reared back and our eyes met. One heartbeat, two, three. We were perfectly still, suspended in the moment, reveling in the way our bodies fit together.

Then I rolled my pelvis and began to move. I found the angle I liked and set a brutal pace. His eyes never left mine and he gripped my hips in desperation as I brought myself to a quick orgasm. My vision blurred, as I collapsed against him, stars exploding behind my eyes. I felt him surge into me, once more, twice more, and then heard his answering groan as his body shuddered against mine.

Thirty-Seven
Sweet Songs & Sticky Salve

I hummed the opening lines of 'Imagine' by Lennon as I ground dried lavender in my pestle. The girls and I had been hard at work the last few weeks restocking the supplies in the surgery, grinding herbs, and prepping salves. We had ordered quite a few items for the *château*, along with the items for Madame Cariou from the apothecary in town. Esme had come with me when I visited her to bring her the supplies she requested, but other than that, I hadn't seen her.

Although I was sure we weren't as busy as Madame Cariou— the *château* had nonetheless been a revolving door of injuries and illnesses, both large and small. The arrival of warmer days had the wildflowers bursting into bloom, scenting the air sweetly, while we planted our seedlings in the kitchen gardens. The lengthening hours of sunlight brought hope and promise, but it also seemed to herald an increase in outdoor incidents.

Thoughtfully, I lifted the ground lavender and breathed deeply of its calming, comforting scent. Humming to myself, I added it to a mixture of sweet almond oil and melted beeswax I had warmed on the brazier, to create a soothing salve for burns. The lavender was known to promote the healing of the skin, and the beeswax formed a protective layer.

I wondered if I should add honey for its antibacterial properties, or if it would make the salve too sticky, and decided to make a batch each way to evaluate it. Carefully I poured the hot mixture into glass pots to cool and harden. I set aside one of the small pots of completed lavender salve I'd made earlier, to bring upstairs with me later. I'd found that it helped me relax and fall asleep more easily when my thoughts raced and kept me awake.

I sensed Gabriel in the room the moment before he wrapped his arms around me from behind and pressed a quick kiss against my collarbone. I turned and wrapped my arms around his neck, lifting my lips to his.

"How do you manage to be so silent that I can't hear you coming?" I demanded with a smile.

He shrugged. "I'm not that quiet, you were just lost in your thoughts. What was that you were humming?"

"Oh. . . just a song I heard once. I'll sing it to you later."

He nodded and handed me a letter that I hadn't realized he was holding. I perused it quickly and pursed my lips doing quick calculations in my head.

"Your friend is coming to visit in. . . " I counted again on my fingers to double-check my math. "About two weeks?"

"*Oui.*"

"Good. We will be ready for him. Is there anything special we should do?"

Gabriel tilted his head as if considering my question, then shook it. "He isn't one much for balls and the like, and there's plenty of that in his life already. We will do some hunting while he is here and let him enjoy his time away from the city." He drew his brows together in thought and added, "It will be good to discuss the finer points of what is happening in court with him. Much as I prefer to be here, there's so little news that makes its way into the country."

I handed the letter back to him and pressing both hands to the small of my back, I stretched, relieving the ache that had coalesced there while I was working.

Gabriel's hands settled on my shoulders and squeezed gently, making me glance up at him, mid-stretch. I raised an eyebrow inquiringly at him.

"How have you been feeling?" he murmured.

"A bit tired, but I'm well otherwise." I shrugged, making light of the discomfort I'd been feeling for several weeks now.

What I assumed was merely stress in the days prior to Esme and Luc's wedding, hadn't dissipated as I expected it to after the excitement had settled down.

"Ava." He didn't raise his voice, but I could hear the exasperation in it regardless.

I rolled my shoulders. *I hate to make a big deal out of something I feel is a passing ailment.*

"Truly, I'm all right," I said stubbornly.

He shot me a wounded look but leaned down and pressed a kiss to my forehead.

"Very well then, I will see you at lunch."

My hands fell to my sides. I felt strangely weepy as I watched him walk out of the surgery. I knew he was upset I hadn't opened up to him. *Was I wrong not to?*

I had always hated dumping my problems on other people and I had to remind myself that it was normal in a healthy relationship to lean on your spouse when you needed them.

I rapidly blinked away the tears I felt gathering and pressed the heels of my palms to my eyes. I took a few deep breaths, taking in the familiar scent of the stillroom and letting it relax me. Suddenly, I felt overwhelmed by a wave of exhaustion, and I hurriedly closed the jars of salve I'd been making, tidied up, and made for the stairs.

Maybe, I should stop pretending everything is fine and listen to my body. I obviously need more sleep than I am getting. A proper lie down was in order.

He strode out of the *château* and made his way to the corral, his long legs quickly eating up the distance to the fenced area behind the stables. Ava's refusal to tell him how she was truly feeling had him feeling flummoxed. He knew she'd been feeling ill; it had been obvious on a few occasions, and he couldn't understand why she insisted on denying it. He rubbed a hand hard over his face in frustration.

They had come a long way since they'd met. She had confided in him about the visions and her suspicions about *la Vicomtesse de Argol*. They'd shared deep conversations about their hopes and fears, and yet. . . and yet he often felt that she was holding a piece of herself back.

He rested his arms on the top rail of the fence and gazed out sightlessly at the horses being worked by the stable lads. She wasn't like the typical lady. Honestly, it was one of the things that he loved about her. Her fierce independence and her self-reliance were unusual and refreshing. She was resourceful, intelligent, and funny. He didn't even mind that she was intensely stubborn. . . other than the fact that she didn't seem to want to trust him with whatever was bothering her.

"Gabriel!"

A hand warmly clasped his back, jarring him out of his reverie.

He turned his head, blinking against the bright sun. "Luc," he nodded. "I was going to come find you soon."

"Well, I found you first." Luc rested one foot on the bottom rail of the fence and nodded toward the corral. "How is everything coming along here?"

In truth, Gabriel had no idea. He hadn't been paying any attention to the exercises the horses were being put through, but he shaded his eyes with his hand and watched them for a moment before answering.

"They're doing well. Flamme is taking after Automne." A note of pride entered his voice as he gestured at a bright, spirited filly that Automne had sired three years prior.

"She's a beautiful horse," agreed Luc. He shifted slightly. "Which reminds me, I spoke to the stable lads this morning and Jean-Paul Le Gall said he expects Minuit's foaling will be soon. He said she's showing all the signs. . . "

"*Merde*," he whispered under his breath.

He wondered if she knew and guessed that she likely did not. A broad smile spread across his face as he turned and made his way back to the *château*, leaving Luc mid-sentence to stare after his retreating back.

My eyelashes lifted groggily and promptly shut again as a frown puckered the skin between my eyebrows. I opened my eyes feeling disoriented and tiredly took in the golden glow of candlelight. *Dammit, I slept a great deal longer than I meant to if it's dark already.*

I stretched sleepily, feeling absurdly comfy. My stomach rumbled, a not-so-subtle reminder that it was empty.

"Good evening, *ma belle*. You must be famished." Gabriel stood up from one of the chairs that sat cozily by the fire and put down the book he'd been reading.

I sat up in bed, slightly embarrassed that I'd slept so late, as he walked over and sat beside me. "What time is it? Did I miss supper?"

Tenderly tucking a stray curl behind my ear, he shook his head, a smile playing around his lips. "I asked Mademoiselle Ollivier to send a tray up for us. I thought we might dine in our room tonight. I didn't want to wake you."

I caught his hand in mine and kissed his knuckles spontaneously. His thoughtfulness was more than I deserved, considering how I'd refused to confide in him earlier today. Tears welled up in my eyes at the thought.

The smile melted from his face and was replaced with concern. "What's this, *mon cœur*? Why are you crying?"

I smiled at him radiantly through my tears and shook my head. "I love you. I don't know how I could be so lucky to have found you."

"I am the lucky one," he said as he frowned slightly. "You frightened me. You're well?"

I nodded and scooted closer to him on the bed, leaning against him, as he wrapped an arm around me.

"Are you going to tell me what's going on with you? In truth?" he asked softly, his lips against my hair.

I sighed. "In truth, I don't quite know." I looked down at my skirt as I pleated the material like an accordion. Noticing my reaction, I deliberately stopped. "I haven't felt like myself for the last month. No, perhaps the last two months. I thought at first that it was the stress and excitement of getting ready for Esme and Luc's wedding, and for Amélie's family to be here. . ."

"And now?" he prompted when I didn't continue.

I shrugged. "Now I don't know. I expect I should be back to normal by now, but I find that I am always exhausted, even when I haven't done anything particularly strenuous. My appetite has been strange as well. I can't seem to stomach *petit déjeuner* and then I am ravenous later in the day. . . " My voice trailed off as the symptoms I was listing coalesced into a flashing neon sign in my head.

Gabriel watched my face as understanding dawned. He smiled, leaning down to kiss the tip of my nose.

"Could you be with child?" he asked delicately, but I could hear the note of hope that refused to be restrained in his voice.

How could I have been so unaware? I nodded once, a tiny nod of affirmation.

"I must be. I can't believe it didn't dawn on me until now." I thought back quickly, trying to recall when I'd last had my courses. I'd never been regular, but it had been an unusually long time. "You're not surprised," I said accusingly at the wide smile that stretched across his handsome face.

"I only just figured it out this afternoon," he admitted. "I realized that the ailments you were stubbornly trying not to complain about were very similar to Amélie's when she was carrying the *bebes*." He shrugged, a little self-consciously. "I sleep beside you every night and it's been quite some time since you weren't—ah, able to—mmh, make love." He muttered the last few words and his face looked flushed under his stubble. I had to hold back a giggle at his obvious discomfort.

I put my fingers to his mouth to silence him and then replaced my fingers with my lips. Pulling back slightly, I studied his face. "Are you happy?"

His eagerness, and joy, shone in the depths of his quicksilver eyes, putting to bed any lingering uncertainties I felt. He swallowed hard as if he was struggling to vocalize his thoughts. He took my hands between both of his, and I felt the strength in them, the calloused fingers, the work-roughened skin of his palms, and he squeezed gently.

"I am utterly humbled, grateful and excited, and a wee bit terrified," he said huskily.

That about sums it up. *Me too.*

Thirty-Eight
Thyme for Pirates

I rose and brushed the loose soil off my hands onto my working apron, glancing down at my basket, and mentally measured whether I'd collected a sufficient amount of mint. It had just begun to unfurl tender, green leaves and I knew it would be far more abundant in another month's time. Judiciously, I eyed what was left and decided that what I had picked would have to be enough until it had a chance to grow more.

Next on my list was checking the thyme and gathering any available oregano. It was quite early in the season for much to be growing, but some of the perennial herbs were beginning to fill in and I was eager to stay ahead of the seemingly endless demands of the *château's* stillroom.

Basket in hand, I moved toward the far end of the garden where the oregano had taken over a corner. I passed the thyme and frowned at the scarce patch, making a mental note to see about planting more. I paused to admire the asparagus, which was growing rapidly and would be ready for harvesting within the next week or two. My mouth watered at the thought of fresh, grilled asparagus with sautéed garlic.

The sound of horses laboring up the hill drifted past the *château* to the kitchen garden where I was gathering. I turned, shading my eyes with my hand against the bright sunlight. We were expecting *le Comte de Saint-Denis*, Gabriel's friend Phillipe, any day now. Nervously, I smoothed my apron down over my day gown and removed my gardening gloves, dropping them and my sheers in with the herbs. I inspected my hands quickly for remaining bits of earth and then shrugged my shoulders to myself. I doubted Gabriel would be friends with the man if he were the type to judge a woman for working in the garden.

I grabbed my bounty, and strode in the most ladylike fashion I could manage, toward our guest pausing to make sure the garden gate latched properly behind me. I arrived just as le Comte was dismounting his horse; a gorgeous stallion with a gleaming, black coat.

I offered my slightly grubby hand and beamed. "*Monsieur le Comte—*"

"To my friends I am Phillipe, please." He gave me a shrewd once-over from beneath heavy-lidded, green eyes, as he bent over my hand. "I see why Gabriel married you," he murmured.

I smiled tentatively at him. I would never get used to the casually suggestive manner in which Frenchmen spoke to women.

"Gabriel will be so pleased you're here. He's dealing with a few things at the moment, but I expect him back before lunch."

He smiled urbanely and gestured to the immaculate gentleman standing beside him.

"My valet, Monsieur Tomas Lacoste."

Monsieur Lacoste bowed low in my direction. "*Enchanté Madame la Vicomtesse.*"

I smiled politely and spotting Jean-Paul, nodded at him to take le Comte's horse's reins. "Jean-Paul will see to your horses, please come in. How was your journey?" I inquired, as I led the way into the spotless hall where Madame Pichon and Monsieur Dubois were awaiting le Comte.

"It was. . . " le Comte paused for a moment. "Enlightening," he settled on.

I raised a brow at him. "That's an interesting adjective. What made it enlightening?"

He raised a self-deprecating shoulder in a shrug. "I have not left the area surrounding my *château* or Paris in some time. It was educational to see what state some of the other parts of *ma belle* France are in."

I frowned. Gabriel was not going to like Phillipe's news from the sounds of it.

"Gabriel will be eager to talk it over with you." I glanced at our butler as *le Comte's* valet carried in two heavy-looking valises, sweat breaking out on his brow. "Monsieur Dubois will show Monsieur Lacoste where you'll be staying." Directing my attention back to Phillipe, I added, "If you'll excuse me, while I freshen up, I'll join you in *le salon* for refreshments in a moment. Madame Pichon will see you in."

I was wiping tears of laughter from my eyes when Gabriel found Phillipe and me in the salon hours later.

"What's so funny?" asked Gabriel, one brow raised as I rose and tilted my face up to receive his kiss.

"Your friend was just telling me about some of your exploits when you visited him at *la université*," I explained.

"Ah, I have a few stories I could share about Phillipe as well," replied Gabriel with a sardonic grin.

He strode over to Phillipe and clapped his back enthusiastically. "Phillipe! It's been far too long. How is Charlotte?"

"She's well. Has the young macaronis falling all over themselves in an attempt to win her hand." He shook his head. "She wants no part of them, of course."

Gabriel laughed. "As stubborn as ever, is she?"

"As hardheaded as Amélie," he said ruefully. "At least she came to her senses and married old Mathieu, eh? How are they, by the way? I don't suppose we might see them while I'm here? I would love to see him."

"Perhaps. I'll send word to them in the morning. I thought we would do some hunting during your stay. I'm sure Mathieu would like to join us for that. I'm awaiting word from one of our shipping contacts as well."

"Excellent." A grin flashed across *Le Comte's* face. "Paris has been far too dull of late. I'm in desperate need of a bit of adventure."

I grimaced and Gabriel, catching my expression, barked out a laugh. "Ava prefers for my life to be a bit less adventurous."

"Ah, well. I cannot blame her. I envy you a wife who cares enough for your wellbeing that she wishes a boring life upon you."

Gabriel paused as he was refilling Phillipe's glass and met my eyes warmly. "I consider myself extremely lucky to have married Ava. I hope that you find such happiness as I have found, my friend."

Taking his glass, Phillipe raised it in salute. "To you and your beautiful wife. May I be so lucky." He downed his cognac in a single swallow.

I lay in bed, still half asleep, languidly running my fingers through Gabriel's hair. These quiet, stolen moments; when it was just the two of us cocooned in our nest of furs and blankets, were my favorite part of the day. The last few weeks had passed in a flurry of activity, and forced repose, with both Gabriel and Esme hovering worriedly over me, constantly checking that I had enough food and rest. It was heartwarming, but I was beginning to feel a bit smothered, and I was hoping that *le Comte's* visit would provide a bit of a distraction from me and the baby.

So far, it looked as though Phillipe was going to deliver in the diversion arena. Gabriel had stayed up late into the night catching up with his friend, and coming to bed more than a little intoxicated, the last two nights. Although I missed his warm, solid presence beside me, I was so tired that falling asleep without him hadn't been as difficult as I imagined it would be.

Mathieu was expected to arrive within the week, and as much as I enjoyed him, I was dreading his arrival as it meant that the men would likely be moving goods again. Although I appreciated the importance of Gabriel's endeavors, I hated the dangerous aspect of it. Just thinking about the potential pitfalls made my stomach clench and twist upon itself with nerves.

"What's wrong *mon cœur*?" Gabriel's deep voice broke into my reverie.

"Hmm?"

"You sighed. What are you thinking about?"

"Oh… I was just thinking about what you said about your work. I expect you have a new shipment arriving?"

"Mmph. We do. Not a moment too soon either. The last two ships didn't make it. I'm hearing reports that those damned Barbary pirates have been raiding unceasingly. I fear that we've lost the cargo from both those shipments."

My brow furrowed. Pirates? Was he serious?

"You haven't mentioned piracy before."

He shifted position, snuggling me down beside him, my head resting on his chest, and wrapped an arm protectively around me.

"To be honest, we've been fortunate up until recently. They've always posed a threat and been problematic, but some of our ships have had to cut closer to the area they tend to operate in. I imagine your family must have dealt with it as well. Roussillon is much closer to the Barbary states. They don't come out into the Atlantic as much, aye?"

He answered me with the assumption that I knew what he meant, but actually, I didn't know. It reminded me how much I hadn't learned or thought of. Sometimes days went by without my feeling like an imposter, and at other times, it slapped me in the face. I longed to tell Gabriel my unbelievable story, but I held back. *How can I tell him now? How upset will he be that I withheld the truth all this time?*

Our entire relationship was essentially built on a series of lies, and it killed me to think about what it would do to us if I told him. *When* I told him, I corrected myself, for I knew it was inevitable.

"Ava?"

I pressed myself closer to him and listened to the steady, reassuring thump beneath my ear in response to his unspoken question. I felt his hand drift up and settle in my hair, his strong fingers seeking the sore muscles in my neck where I store all my anxiety. I could feel my nerves melting away as he gently kneaded. My eyes felt heavy. It was ridiculous. I had a full night of sleep, yet I was still so very tired. Perhaps, I would stay in bed just a little bit longer.

Thirty-Nine
Roots and Rot

The waiting was the worst by far. No one could convince me otherwise.

The men, Mathieu, Phillipe, and my dear Gabriel among them, had all left in high spirits early this morning. I knew better than to expect them back for several days, but I couldn't help but jump in anticipation at every little noise. A deep foreboding filled me, that I couldn't seem to shake. I'd forced myself to smile cheerfully when they left, but I'd been teeming with dread inside.

It didn't help that I'd had unusually vivid dreams, or nightmares rather, the last few nights. They felt so viscerally real that I'd woken up with tears on my cheeks one time, and Gabriel had awoken me when I'd been screaming brokenly in my sleep another time.

The dreams were a jumbled mess of the past and events that hadn't happened yet. I replayed Carri's fall overboard like a broken record. Confusingly mixed into the disjointed scenes of terrifyingly stormy seas, were visions of blood, prison, and guillotines.

Were my dreams a portent of the Revolution to come? Were they a warning to leave and go back to my own time? It wrenched my heart to think of leaving Gabriel. Not that I had any idea how such a thing might even be accomplished. How did one travel through time? It had happened to me accidentally, and I still wasn't sure what the catalyst had been. But I had found an unexpected love here, friendship as well. My newfound family was balm to my battered soul, and I knew that absolutely nothing awaited me back in the twentieth century.

I sighed and gathered my shawl and my foraging basket. Some fresh air and a bit of productivity would do me good. Perhaps, it would even take my mind off my fears. *The men will be fine.*

I walked through the gardens and made for the path that led away from the cliffs and toward the woods, immediately spotting a cluster of mushrooms growing near the base of a rotting tree, set down my basket, and began cutting them away. I took a deep cleansing breath of the resin-scented air as I carefully packed the mushrooms into my basket. If I found more, we would have enough for stew. My mouth watered at the thought.

I glanced over my shoulder and smiled to see Esme approaching. I leaned into her embrace and pulled back to study her face appraisingly. She looked a bit wan and downcast, not unlike how I'd been feeling earlier today.

"What's wrong?"

Her eyes filled with tears even as she shook her head in denial. Surprised at her reaction, I set my things down and wrapped my arms around her. This was the cue for the floodgates to burst open. I could do nothing but hold her and make shushing sounds like one would make to a small child, as her petite body was racked with sobs.

Her tears soaked through my shawl as I gently rocked her. Little by little, the torrent subsided, and she eventually lifted her head off my shoulder, sniffling and red-eyed. I pulled a clean handkerchief from my pocket and handed it to her wordlessly. She wiped her eyes and blew her nose before giving me a watery smile.

"Thank you."

"You would have done the same for me," I replied simply.

"Aye." She nodded in acknowledgment.

"Do you want to talk about it?"

A long sigh shuddered through her frame and her shoulders slumped. "I'm worried about Luc. He insists that he is fine, but I can tell that something is amiss. . . and to be honest, I hate this business with the shipping. He says that it's perfectly safe, but of course it isn't. What if they get caught?" she bit her lip in consternation.

"It's not safe, Esme. We all know that there are risks involved with what they are doing. The men know it too, although I suspect they pretend there isn't because they thrive off the adventure, and don't wish to worry us." I paused and ran my tongue over my lips, wondering what I should say and what I shouldn't. I took a breath. "What they're doing is noble, their intentions are pure. But I understand if you prefer that Gabriel not involve Luc any longer—"

"*Non*," interjected Esme. "Luc would never forgive me for going behind his back."

"Of course, he would forgive you," I protested.

"Well. . .yes. Perhaps he would. It's more that I couldn't live with myself if I prevented him from taking part with the rest of the men. He would have to decide to stop on his own."

"I understand," I said sympathetically, knowing there was nothing else to say on the matter of smuggling. "Was there something else? You said something is amiss."

"That's likely what has me more worried," she admitted a line forming between her brows. "He's been complaining of stomach pains the last week or two. He's making light of it, but I see the look on his face sometimes. He's in far more pain than he's letting on."

I gripped both her hands in mine urgently. "It just began? Are there other symptoms?"

Esme drew back slightly in alarm, surprised, no doubt, at the note of panic lacing my voice.

"*Oui*, it began after we were married."

"Other than that, what else has changed? Is he eating anything different?"

"No—no," she stuttered. "I don't believe so. What's wrong? Your reaction is not what I expected." Doubt was edging its way into her expression.

I shook my head, unable to put my thoughts into words. "Try to think, try to remember if anything has changed. Let me know as soon as you figure it out. Tell me immediately if it worsens."

She took a step back, concern etching lines into her face. "I will," she answered with determination. "I must go. I will see you tomorrow."

I nodded mutely and watched her hurry away, unease clawing its way up from my belly to my throat. Turning around, I retched neatly onto the exposed tree roots behind me.

Forty
A Bitter Bite of Steel

Gabriel soundlessly shifted his weight from one foot to the other. He was crouched down, hidden behind the limestone rocks and shadows, waiting for Luc's signal from further down the beach. His legs were beginning to cramp, they'd been anticipating the ship's arrival for an unusually long time. Beside him, Mathieu changed his position as well.

Neither man spoke, but a sense of disquiet seemed to fill the silence, broken only by the distant sound of crashing waves and the occasional briny, breeze. On the cliffs above them, Phillipe and Armand waited with the horses in a small copse of trees.

He let out a silent breath, and thought longingly of Ava, waiting for him at home, carrying their first child in the safety of her womb. Her slender body wasn't yet showing the signs of pregnancy, but the midwife had assured them that this was not unusual for first babies. He was unable to hold back a smile as he pictured how she would look in a few months; belly round, long, curly hair flowing down her back. He felt himself get hard at the thought and groaned internally. He shifted, unobtrusively seeking relief from breeches that were suddenly too tight.

The tension in the air mounted as the minutes crept tortuously by. *La bite de la baleine* had assured them that tonight was the night, but the utter lack of movement on the beach made Gabriel leery. He and Mathieu had met dozens of ships and moved countless goods across the dark countryside over the last few years. Their operation generally ran smoothly. They seldom ran into trouble with the authorities. Over the last few months, however, the situation across France had devolved. He was beginning to feel that the time to continue to smuggle in relative safety was rapidly coming to an end.

He glanced at his pocket watch, waiting for the clouds to part so that the moon might illuminate the time for him. The light briefly flashed across the rocks where they were hidden. Half past ten. They'd been waiting for hours. As the heavy, opaque clouds scudded across the face of the moon, it lit up the sea for an instant, giving Gabriel a glimpse of a ship approaching stealthily in the dark. The hairs on his arms prickled in trepidation, as the slight breeze shifted.

Almost noiselessly, Mathieu spoke under his breath, "Something is not right."

Gabriel nodded imperceptibly.

Why hadn't Luc and Timothée given the signal yet? If he had spotted the ship, surely, they had glimpsed it as well. A horse's whinny carried to them in the abruptly still night air, and in the split second of silence that followed it, Gabriel could hear his heartbeat rushing in his ears.

"*Merde,*" he swore softly. "*Fils d'une chienne sournoise et menteuse.*"

The tranquil evening was rent by a cacophony of sound as a bullet ricocheted off a nearby rock and buried itself in the sand less than a foot from where Gabriel and Mathieu were hidden. The dark was suddenly filled with the screams of men and horses. Gabriel sensed that Mathieu was about to leap out of their hiding spot in retaliation, and his hand snaked out and grabbed his friend's arm, stilling him, and pushing him further down behind the rocks.

"Fool! They don't know where we are," he hissed. "Don't give our position away."

"But—"

"*Non*. Think, Mathieu. What weapons do you have on you?" he demanded, as he swiftly and silently loaded his rifle.

Mathieu let out a muted rush of air, as he assessed the situation and reined himself in. Gabriel checked his knives, powder, and shot as he waited for his friend to load his rifle. Their eyes met wordlessly in the chaos around them and in perfect unison, with the practiced movements of men used to watching each other's backs— they moved. They stuck to the shadows, making no sound as they crept in the sand toward the fighting.

The uncommonly dark night, and the drifting smoke settling like fog over the beach, made it difficult to make out who had attacked his men, but as the moon played peekaboo with the clouds he caught a glimpse of the unmistakable French naval uniform. He spied Timothée fighting them off three against one and sped in his direction. Mathieu advanced toward Luc who was holding off two men, his back up against a sheer cliff.

Gabriel rushed at an older naval officer and rammed him with his shoulder from behind just as the man was about to smash Timothée over the head with his rifle. Timothée spared a split second to toss Gabriel a grateful look and then continued to circle, crouching low, one knife in each hand. Gabriel spun and kicked the second officer's rifle out of his hands, and then hurtled himself on top of him, grappling to restrain the man.

He caught a glimpse of his opponent's face and was surprised to notice that this one was young, younger than Gabriel was. His face was smooth and unlined, and his eyes were light and gleamed in the fickle moonlight. The boy fought with a wiry strength and rage that made him astonishingly hard to hold down. Gabriel registered this with a faint sense of surprise, which the younger man took advantage of, bucking Gabriel off and then rolling over, wrestling him down into the sand.

Gabriel grunted as the air whooshed out of his lungs, and cursed to himself as he twisted, trying to wrangle him off. He reached down for the knife hidden in his boot and managed to get his fingertips on the hilt. Straining, his fingers slippery with sweat, he struggled to wiggle it free.

'*Dieu, merci,*' he silently sent up when he had it snuggly in the palm of his hand. He raised his knee, seeking to disable the muscular young man as he brought his hands up to his face, seeking to thrust him off. He felt hands on his throat, thumbs pressing down against his windpipe, and knew he had to move before he lost consciousness.

Grasping a handful of cold sand, he closed his eyes and shoved it into his adversary's face. He felt the boy's body stiffen in shock and took his element of surprise. He locked his legs around his body, and using his weight, and the momentum he'd gained, he rolled them down the slope of the beach toward the water's edge.

They landed in a tangled heap, gasping, but Gabriel was now on top; an advantage he wouldn't lose again since he was the heavier of the two men. He pressed his forearm across his throat and raised his dagger, pressing it warningly against his neck.

Panting, Gabriel opened his mouth, but before he could utter a word he felt bitter-cold steel slip between his ribs. Pain rippled across his torso, but his adrenaline was so high, it barely registered. He forced his arm down harder on the boy's throat, feeling vindicated when the young man began to panic, the whites of his eyes showing as they rolled frantically. His mouth opened, silently gaping like a fish out of water, taking its strangled last breaths. Gabriel heard a sound behind him, and then the world went black.

FORTY-ONE
COGNAC STITCHES

He'd been aware of the steady, rolling movement in some distant, detached manner for some time. He felt like he stood outside of his body; watching a party of travelers as they jostled their way uncomfortably down the rutted, dirt lane. There was a vague, hazy, throbbing discomfort that kept time with the constant clopping of the horse's hooves.

The men were talking quietly and soberly amongst themselves. For the most part, the words were unintelligible, but bits of conversation drifted into his consciousness, and he attempted with the aloof interest of a casual observer to make sense of the words.

"—much longer?"

"At least another day. . . Will he—"

"—blood. . . Should we stop at— "

Something jostled him and an agony of pain bloomed across his body, stealing the breath from his lungs.

When the velvety, black curtain lifted again, his left arm was prickly and numb, his head felt like it'd been stuffed with cotton, and his mouth was as arid as a desert. Through cracked, chapped lips, he tried to form words. But, no one heard him over the unceasing beat of dozens of hooves rhythmically hitting packed earth.

He licked his lips and tried again. "Water," he croaked.

The nauseating motion of the horse came to an abrupt halt and a moment later someone was holding a water skin to his mouth. He gulped greedily, thirstily, but it was taken away too soon, he was still parched. He felt water dribble down his chin and feebly tried to wipe it away, but his hand didn't respond to his brain's command.

"Slowly, *mon ami*."

Gabriel knew that voice. Trying to place it, he blearily opened his eyes. Phillipe's blurry face stared back at him in concern.

"How do you feel?"

"Terrible," he said concisely and promptly threw up the contents of his stomach.

The remainder of the everlasting, hellacious trip passed in a muddle of fitful sleep, broken by unbearable pain, nausea, and hallucinations once the fever set in. When they carried him into the *château*, he was barely cognizant of the change in scenery except for the moment when he caught a glimpse of Ava's beautiful, pale face.

"What happened?" I asked briskly as they gently laid him on the bed.

Breathe.

I wanted to scream and cry and throw things, but I had to hold it together for Gabriel. I listened attentively, while Mathieu explained that they'd been set up by their informant. Sold out to the Navy, who was apparently under orders to crack down on the smuggling that was running rampant across the country.

"There was a fight?"

Phillipe, sporting an impressively black eye, nodded. "It was an ambush. We were vastly outnumbered, there were at least twenty of them. Gabriel was cut. . . I don't know how bad it is, but it hasn't stopped bleeding, and he was smashed on the back of the head with a rock."

I took a deep breath in an attempt to steady my nerves.

"And the rest of the men? Is everyone else all right?"

"Gabriel was injured the worst. Timothée has a broken arm and a few shallow scrapes. It's nothing serious."

Mademoiselle Noemi hurried into the chamber with Esme and Luc hot on her heels. Esme was already directing Noemi to get hot water and cloths for bandages, as she set up the items she had grabbed from the stillroom on the table by the bed. Her worried gaze met mine before she concentrated her attention on Luc.

"Fetch Madame Cariou. Tell her it's urgent."

Luc brushed a quick kiss against Esme's cheek before he bowed to me and made his way hurriedly to the door. Madame Pichon appeared, and Esme sent Phillipe and Mathieu out with her.

"See that the men are fed," she ordered competently taking charge.

Madame Pichon glanced at me, and I nodded simply.

"Mathieu, Phillipe. . . Thank you for getting him back so quickly. Once we've stabilized him I'll send for you, and you can tell me the rest."

Mademoiselle Noemi reappeared with buckets of fresh water and after setting them down, she pulled a small stack of clean rags from her apron pockets. She hovered nervously by the table until Esme addressed her.

"Thank you, Mademoiselle Noemi, you may go. Please bring Madame Cariou up as soon as she arrives."

I scarcely noticed as they left, and I turned helplessly toward Esme. She wasted no time, embracing me closely for a moment, knowing intuitively that I needed the comfort desperately. Then she was all business.

"The knife wound first," she said briskly, opening the buttons of his overcoat, and waistcoat within seconds. Pushing the material back, I noticed that she faltered for an instant when she saw that his linen shirt was steeped in blood. The outermost layers of his garments were stiff where it had dried, but fresh, crimson blood was still seeping slowly through his shirt.

I took scissors from the table of supplies Esme had laid out and began cutting away the cloth so we could work unhindered. The right side of his body was completely drenched. I took a deep, steadying breath, and continued doggedly cutting away his linen until I revealed a hastily wrapped bandage that might have been white at one time but was now solidly burgundy. Without pausing, I cut the bandage away as well, until Esme and I could view the source of the constant trickle of blood.

Located on the right side of Gabriel's torso, was a deceptively small cut. The edges of the skin were jaggedly torn, as though the knife hadn't been as sharp as it might have been. The result was not a clean slice; but rather, a mangled mess of skin and tissue.

Esme handed me a clean cloth with warm water on it and I began to tenderly wash the area surrounding the wound, as she busied herself with another wet rag, this one presumably cool, which she placed on his forehead. As I worked on him my brow furrowed and I looked up at Esme questioningly.

"Do you think there's internal damage?"

She frowned. "I don't know." She ran her fingers over his ribs, counting under her breath, stopping just above the cut. "This is about where his liver should be. I don't know how deep the wound is; the entrance is relatively small. There's no way to see without injuring him further."

I bit my lip. "His liver should be able to repair itself if it is damaged, right?"

I knew already that the liver could regenerate itself, the only organ in the human body able to perform such a feat, but I was in sore need of reassurance that Gabriel would be okay.

Esme hesitated. "I believe it can, yes. . . although that's likely a better question for Madame Cariou. It's quite lucky that the injury is on the right side of his body. There are so many more organs to contend with on the left."

I crossed myself and moved on to the next question on my mind. "Stitches?"

"Absolutely. That wound is too big to close on its own."

"Can you hand me the bottle of cognac?" I asked.

She raised a brow at me but handed it over without a word of protest, watching with a faint air of skepticism as I poured the alcohol onto a clean rag and pressed it against Gabriel's injury. Carefully removing the rag, I splashed a small amount of additional cognac directly onto the wound, trying to aim it so that it went into the cut itself. I was worried most about infection if sand or dirt had gotten into it. Judging from the heat radiating off his body, and the way he was mumbling brokenly in his sleep, it had likely happened already.

"Should we wait for Madame Cariou?"

"*Non*. He's waited for days already. I don't think we should wait any longer."

"Can you?" I motioned toward the glass jar of sutures. "I don't think my hands are steady enough right now."

"Of course, Ava, you needn't ask."

We switched positions and I pulled a chair up the head of the bed and sat while Esme got to work. I brushed a stray lock of hair back off his forehead and noticed that it was full of sand. Taking another rag, I gently sponged the dirt, grit, and sweat off his face and neck before moving slowly down his body. His skin was stippled in goosebumps despite the beads of perspiration that stood on his forehead and temples. He was burning with fever.

I stood up and moved to the end of the bed, removing his leather boots and stockings. Then I pulled blankets from the carved, cedar chest that sat at the foot of the bed and carefully placed them over his lower half, before sitting back down.

I stared down at his chiseled face, stubble darkening the usually smooth planes and curves of it. His lips, normally so full and soft, were dry and cracked. I grabbed the pot of lavender salve and gently applied some to his mouth, running the tip of my finger across his kissable lips. His breath fanned out against my hand. It seemed steady at least. Tenderly, I turned his head so that he faced away from me and ran my fingers over the contours of his skull, searching for the injury that Phillipe had mentioned.

It didn't take long before I found a clump of hair, stubbornly glued with what I could only assume was dried blood. Beneath it was a sizable, swollen lump. I dipped a fresh rag in the bowl of water beside me and went to work on the matted hair, using my fingers to carefully separate the strands. I got the area as clean as I could manage given the circumstances, finishing just as Esme tied off the last stitch. She snipped the end off and stood up, stretching her lower back out.

"How's his head?"

"It must have been hit quite hard; it's still swollen. But I imagine it will heal all right. I'm more worried about his side."

She nodded, "I want to put a bandage and ointment on it, but we should wait so that Madame Cariou can see what we've done first." She side-eyed me. "I don't suppose you can stomach a bite to eat? I was thinking of having Mademoiselle Ollivier make me a plate."

"I'm famished actually," I admitted. "Can we eat here though? I don't want to leave him."

She shot a smile at me. "Of course. If I see the men, I'll have them come back up and fill us in, shall I?"

"Please. Thank you, Esme."

FORTY-TWO
"A Good Navy is not a Provocation to War. It is the Surest Guarantee of Peace."
-Theodore Roosevelt

I nibbled on a piece of cheese, before picking up my goblet of wine and taking a lengthy, strengthening sip. Carefully placing it back on the table, I raised my *serviette* to my mouth and dabbed. I chose a plump, red cherry, and paused with my fingers in midair as Phillipe and Mathieu took turns explaining what had transpired during their misadventure.

"I'm quite sure it was *la bite* that gave us away to the Navy—" muttered Mathieu angrily.

"*La bite*?" I interrupted questioningly.

"*Oui*. One of our informants. Nothing else makes sense."

I nodded and popped the cherry into my mouth, savoring the sweet, tart burst of flavor.

"So, explain to me how you were all able to get away? Presumably, the Navy didn't just let you all leave?"

"Ah, that's where *le Comte* comes in." Mathieu angled his head toward Phillipe.

"We lost the fight, that much was clear. But when I explained who we were, and demanded to see their officer in command, their attitude changed a bit." Phillipe smirked, but Mathieu's face grew serious.

"It was *Commandant* des Rochefort," he interjected concisely.

He said it just as I was swallowing a piece of cheese and I choked in surprise, sputtering. Both men jumped up in alarm, but I flapped my hand at them and swiped at my streaming eyes.

"I'm all right," I managed.

Mathieu gave me a narrow, disbelieving look, but continued speaking. "I thought you would remember the name. Gabriel mentioned him to me after you returned from Nantes. I didn't think it likely that we would run into him so far from his base, but perhaps he's been moved. . . " he mused.

I raised a brow in question, my throat still smarting from my near-death experience. I cautiously took a sip of wine.

"Somehow, Phillipe convinced the Navy that it was all a misunderstanding. It was quite a brilliant performance," he added admiringly.

Phillipe shook his head humbly. "I just thought we should pretend we were on the same side as the Navy. That we had heard about a smuggling ring in the area and had sought to provide support to the monarchy in a part of the coastline that we didn't think had a large, active presence of the Navy."

Mathieu chortled. "You should have heard him explaining to des Rochefort that while we had no idea who the true smugglers were, we heard rumors that they were expecting activity that night. He said there was no time to send word to the Navy for backup, so we took it upon ourselves to catch them."

Phillipe shrugged modestly. "Of course, we had no idea that the Navy was so close and already hot on the trail of the smuggling ring."

"Of course," I managed wryly.

I had to admit, it'd been a solid plan and had obviously worked since they were sitting before me now. I wasn't sure I would have thought up a plausible story that quickly myself.

"I imagine it helped that you are who you are," I added.

Phillipe and Mathieu both inclined their heads, silently acknowledging that the status of their birth likely played a part in saving their necks.

"Did des Rochefort recognize Gabriel?"

"As a matter of fact, he did," admitted Mathieu. "But Gabriel was unconscious the entire time that we were in the Navy's custody." He raised an elegant shoulder in a shrug. "So, he was unable to question him."

I grimaced and wondered if it would have had an influence one way or another.

"He didn't mention me, did he?"

"*Non,*" replied Mathieu softly. "I don't think you're in any danger from him. He wouldn't go after the wife of a noble. He's likely forgotten about you."

I rather doubted it. Men like des Rochefort didn't tend to forget women who had the balls to stand up to them and call them out for what they were. I left it alone for the moment, although the reappearance of *le commandant* made my stomach churn uneasily.

I stood up. "Thank you both for telling me the rest of the story and bringing him home safely."

"He would have done the same for us," answered Phillipe.

He was right of course, but I was grateful regardless.

"Has Luc returned? Has there been any word of Madame Cariou?"

The men exchanged a cautious glance, before Phillipe spoke, "No, her cottage was empty. Luc returned a little while ago."

I frowned and briefly wondered where she might be. "Right then, Esme, do you mind helping me bandage Gabriel's wound before you leave?"

"Of course, Ava!" she exclaimed, brushing crumbs off her hands as she stood and moved to the washstand.

Phillipe moved toward the bed. "We'll help."

I nodded my appreciation, moving Gabriel's dead weight to wrap the bandages around him would be much simpler with the men to lift and turn him.

Once the ointment was applied and the cloth was tightly bound about his torso, I hugged Esme and thanked the men.

Mathieu hesitated briefly before speaking his mind. "Are you staying with him tonight? Should you not try to get some sleep?"

I smiled at him appreciatively. "I'll get more sleep here, knowing I can hear him if he needs me than I would get in a separate room. But thank you."

Mathieu nodded unhappily. Phillipe sketched me a little bow and they all left, leaving Gabriel and me blissfully alone. Finally.

Untying my wrapper, I snuffed out all but the candle closest to the bed and cautiously crawled under the covers next to Gabriel, taking care not to bump into him. I curved my body protectively around his and closed my eyes tiredly. The reassuringly steady thump of his heart beneath my hand lulled me to sleep.

Garbled muttering and a muffled shout dragged me from the depths of a deep and dreamless sleep. I was so tired it took several long moments for the thrashing of Gabriel's arms and legs, and the events of the day to come flooding back to me. Sleepily I urged my sluggish limbs to react. My hand brushed over Gabriel's face in an attempt to soothe him, but I snatched it back as though scalded, my exhaustion ebbing away in a flash.

His skin felt dry and papery, like tinder about to burst into flames. I sat up and noted how far the candle had burned down. The early dawn light was creeping around the edges of the closed shutters, searching for a way in. I rubbed my hand over my face and stood. I hurriedly moved to the basin of water and wringing out a cloth laid it over his forehead. I half expected the rag to sizzle and steam from the heat of his body.

Where is Madame Cariou?

I thought it odd that Luc hadn't found her last night, but I'd been too tired to fully question her absence. Now, as I shrugged into my wrapper and tied the belt, I fought to recall what the men had said and remembered the look Mathieu and Phillipe had exchanged when I inquired.

I rang the bell and waited anxiously until I detected the hurried patter of footsteps tapping lightly down the corridor. I opened the door for Mademoiselle Noemi, who looked presentable but still half asleep. She bobbed a quick curtsey, her face flushed and concerned.

"Is his lordship well, Madame?" Her voice was threaded with a discernable ribbon of fear.

I managed a smile.

"He'll be quite all right, Mademoiselle. *Le Vicomte* is a bit feverish at the moment. Could someone please rouse Madame Esme to help me?"

"*Oui*, of course!"

"Oh, and by any chance, do you know where Madame Cariou might have gone?" I asked, striving for nonchalance.

She frowned in momentary concentration before her brow cleared.

"No Madame, but I will see if she left word with anyone."

"Thank you. I thought perhaps she mentioned it and I forgot."

"No wonder, Madame. It was a stressful afternoon and evening for you," she offered softly.

"Twas," I agreed. "Thank you Mademoiselle. Could you bring up fresh water, and if Madame Bleuzen or Mademoiselle Ollivier are in the kitchen, could you ask them to send a tray up?"

"*Oui,* Madame. They are already at work. I'll have something sent up directly."

As soon as she left I moved back to the bed, lifting the cloth from Gabriel's forehead and gently replacing it with a fresh one. I pressed the back of my hand to his cheek and winced at the heat radiating off him.

I closed my eyes, crossed myself, and offered up a swift, heartfelt prayer, wrenched from the depths of my being. Surely, having cast me into another time; alone and away from everyone I knew; God wouldn't also snatch away my newfound, tentative, hope and joy in life. Would he?

What will I do if Gabriel doesn't recover?

Tears sprang to my eyes, threatening to breach the dam and overflow onto my cheeks if I continued to wallow in self-pity. I shook my head, willing the moment of weakness away, and forced myself to focus on what I could do for Gabriel.

I lifted his head and managed to prop him up slightly with another pillow. His lips were dry, cracked, and colorless, so I tenderly rubbed a bit more of the lavender salve on them. Once Esme or Noemi returned, I would have them help me give him some water to drink. As I moved about, trying to make Gabriel more comfortable, my thoughts returned to Madame Cariou.

Where is she?

Forty-Three
"The Art of Dreams"
-Thomas Browne

The hours passed in a blur of colors and sounds that melded slowly into days. Time became hazy and indistinct, the way the sky and sea become indistinguishable from one another when fog rolls in, obscuring the horizon and making it impossible to tell where one ends and the other begins.

My world shrank to the confines of our room, revolving around Gabriel, as the fever raged within his body, and fought to obliterate the infection. Madame Cariou never appeared at the *château*, and no one seemed to know where she'd gone. It irked me every time I thought about it, so I tried valiantly to put it from my mind. My success was limited.

By the fifth day, Gabriel was noticeably thinner; the skin on his face stretching over his finely chiseled bones. On the sixth day, the pus and blood that had been seeping from his wound finally began to scab over. I watched anxiously for red streaks, a sign the wound was still infected. His incoherent ramblings in the depths of fevered hallucinations punctuated my days and nights.

I knew I wasn't bearing up well, when on the eighth day, Esme and Luc, sharing looks of concern, insisted that I bathe and sleep in one of the other rooms.

"You must take a break, Ava. If not for yourself, then for the sake of the child you carry."

I shook my head in protest, "I'm fine. Thank you, but I need to be here, in case he wakes up."

"Ava, please. Look at yourself." She took my hand and tugged me toward the small hand mirror that sat on my vanity.

I glanced at my reflection and had to admit— internally at least— that I looked terrible. Worse than Gabriel, perhaps. My hair was unkempt, my face looked wan and pale, and dark circles made my eyes appear sunken.

Sensing my hesitation, Esme pressed her advantage.

"Luc and I will be here with him. If anything changes, I promise to fetch you immediately."

I swayed on my feet as a wave of dizziness overcame me, and Esme took my arm, firmly leading me toward the door. As she half-dragged me into the corridor, she threw a glance over her shoulder at Luc.

She led me into one of the rooms we reserve for guests where a steaming bath, liberally scented with rose oil, awaited me. Clearly, they'd felt it was a foregone conclusion that I would give in. Fortunately for Esme, I was too tired to be miffed as she directed Noemi and Adrienne to help me undress.

I sank into the warmth of the tub and let the heat soothe the stiffness from my body. Tears welled up in my eyes as my muscles relaxed in increments. For the last eight days, I'd fueled my body out of sheer willpower, but I was beginning to show the signs of stress fractures, cracking the facade I'd been stubbornly showing everyone.

Wordlessly I let them wash my hair and body, and massage oil into my skin. When I stood up, letting the rapidly cooling water cascade back into the tub, another ripple of light-headedness washed over me. Adrienne wrapped a warm, plush cloth around me, and Noemi helped me step out, feeling as shaky as a newborn foal on her feet. They dressed me; brushed and plaited my hair, and tucked me into bed like a child. I sank into the open arms of sleep without a murmur of dissent.

The dream was vicious, as it always was. As I fought my way out of it, images from the nightmare rose to the surface, the way a leaf submerged in a dark pond will slowly reemerge from the depths, reflecting ghastly images of Dante's frozen hell into my consciousness.

The sweat on my skin was rapidly cooling, making me shiver. As I lay in the dark, it dawned on me that the dreams always seemed to strike when I was most vulnerable. There was something to that, I was sure of it, but there was no time for me to delve into it as the panic struck. Desperate to know how Gabriel was, I frantically tore at the bedclothes, which had wrapped sinuously around my legs, shackling me to the bed, and barreled down the hallway, bursting into our bedchamber.

Esme and Luc were sitting with their heads together, deep in heated conversation when I shoved the bedroom door open so hard it smashed into the stone wall. Their faces mirrored each other's shocked expressions before Esme jumped up and hurried to me.

"He's all right, Ava. There's been no change."

I sagged against her in relief, but straightened up within seconds, eager to see him for myself. "Thank you," I said as I approached the bed. "The two of you can go get some rest now, I feel much better since I got a bit of sleep."

They exchanged dubious looks at my outright lie. But Luc stood up and walked to Esme, bending to say something I couldn't catch in her ear. As I glanced over my shoulder at them, I noticed Luc seemed to have lost a few pounds. He appeared worn down and there were creases of pain bracketing his mouth. In a flash, I recalled the conversation I'd had with Esme. . . had it only been a week or two ago? It felt like a lifetime.

Amidst promises to check back in the morning, they walked out the door, Esme's hand tucked protectively into Luc's arm. I felt icy fingers of dread creep down my spine and settle in the pit of my stomach. I was certain that the illness I had foreseen for Luc had already begun to manifest. Frowning in concern, I told myself I would speak to Esme about it when they returned the following day.

I gazed down at Gabriel; watching the peaceful, regular, rise and fall of his chest, and felt my own anxious heartbeat gradually slow to match his. I let out a long, unsteady breath and felt some of the tension from my nightmare ebb away, like refuse being washed out to sea on a tidal change.

I lifted the blankets and edged into bed beside him. I was still tired to the depths of my bones. I wished he would wake up and smile at me. I ached for his warm, comforting touch. I missed the deep, steady murmur of his voice. I rested my head on his shoulder and closed my eyes.

"Please be okay," I whispered forlornly.

My hand drifted gently down his face, then back up to thread through his hair. I pressed my fingertips into his scalp, massaging it in tiny circles. The first time I'd massaged his head and neck he'd closed his eyes and groaned in ecstasy. A small smile touched the corners of my mouth as I remembered where that massage had led. I shifted closer to him, willing him to wake up.

"I need you. I love you. Don't leave me here alone."

Forty-Four

> "At the head of the harbor is a slender-leaved olive, and nearby it, a lovely and murky cave sacred to the nymphs called naiads."
>
> -Homer, The Odyssey

Gabriel's eyes were dry, and itchy, like he'd taken handfuls of sand, and rubbed them over his face, scratching his eyes until they burned. His mouth was parched, and his tongue felt thick and sluggish.

Moving his limbs was an insurmountable obstacle. He'd been weighed down, as though he'd walked along the beach filling his pockets full of smooth, heavy, ocean-tumbled stones, in preparation to be thrown into the deep green depths of the sea, so he would sink, sink, sink relentlessly down to the bottom, eventually lying amidst the waving fronds of seaweed, in the cave of the nymphs.

He welcomed it.

But something held him back. Something whispered that it was not his time. Someone was waiting for him.

His lashes lifted slowly, painstakingly. He imagined it might feel nicer to have them pried open with rusty pliers. The early morning sun seeped through the chinks in the shutters making everything hazy. Dust motes danced in the soft, golden light. Or perhaps, his eyes needed to adjust after their lack of use. There was a warm, solid weight pressed against him. Comforting and familiar.

Ava.

He plucked her name into his consciousness before he could even focus on the gilded curves of her precious face and held it to his heart like a talisman against evil. Her petite, compact body was nestled against his side, tendrils of dark, silky hair escaping her plait to curl against her neck. With a herculean effort, he lifted a hand to brush away a strand that was stuck to her cheek. She stirred and whimpered in her sleep but didn't awaken.

He studied her in the gloomy light. Took in the delicate, violet shadows beneath her eyes and wondered how ill he'd been, and for how long. The last thing he remembered was the fight on the beach. He'd been stabbed. . . he flinched slightly as he remembered, feeling the answering sting in his side where the icy metal of the knife slid between his ribs. *What happened next?*

Dieu, his head was pounding.

He shifted slightly, turning his head to take in the rest of the chamber. He was home, so they had gotten away or been released. Where were Mathieu, Phillipe, Luc, and the others? Had everyone made it out safely? His body tensed as his brain struggled to catch up and figure out what might have occurred.

Merde!

How long had he been unconscious?

Ava stirred and sleepily parted the heavy fringe of her eyelashes, revealing the calm, sea-green eyes that Gabriel loved. As if she sensed the change she lifted her head to look at Gabriel in astonishment, before throwing her arms around him. Weakly, he managed to wrap an arm around her lean, soft body. Crying, she lifted her tear-stained face to study his face, as though she could barely believe he was awake.

He opened his mouth to ask her the questions that were bursting in his head, but his voice came out like a frog's croak. She leaped out of bed, lithe as a dancer, poured him a cup of water from the jug on the table, and carefully lifted his head as she held it to his mouth.

He drank deeply, draining the contents in mere seconds.

"More," he managed.

She shook her head. "Wait a moment. That's the most you've had in days. I don't want it to come back up."

He would have argued with her if he didn't feel as weak as a newborn infant, and if her face didn't look so stern.

He took a breath, filling his lungs with sweet air. He could smell Ava's favorite rose oil wafting from the furs in their bed and her body.

"The men?"

She gave him a soothing smile. "They are all well. You were the only one seriously injured. Timothée has a broken arm, but it's been set, and I think it will heal nicely."

Gabriel felt some of the tension melt from his muscles. "What happened?"

She raised a brow as she fussed with the blankets. "You don't remember?"

He struggled to sit up in bed. He felt he was at a disadvantage lying there like an invalid. The room began to spin, forcing him to close his eyes to gain his bearings. Ava carefully propped him up with extra cushions and pressed her soft, cool hand against his brow anxiously.

"How do you feel?"

"Fine," he answered short-temperedly, feeling dangerously close to nausea.

She withdrew her hand, hurt clouding her normally clear, sparkling eyes. She sat on a chair beside the bed and carefully folded her hands in her lap, studying them for several long seconds before she lifted her head to meet his eyes. He felt a pang of regret for being the one to put that expression on her face.

"Ava—"

She raised her hand to stop him. "I only know what Mathieu and Phillipe told me. You were ambushed on the beach by the Navy. I assume you remember that?"

"Aye."

"You were wounded in the side, I think your liver was damaged, but you were incredibly lucky. A few *lignes* away and I don't know what would have happened." Her voice wavered and she paused to regain her composure. "You were hit on the back of the head as well. . . I don't know what with. Phillipe somehow managed to convince the Navy that you were on their side, and it was all a misunderstanding. He can tell you the story better I'm sure, but suffice it to say, they let you all go. You were largely unconscious on the way home, and by the time you arrived here, you were already feverish." Ava stopped again to take a deep breath before continuing. "Mathieu told me that des Rochefort was heading the inquiry into the smuggling ring. He's not here any longer. He left to return to *Trégoudan* two days ago. He didn't want Amélie to worry over much at his long absence."

"*Nom de Dieu.*"

"Quite. Mathieu said that des Rochefort recognized you."

"*Putain de bordel de merde.*"

"Mathieu didn't seem to think that he would be inclined to come looking for me but I'm not sure if I trust that assumption."

Gabriel raised a trembling hand, internally cursing his weakness, and passed it through his hair. He winced when his fingers skimmed over the tender spot at the back of his head. "Ava, I'm sorry. I'm not feeling fine. I didn't intend to be irritable with you."

He reached out a conciliatory hand in supplication. After a brief hesitation, she placed her petite, but surprisingly strong hand in his, and he curled his fingers around it gratefully. She closed her eyes temporarily and he could see the battle for control on her face. When she reopened them, they were swimming with tears.

It felt like a dagger to the heart.

"I was worried about you," she said in a small voice.

He rubbed his thumb in circles across the back of her hand, reveling in the soft, smooth skin. "Come here," he said roughly.

She stood and delicately sat on the edge of the bed.

He flashed a shadow of his wicked smile, though his eyes were still tinged with pain. "Closer."

After a moment's hesitation, Ava lay against him, her head resting against his chest. He snugged her close against him and let one hand settle on her back, caressing the familiar contours of her body through the silk of her wrapper, and let the other find its way into her hair, threading through the smooth, thick strands until it was cupping her scalp.

He felt a dangerous, telltale hitch in her breath, and he closed his eyes, furious with himself for causing her a moment's pain.

Neither of them said a word.

Forty-Five
Cariou's Coincidence

I was spooning broth into my cranky and belligerent Frenchman when Esme and Luc showed up later that morning. Gabriel was frustrated with his invalid status, itching to get up and move about. I had left a few minutes earlier to fetch more salve from the stillroom and had returned to find him sitting on the floor doubled over in pain. He had stubbornly tried to get out of bed, even though I'd warned him that he needed to regain his strength first.

Luckily, Phillipe had heard the thump Gabriel made when he fell and was able to help me get him back onto the bed. Afterward, Phillipe sat with him, filling in the gaps in his memory and adding details that I missed, while I met with Éloise and Isabelle for the first time in days.

They updated me on how everything was coming along in the garden and still room, and we discussed what we needed to concentrate on. Our stock of laudanum was running low according to Éloise, and I made a mental note to add it to the list of ingredients we needed from the apothecary the next time someone traveled from the *château* into town.

Striving for nonchalance, I asked if Madame Cariou was back. Isabelle had shrugged a slender shoulder, letting it fall in a thoroughly Gaelic manner.

"Monsieur Le Gall, who works in the stable— he told me that she was seen in Argol."

I raised a brow, even as the tiny hairs on my arms stood on end. "In Argol? Who saw her there?"

"Monsieur Le Gall said that when he and Monsieur Tremblay took Madame Pichon into town, he spoke to an old friend of his, who saw Madame Cariou in Argol."

"But. . . " I said slowly, even as my mind raced. "How is Madame Cariou known in Argol?"

"You did not know?"

"Know what?"

"She is from there."

After that, Isabelle and Éloise left, as did Phillipe, leaving Gabriel and me alone for a bit. While Gabriel slept, I let my mind turn over the information I'd been given on Madame Cariou. What did it mean? I was certain there was a connection that was eluding me. When Luc and Esme arrived I was still ruminating on Madame Cariou's absence.

I spooned the last of the broth up for Gabriel and moved the tray to the table by the fireplace.

"Sit, Luc," I said, standing up from my chair. "You can keep Gabriel company for a while? I need Esme in the surgery."

"Of course," answered Luc good-naturedly.

I watched carefully as he sat, noting how he winced and seemed to melt into the chair afterward. It was obvious to me because I was searching for signs of discomfort, but I could tell he was trying valiantly to control his expression and not give away that he was feeling unwell. I said nothing, although when I looked up I found Esme watching me.

I leaned down to brush my mouth against Gabriel's and then turned to take Esme's hand. She followed me willingly down the stairs but, she was strangely quiet and subdued. Not at all her normal chatty self. This, in and of itself, was an indication that something was amiss. Dread coalesced in the pit of my stomach as we walked down the corridor that led to the still room.

The door stood ajar, inviting us in with the familiar herbal smell I was coming to love. I sat at the table, and poured a splash of cognac into two cups, gesturing with my hand that Esme should sit.

I sat quietly and waited while she pursed her lips and picked up the cup, thoughtfully turning it between her hands, as she decided where to begin. "Gabriel awoke this morning?"

"Yes, thank God," I answered, fervently crossing myself.

She smiled, sincerely. "You must be feeling so relieved. I know how worried you were about him."

"I am. It made me realize how afraid I am of losing him." I picked up my cup and stared down into its amber depths.

"You love him." It was a statement.

"*Oui,*" I whispered, inhaling the fortifying scent of the liquor.

"And I love Luc," she added simply.

I looked up at this. "I know you do." I paused briefly and then added, "What's wrong with him? Is it his stomach?"

She nodded, her face etched in concern. "Do you remember what I told you? It's getting worse."

I took a small sip of my drink and held it in my mouth, savoring its taste for a moment before I swallowed it. "I remember. . . Esme, have you thought about what I said? What has changed? Is he eating differently?"

"No, I don't believe so. Madame Allard has been his housekeeper for years."

"What about herbals? Has he started taking anything? From Madame Cariou, perhaps?"

Her brow furrowed as she thought. "Madame Cariou? No. What need would he have for taking something from her?"

"I don't know. I'm simply trying to think of all the possibilities. It worries me that he is getting worse."

She bit her lip in consternation. "It worries me too."

I sighed, frustrated that we weren't getting anywhere. "Well, please let me know if something comes to you. I want to help."

"I know you do, and I will."

I smiled at her and took a sip of my cognac.

"Speaking of Madame Cariou. Have you heard? She's back."

I almost stood up from my chair. "What? When?"

Esme shook her head, sending a few loose tendrils of chestnut hair flying. "I heard this morning. I don't know if she arrived yesterday or today."

"Well, where has she been?"

"I heard Argol."

It couldn't be a coincidence that she'd heard the same, I thought to myself. Aloud I said, "What's in Argol?"

"Apparently, she is from there. She seems to be keeping mum on what brought her back though."

I sat back in my chair while Esme sipped on her cognac thoughtfully. I watched as her bright blue eyes suddenly narrowed and flashed to meet my gaze.

I raised a brow at her suspicious look. "What?"

"I just thought of something."

"About me?"

"*Non*, about Madame Cariou. . . and Luc."

I waited a beat, then another, but Esme didn't elaborate.

Finally, I sighed and put my cup down. "Well, I should go back up and relieve Luc. Maybe Gabriel is awake now."

Esme nodded distractedly. "Let Luc know that I'm waiting here for him?"

"Of course," I murmured soothingly.

As I walked away from her, my mind sifted through and cataloged everything I knew about Madame Cariou. I had the nagging feeling that I was missing something vital, but the pieces stubbornly refused to fall into place.

FORTY-SIX
FILLING THE SILENCE

I carefully dug into the soft soil and transplanted thyme into its designated garden patch. Esme and I had gone on several foraging missions with Isabelle and Éloise over the last week and I was pleased with the success we'd had. Several herbs and plants with medicinal qualities had been found, which we added to our expanding garden.

I sat back on my heels and replaced my small trowel in the basket beside me as I surveyed our progress thus far. I took pleasure in seeing the early cucumber and squash vines sprawling up their stakes, the orderly rows of vegetables marching neatly down the length of the garden, the rioting flowers bursting into colorful bloom. I watched a fat bumblebee drowsily fly by, drunk on sweet nectar. It filled me with a satisfaction that surprised me. My former self would scarcely recognize me.

The garden gate swung open, nearly soundless, but my ears picked up the sound in the stillness and I turned my head to see who approached. I resigned myself to an uncomfortable conversation when I recognized the errant Madame Cariou's silhouette walking down the path toward me. It'd been a full week since I'd heard of her return, but she hadn't seen fit to make her way to the *château* to check on Gabriel during that time.

He was healing nicely, regaining his strength more slowly than he would have liked, but I was pleased with his progress, even if he was not. I heard through the grapevine that Madame Cariou had been visiting a childhood friend in Argol. Perhaps it was true. Regardless, I was miffed by her obvious disinterest in Gabriel's recovery and wondered at her extended absence.

"My lady." She curtseyed prettily when she got to me.

I nodded my head and gave her a cool smile in return. "Madame Cariou, to what do I owe the pleasure?"

She faltered briefly at my detached welcome and furrowed her brows as though she couldn't understand why I might be distant with her.

"My lady, I have come to see how my lord is healing. I apologize that I was unable to come sooner."

Her face looked smooth and earnest. I said nothing, merely lifting a brow in response. Let her squirm a bit. There could be no explanation for staying away as long as she had and she knew it as well as I did.

"I'm ever so sorry for not being here when *le Vicomte* arrived injured. I traveled to Argol to visit my closest girlhood friend. We hadn't seen each other in years."

The longer I remained silent, the more she sought to fill the void with words. They tumbled out over each other, the slightly desperate edge in them betraying her fear that she had perhaps pushed my limits too far.

"Mayhap I should have come to the *château* sooner, my lady. In truth, I was quite busy with several ailments to deal with when I returned. . . and of course, I heard that you and Madame Esme did an excellent job in my absence and that my lord is healing well."

I had to give her credit for pressing on. That last bit was a shameless attempt to flatter me out of my displeasure with her. In truth, she was an excellent actress. If I didn't have a premonition that she was responsible for the downturn in Luc's health, I would probably believe her. As it was, I knew better, but I couldn't let her know what I suspected. There were still missing pieces needed to complete the puzzle. *'Keep your friends close and your enemies closer'*. . . Who had said that?

I forced a warm smile onto my face. "Thank you for saying that, but my skill cannot hope to compete with yours. I was so very worried for *le Vicomte*, you can understand why I hoped for your expertise. Did you enjoy a nice visit with your friend?"

"I did, my lady. It was lovely to see her and her children. Thank you ever so much for your understanding. With your permission, I would see how *le Vicomte* is faring." The relief on her face was evident.

"Yes, of course. I believe he's in the library at the moment."

I gathered my basket and led the way through the garden back to the *château*.

The rain pattered softly but steadily against the shutters as I lay in bed, idly tracing my fingers along Gabriel's collarbone, to his shoulder, down his arm, and back again. I loved the contrast between the smoothness of his skin and the coiled strength that lay just below the surface. His arm was curved around my body, holding me snuggly against the warmth that radiated from him. These were some of my favorite moments. When we were cocooned in the safety of our room, away from the world and its intrigues. Where I could forget for a few minutes all the heartache in my past.

I broke the serenity of the moment by asking one of the questions that had been brewing in my mind. Luc had rapidly deteriorated over the last weeks while Gabriel healed. The two of us had visited Luc earlier that afternoon, and as we walked home, shocked into silence by how ghastly he looked, Gabriel made the observation that nearly stopped me in my tracks. 'He seems to have what my papa had.'

"When your father took ill, who treated him?"

"*Docteur* Henri," he answered, affection clear in his voice.

"Is he still around? I haven't heard you mention him before."

He shifted slightly. "As far as I know, he is, although I haven't seen him in years. He moved away from the village two or three years after my papa passed."

"Do you think we might be able to find him?"

"Well, aye, I suppose we could. Why do you want to find him though? He was not able to help my father."

"I know," I said softly. "But you thought him a skilled *docteur*, did you not?"

"*Oui.*"

"Perhaps he has some insight into what is wrong. Maybe he has learned something since your father's case. It's worth asking, is it not?"

"If it saves Luc, it is certainly worth it *mon cœur*. I will begin to inquire on the good *docteur's* whereabouts in the morning."

But the morning brought fresh surprises, of the unpleasant variety. Gabriel found me nestled in one of the large window seats in the library, reading a collection of Shakespeare I'd found. I was deep into *Macbeth* when he strode in carrying a letter. Based on the grim expression in his dark gray eyes, it wasn't good news.

He silently handed it to me and sat beside me, patiently waiting while I read the missive.

1st June 1788

Monsieur Gabriel Chabot
Vicomte Landévennec
Château Landévennec

My dear Gabriel,

It is with a heavy heart, that I write to inform you that my beloved husband Jean Auclair, le Vicomte de Argol has left this earth and gone to his heavenly reward. I am heartbroken to be left widowed once more. It brings back heartbreaking memories of when I lost your dear Papa.

I will write more when I am able, but I knew you would want to know of your friend and my husband's passing. I regret that I did not write you under happier circumstances.

Your Loving Stepmother,

Madame Adele Auclair
Vicomtesse de Argol

I quietly placed the letter in my lap, and sent up a silent prayer for *le Vicomte de Argol's* soul, crossing myself at the end. My hand reached out for Gabriel's and my eyes sought his out. His face was inscrutable, but his gaze held fury. I swallowed down the lump in my throat. Without question, at least some of that anger was directed at himself. We had suspicions but lacked the necessary evidence. Whether or not his stepmother was responsible in some way, for now, two husband's deaths was a question we could not answer with any certainty. In a world where people died over simple infections, and infant and maternal mortality rates were through the roof, two husbands dying didn't raise many eyebrows.

"I'm sorry," I said softly, knowing how inadequate it was.

He turned my hand over in his and studied our linked hands in silence. I waited while we sat, listening to the water drumming steadily outside, each of us absorbed in our thoughts. It was a long while before Gabriel stirred.

"I've sent out a few inquiries about *Docteur* Henri. As soon as I hear something I will let you know."

"Speaking of Luc, when you see him next, can you delicately probe about and find out if he's doing anything different that could be causing his illness?"

Gabriel raised a brow. "Something he is doing differently? You think he's bringing it on himself?" he asked incredulously.

"I don't think he's knowingly doing something that would harm him, but people often take things they are led to believe will help them, that are actually detrimental to their health."

He drummed his fingers on his leg absentmindedly. "Like what?"

I shrugged. "Taking an herb, a tea, or a posset, or I suppose it might even be an ointment or a salve that he is told will help him feel better. . . it could be something in his food— although I'm disinclined to think that's the case for Luc. Anything really, but, it would have to be something that is a fairly new addition to his routine."

"How new, would you say?"

"Since he married Esme."

This time both brows shot up in disbelief. "You don't think—"

"No. I don't think Esme has anything to do with this."

The relief on his face was evident. "If the weather relents this afternoon, I'll head down to see him today. Otherwise, I'll try to stop by tomorrow."

I leaned in for a quick kiss. "Thank you."

He stood to leave. "I'm going to see about keeping Phillipe busy over the next few days, he's planning on leaving soon." He hesitated briefly. "How would you feel about visiting him after we get the harvest in?"

"I suppose it will depend on how I'm feeling. I might be a bit nervous about traveling so close to when the baby is due unless we have Esme or a midwife with us."

He rested his hand protectively on my belly, which was still quite flat, although I swore it was beginning to curve, just the slightest bit. His eyes crinkled at the corners.

"We won't do anything to endanger you or the bebe, *mon cœur*." He lifted my hand and brushed my knuckles with his mouth.

Forty-Seven
Cantarella

I sat fidgeting with my handkerchief, running my fingers over the embroidered scalloped edge over and over, the familiar pattern soothing me. The late afternoon sun streamed in through the high windows of *Docteur* Henri's salon, making it unbearably hot. I shifted slightly, the fabric of my shift clinging uncomfortably to my damp skin beneath the layers of cloth stays and the bodice of my gown.

"Ava, relax, *mon chou.*" Gabriel sent me a calm smile from across the room. "I'm sure the *docteur* will join us in a moment."

Gabriel somehow managed to track down the *docteur* of his youth. He had set up shop in a small village a little more than a day's ride from home. After a flurry of letters back and forth, we'd agreed to visit him to see what we might uncover.

The day following our receipt of *la Vicomtesse de Argol's* letter, Gabriel and I visited Luc and Esme. What transpired was a nearly precise reenactment of the vision I'd had the night of their nuptials. The key difference was that Gabriel was present when Esme bemoaned the fact that Madame

Cariou's tea wasn't helping Luc. Our eyes had met, his in blank shock, mine in resigned misery. It put paid to any uncertainties I'd felt about my premonitions.

I pulled Esme aside that afternoon.

"It's in the tea, Esme."

"It can't be, he's only just begun to take it in the last week!"

"You need to find out what he was taking from her before this."

She shook her head, confusion clear in her bright blue eyes. "I don't think he was taking anything else from her, Ava."

Frustrated, I grabbed her shoulders and gave her a little shake. "Stop being in denial Esme! This isn't happening by accident. For some reason, Madame Cariou has given Luc something that is making him ill. Don't be pigheaded! Throw away whatever she has given you, and if she comes with fresh supplies, get rid of it."

She looked at me, eyes wide with shock, and then her gaze slid over my shoulder.

Gabriel's deep, authoritative voice cut in. "Esme, would you please give Ava and me the tea instead of throwing it away?"

I shot him a questioning look, both eyebrows raised sky high.

"Fine," muttered Esme, stalking away and returning a moment later with a bag of possets which she grudgingly deposited in Gabriel's out-stretched palm.

I crossed my arms and tapped my foot, gearing myself up to ask Gabriel why he wanted them.

He shot me a warning look, his eyes begging me to keep mum.

"Thank you, Esme," he said quietly. "We mean to help you figure out what's going on with Luc. As soon as we have answers, I'll let you know."

She practically deflated in front of us, shoulders slumping, eyes filling with tears.

"Thank you both."

I hugged her and we left, walking back to the château in relative silence.

It dawned on me what he planned to do with it when we got back to the *château*. I'd watched, admiring how his critical mind worked, as he soaked bits of bread in the steeped tea and fed it to a mouse, one of the stable lads trapped.

While letters flew back and forth between Gabriel and *Docteur* Henri the mouse sickened and died.

I'd tentatively asked Gabriel if he recalled his father drinking anything different before his death, but he merely shrugged. *'It's not the sort of thing I would have paid attention to then. I'd not have thought of it now honestly, if it weren't for you,'* he'd replied.

The door to the salon opened, yanking me out of my reverie and *Docteur* Henri strode in, beaming widely at Gabriel. I was surprised by his obvious vigor. I'd imagined a much older, frail-looking man.

"It is so good to see you *Vicomte*—"

"Please! *Docteur* Henri, to you I am simply Gabriel."

The *docteur* smiled sheepishly. "Of course, of course. It's been so many years. . . You were just a lad when I saw you last," he responded warmly, drinking in his face like a long-lost friend. His eyes roamed the salon until they settled on me, and his smile grew wider. "Is this your beautiful wife?" He waggled his eyebrows playfully at Gabriel.

A dull red crept up Gabriel's neck and ears and I realized with no small sense of mirth that he was blushing. I had never seen Gabriel look discomposed. He recovered quickly though, stepping to my side to make the proper introductions.

We sat while Gabriel and the *docteur* exchanged reminisces and I sipped my tea, looking on with a pleasant smile plastered to my face.

Finally, *Docteur* Henri leaned forward and said, "Now, Gabriel, it is wonderful to see you, but I know that something serious must have impelled you to seek me out. What's wrong?" His gaze flicked to assess me, but my obvious, glowing health made him quickly discard the idea that I was ill.

Gabriel took a deep breath, the furrow between his brows growing deeper. "You remember the circumstances of my papa's illness?"

A shadow crossed over the *docteur's* face. "Of course, Gabriel. It haunts me that I was unable to help him." He sat back in his chair and looked down at his hands, rotating a thick, gold band on his right ring finger, lost in thought for a moment, before looking back up at us. "In my line of work, I see a lot of illness, misery, and death. I won't say you become immune to it, but to a degree, you come to expect it. There are cases, however, patients; who take you by surprise, who stick with you and visit you in your dreams. Years later even. Some because they are incredibly young, some because you don't know what went wrong. Your father was one of those patients."

Remembered grief flickered in the gray depths of Gabriel's eyes. He swallowed convulsively before asking, "Did you have any ideas at the time, or since then, of what was wrong? Any suspicions?"

The *docteur* raised a thick salt and pepper eyebrow. "Suspicions? At the time, I was flummoxed by his symptoms. It didn't seem to match any of the diseases I was familiar with. As I said, however, your papa's case troubled me, and I did exchange notes whenever I had the opportunity to with other physicians. In all the years since then, there has only been one who seemed familiar with his illness. I couldn't reconcile what he told me to what I knew of your family though."

I leaned forward, unable to help myself. "What did he think it was?"

"Poison," he said flatly.

Gabriel sat back, deflated at the confirmation of my intuitive distrust of his stepmother. He let out a shaky breath. "*Docteur*, what were your impressions of my stepmother?"

"Gabriel! You can't think—"

"I do," he interjected quietly.

Docteur Henri shook his head in disbelief.

"I don't know if you've heard, but she remarried this last year, to *le Vicomte de Argol*."

At this, *Docteur* Henri looked up questioningly.

"I received word from the new *Vicomtesse* de Argol that her beloved husband passed at the end of May," Gabriel said softly.

The *docteur* blanched as I added, "We saw them in March, at a wedding. I felt strongly then that de Argol's symptoms suggested he was being tampered with."

"I have never been able to reconcile what reasons humans have for harming each other," he said in a defeated voice. "I didn't know your stepmother well, Gabriel, but it never would have occurred to me that she would commit such a heinous crime. Your father was a gentle and kind man. I can think of no reason why she would have wished him ill."

"Nor I," came the subdued response.

I sighed. "People who murder don't typically need a cause. Could greed have motivated her though?"

Gabriel frowned thoughtfully. "I don't know what her finances looked like prior to marrying my father. I suppose it could have been. She was well taken care of as the dowager *Vicomtesse de Landévennec* though. Why remarry and commit murder again?"

"Did de Argol have children? Is she wealthier now that he has been disposed of?"

Gabriel nodded slowly. *"Non, no heirs."* His gaze looked glassy; his thoughts distant from the *docteur's* boiling salon.

"It could be about power and control, there are people who simply enjoy wielding it," I suggested, carefully flattening my sweating palms against the fabric of my skirt.

"This is true," agreed *Docteur* Henri. *"Le bon Dieu* knows that I will never understand that part of human nature, but it does us no good to pretend it doesn't exist simply because we cannot fathom it."

"Perhaps the more relevant question is, how did she poison her husbands? Where did she learn the skill?" I delicately submitted. "We think we may be seeing similar symptoms in our friend Luc. If we want to help him, we need to know if there is a remedy," I reminded Gabriel gently.

This seemed to pull him back to the present. I waited as his eyes cleared and his posture straightened. *"Oui, oui,* you're right Ava." He directed his gray gaze back at *Docteur* Henri. "Did your colleague suggest a specific poison?"

"The most likely poison is arsenic, it's relatively easy to obtain, simple to mix into food or drink, and it could even be absorbed through the skin if it were added to a salve. If I wanted to poison someone, it would be my first choice."

I nodded, unsurprised. What little I knew of poisons indicated arsenic as well. It had been used for centuries and been the favorite of many infamous persons over the years; the Borgia family came to mind. The trouble was I had no idea what might be used to detox a poisoned person.

Gabriel's gaze skipped back and forth between *Docteur* Henri and me and our obvious agreement. "So, what can we do to help Luc? Will he recover?"

Docteur Henri sighed and spread his hands out, palm up. "In truth my son, I do not know. I imagine it will depend on how far the damage to his organs has gone. I would prescribe a diet rich in fruits, nuts, and vegetables. He should avoid meat. It's my personal belief, that spending time outside in the sun will help. It will be a long road for him, and he may never fully recover, if he does at all."

It was not a very, auspicious recommendation. But at least he had a chance. Gabriel looked as though he'd been punched in the stomach. I realized then that he hadn't allowed himself to believe that Luc might not recover from this ordeal.

"Thank you *docteur*." I stood, gently touching Gabriel's shoulder to recall him to the moment.

His eyes caught mine, the misery in them taking the breath from my lungs.

"I do so hope your friend Luc makes a full recovery. I'm sorry I couldn't be more helpful." The good doctor looked genuinely distressed.

"You've been immensely, helpful," I replied soothingly. "At least we now have a direction to move in, and confirmation as to the cause of his illness."

He shook his head sadly. "Nonetheless, I wish I had seen you again under better circumstances Gabriel."

"I do as well, *docteur*. Thank you for everything. I will stay in touch now that we've found each other again." Gabriel stood up and shook *Docteur* Henri's hand heartily.

"Are you staying in town tonight?"

Gabriel shook his head regretfully. "Unfortunately, not. I rather want to get back as quickly as we can."

"I quite understand my dear boy. Safe travels to you both." He bowed low over my hand. "It was a pleasure to meet you, my dear."

FORTY-EIGHT
SACRIFICE

We returned to *Landévennec* in an unspoken race against time, hoping we weren't too late for Luc. When we arrived, the sun was low in the sky, splashing vibrant sorbet hues across the heavens. Foregoing the *château*, we rode straight to Esme and Luc's, nestled amidst the pines about a thousand fathoms from our home.

Gabriel jumped down from Automne and helped me down, rubbing his hand affectionately against the bay's flank before carefully tying his reins to the post. Esme was waiting for us. She flung the door open before their housekeeper could get it, her face betraying her anxiety.

"Gabriel, Ava, what brings you here so late?"

I took both her hands in mine and took in her exhausted countenance. "We have some information that may help Luc. How is he?"

"The same, I think. I've seen no improvement, though he hasn't used anything from Madame Cariou. . . Will you tell me what is going on?" she pleaded.

"Is Luc awake?" interjected Gabriel before I could speak, squeezing my hand warningly in his.

Esme nodded.

Realizing Gabriel's intention, I said, "Why don't we sit down and tell both of you together?"

Esme pressed her lips together tightly as she led the way upstairs to their room. "Luc?" she called, opening the door slightly before she opened it fully and let us in.

Luc struggled to sit up in bed when he saw Gabriel and me, grimacing in pain as he pulled himself up. "Gabriel, Ava, how are you? Is everything well?"

"All is well with us my friend. We are here because we think we have information for you," Gabriel answered seriously.

Esme protectively moved to stand by the head of the bed, clasping her hands together, her face like a statue, as if she intended to fight us off if we gave Luc unwelcome news.

I gave her a sympathetic look, but she resolutely avoided my eyes.

Gabriel cleared his throat and began, "We spoke to *Docteur* Henri about Luc." Esme's eyes flew to his face. "You remember him, Esme?"

"*Oui*, of course," came the soft reply.

Gabriel nodded, satisfied. "We spoke about my father's illness, and how similar Luc's seems to be to his." He stopped and looked at her and she nodded in agreement. "We believe my papa was poisoned by my stepmother."

The shock in the room was palpable, but my eyes were on Esme's reaction, and I thought she didn't look as surprised as one might expect, considering the accusation.

Luc broke into the silence incredulously. "You think I am being poisoned?"

Gabriel's eyes were steady on Luc's face. "*Oui*."

"But—"

"We believe *la Vicomtesse* de Argol, my stepmother, has killed *le Vicomte* de Argol as well. We don't fully understand the connection, but Madame

Cariou is from Argol, perhaps she gave the poison to *la Vicomtesse. . .* We aren't sure."

"You cannot mean to say that you think Madame Cariou is—"

"She most certainly was poisoning you, *mon ami*. The tea she gave you killed a field mouse, in a matter of days. We tested it out. The only question is why."

Esme opened her mouth and then shut it without saying a word. I watched her narrowly, pinpricks of unease beginning to tease the fine hairs on my arms into a standing position.

Finally, Esme looked at Luc. "What were you taking from Madame Cariou?"

Luc plucked the coverlet on their bed into little mountains and his ears turned bright red. "She offered me a tea, guaranteed to increase my vigor and make my seed take hold."

"She offered it to you?" she asked evenly. "You didn't seek her out for a remedy?"

"*Non,*" he mumbled. "She came to me, just before we married. I didn't think it could do any harm. She's a midwife after all. . . bringing *bebes* into the world is her work."

Esme muttered something I couldn't hear under her breath. The silence in the room stretched out as everyone pondered the ramifications of what had been revealed.

"Is there a remedy for what ails me?"

I looked up to find Luc staring stoically at me.

"*Docteur* Henri thinks there is a chance you may heal, as long as the damage isn't too far gone. It will take time. He suggested a special diet. . . " I trailed off and looked at Esme. "We'll go over his suggestions with Madame Allard and you." She nodded, pressing her lips even closer together. "Gabriel and I are hopeful, Luc. But we don't know anything with any certainty."

He nodded and took a deep breath. "I am willing to try whatever the *docteur* recommends. What do you intend to do about Madame Cariou?"

"Leave that to me, Luc." There was a deceptively quiet thread of steel running through Gabriel's voice. "I do not forget that her husband also passed away, with what appears to be the same illness that you, my papa, and *le Vicomte* de Argol had."

We left shortly after we went over *Docteur* Henri's recommendations for Luc with Esme and the sweet, portly Madame Allard. There was a heaviness in the air and in my heart, as we ambled back to the *château* with the silver, light of the moon guiding Automne.

I desperately wanted to sleep late the following morning. The days of travel wore me out, and I was heartsick over our meeting with *Docteur* Henri and having to break the news to Esme and Luc. Even though I wasn't surprised by our findings, my stomach was sick at the confirmation of my suspicions.

I was gently awoken by a grim-faced Gabriel far too early for my liking. I pried open my gritty eyes to find him dressed and impatient to go. I scowled at him as I pulled his watch out of his pocket and glared at the ungodly hour.

My eyes found his in unspoken inquiry. I knew he would only wake me for a good reason.

"Esme is missing."

I sat bolt upright. "What?" I exclaimed.

"Madame Allard arrived just as I was about to leave for Madame Cariou. She says that Esme slipped out shortly after we did last night. This morning Luc told her that she hadn't returned. He awoke in the middle of the night and realized she wasn't back, but the poor man was unable to do anything until Madame Allard brought in his breakfast."

I pushed back the blankets and scrambled out of bed. "Help me get dressed."

He gently put a hand on my shoulder and turned me around to face him. "Wait, Ava, do you have any idea where she might have gone?"

I slowly shook my head as I ran through options and rejected them. Then, horror dawned as fear congealed in the pit of my stomach.

He noticed my sudden pallor. "What, Ava? What are you thinking?"

"I think she went to Madame Cariou."

"Are you sure?" His voice was strained.

"No, of course not. But I think it's possible that she meant to confront her."

Gabriel nodded, his eyes bleak. "Then she's in danger."

"I'm coming with you."

"Absolutely not Ava. I will not risk you. I do not know what she is capable of. . . if she would harm you." His face was drawn tight with fear. I opened my mouth to argue, but he leaned down and desperately pressed his mouth to mine. "Please, Ava. Stay here where I know you are safe."

Unable to ignore the pleading in the dark depths of his eyes, I acquiesced. "I will stay, but I want to know who is going with you. You're not going alone." I ruled.

"Timothée and Georges are coming with me. They are waiting downstairs already."

"Alright," I whispered, hearing the palpable fear in my voice, and hating it. I pulled him to me for another kiss. "Be careful, my love."

Unable to fall back asleep I rang for Adrienne to help me dress, and after a quick *déjeuner*, I found myself in Gabriel's study seated at his desk, with a fresh sheet of parchment in front of me, tapping a quill thoughtfully against my lips.

I'd come in to write a letter to Amélie to pass the intolerable hours of waiting, but I was incapable of writing a single word. I felt like a hamster scrabbling on a wheel, going round and round, with no end in sight.

After I sat for an interminable length of time, I stood up, my parchment still a fresh, blank slate. Perhaps, a walk outside would help. I set off with my basket and foraging tools intending to head for the forest to gather more specimens for the garden but wandered down the sandstone cliffs to the rocky beach below instead.

Until now, I had largely avoided the seashore. The part of me that had always loved the endless, crashing of the ocean had shied away from it since Carri's death and the shipwreck. Today though, the warm, salty air and the rhythmic pulse of the aqua waves called to me and soothed my tumultuous thoughts.

I removed the blanket I usually knelt on for foraging, from my basket and spread it on a small sandy patch, sitting I drew my legs up, wrapped my arms around them, and rested my chin on my knees. I stared out at the invitingly, clear water, my eyes drawn to the predictable pattern that the ebb and flow of each wave created, perfectly timed, one after another, after another.

My mind skipped back to last night, and Esme's reaction as I picked apart everything that had been said. I couldn't get the expression on her face out of my head. I examined it from every angle, turning it this way and that, like a crystal held up to the sun, probing every facet of it, watching how the refracted light bounced back at me. Instinct told me she went to Madame Cariou, but why? Did she think that she wouldn't be harmed? Did she go in anger? Was she unable to think clearly about the foolhardiness of her venture and the danger she was putting herself in?

I sighed, rested my forehead against my knees, closed my eyes, and listened to the breakers. The gentle swoosh of water against sand, the way it trickled back through the rounded, weather-beaten stones, creating a kind of timeless music. Incrementally, I found myself relaxing, the anxiety that gnawed at my insides receding in time to the ebb of the tide, slowly inching its way further from me.

The gentle breeze carried my name to me, breaking through the fog. I awoke with a start; shocked that I'd been lulled into sleep by the sea. I lifted my head groggily, my neck stiff, and peered up at the cloudless, azure sky. The sun was at its golden height, shining down mercilessly, glinting off the silver edges of the water. I've been here for hours. . . *How long has Gabriel been searching for me?*

I stood up, working the kinks out of my back and legs, and looked around for the source of the sound.

"Ava!"

I glanced up, shaded my eyes with my hand, and spotted Gabriel at the head of the cliff. I waved my hand until I knew he saw me. I gathered my blanket, carefully shaking the sand out before refolding it and placing it back into my basket, as Gabriel and Automne picked their way down to the beach.

I opened my mouth to ask Gabriel how it had gone, but one look at his face told me everything I needed to know. He swung down from Automne and gathered me against him, fear making him rough. Pressed against his length I could feel the wild galloping of his heart and feel the slight tremble in his hands.

"*Dieu*, Ava. You frightened me."

I wrapped my arms around him tightly, squeezing in apology. "I came down here to think, I was going crazy sitting in the *château*. I must have fallen asleep. I'm sorry."

He ran a hand gently over my ocean breeze tumbled hair, and took a deep breath, letting it out slowly. "It's all right. I know you were tired, it's no wonder you fell asleep."

I leaned back slightly, looking up into his face, searching the tired eyes, and noting the grim lines around his mouth. "No Esme and no Madame Cariou?"

He shook his head, bewilderment clouding his features.

"Did you go anywhere other than Madame Cariou's cottage?"

"We searched the area around it and checked back at Esme and Luc's, in case they somehow ended up back there. . . come." He gestured toward Automne, helping me up behind him. "Timothée and Georges are waiting for us at the top. Le Gall has joined us as well."

I wrapped my arms around his middle and securely held onto my basket. Gabriel clicked his tongue softly to Automne and urged him back up the narrow, winding path that led from the beach to the cliffs. The sun was warm on my back and for a moment, I closed my eyes, wishing we were just a man and a woman out for a romantic horseback ride. The breeze teased tendrils of Gabriel's hair out of its binding and tickled my cheek. I sighed and opened my eyes. *Where is Esme? She wouldn't go with Madame Cariou voluntarily, would she?*

My stomach churned uneasily. Automne huffed as he reached the summit of the cliffs and dropped his head to lip up some grass while Gabriel paused to confer with the others.

"Shall we split up?" offered Le Gall.

"Nay, we don't have enough men. If one of us finds them, how will we get word to the others?" put in Georges shrewdly.

"We could gather more men?" suggested Timothée, his arm still in a sling from his break.

Gabriel chewed on his lip for a moment, considering our options, before huffing out a small breath. "We'll stay together. There's no need to involve others just yet. As we pass tenants, we'll inform them to keep an eye out. 'Tis a busy time of year, I won't take them away from their work unless necessary."

"Right then, let's go," said Georges gruffly.

"We'll stop by the *château* for lunch first," ruled Gabriel. "We may be searching for quite some time."

My belly grumbled at this suggestion, and I realized it was well past lunchtime already. Gabriel nudged Automne with his knees and led the way back home.

Within half an hour, the group was back underway; wineskins full, bags stocked with fresh bread, chunks of cheese, sausage, fresh plums, and apricots. We munched companionably as we searched the cliffs and woods and questioned the tenants. There had been no sign of either Esme or Madame Cariou, and as the hours of the day slipped away, and the sun began its slow descent, the unease among the men grew.

"Where could they have gone?" muttered Timothée, his gruff voice betraying his fraying temper.

"They must be on foot; they cannot have gone that far," pointed out Le Gall reasonably.

"Aye, but no one has seen them. They must be holed up somewhere," replied Timothée.

"Are there any uninhabited cottages or buildings nearby?" I asked.

Gabriel frowned. "The old Kirouac place mayhap, though it's been empty for years. The roof is threatening to cave in."

"It's a starting point, and we have no other ideas," said Georges, turning his black gelding's head toward the far edge of the property.

We made good time, wending our way to the outskirts of our land where the Kirouac cabin sat. Throughout the afternoon, clouds had gathered overhead, turning the beautiful day overcast to match our moods. I squinted up through the towering trees at the threatening sky. The air felt oppressively heavy, and the temperature was beginning to drop; weather was on its way.

Gabriel lifted a hand in silence when we approached the edge of the pines that crept close to the abandoned cottage, and everyone halted, the horse's hooves rustling as they shifted nervously in the pine needles that thickly carpeted the forest floor.

All I could hear was the sounds of men and horses breathing. Other than that, the stillness was complete. It was as though the birds, squirrels, and rabbits were all waiting and listening for a sign. I squinted at the small stone cottage in the clearing ahead of us. The chimney had partially collapsed and missing roof shingles exposed the beams. The grass was high as my knees and honeysuckle scrambled up the exterior walls of the house, scenting the occasional breeze sweetly.

"Look," Le Gall pointed at a trampled area of overgrown grass in what must have once been the garden, a broken wood fence still stood, haphazardly delineating the perimeter. "Someone has been here."

Gabriel slowly surveyed the property. "All right, Le Gall, stay here with my lady and the horses. Timothée, you take the back, Georges, you check the perimeter, I'm going through the front."

I took a breath, prepared to argue, but a single look from Gabriel quelled me. The men nodded in agreement, dismounting, and tying their horses to sturdy branches, checking their belts for knives, and then melting back into the forest.

I scarcely dared to breathe as I watched them quietly and stealthily approach the house from different angles. Le Gall shifted from one foot to the other impatiently, and I wondered if he was annoyed that he'd been left behind to babysit me. I eyed him from under my lashes, noting his obvious youth. *I bet I could convince him to bring me closer to the house.*

Prepared to test my theory, I sighed forlornly, caught his eye, and gave him a sympathetic smile. "I hate being left out of the excitement, don't you?"

He grimaced, "Aye, my lady."

"I don't think there would be any harm in us getting a bit closer," I suggested.

I sensed his hesitation as we watched Gabriel plaster himself against the house's outer wall and creep toward the door. Le Gall leaned forward, his yearning to be with the men obvious. He glanced back at me and straightened up, shaking his head ruefully.

"Nay, my lady. *Le Vicomte* has entrusted me with your safety. I cannot break his confidence."

I swallowed my defeat as gracefully as I could. I knew it was a long shot, I had seen firsthand the loyalty Gabriel's men had to him. It was generally something I appreciated, but it was standing in my way right now and I knew that I needed to witness whatever was about to happen to understand how all the pieces of this puzzle fit together.

I watched breathlessly as Gabriel entered the cottage, the door swinging open surprisingly easily, and disappeared into the shadowy depths. I caught a flicker of movement at the only window, and then, nothing. The minutes dragged by painfully, as I shifted from one foot to the other. *He must be done searching the cabin by now.*

Gabriel moved slowly and stealthily, keeping within the tree line until he'd circled to the right of the house, then crouched as low as he could, letting the wild grass and overgrown brambles camouflage him as he approached the ramshackle cabin. Once he reached the building, he plastered himself against the outer wall and willed his heart rate to slow, deliberately breathing slowly and steadily. He pressed an ear to the wall of the house, listening for any sound that might indicate someone was within. Nothing.

Step by careful step, he inched his way to the front of the cabin, ducking beneath the window, until he made it to the front door. He paused again, listening, and let his gaze rove over the woods until he glimpsed Ava's red gown through the trees and thick underbrush. He closed his eyes and willed his stomach to stop churning; he should have left her in the safety of the *château*.

He forced himself to tear his eyes away from the forest, put a hand on the door, and pushed it open. He held his breath, and slowly let it whoosh out of his lungs when it swung inward soundlessly. Gabriel ducked in quickly; stepping lightly on the old, creaky floorboards, and positioned himself behind the door while he waited for his eyes to adjust to the dim light within.

One hand on the dagger at his waist; he carefully took in the interior of the old, house. Chinks in the walls, and the partially collapsed roof shed rays of light over the old stone hearth. He carefully moved through the small house, checking underneath the table and beds. He had just completed a thorough circuit of the small space when he heard Timothée shout.

Heart racing, he burst out of the cabin and ran toward the back garden where he thought the shout had come from. He almost stumbled over a partially buried rock as he pushed his way through the thick growth, thorns snagging and tearing at his breeches, as he yanked his dagger free of its sheath. The weight of the hilt was comforting in his grip as he rounded the corner and skidded to an abrupt halt.

Esme was laid out on the grass, arms, and legs akimbo, reminiscent of a starfish, with meadow flowers strewn about her in a wide circle. Madame Cariou knelt at her head, a wickedly sharp blade in her hand, and regarded him coolly. Georges arrived a few seconds after Gabriel, and the men arranged themselves in a semi-circle around the women.

Gabriel stared at Esme, trying to discern whether or not she was still alive. Her eyes were closed, and she lay eerily still, but he could see no blood or telltale wounds. His gaze caught on Madame Cariou's dark, amused eyes, and he felt a pit of fear coalesce in his stomach.

"You're wondering if she is still alive."

"Aye," he managed.

"Luckily for you, she is. Which means you gentlemen have arrived just in time to watch her life's blood ebb away."

Gabriel moved toward her rapidly, but she moved faster than he could have imagined, hauling Esme up against her, and pressing the glinting, silver knife against Esme's throat. He froze.

"You won't take a step further," she said simply.

"I'm sure this is all a misunderstanding, Madame," he tried, shifting just the tiniest bit closer.

She cocked her head in amusement. "Not at all, my lord. Nor will you shift your feet in my direction, or this will be over far too quickly for my liking."

"If you kill Esme, you lose your chance at life yourself, Madame."

She threw her head back and laughed maniacally, sending shivers down Gabriel's spine. "You don't expect me to believe that you intend to let me walk away from this garden, regardless of what happens to Esme, do you?"

"Why wouldn't I? As long as Esme remains alive, you are not a murderess," he answered reasonably. *Maybe she would believe that he wasn't aware of her other victims.*

He saw Georges shift his feet in his peripheral vision and sensed that the men were losing patience. He kept his eyes trained on Madame Cariou and Esme. *Would she really kill her? Would she have done it already if they hadn't found them?*

His eyes caught a glimpse of movement by the cabin, and his heart froze in his chest. Surprise made him move involuntarily.

I started toward them resolutely; halting in my tracks when I heard a shout from the back. The men burst out of their various hiding places and moved as one toward Timothée's voice. Even Le Gall perked up and had to visibly stop himself from running to join them. I strained to hear what was happening, but only a handful of disjointed words drifted toward us.

Minutes ticked by as the sky darkened and a sudden gust of wind rustled through the leaves. I stole another glance at Le Gall, he looked as impatient and sick with anticipation as me and rubbed my sweaty palms on my dress. The wait was excruciating. *They must have dealt with whatever threat Madame Cariou posed by now, right?*

Resolved, I placed my basket on the ground beside the horse and moved resolutely toward the fringes of the woods.

"My lady!" hissed Le Gall in a frantic whisper.

I threw a smile over my shoulder at him. "I'm sure it's fine now. I'm going to see if Esme is all right. You can come with me if you like." Without another backward glance, I continued walking toward the house, sure that Le Gall would not physically try to stop me.

I moved purposefully through the knee-high grass, expecting to hear him behind me within seconds. As I was nearing the cabin, I heard him fall into step beside me. Oddly, I could no longer hear anyone speaking as we approached the back. My hackles rising, I put out a hand to stop Le Gall and motioned him against the wall of the house. I knelt in the tall grass, sidled over, peered around the corner, and felt my breath back up in my lungs.

Madame Cariou's petite frame stood in the middle of the old garden, her back to us. Esme's limp body was pulled up against her, her long, white neck lolled back, exposed. There was a knife in the hand she held against Esme's throat, its wickedly sharp edge glinted in the sun. Gabriel and the men were ranged in a semi-circle around them, clearly at an impasse.

Something in the way Madame Cariou stood told me the threat she posed to Esme wasn't an empty one. She would not hesitate to cut her throat if the men made a move in her direction. I let out a quiet, shaky breath, and offered a silent prayer.

Gabriel's gaze ranged over the landscape slowly, and halted, staring right at where Le Gall and I were hidden. *Did he see me?*

There was a flash of silver as Madame Cariou threw her knife, with shocking precision at Georges, catching him in the bicep, and whipped another dagger out of her skirt, replacing the one at Esme's throat, faster than I could draw breath.

Georges grunted in surprise and looked down at his arm. With his right hand, he pulled the weapon out, grimacing as the crimson stain on his shirt grew alarmingly. "What did you do that far?" he demanded.

"Your friend, *le Vicomte* moved," she replied lazily.

"That was unnecessary, Madame. Let Esme go, and we can work out the rest," Gabriel spoke in a calm, even voice.

Madame Cariou cocked her head and laughed lightly. "There's nothing to work out, my lord. Esme made a mistake, and she must pay the price."

"What mistake was that? There's no need to make a hasty decision in anger, Madame. As long as Esme is unharmed, we can discuss everything in a civilized manner."

She scoffed. "Men do not understand how to be civilized."

"I beg your pardon?" His voice was deceptively soft. Gabriel shifted his feet and her entire body tensed.

"You heard me the first time. . . *my lord.*" She emphasized the last few words sarcastically.

"I'm not sure where the animosity stems from Madame." He sheathed his dagger and lifted his hands, showing her that he was unarmed. "May I come closer?"

She shook her head vehemently. "Take a single step and she's dead. You'll never reach her in time."

"It doesn't have to be like this."

Timothée blurted out, "This is ridiculous, why are we letting her get away with this?"

Gabriel's eyes flashed dangerously, effectively shutting him up.

Madame Cariou chuckled. "My, my. I must say I wasn't expecting to be entertained this evening. Go ahead and tell my lord how he should manage me."

Even from a distance, I could see the red flush of embarrassment and anger on Timothée's face.

The situation was worsening and they were no closer to negotiating Esme's safe return. I glanced up at the ominous sky. The wind now blew consistently, rushing through the long grass, and whipping my hair loose. I squeezed my eyes shut and tried to think. *Perhaps I could create a distraction that would give the men enough time to act without harming Esme?*

I heard a whoosh next to my ear, the disturbance in the air so near, I felt it caress my skin. I opened my eyes and caught the startled look of relief on Timothée's face as Madame Cariou crumpled in a heap and the men rushed forward to extricate Esme from her slackened grasp.

I ran toward them, Le Gall one step behind me, and knelt beside Esme, my fingers frantically fumbling for her pulse. I finally found it, faint but steady. *Thank you, God.*

I looked up as the first raindrops began to fall to find all the men staring at me.

"She's alive," was all I could manage.

Behind me came Georges's voice, "She's not."

I turned to inspect Madame Cariou's prone body, lying at an impossibly strange angle. Le Gall's arrow had hit its mark with impeccable precision. I let out a shuddering breath, pity for her washing over me.

"What made her do it?" I wondered aloud.

"You'll likely never know," said Gabriel softly, holding his hand out to help me. I stood and leaned against him as he held me crushingly close. In the aftermath, I found myself shaking uncontrollably from the adrenaline rush.

We waited in shocked silence while Le Gall left to gather the horses and walked back toward us. With Georges's help, they broke the shaft of the arrow off, and then they hoisted Madame Cariou's body up, laying her across the gelding. The horse shied at the smell of blood, but Le Gall swung up behind the body and leaned forward, patting the horse's neck, and murmuring to him soothingly. After a moment, the frightened animal stopped stamping his hooves and calmed.

Rain began to fall gently and steadily, and the wind died as we headed back into the forest. It felt like a benign summer shower, washing away the ugliness of the day. Esme rode back in front of Georges, slumped over and unconscious.

As we neared the *château*, Timothée broke off and rode ahead to Luc and Esme's, bringing him news that she'd been found. Whether or not she was safe was another story. No one knew what Madame Cariou used to drug her, I hoped that the fact that she was still alive was a good omen.

Forty-Nine
Her Story

It took two excruciatingly long days for Esme to regain consciousness. In the interim, we quietly laid Madame Cariou to rest and moved Luc temporarily into the *château* so I could oversee his recovery and so that he could be near Esme.

I wanted desperately to know what transpired between Esme and Madame Cariou, but I waited, albeit impatiently for her to be ready to talk. On the fourth morning, she found Gabriel and me discussing our proposed trip to see Phillipe in the study.

"I'd like to tell you about Marguerite now," she said shyly.

Gabriel sensed my momentary confusion and squeezed my hand gently. She meant Madame Cariou, I realized, suddenly noticing that no one had ever called her by her given name, odd in and of itself, but also noting that Esme knew what it was.

"Of course," I said softly. "Only if you're ready."

She took a deep breath and rubbed the palms of her hands on the skirt of her dress, smoothing it down self-consciously. "I'm ready. I told Luc earlier this morning."

I gestured that she should sit, and sat myself, while Gabriel busied himself with pouring glasses of wine.

"The story begins when I was nine years old," she began quietly.

I looked up in surprise but didn't interrupt her.

"My *maman* and I traveled to the village of Argol to see the midwife there, for my *maman* had suffered from many miscarriages over the years and was beginning to despair of ever having other living children. The midwife, of course, was Marguerite's *maman,* and while our mothers consulted about the state of my mother's womb, Marguerite and I became instantaneous friends."

Gabriel and I listened, rapt, our glasses of wine forgotten in our hands. Esme took a deep shuddering breath before she continued.

"We did not bond over the normal things children bond over. My father—" She paused and looked at Gabriel. "You never knew my papa, but he was an awful man. He would beat my *maman* all the time but as I grew older, he began to notice me, and he—" she stopped and sniffled. "He—"

I held my hand up. "Esme, please, you don't have to do this if you don't want to."

"*Non*. I have kept this to myself for all these years. It's time people knew what my papa was. He used me like his whore," she spat out.

I closed my eyes, aching in misery for my friend. The silence in the study was deafening.

"Marguerite understood. Her papa had also been a monster; but she had so much knowledge in herbs, even at that age, that she had learned from her *maman*. She poisoned her father, and she gave me what I needed to kill mine."

She let the words, the admission, hang in the air for a long time, waiting for our recriminations. But neither Gabriel nor myself uttered a word.

After several long minutes, she continued. "I did not live near enough to Argol to maintain contact with Marguerite, and we moved here shortly after my papa's death." She shrugged. "I thought of her often, she freed my mother and me, saved my life mayhap, but life has a way of biting back when you least expect it. We settled in. Your family was so loving, Gabriel, it made me wish my own family had been like that. When your papa took ill, it didn't take me long to realize what was happening. I recognized the symptoms but I didn't know how to help him. . . I knew of no remedy. I suspected that your stepmother obtained the poison from Marguerite's mother, but of course, I could not verify that. I didn't even know if they knew each other, or if she got it from another source."

Gabriel's face was ashen, his glass of wine sat untouched on the table. I leaned against him in silent support and felt a fine tremor run through his body.

"You must understand Gabriel," she pleaded. "I was only a child, and I was terrified of what would happen if I came forward. I thought *Docteur* Henri would be able to heal him, and when it became clear that he could not, it was too late."

"I understand," he rasped out, his voice sounding strangled. "I'm not angry with you Esme. You didn't kill him."

She visibly deflated at his words, nodded to herself, and continued. "As you know, eventually I left with Amélie to *Trégoudan*, and while I was gone, Marguerite married and somehow ended up moving here. You can imagine my surprise when I visited with Amélie and found Marguerite living here. We struck our friendship back up immediately; it was as though all the years in between had never happened."

"But—"

"You're going to suggest that surely once I realized she was murdering her husband, I would have said or done something," guessed Esme. "In truth, I didn't even question it when she killed her husband. . . She confided in me that he beat her so badly she was afraid he was going to kill her, and I had no reason to disbelieve her."

"But he was friends with Luc," interjected Gabriel.

"Aye, but I didn't really know Luc at that time."

Gabriel was quiet and I said nothing. I thought about Madame Cariou's claim that Monsieur Cariou beat her and I thought about the vision I'd had of Jeanne. I knew that there was nothing to prevent men from physically abusing their wives in the eighteenth century, hell, even in the twentieth century when there were laws against spousal abuse, it still took place with shocking frequency. *Was her claim true though?*

Gabriel's thoughts must have mirrored my own because he fidgeted with the tassel on a cushion and then spoke. "I cannot say with certainty that Monsieur Cariou did not strike Madame Cariou," he began, "but I never saw or heard any evidence of it. Such things have a way of becoming common knowledge, aye? Certainly, it would have been mentioned. . . if at some point she was thrashed within an inch of her life."

Esme hunched her shoulders. "Luc said the same. That he was a gentle, caring, solicitous man, completely lacking in temper." She lifted her gaze to pin us with her agonized blue stare. "It matters not. I believed her then, and they are both in the ground now."

"What about Luc?" I asked, my mind swirling with everything she'd revealed thus far.

"I asked her the same thing when I went to her. I suspected that she was poisoning him, but truly, I could not understand why. I didn't even know that he was taking that blasted tea for virility from her!" she exclaimed angrily. "I thought we were friends, but the way she behaved. . . I can't reconcile it to the girl I met all those years ago."

"But Esme. . . you never told me you knew her. In fact, you came to me with that story about how she didn't want to help teach us her skills. Why did you lie to me?"

"Twasn't a lie. 'Tis true, I didn't say I knew her. I was perplexed by how she acted when Luc and I announced the banns. I thought she would be happy for me, but she told me I hadn't learned anything about men if I was getting married of my own accord." Her eyes looked far away, recalling a conversation only she could remember. Then she shook her head. "She told me that she did it for me. To save me from my stupidity, because 'twas surely only a matter of time before Luc showed me his true nature."

"Her experiences early in life poisoned her against men. I can't say that I blame her," I mused.

"But Esme, you know she had a reputation for going with men, aye?" I could tell by the uncomfortable look on Gabriel's face that he was trying to tread lightly.

She shook her head vehemently.

"I don't understand why she would have done that if she hates us all so much..."

She shrugged. "I think that in the end, I didn't know her at all. After she called me an idiot for marrying Luc, she told me she tried to seduce him, but he was too much of an imbecile to go with her... In truth, she was a very lost and broken soul." She raised eyes awash with tears. "Truly all I care about is how to heal Luc. I asked her if there was a way to reverse the effects, but she laughed in my face."

"The only way we can hope to help him regain his health is by doing what we told you the other evening," I responded gently.

She looked down at her lap and spread her fingers out on the fabric of her skirt. It was then that I noticed she was trembling.

"What if he doesn't recover, Ava?"

I took a deep breath, feeling my stomach clench at the fear in her voice. I couldn't lie to her. "He may not, Esme. We can't ignore that possibility. All we can do is try what *Docteur* Henri suggested and pray."

In a voice so low I had to lean forward to hear her, she asked, "Do you wish me to leave?"

I closed my eyes, feeling the misery in her voice in the depths of my soul. I wanted to leap up and assure her we would never ask her to leave, but I checked myself. She had killed someone. She had stood by and said nothing when two others had been poisoned. Would Gabriel see what I saw? Or would he only see the crimes she'd committed? The silence stretched out for what felt like an eternity.

Finally, Gabriel stood up. "Thank you for telling us Esme. I need to think about everything you've said." I stood up, prepared to argue her case, but he sent me a quelling look. "I don't forget that you were a child when most of this happened, but there is much I need to consider."

Esme bowed her head. "I understand Gabriel, thank you."

"You can stay here with Luc for the time being, of course," he added formally.

He reached his hand out to take mine, tucked it snuggly on his arm, and guided me out of the study, leaving her sitting forlornly in her seat.

FIFTY
THE RISE OF THE GUILLOTINE

I stared up at the ceiling and tangled my fingers in Gabriel's hair as he lay with his head on my stomach. I couldn't stop thinking about Esme's words and what she'd revealed. Not only about herself but, about the doomed Madame Cariou. I rubbed the thick strands between my fingertips, massaging his scalp in tiny circles, and let the story replay in my head.

There were holes in Esme's story, things that didn't seem to line up quite right. I'd seen the look on her face when she divulged the way her father had used her. . . I didn't think she could have faked the naked loathing in her expression. But I also couldn't understand why she hadn't confronted Marguerite sooner if she'd suspected she was poisoning Luc. For that matter, why hadn't she asked Luc himself whether he was using any herbals from Madame Cariou?

"You're thinking of Esme," came Gabriel's deep voice.

"Aye."

He sighed and lifted his head to look at me. "I don't know what to do," he admitted.

"Do you believe her?"

He shifted, resting his head on his propped-up hand. "I've known her for most of my life. I knew her papa was not a good man, although I never suspected the extent of it. If what she said is true, and I believe it likely is— then the man deserved to die."

"I agree."

"The law would not look kindly on her killing him, mind? But I see no reason for anyone else to know the truth of what happened."

I let out a breath I hadn't realized I was holding. "What about the rest?"

"She is not responsible for what happened to my papa. That responsibility sits squarely with *la Vicomtesse* de Argol, and if I ever figure out a way to prove what she did, then you can be sure that I will make sure she pays." There was a hint of steel and scarcely suppressed rage in his voice that made me shudder to think of what would happen to his stepmother if he ever had the evidence.

"Do you remember the night of Denis Bleuzen's death?"

"Aye," he said softly, grief in his voice.

"Do you recall that you were in the surgery alone with Madame Cariou for a little while before I returned? I felt like I walked into an uncomfortable conversation. I meant to ask you before, but I forgot."

"Mmph. She made a comment to the effect that Éloise and Madame Bleuzen were better off without Denis."

"Why would she say that?"

"That was my response. She said, *'All men are brutes'.*"

"Hmm. Well, it does seem that she felt that way. Do you suppose that Madame Cariou went to Argol to see *la Vicomtesse*?"

"If my stepmother originally learned how to poison men from Madame Cariou's mother, as Esme suspects, then it is possible, aye? I suppose we might begin by finding out whether Madame Cariou's mother still lives."

"She told me she passed away when she was sixteen."

"Hmm, well, that's something we should verify. I'm not taking anything she said as the truth right now."

"True. . . and Monsieur Cariou?"

"I'll discreetly ask about it, but Ava, you must understand that such things are generally not a mystery. I know which of my tenants enjoy their drink a bit too much, which ones like to fight and gamble, and aye, even the ones that are unrestrained in the abuse of their wives."

"But—"

"You're going to ask me if it isn't possible that the man was particularly good at hiding his beastly nature, and of course 'tis possible. After all, his wife had secrets that went largely undetected for years. But that's why I intend to dig around a bit."

"You cannot hold Esme responsible for something that Madame Cariou lied about or did to her husband though."

"*Non*, I cannot, and I would not. I wonder why she didn't come forward though. It bothers me, aye? I always considered her to be like a sister to me. Mayhap that is why I'm struggling so much with this."

"And Luc is your friend," I added judiciously. "It's difficult to be clear-eyed about crimes that affect our families and friends."

"Aye, it is." He took a deep breath. "Speaking of friends, Ava. I received a letter from Phillipe before supper today."

I turned my head to look up at him. "Oh?"

"He stopped in Paris for a few days on his way home. He says that confrontations are worsening. *Le Roi et la Reine* are as oblivious to the miseries of their subjects as ever. He fears this winter will be catastrophic for those already struggling, and despite this, the taxes continue to mount."

With a flash of clarity, I realized this was my moment. I had to tell Gabriel about what was coming. I pushed myself into a sitting position, pulling the bedclothes onto my lap.

"There are things I need to talk to you about," I began. "Things you need to know concerning what is going to happen over the coming years."

"Have you had a premonition?"

I shook my head. "I should start at the beginning, though I hardly know where to begin. What I'm going to tell you is going to sound insane, unbelievable, but I swear to you, on our love, on our marriage, that it's the truth, though I still can't understand or explain most of it."

Gabriel propped himself up with cushions against the headboard. "On our marriage, eh?" A ghost of a smile accompanied his attempt to lighten the suddenly somber mood, but his gray eyes betrayed his apprehension.

I raised my knees and wrapped my arms protectively around my legs. Anxiety swirled through my body as my palms began to sweat and my heart rate picked up tempo.

"I was born on July fourteenth, in the year of our lord nineteen hundred and sixty-four." I paused and looked at him. He stared back at me, mute. "I always thought it was interesting because I was born on the anniversary of the storming of the Bastille, which of course, hasn't happened yet."

I watched his lips mouth the words, "Storming of the Bastille," to himself.

"It will happen next year, in 1789."

His gray eyes stared at me, and he suddenly reached out with both hands to take mine, gripping them tightly. "How can you be here with me, when you haven't been born yet?"

I shook my head, my eyes feeling hot with the threat of tears. "In 1987 when I was twenty-three years old, I was on a sailboat circumnavigating the world with my best friend Carri when our boat wrecked. Don't ask me how, because this is one of those things that I cannot understand no matter how much I have thought about it— but somehow, you found me on the beach in 1787."

I paused and raised my eyes to Gabriel's to measure his reaction. He comically opened his mouth to say something, before snapping it shut again.

"You can imagine what a shock it was to me. . . still is, to be honest. But once I got over that, what was perhaps the bigger surprise, was where I'd landed, in history."

"The storming of the Bastille," he repeated. Understanding, but not understanding the significance.

I closed my eyes, took a deep breath, and reopened them. "In August of this year, the royal treasury will be declared empty. Next year, what will come to be known as the French Revolution will begin in earnest. On April 25th, 1792, the first criminal faced capital punishment via the guillotine, which is a machine built to behead people swiftly and efficiently. They will do it under the guise of humanity, claiming it a kinder death than burning at the stake, hanging, or racking on the wheel. Perhaps it is." I could hear the telltale hitch in my voice, precluding tears, and paused, trying to regain control.

"It will be the beginning of what history will dub 'The Reign of Terror' and it will be used as the primary form of capital punishment in France until after my birth, in 1977. On January 21st, 1793, they will behead King Louis XVI with the guillotine. The queen will follow him in death on October 16th, 1793."

"We will kill the king." His voice was full of disbelief.

"Aye. The guillotine became one of the symbols of the French Revolution. We will behead at least fifteen thousand people with it, many of them in the aristocracy, though many more will be commoners. Thousands will die of other causes in the name of equality over the next few years."

He shook his head in denial, and I closed my eyes to it, nausea swirling in my stomach and threatening to erupt at any moment.

When I reopened them, they were swimming with tears. I looked directly into his shocked face. "War is coming."